CREATURES MOST VILE

CHELSEA LAUREN

ZENITH PUBLISHING

ZENITH PUBLISHING

To my confidant and fellow fangirl
This is for you, Mom

CONTENTS

Chapter One

Mother above, it was too loud—always too loud.

Chairs screeched on the tile floor. Chalk squealed against the board. Eithan *tap tap tapped* his pencil on the desk.

They would hear it. They always did. The only thing that stood between me and the monsters prowling the forest was time. If only I could make it stand still.

How did no one notice? Why did no one care? The senior class milled about the room, chatting and carrying on as if there was nothing to worry about. As if nothing dangerous lurked beyond these brick walls. I wanted to snap Eithan's pencil and scream at them to shut up, but that wouldn't help my noisy dilemma, now would it?

Cassandry would say I was being paranoid. *These small noises won't penetrate the walls*, she'd insist. *No creature could hear us*. She'd assure me that the patrolmen would protect us, and if there were an attack, the Guardians would come save us. I'd simply nod along because it'd break her heart to know her words were all for nothing.

I thought we had been quiet enough that day by the creek all those years ago, fishing line fed slowly into the water and our bodies lowered silently onto the rocky shore. But I had been wrong—unforgivably wrong.

A silvery tail splintered his ribs.
Blood spewed out his mouth.

I blinked to blot out the memory.

I'd never make that mistake again.

I bounced my knee and stared out the window. No monsters stalked the grassy clearing, only patrolmen. They stood at attention around the perimeter of the school. Some were stationed in treetop stands, crossbows wedged in the crooks of their shoulders and sights trained on the emerald canopy sprawled before them.

Bellwarn Central School patrolmen, providing top-of-the-line protection against the beasts of the Portemor Mountains. What a joke. A cruel and deadly joke. They were no match for the Portemor monsters, just incessant flies against their fangs and claws. Everyone knew it, too, but it was easier to pretend they would save us all than accept the fact that we were defenseless. Helpless.

Hopeless.

A hand squeezed my shoulder and I turned to find Cassandry's beaming face, soft brown curls tumbling off her shoulders. "And you say I'm the vain one."

"Yeah, and I'm sure those curls you spent all night setting would agree." I reached out and tugged on one of them.

"Hands off!" She batted my hand away, then gestured

to the window. "You and me both then, since you're always gazing at your reflection in the window."

"Oh," I chuckled. "You know that's not what I'm doing."

She sat at the desk behind mine. "Hey, don't get me wrong, I get it. I would too, if I had eyes like yours."

I looked at my reflection. The glass muted the green specks in my hazel eyes. They practically looked gray —*blah*.

"I think Confinement is messing with your head," I said.

"I'll be sanctioned for travel soon! Graduation is only a couple weeks away."

Before I could say anything, the light bulb above the chalkboard began to flash. The alarm light silenced all those incessant noises, blanketing the room with its message: Monsters prowled nearby, bellies empty and fangs aching to tear into their next meal.

Blood drained from my face. My heart raced beneath fragile ribs.

The sharp crack of bone.

No. I shook my head. *Not now.*

I focused on the alarm light before the memory could resurface.

Maybe if I let the light coat me, like a balm or a shield, I would be safe. Let it soak through to the bone and mold me into the brick walls. Then I could hide from the beasts lurking just beyond the window, desperately sniffing me out. But these were the ideas of a girl who could hope and dream of a different world, a safe world. That girl died some time ago beside a brook trickling with crimson water.

The classroom was muted chaos. Students scurried through a maze of desks to the far corner of the room, careful to not skid their shoes or chairs. I stayed rooted in my seat.

I bit my quivering lip. *Stay silent.*

I calmed my bouncing knee. *Be still.*

Please, please, please don't let them find me, I pleaded. I begged. To the Mother above. To anyone who would listen. I was desperate. Some people would never admit that, but I couldn't care less. Survival mattered more than pride.

The teacher dragged a box of mallets out of the closet and began passing them out. Some believed it a useful weapon, but it was simply another charade of security, just like the patrolmen.

Cassandry crawled out of the corral of students. She came to my knee, her bright blue eyes settling on mine. "Anora, come on."

Fear numbed my mind. Nothing existed except the threat of teeth and talons nearby. I broke out in a cold sweat. My eyes glazed over. My breath quickened.

"We're safe here." She claimed this every time there was a lockdown, but it was never reassuring. It didn't matter that this building was the only one left standing from Old Bellwarn, that it had survived countless attacks. Against their wrath, their insatiable hunger, it would eventually collapse to rubble like everything else.

I imagined a winged beast shattering the window with its barbed tail. Black talons slick with blood screeched against the broken glass edging the window frame. The wall crumbled away, brick by brick, bringing the creature closer and closer . . .

The urge to scream came in a crashing wave and I bit my lip to hold it in. To stay silent.

I shook my head to knock the illusion loose, as if that were enough to keep the visions at bay. It had never worked before. Why should this time be any different?

"Anora, we have to move," Cassandry whispered.

She lifted me from my seat and guided us to the back of the room. Crouching with the other students, I spotted Eithan cowering in the back of the horde, too far to reach. My classmates' eyes were widened in fear, their knuckles white as they gripped their mallets. Maybe if they hadn't been so noisy, if they held this fear in their hearts all the time like I did, none of this would be happening.

Cassandry handed me a mallet while our teacher locked the door and secured the shutters. The room would've been pitch black if not for the momentary flash of the alarm.

The world slowed to stilted movements in the brief flashes . . .

Students clung to one another.

Heads swiveled, eyes darting around the room.

Cassandry pulled me in close.

Silky curls brushed against my cheek.

And in the darkness, the past sprang to life . . .

The creek babbled over smooth rock.

Fish waded in the stagnant pools pocketed along the edge.

Two splintered fishing poles floated among them.

A serpentine creature launched over the water and coiled around him.

His last word of advice clung to the wind and my heart.

"Run!"

It was a creat! A Portemor monster—real, ravenous, and right in front of me. I had to get out. I had to run. The serpent had already devoured him, there was no changing that, but I couldn't let it snatch me too.

I started crawling away, but before I made it far, the beast pulled me back. I shook it off. When the creature grabbed me again, there were more tails. Sharp scales dug into my skin as tails wrapped around each leg and another weighed along my spine. Where had they all come from?

The whip of a tail down my back.

My sobs morphed into screams as I sprinted through the woods, trailing blood.

No. No, no, no. Please, Mother, I didn't want to die like this. Anything but this.

I fought the creat's grip, but it had me pinned. I gripped my mallet and swung blindly. Before I hit anything, it coiled around my wrist and ripped the hammer from my grasp. I opened my mouth to cry out, but before I uttered a syllable, a tail slithered over my mouth. My voice grew hoarse behind it.

The beast flipped me onto my back. I expected glowing red eyes to pierce mine, to call on my blood and drink their fill, but was met by a pair of sapphire ones. They were round, full of worry, and . . . human?

No monster pinned me. It was Cassandry that sat astride my torso, shushing softly. Instead of a serpent gagging me, her hand was clamped over my mouth while the other petted my flaxen hair. Classmates restrained my arms and legs, not a beast.

Tears blurred my vision. It had happened again. *Why?* Why did this always happen to me? I really shouldn't be surprised. Flashbacks always came at the most inopportune times, but that didn't stop me from hoping and praying it was the last time.

Cassandry drew my focus back. I desperately searched for her in the darkness, locking onto her eyes in the momentary flashes of light. My friend guided me through deep breathing.

In and out . . . In and out . . .

As I slowly regained my composure, Cassandry motioned for the others to release me. I remained lying down and focused on breathing, on keeping those memories from worming their way back in. My friend knelt beside me and resumed stroking my hair. A solitary knock at the door jolted me and she shielded me in her arms.

Our teacher unlocked the door and eased it open. In the next flash of light, the principal materialized.

After whispering with our teacher, she addressed the class. "It was a false alarm. Nothing to worry about." She promptly left our class for the next.

I let out a long breath. My head still ached from the flashback, but the relief of knowing it was a false alarm eased the pain.

The alarm stopped flashing and our teacher removed the shutters, flooding the classroom with natural light. I watched him approach through squinted eyes.

"Are you alright, Anora?"

With a cursory glance, I noticed every eye was on me. They gawked as if I were about to sprout fangs and feast upon them. As if this was the first time they'd witnessed one of my attacks. They acted like I was the only one who had been scared. Maybe my reaction had been a bit more conspicuous than theirs, but they all had fear in their eyes.

How did they forget that so easily? My cheeks warmed and I glowered.

"What do you think?"

He stepped back, appalled. "No need to be so snippy."

I glared at him as he walked away to check on the other students. Of course I was at fault for not being gracious for his empty display of concern. *Are you okay?* They never really wanted to help. The knee-jerk response of *I'm fine* wasn't just expected—it was demanded. Answering any other way meant you were being dramatic. *Snippy*.

"And *she's* going to be a nurse," Victon scoffed. "Mother save us."

A few students laughed along with him. The teacher pretended to not hear Victon's remark as he readied for class.

"Say that the next time you're at the infirmary and see where it gets you," I shot back.

A mischievous sneer spread along his narrow face. "Tough words for someone who just had a mental breakdown over a false alarm."

"Come off it, Victon." Cassandry stepped forward with a scowl. "Like you weren't about to piss yourself."

"Like it even matters to you!" He turned his venom on her. "You'll be safe in Celepheria and won't have to rely on *her*."

His beady eyes pinned me with disgust. I returned the look. Victon could never stand it when people challenged him. When someone stood up for themselves. That was probably why he hated me so much.

Our teacher finally stepped in. "That's enough! Everyone settle down and open your books."

"Don't listen to him, Nory." Cassandry's pale complexion smoldered with rage.

With the tension somewhat dissipated, Eithan found it safe to approach. "Yeah, you're going to do great." His warm brown eyes brimmed with concern.

I released a breath and tempered my nerves, but simmering in the back of my mind was doubt, a fear that Victon was right. With a nod, I said more for myself than anyone else, "Right, right."

Eithan tilted his head with a questioning look but left it alone. He adjusted his thick-rimmed glasses and sat at his desk. I remained standing, my limbs jittering like a live wire.

Students settled into their seats and flipped open their textbooks as the excitement of the lockdown and our spat subsided. Everyone acted as if nothing had happened. False alarms were common enough, and more of a relief than anything, but how could they let go of their fear so easily? My mind was still trapped outside in the clearing, waiting for a monster to show itself. My heart was on that creek bed where my blood and his ran together into the stream.

Victon had only granted a brief reprieve.

All I wanted was to run home, crawl under my bed, and hide from the world and all its sinister things. Leaving the school alone would be too dangerous though, so I stayed and tried to forget the horrors of the day like everyone else did so effortlessly. I sat beside Eithan, knee bouncing and fingers fidgeting with the hem of my sundress. I glanced at him out of the corner of my eye. Admiring him always worked a charm on my restless mind.

The sunlight brushed his brown skin with a golden

hue. He chewed his lip as he looked over the lesson in his textbook, pushing his glasses into place. So intent on the passage he read, he didn't notice my gaze. His eyes flitted across the text, fingers fiddling with the corner of the page like a horse nudging at its gate.

In those eyes, all of my fears vanished. On those lips, every worry was silenced. I imagined Eithan leaning in to meet my lips. He would hesitate at first, then softly lay his upon mine . . .

"Uh, are you alright?" Eithan whispered, bringing my daydream to a crashing halt.

I had scooted to the edge of my seat, practically leaning on his desk. I fumbled back into my chair and stumbled over my words. "Oh—yep! Sure! All good."

"Okay . . ." Eithan turned away, scooting his chair in as far as he could.

My tan cheeks burned. No matter how many of these intense-awkward moments happened between us, Eithan always turned away and left me to stew in embarrassment.

I looked to Cassandry for comfort. She was waiting with a sympathetic pout. "One day he'll catch on. Be patient."

"After graduation, though, you'll both be on your way to the university while I'm stuck here."

Before I turned away, Cassandry squeezed my arm. "Don't give up. Who knows what fate has in store?"

With a forced smile, I faced the board. Our teacher started rambling about graphs he'd drawn. Chalk dust clouds plumed as he erased and redrew one of his diagrams.

The lesson passed in a blur of graphs and equations. The teacher's droning voice grazed past my ears, my mind too full of daydreams about stolen kisses with Eithan in the library—the best remedy for fending off troublesome memories.

Cassandry tapped my shoulder to signal that class was over. We gathered our books and walked down the hall, joining the growing crowd of students mobbing the cafeteria.

While everyone was drawn toward the counter by the scent of chicken nuggets, I was busy searching the crowd for a tiny flurry of brown curls. Where was Liam? I needed to check on him after the false alarm.

As the horde bottlenecked into a single-file line, Cassandry tugged on the skirt of my dress so I'd keep my place. Tray after tray slid down the metal counter past mounds of food. I grimaced at the slopping sound the beans made as they were spooned onto my tray. After collecting our rations of chicken and carrots, my friends and I entered the fray.

Cliques of every age swarmed the tables by the windows on the wall opposite the serving station. The cafeteria was the second-largest space in the school, and everywhere past the windows was consumed by shadows.

Knowing better than to try for a window seat, we meandered to a small table shoved in an unlit corner. We slid into our seats and took note of where the overseers were posted. There were four, one along each wall. They scanned the room for monsters hiding among us. In this case, the monsters were any rowdy children—or rather, any kid that sneezed or coughed too loudly. Most students scowled when they hushed them. I didn't mind. They seemed to be the only people in the entire school besides me who understood the importance of silence.

Soft murmurs and reined-in laughter floated through the cafeteria. My friends dived into their meals while I scanned the crowd for Liam. A bundle of curls bobbed among a gaggle of little ones running for one of the last lit tables. *There!* My chair screeched as I jumped up, earning a glare from a nearby overseer. Cringing, I quietly tucked in my seat and whispered, "Sorry."

Liam's bunch lost the window table and retreated to one in the middle of the room. I weaved through a sea of students, stepping sideways when one refused to scooch in their chair. Liam hopped out of his seat once he noticed me, a smile dimpling his cheeks. He rushed over, shoes pattering on the tile floor, and nearly knocked me over with his embrace.

"Jeez, easy there." I knelt down. "I take it you're alright."

The overseers rushed over to shush us and I nodded our compliance.

"Did you have another . . . ?" He trailed off in a whisper.

"Cassandry helped me through."

"Sorry I wasn't there."

I rested my hands on his shoulders and smiled. What did I do to deserve such a sweet little brother? "Don't worry yourself over me."

"Then who'll make sure you don't miss the bus when you're cuddling in the library with *Eithan?*" He mocked a kissy face.

Sweet? I meant annoying.

I shushed him as vehemently as an overseer. Heat flared my cheeks as I looked over my shoulder to make sure Eithan wasn't listening.

"Stop it, Liam! That isn't funny *or* true."

"Sure it isn't." He winked.

I couldn't help but laugh at his scrunched-up face. "You're such a dork."

He stuck out his tongue and scampered back to his table.

Flopping back into my seat, I dug a fork into the pile of steaming carrots. I wrinkled my nose at the stench and forced myself to take a small bite.

Pushing the rest to the edge of the tray, I asked Cassandry, "How's packing going?"

She batted her curls. "Terribly, we only have one suitcase to cram all of my clothes in. It's proving impossible."

An overseer bustled over to shush her. She had never quite figured out how to dampen her boisterous voice.

"There will be plenty of places to buy clothes in Celepheria," Eithan pointed out in an appropriate tone. "They have real stores with limitless options. There's no need to bring so much."

"I *know*, Eithan. But I like my clothes. If I leave them here, I won't ever wear them again."

"You can when you visit in the summer," I reminded her. She had been forgetting lately that her travel sanction was approved for every summer she was at the university.

"Oh, right," she murmured, then quickly followed with, "You're not bringing anything then, Eithan?"

"Only my notebooks. The biochemistry department is intrigued with my theories on—"

She held up a hand. "Spare me the lecture, just this once."

Eithan scowled, the look he gave when churning up the perfect comeback.

Before they could dive into one of their daily arguments, I said, "What will I do when you're both at the university and I don't have your bickering to keep me entertained?"

Cassandry frowned and laid her hand atop mine. "I wish you could come."

"Ah, well, I've been meaning to spend quality time with Victon, anyway."

My joke didn't land. My friends looked at me with sad eyes and Cassandry squeezed my hand. I could tell she was trying to come up with something encouraging to say by the way her mouth hung open and her eyes wavered, but there were no words that would soothe the ache in my heart. I should be happy for them. They were fortunate to escape this Mother-forsaken mainland and its strict Confinement Laws. But loneliness and jealousy had a tendency to smother such things.

Even knowing they would travel home for the summer didn't ease my sorrow—especially with the rest of the year looming ahead. They'd be thriving in safety on a faraway island while I lay awake every night wondering if I'd survive it, praying a beast wasn't scaling my home or clawing at my shuttered window. While they sat cozy in their lecture halls, I'd be scrambling between eviscerated patients while struggling against the flashbacks threatening to consume me at any moment, any trigger.

Yes, they'd be home next summer, but a sense of foreboding scratched at the back of my mind that I might not be alive to see them.

Chapter Two

The near-silent hum of the school bus's engine vibrated the steps. The bus driver twirled her gray hair around her fingers, eyeing her third group of the day to transport with disinterest.

Cramped together on a bench seat, Cassandry and I spoke in the softest whispers. The school bus was padded with soundproof cushions, but I didn't trust that it was enough to cancel out a bunch of schoolkids' voices.

Our conversations usually revolved around Cassandry, and these days, the focus was all on Celepheria. I pushed my bitterness aside while we daydreamed of all the things she'd do there. She would stroll along the beach and discover how it feels to have wet sand mush between her toes. She would wander the city with no fear of something prowling in the shadows. That part was the hardest to imagine. I could pretend mud after a rainstorm was sand if I closed my eyes. But safety was one thing I could never pretend to know, no matter how tightly I squeezed my eyes shut.

When the bus pulled in front of our house, I ushered Liam off and we headed down the dirt path.

The house was painted in forest greens and earthy browns, blending in with the surrounding foliage. It fit snugly in the small clearing, the edges of the covered porch skirting the low-hanging branches. A small shed hid just within the tree line. The sight of it stung, even after all these years.

I imagined my father, tawny complexion smattered with grease, peeking out of the shed door to greet me after a long day of school . . .

He stepped out of the shed, fishing poles and tackle box in hand.

"I need your help, kiddo. We need to put some food on the table."

"Why can't we go to the market?"

"Well, things've been a little tight. Mom's real busy with her sewing, though."

"But it's not enough," I said for him.

"You're too smart for your age. What are you, seven?" he joked.

"I'm eleven, Dad."

"Oh, right." He smirked and handed me a pole. "I forget how fast time goes."

I wanted to stay with him in that moment forever, but Liam, too young to know the ghost in the clearing, tugged on my dress until I left the memory behind.

Once inside, we kicked off our shoes and bounded for the living room couch. I nestled between the lumpy cushions and scratched my feet against the rug. Liam rambled on about his day, talking over the whir of Mom's sewing machine that drifted down the staircase.

"That jerk, Thenton, came and ripped my picture. I was drawing a flower for Mommy and he ruined it." He pouted.

"You know if you have any issues to come get me."

He shrugged. "I thought I could handle it."

"What's that supposed to mean?"

Liam looked around to make sure the coast was clear, then lifted his shirt to reveal a fresh bruise growing on his belly.

"No!" I gasped. "Did you go to the nurse?"

"The teacher sent us both." A smirk flickered on the edge of his mouth.

"Both?"

"He'll have a black eye tomorrow."

"You punched him back?"

"Technically I didn't punch him *back*," he said smugly.

I sat back, stunned. He started it? Where was this tough-guy Liam coming from? He'd never acted out like that before, at least not that I knew of.

"He may deserve it after all he's done, but that doesn't make it right."

Liam rolled his eyes.

"You can't be starting fights. I'll tell Mom if—"

Liam shot forward, his brown eyes wide with fear. "No, no! Mom can't know!"

"Well, promise no more fighting then."

"Okay, fine," Liam said with a pout.

I scoffed. So much attitude in such a little person.

The creak of the back door echoed through the house. My stepfather moseyed into the family room, the monthly newspaper tucked under his arm. His wrinkles deepened around his thin mouth as he smiled.

"Hey there, kids."

We both smiled and greeted him in return as he sat in the chair beside the radio.

Bill hid his crystal-blue eyes behind his newspaper. The front of the Bellwarn Observer showcased another headline about the creatures from beyond the mountains. This one featured a large, hairy beast with claws as long as scythes and a snout lined with rows of teeth. It was subdued by red-hot iron chains. In the corner of the photo was an inlay of the Guardian who had captured the beast. He was garbed in the traditional Guardian jumpsuit, a charcoal-gray fabric accented with cobalt-blue stripes at the collar and down the sides. The Guardian insignia was embroidered on his breastplate, a phoenix rising from flame. The Guardian's umber face was broad and his smoldering eyes seemed to burn through the page. I didn't have to read the article to know he was Guardian Bron. His gift was a soul of embers. To touch his skin would be like touching a hot iron.

I nodded my head toward the paper. "How'd he do it?"

"Got a chain wrapped around its neck. It didn't die though, just passed out from the burns. They kept this one for training. Past few years there's been ten times more sightings than before. I wonder how the Guard catches as many as they do," Bill pondered.

I looked at the image of the beast, its yellow eyes stared wildly back. I turned away. I'd had enough creat torment for one day.

Upstairs, the soft click of a door shutting was followed by the patter of footsteps down the hallway. My mother's skirt billowed around her calves as she swept down the stairs, grocery boxes in tow.

"How was school today?" she asked.

"There was a false alarm," Liam answered.

Her hazel eyes shot to mine. "How are you doing?"

"I survived."

"That's not what I mean."

"That's the best I got."

Mom narrowed her eyes to look for cracks in my rough shell, waiting for a mess of emotions to spill out. If she looked long enough, she wouldn't be disappointed. I felt like an egg whose shell was spiderwebbed with a bunch of tiny little cracks and the slightest fumble would break me. Would the tough-girl act hide it from her?

"Okay, well . . ." she trailed off. "We were planning to go to market."

"I'm not going," I stated, sinking into the couch. Mom saw through my front—no use in keeping it up anymore. Especially when that would require pretending I was okay with risking my life going to market. After the day I'd had, that was the last thing I needed.

"We don't have much to make a meal out of, Ruth," Bill indicated, peering over his newspaper.

They looked at each other, holding a silent audience as if I had no say at all. Liam perched on the arm of the couch, awaiting their reply, while I burrowed farther into it.

"It was a false alarm," she said. "And now that I've been paid, we can get meat, something we haven't had in a while."

"Still not going."

"Anora—"

I cut her off by stomping toward the stairs. "Go without me."

"I'm sorry, Nora bug, but we need your help carrying the boxes," she said.

As I stood halfway up the staircase, I struggled between needing to curl up in bed and helping my parents. If the plan was to buy that much, it'd be too heavy a load for my mother and Liam, and with my stepfather's backache, he really shouldn't be doing much lifting or hauling of any kind.

I ceded with a huff. "Fine."

She let out a sigh of relief and led Liam toward the door.

As we slipped on our shoes, Mom grasped the door handle and recited her warning. "If something happens, you run. Run as fast as you can."

"Mom, we know what to do," I said, not in irritation, but for her reassurance.

"I need to remind you. Just in case."

The canopy from the surrounding woods draped over the road, casting refreshing shade. The forest was deathly silent with not even the coo of birdsong or the buzz of cicadas in the distance. The scent of rotted leaves swamped the air.

We marched in a tight line behind my stepfather. Bill scanned the woods, one hand holding a grocery box and the other resting on the hilt of the knife hanging off his belt. The sight provided no comfort.

No one spoke as we made our way to the farmers' market. Being out in the open, taking in the lush greenery and life of the forest, reminded me of how much I absolutely hated it. There were so many places for monsters to hide, but no place for a girl to do the same. The forest might offer a thicket of bushes or the hollow of a tree, making you think you're safe, but the monsters always sniffed you out. *Always.*

There was a rustling nearby, and we halted. Adrenaline surged and I stiffened. My stepfather's knife whistled as he whipped it out of its sheath.

The flash of fangs.
The flick of a scaly tail.

I squeezed my eyes shut against the past, then forced them back open to scan the woods. At a moment like this, I couldn't let the flashbacks take over.

A blur of tan darted through the woods. My breath hitched, holding back a scream. Just as I turned to sprint away, a doe burst from the trees and leaped across the road. We stared after it as it ran through the woods. My heart did not slow. My feet itched to rush back to the house and hide under my bed.

"It's fine. We're fine," my mother reassured us, her murmur so soft it blended with the lazy summer breeze.

Regardless, we picked up the pace.

A large clearing emerged, revealing a dozen wooden stands spread throughout. Some were small tables lined with homemade jams and syrups. Others were larger benches displaying baskets of locally grown vegetables. Purveyors perched at their posts, one eye on their goods, the other on the woods behind them.

Mom eyed the fruit and vegetable counters. She instructed me to help her while Bill and Liam placed our order at the Ice Box.

"When you're done helping your mother," Bill said,

"I'll treat you to an ice cream cone." His voice was a near-silent whisper, as our voices had to be whenever we spoke outside.

"Really?" I whispered my surprise for such a rare treat.

"Consider it part of your graduation present." He winked.

"Do I get one too?" Liam asked.

"Sure, squirt."

Liam dashed for the run-down shack, and Bill ambled along after him, stifling his chuckle.

I followed my mother, grocery box upright and ready to fill. It was too early in the season for summer fruits. Our choices were either a few unripe berries or nothing. Mom scrunched her nose at them and picked up a package of half-green strawberries.

The young farmer's outside voice was barely audible. "They should ripen in a few days."

My mother blushed. "Yes, I'm sure they will."

The vegetable stand was similarly bare. My mother hid her disappointment as she picked a bundle of lettuce, a handful of carrots, and some red potatoes.

I helped her load the box. "Need any jams or anything?"

"Yes, but I'll get it. Go get your ice cream."

Without protest, I headed toward the Ice Box.

At my stepfather's side, Liam bounced on the balls of his feet. I joined them in line.

In the rear of the Ice Box was construction. Ladders leaned on either side of the shack while men hammered on new wood siding. The men and the Ice Box were encapsulated by an iridescent bubble that left only the shack's ordering window exposed. The opalescent bubble served as a noise-canceling barrier. The banging of hammers and the snarling of handsaws was reduced to a soft hum. The bubble was one of the rare technological marvels to come out of Celepheria—one of the few things they ever bothered sending to the mainland.

A construction worker, leaning against a horse-drawn wagon loaded with supplies, waved for Bill to join him.

My stepfather gave me his shopping box and a handful of coins. "I gotta go help them for a minute. Get our usual order—and two small cones, of course."

Bill joined his fellow worker. He reached for a seam in the soundproof veil and revealed a small opening. As they walked through, the thump of hammers filled the clearing. Then, as quickly as the racket came, it was subdued to a purr when the veil closed behind them.

We were next in line and ready to order when a rumble entered the clearing. I smiled when a compact car pulled into the market. Only one family in Bellwarn could afford a vehicle and the gasoline delivered annually from Celepheria. Abandoning Liam with our grocery boxes, I sprinted toward the car.

Cassandry bounced out of the back seat, already beaming and barely able to rein in her outside voice. "Hey!"

"We're getting ice cream, want to join?"

She turned to her dad. "Can I get ice cream with Nory?"

"Of course, pumpkin. Here," her father said as he took out a high-value coin. "Get Anora and Liam's too."

I thanked him, a twinge of shame in my words, then hooked my arm in Cassandry's and strolled toward the Ice Box.

"I'm surprised you guys came on a weekday. Don't your parents work late?" I asked.

"Typically, but there haven't been many high-risk patients lately. That last attack was a couple months ago already."

"Don't jinx it."

"So superstitious." She flashed a devilish smile. "They're excited to start your nurse training."

"I'm nervous," was all I revealed. Victon's cruel, and possibly true, words from earlier rang through my mind.

"You'll do fantastic! Don't worry about it."

I didn't tell her how impossible that was. Maybe if she had anxiety, unpredictable flashbacks, and a family relying on her to not screw up the highest-paying job in town, she would understand.

Cassandry laced our fingers and led me to the horses hitched by the Ice Box. She slowed as we neared, trying not to startle them, then began petting their noses. The husky brown horse whinnied and leaned into her touch.

"Oh, aren't they so beautiful?" Cassandry said adoringly. "In Celepheria, people can have horses as pets. Can you imagine? They ride them along the beaches, not a care in the world."

I admired my friend as she looked into the horse's eyes, unable to fathom what that kind of freedom felt like.

"They have dogs too, just for their companionship. Wouldn't that be amazing? I want a dog so badly. A spunky little thing that I could chase around the beach and cuddle with after a long day." Cassandry's face turned sullen then, her eyes glazed and distant as she pet the horse. "I won't be coming back."

"What?" I tilted my head and crinkled my eyebrows.

"What're you talking about?" She couldn't possibly mean never come back *home*, because that would mean in two weeks I'd be saying goodbye to my best friend—not just until next summer, but forever.

Her focus shifted to the torn-up ground the horses dug at. "I've been putting off telling you. I didn't want to ruin our last few weeks together, but I hate lying to you."

"You're scaring me."

Her eyes were lined with tears. "There are more opportunities for me in Celepheria. Not just for school, but for a life."

"But your family is here. Your friends are here. Your *life* is here." The words tumbled out faster and faster. My voice became shrill. I took a breath and slowed down, needing to keep my outside voice in check. "What about coming home for the summers? I thought you wanted to teach Government here after you graduate from the university?"

"Traveling every summer—it's too expensive and dangerous. And there are a lot more job options there. Ones where I can actually participate in politics rather than just teach it." Tears streamed down her face. "I understand what I would be leaving behind, but I can't take this lifestyle anymore. I want to be free, and the people in Celepheria are."

"But everyone flocks there. Half the people are begging on the streets!"

"Really, Anora, come on." She became defensive, her volume bordering an inside voice. "My seat at the university is my ticket in. Afterward, I'll find a job that makes decent money so I can afford to live there."

A flood of memories scrolled through my mind. Little

Cassandry shuffling toward me in our kindergarten class-room, paper and crayons hidden behind her back as she asked me to help her color a rainbow. Chasing each other and playing tag in the gymnasium at school. Scrunched together on my bed, throwing our heads back as we laughed at some ridiculous joke. If Cassandry never came back, those memories would be all I had left.

"But I—I just don't understand," I said. "I won't ever see you again if you stay there."

Cassandry wiped away my tears, her voice soft again. "You could come with me. You can stay in my dorm and find a job. You'd be free to do whatever you want."

I shook my head. "Breaking Confinement would make me an outlaw. Besides, my family needs me. There's no one to keep the house up once Bill retires."

"I know . . ." Cassandry trailed off, then painted on a weak smile. "Let's go get that ice cream."

I forced my own smile as we hooked arms again, my grip tighter than before.

I held back the rest of my tears as we headed for the Ice Box, tucking those sweet, painful memories into the far reaches of my mind.

An orange hue soaked into the blue sky as the sun slipped below the tall pines.

Arms crossed atop the grocery box filled with eggs, meats, and cheese, I savored my raspberry ice cream with every lick of the cone. Partly because it was delicious, but also to distract from the tension between Cassandry and me.

She sat at the picnic table, relishing her double scoops. Did she feel the same hurt I did? Probably not. She had a future to look forward to, full of new people and opportunities. All I had was her and this quiet life. What would I do without her?

I finished my dessert, grabbed our shopping boxes, and told Liam it was time to go. He frowned, but with a quick glance at the changing sky, he hopped off the bench.

We headed toward the cluster of tables and stands where farmers packed their goods into carts and wagons. Cassandry spotted her parents on the other side of the market. We bid her goodbye and safe evening before she ran off.

Mom and Bill were chatting with the construction workers as they packed up their equipment and we joined them. Bill helped them load their tools as he explained the layout of the renovations he was completing on a villager's home. His back strained as he struggled to lift a tool box into their wagon. It slipped from his grip and landed in the wagon with a *thud*, startling the horses. The horses whinnied and kicked their front legs in the air. The men pulled on their reins, willing them to calm down. The horses shook their heads, pulling back on the reins. The men tried to calm the horses, to keep them quiet, but to no avail. They wouldn't.

Mother above, they were being so loud. *Too* loud. Their neighing was as good as a dinner bell.

Everyone at the market focused on the horses. My heart galloped alongside the kneading of their hooves. I inched closer to my stepfather, grabbing onto his sweat-dampened shirt. My mother dug her grip into Liam's shoulder as her eyes frantically searched the woods.

In the distance, sticks crunched under heavy feet. Tree trunks cracked like they were snapped at the root. With every passing moment, the rustling became louder, more fervent. Then, on the edge of the clearing, the trees shook violently and bowed as a beast emerged from the shadows.

Chapter Three

The creat stretched its legs and stomped into the clearing. Hairless gray skin clung to the beast's thick muscles and distended gut. A guttural roar shook the ground as it lifted its head to the sky. The beast lowered its boarish snout. Sharp tusks, dripping blood, hooked around its nose. Milky eyes swirled as it surveyed us.

I held my breath and stiffened my muscles.

Was this real? Please, Mother, tell me this was simply a hallucination—terrifying, but not a real threat. Not real tusks or real claws ready to tear the flesh from my bones. I hoped, prayed, and begged that was all this was.

The horses cried out, kicking and pulling at their restraints. Their handlers, frozen in terror, didn't stop them as they broke free and stampeded down the road.

The creat was not fazed by the horses, silver eyes trained on the easier meal. The beast held out both arms, white claws outstretched as if welcoming an embrace. It began to twirl in place, faster and faster as it propelled into a dizzying spin. The wind whipped around the creature until it was enveloped in a tornado. Spinning like a top, the monster made its way toward the market.

People started to scream then—ear-piercing screams. No sense in using outside voices when the monster had already found us. A couple of men knocked into my shoulder as they sprinted past and jostled some sense into me. This was not a vision, but a horrifying reality.

Everything around me grew fuzzy. All I could hear was the trill of my heart. My knees wobbled with fear. My bladder threatened to empty as I beheld pure terror raging toward us. But then, I heard his voice.

Run, my sweet girl.

I snapped out of my trance and dropped the boxes. Eggs smashed. Strawberries scattered.

I bolted toward the forest, looking over my shoulder to make sure my family was close behind. My dress billowed up my thighs.

Sprinting through the trees, I dodged trunks and hurdled over logs. I didn't notice an upturned root hidden beneath a clot of leaves in time and jammed my foot. I toppled over, landing hard on my side. I winced, biting back a wail of pain. When I looked up, the beast began its carnage.

Every stand and wagon it spun toward exploded into splinters and nails. People that hadn't reached the trees were hit by the shrapnel, crying out and falling to the ground. The creat tore into Cassandry's vehicle, flaying it and scattering metal into the wind. More shouts of pain whistled through the air as people dropped to the ground, metal sticking out of their backs.

In the midst of its own gusts, the monster reached out,

grabbed a person, and dragged her into the whirlwind. It was the young farmer from the fruit stand. Her cries of terror cut through the clearing like a blade. She dug her fingernails into the ground, trying to claw her way out of the monster's grasp, but was quickly swallowed by the creat's winds. Her blood-curdling scream was cut short by a snap and a crunch. Blood splattered, dying the tornado scarlet.

I quivered. Tears drenched my face. Breaths came in shallow, quick bursts. My head felt light, heavy, and about to burst all at the same time. No matter how many times I witnessed horrors such as these, it never got easier. It only got harder and harder, my broken heart only able to take so much.

Fangs unhinged as the serpent whipped across the brook.

Its red eyes homed in on me, calling my blood, drawing it to the surface.

Before those fangs could sink into my flesh, he dove in front of me.

Blood sprayed alongside his cries of pain.

"No!" I wailed.

I reached up for him. Maybe I could pry him loose. Maybe I could save him before—

Blood splattered out of his mouth.

I cried out and curled into a ball, spiraling into my new reality. I squirmed on the forest floor, trench deep in his blood while the serpent feasted on his flesh above me. The leaves would camouflage me if I sunk deep enough. Maybe even bury me alive. It would be a more peaceful death than his, an end that should've been mine.

Before I could accept my fate, something yanked on my arms.

I screamed and looked up, expecting to find that serpent tangled around me. Instead, I found my mother pleading.

"Get up, Anora."

Her words sent the flashback scurrying away. There may not be a serpent about to devour me, but a very real threat tore through the clearing behind us.

I pushed through the piercing pain in my foot and dashed through the maze of trees. As we headed farther into the woods, the shouts and cries from the massacre subsided under the growling of the monster and the grunting of something much more . . . human? It sounded more like a war cry than one of fear. Looking back through the trees, I caught glimpses of the battle unfolding and stopped fleeing.

The creat had stopped spinning and circled something in the middle of the clearing, a woman garbed in a gray and bright-blue jumpsuit. The slick material glistened in the lingering light. Her jet-black hair, tied in a ponytail, glinted too.

It was Guardian Yllaria—the Mimic.

She circled the beast, assessing its movements as it began to spin once again. Then, just as the beast had, she lifted her arms out to the sides and began spinning on her tiptoes, faster and faster until she became a whipping wind as well.

Guardian Yllaria rammed against the beast's tornado with her own. The creat flew across the clearing and slammed into the trunk of a sturdy pine. Its back nearly snapped as it bent around the wood.

With a scream, the Guardian broke her whirlwind and fell to the ground, cradling her arm. She stumbled to her feet, then dashed toward the beast, a dagger winking in her hand.

Before the beast could stand, she reached out with her blade. She aimed the knife for the creature's middle, but the beast sliced down with its claws. Guardian Yllaria cried out again and crumpled to her knees. The boar stood and bellowed at the Guardian in triumph.

She stayed on her knees, whimpering at the lancing pain. The creat raised an arm, balled its meaty hand, and aimed for the cowering Guardian.

I braced myself for the blow, ready to dash through the woods once the monster was free to demolish whatever lay in its path.

But then, a flash of gray.

The beast's wail pierced the air as its innards spilled onto the forest floor. The boar cried out once more before it slumped to the ground, clawing at exposed organs. The Guardian strolled up behind it and dug her dagger into its throat. The creat's head lolled on the ground as its last dregs of life bled onto the dirt.

Guardian Yllaria stepped out from behind the beast's carcass, chest heaving. She collapsed to the ground, wincing as she clutched at her arm, then her face.

A crowd trickled into the clearing. Bill hobbled forward to join them. I went to follow, but my mother's nails dug into my shoulder.

"Are you okay?" She scanned my body for cuts and bruises.

"I sprained my foot," I answered, the pain throbbing down my heel.

"We'll have the Willards look at it."

"I think they have more pressing patients." My voice was shaky as I looked toward the clearing. Several people lay in pools of blood with wood and metal lodged in their backs and sides. Their moans replaced the roars echoing in my ears. I closed my eyes to escape the gore, but behind my eyes lurked a serpent twined around my father's bloated, purpled body. I opened my eyes just as quickly as I shut them. I should've known better.

There's no such thing as escape.

"Well then—I . . ." She searched for a remedy. "I'll wrap it when we get home."

She caressed my face and I leaned into her hand. Tears filled her hazel eyes as she looked from me to Liam, who clung to her skirt with a numb expression.

"Let's go," she said, pulling us toward the clearing, the carnage.

I limped into the clearing just as Cassandry and her parents emerged from the trees and raced for the fallen Guardian. The closer I got, the clearer the gashes maiming her olive skin became. Blood gushed down her cheek and neck from the two slashes adorning them. Flesh hung off her face in jagged chunks. Her hair was matted from the blood coating her neck. The cut on her arm was smaller, but leaking a fair amount of blood all the same.

Cassandry's father examined the Guardian's arm while her mother focused on her face.

"Don't worry about me. Help your wounded," Guardian Yllaria insisted.

"After that—what you did—it's the least we can do," Mrs. Willard said.

"It would be an honor," Mr. Willard added.

"I'll be okay. We have supplies at the base. So please, help the civilians," she urged.

The doctors nodded. "Thank you for saving us."

"Not a problem." The Guardian nodded in return as they made their way toward the wounded.

Cassandry joined her parents, helping them assess and move their patients. From a distance, I couldn't see any major injuries on her, just a glazed look as she trudged along. They, with help from some uninjured volunteers, started down the road toward the infirmary.

I took a step forward, ready to follow after them. This seemed a better time than any to start training, but my mother had a different idea. Before I got far, she clutched her fingers around my arm and pulled me back.

"I know you want to help," Mom whispered in my ear, "but I'm not letting you out of my sight."

I nodded and leaned into her side. There was no use arguing, and a part of me was relieved for it.

Guardian Yllaria summoned the strength to stand, and a couple of men rushed to her side, but she waved them off.

"Don't worry about me."

They kept their distance, ready to catch her if she fell. She stumbled to her feet, her face bloodied and wrinkled in agony. She surveyed the carcass of the beast, grimacing at the vile smell.

The mangled remains of a corpse lay among its intestines.

I gagged and covered my nose and mouth with both hands. The farmer's face, her screams, tore through my mind. I fell on quivering knees and retched. A soothing voice cooed, a sound that comforted me after all my nightmares, real or dreamt. After I finished heaving my ice cream onto the blood-speckled grass, my mother pulled me into her arms and away from the grisly scene.

As I burrowed into her embrace, Guardian Yllaria gave me a pitying glance, like a grown-up would a crying infant. I scowled back at her.

"I'm sorry we didn't have time to send a warning over the air," she said. "Six of them came out at once. We stopped three, but the others got past the fence."

"Is it common for them to come in packs like that?" Bill asked, massaging his lower back.

"Yes, it's been happening a lot lately, but usually only two or three at a time."

A construction worker chimed in. "We appreciate everything the Guard does."

"We're happy to. It's what we're born to do." She waved toward the gore. "I'll go fetch the Clean-Up crew to take care of this. And kid," she added for me, her pitying look returning. "I know how hard all of this is, but just remember that the Guard will always be here to protect you."

"Liar," I muttered, thinking of all the farmers making a living and fathers saving their daughters that had died in a scarlet-soaked clearing like this one.

"Anora—" Mom scolded.

Guardian Yllaria cut her off. "It's alright. Have a safe evening."

Then, with one hand wrapped around her bleeding arm, she dashed down the road.

She had just fought off a creat and lost so much blood. How did she have the energy to sprint all the way back to her base? I'd never understood how Guardian abilities worked, but I supposed being a regular citizen meant I didn't have to. All I had to do was trust in them and believe they would save me, but look what good that did the farmer.

By the time she left, the sky had traded its dark orange hue for an evening purple, a red moon peeking over the treetops. A chilling breeze swept through the clearing, raising goosebumps on my arms.

With our groceries and boxes lost to the wind, we began the somber journey home. Mom gripped Liam's hand and mine. My stepfather clutched his back, a wince wrinkling his tan face, as he led us down the road. I kept my concerns silent as I limped down the road behind him. My foot throbbed with each step.

Dusk settled into night. The moon shone over the canopy to light the path home and keep the nightmares that crept in the woods at bay.

It's said that the Mother watched over us from the moon, to provide light and protection for Her creations in the ominous dark of nightfall. Normally, the moon shone bright blue as her sign that all was well, all was safe. But when the moon cast a harsh red glow, it was Her warning that something terrible was coming. The warning could be for a day later, sometimes a week. It could be a sign of an impending creat attack, or a personal omen for an unfortunate soul.

That night, the Mother's warning was clear in the red haze. The attack was already over—could another one be coming so soon? Or, was someone out there about to live their worst nightmare?

I could only pray it wasn't me.

My parents had turned locking down the house into an artform.

Bill fastened three sets of locks and deadbolts on the front and back doors. He placed thick wooden brackets across both for good measure. Mom secured the wooden shutters and reinforced them with iron bars, sending the room into complete darkness. She blindly turned on a lamp without so much as bumping into the table. Dim light cast shadows on the gray walls and plank floors. They both hurried upstairs to barricade the rest of the windows.

Once the house was secured, Mom efficiently wrapped my throbbing foot in a tight bandage. I should've insisted on doing it myself as practice, but I couldn't muster the strength or drive. When she finished, utter silence weighed on the room. I turned on the radio and wiggled the dial until the news came in clear.

The tail end of the report stated, "—on both Bellwarn and Heneth this evening. We have officially broken last year's attack record."

"Can I change it?" My question came out more like a statement. We had just lived it—Why listen to it all over again? I'd had enough attacks for one day.

"Yeah, sweetie, you can," my mother said softly.

I twisted the knobs until I heard the soothing plink of a piano, albeit a bit grainy. The graceful melody flooded my aching head, fighting off the torturous memories banging at the door. Nestling between my parents, I closed my eyes and let the music consume me.

Chapter Four

The glade was laden with a dense fog. I rubbed my arms to fend off the chill. My fingers skidded along the sleek fabric of my shirt. With a cursory glance, I realized I was wearing a gray and blue jumpsuit. A shiver ran down my spine. Why was I in a Guardian uniform? The Portemor Mountains would have to crumble to the ground before I battled a creat.

The earth quaked and threw me off balance. I slammed to the ground and my head struck a boulder. Wincing, I rolled onto my side, curled into a ball, and cradled my head.

The glade shuddered again. I surveyed the surrounding forest and spotted a shadow gliding between the trees. Blood drained from my face, as if it too wanted to hide. I sank onto my belly, trying to blend into the tall grasses.

This was it. The creat would sniff me out, tear me to bits, and I'd be gone. There was no stopping it—my inevitable end.

I closed my eyes so tightly my eyelids ached. I breathed heavily into the wet earth, condensation built up on my lips and nose. The ground rumbled. A boom sounded from every direction. My body shuddered and eyes refused to open.

Hot breath that smelled of carrion swamped the air. I whimpered, tears mixing with the sweat and dirt on my face. A sharp nail scraped down my spine. My sobs were muffled by the soft dirt. A deep sneer reverberated through the glade as the beast toyed with its meal, slowly slicing its claws down my back, along my scar. I screamed from the agony, the pain, the fear. The creature clenched its thorny claws around my waist, lifting me to its nose. Its wet snout smeared the blood on my back as it sniffed. I cried out from the burning pain that shot through the gashes.

Anticipating my death hadn't made it any less painful . . . any less terrifying.

The creat turned me in its palm, huffing hot air in my face. I gagged as the smell of death washed over me. It squeezed me, suffocated me. I struggled for breath, clutching at my throat. Just as my last breath slipped away, I opened my eyes—

Thud! I crashed onto my bedroom floor, cocooned in a blanket. My injured foot ached. Panic bloomed in my chest like a revving engine as I searched for a creature hiding in the shadows. The sight of my cluttered room, free of monsters, eased my breathing.

It was only a nightmare. Another to add to my growing collection.

My body and blankets were drowned in sweat. I wriggled out of the swaddle. My shorts sagged on my hips, thoroughly soaked. Whole droplets slid down my legs. My hair, ruffled in a loose braid, hung heavy and damp on my neck. Grimacing, I examined my bed. The sheets and mattress were sopping wet with sweat or urine, or both. *Gross!* I balled up the blankets and peeled off my pajamas. Even the carpet was soaked and squishing beneath my toes. *Ew*, was it even humanly possible to pee this much? I wrapped myself in a robe and stepped into the hall.

The hallway was dark, the shutters not yet lifted. A small shaft of dawn peeked through the crack between the windowpane and the shutter. I hobbled down the narrow hall, avoiding the squeaky planks on my way to the bathroom.

With a flick of a switch, bright light flooded the room and reflected off the white tile. I blindly searched for a towel and groped for the shower faucet. As the water warmed and my eyes adjusted, I glanced in the mirror. My wheat-gold hair looked dark brown from being soaked. The scar tissue that slashed up my back and peaked at my shoulder shimmered with moisture. Water beaded on the faint freckles scattered across my tan cheeks and nose.

There was just too much water for it to have all come from me, right? It was physically impossible. I sat on the lip of the tub and mused.

Maybe a strong storm broke my window and blew through the room? No, the window was closed. At least, I believed so—that seemed like something I'd notice right away. The whole room would've been destroyed too, not just the bed.

Hmm. What could it have been?

I scowled when the most obvious explanation came to me. Leaving the shower running, I limped down the hall. My bathrobe swished against my calves.

I stormed into Liam's room. "What is *wrong* with you, you little twerp?"

Liam jolted out of bed, rubbing his eyes. "What?"

"You know *exactly* what! You decided it'd be funny to dump water on me."

"Hey, hey, what's goin' on in here," my stepfather mumbled as he stumbled through the doorway, sleep weighing down his eyelids.

"Liam dumped water on me while I was sleeping. My bed is *ruined*!"

"No, I didn't!" My brother rushed to his feet, seeming more awake after the accusation.

"You *liar*."

"Don't you speak like that under my roof," Mom commanded from the doorway, her arms crossed and face stern.

"But look what he did!" I held out my wet arms as proof. "And my whole room is drenched."

"I didn't! I swear!" Liam pleaded.

Mom stepped into the room. Her judging glare made me antsy and I blurted, "Don't believe me? Go look."

With Mom leading the pack, we piled into my room.

"See! How else would you explain it?"

"What the . . ." my stepfather trailed off with a baffled look. "It's all over the floor and wall too."

In the surprise of the morning, I hadn't noticed that the pale yellow wall behind the bed was splattered with water. Maybe it *had* been a storm. I looked to my window —it was still shuttered, still intact.

Silence fell as we all took in the strange scene.

Mom circled my bed, avoiding the waterlogged carpet, confusion creasing her freckled brow. She felt the blankets, the mattress. "This is a lot of water."

"He probably had a bucket or something." I scowled at my little brother.

"Sis, I swear, I didn't." His thick eyebrows raised in supposed innocence. What a faker!

"Okay, let's not get into this now," Mom commanded. "We'll talk about it later."

"But my room is destroyed!"

"No, it's not, Nora bug. We'll clean it up and it'll be fine. Now, go take your shower."

Glaring at my brother one last time, I headed for the bathroom and left my bemused family in the bog that was once my bedroom.

My parents insisted there was no way little Liam could lift and dump a bucket filled with that much water. Reluctantly, I agreed and began searching for another explanation.

Mom had taken the sheets and pillows, leaving the damp mattress to air dry. The wall was dry, returning to its soothing shade of daffodil. I sat at my oak vanity cluttered with brushes, hairpins, and ribbons. In the mirror, I looked past my reflection to the bed.

Where could that much water have come from? Had a pipe burst? But then there would be a gaping hole or crack in the wall or ceiling. I looked to the window beside my bed again. It hadn't been broken by a storm, but could it have been opened by someone, or something, else?

Stepping toward the window, I examined the shutter locks: sealed. I unlocked the shutters and revealed a sealed, unbroken window on the other side. Maybe it had been closed afterward . . .

I pictured a slender creature slithering through the window and down the wall. Lifting its pointed head in the darkness, it peered down at me with glowing green eyes.

A chill wriggled up my spine and I slammed the shutter shut, locking it.

"Everything alright in here?" Mom inquired, a laundry basket pinned to her hip. "How's your foot?"

"A little sore. I'm trying to figure out what happened."

"It's just one of those fluke things you can't explain. Don't worry yourself about it."

"You don't think something broke in, do you?"

"Oh, dear, no. This house was locked up tight. There's no way something got in," she insisted, though worry deepened her wrinkles as she surveyed the room.

I nodded absentmindedly. My room was a cluttered mess, but it was exactly how I'd left it the previous night. I glanced over my body; no strange cuts or bruises or bites.

I sighed, pushing curiosity to the back of my mind. "Need any help today?"

"No, just finishing the laundry then getting some sewing done. You rest and enjoy your day off, okay?"

"Sure," I said with an unconvincing smile. Instead, my mind kept churning for an answer.

When I tired of picturing sly cretins sneaking into my room, reaching for my throat, I dug into my backpack and pulled out final exam notes. They sat in my lap, my eyes unable to focus on the page. With a sigh, I tossed them on the floor. How ridiculous to think homework could actually distract me from such thoughts.

Food ended up being the distraction I needed. Piecing together a lunch from the scraps in the pantry was a challenge. While nibbling stale bread and dried fruit at the kitchen counter, I spied Liam sprawled on the living room rug playing with the wooden animals Bill carved for him. He tweeted and howled for his figurines while they flew through the air. A smile tugged at my lips, and I knew what I had to do.

The sunlight burning through the kitchen window warmed my feet as I slunk along the wall. I ducked behind the couch and crept around the corner, ignoring the ache in my foot.

His feet lay on the rug, completely exposed. Before he could notice me, I dove for his toes and began tickling. Liam shrieked in surprise and swatted me away.

"Quit it!" Liam demanded through his laughs.

Letting go of his feet, I chuckled. "I definitely got you back for the last time you ambush-tickled me."

"Barely, this totally doesn't count." He tucked his feet under him in defense.

"Oh please, this does too! Don't be a sore loser." I reached to tickle him again.

He squirmed out of my reach and furrowed his brow. "No, I'm not. And I'm not a jerk that splashed you with water this morning, either."

He looked down and fiddled with a whittled rabbit.

I tilted my head and sighed. Looking at him now, so

small and innocent, I didn't know how I could ever accuse him of such a thing. The only monster in the room that morning had been me.

"I know you didn't, Liam. I'm sorry for what I said. I was upset and confused and, well . . . can you forgive me?"

"I don't know. I guess." A small smile crept onto his face. "On one condition."

"What?"

"Tonight is my night for dishes." He flashed a devilish grin.

"Fine, fine. I'll do the dishes tonight," I accepted, getting to my feet. A small price to pay and a far better offer than I deserved.

"Good doing business," Liam said as he flipped onto his stomach, resuming his play.

With a weight lifted off my heart, I shuffled out the front door and down the porch steps.

Just inside the line of trees, shadowed by branches, was my father's shed. It was small, weathered, and sagging. The step leading inside was broken and replaced by a thick, flat stone.

This was where my father had spent most of his time. Even though it was less protected than the house, I never felt afraid in it. We would stay out here for hours: him, bent over his work; me, reading or coloring in the door-frame. That broken step was where I would stifle laughter until my chest hurt from his goofy jokes and silently cry in his strong arms after being bullied at school. That single step held my childhood secrets, my all-grown-up dreams. Their true keeper was gone, so that his little girl could have a chance to make those dreams come true. A tear slid down the curve of my smile as I poked my head inside.

Bill sat on a stool, hunched over a workbench with screwdrivers and wrenches scattered haphazardly about.

"Whatcha up to?" I asked with my near-silent outside voice.

My stepfather peered over his shoulder, his smile gathering wrinkles. "Hey there, kiddo, come on in."

He swiveled on his stool and wiped grease-coated hands on his fraying overalls. As he showed me the broken radio he was repairing, I noticed his slight wince and hand pressed to his back.

"You're hurt."

"I'm fine." He waved it off. "Pulled a muscle, is all. How's your day off?"

"You should be resting. Sitting on this stool all afternoon is only going to make it worse."

"It's not that bad, I promise." He smiled. "Now, tell me about your day."

"It's been fine." I fiddled with a scrap piece of wood on the bench.

He inclined his head. When I didn't divulge anything more, he leaned back on his stool. "It's okay to be scared, you know. It's okay to not be okay with what happened."

I shifted my posture. I should've known he'd want more than that obligatory response. Unlike most, Bill actually cared. "I had another nightmare."

He wrapped me in his arms. His warm embrace and the smell of grease soothed me.

"I understand why you're afraid. You have every right to be. Use that fear to stay alert and safe. You did exactly what you should've done yesterday. You ran. You ran as hard as you could. You were so fast that no one could keep up with you." He chuckled. "I'm proud of you, Anora. You saved yourself and that's exactly what your mom and I want."

"But it's not enough. They're faster." I shuddered.

"Don't think that way." My stepfather's eyes locked on mine. "You are a survivor, Anora. Don't *ever* doubt yourself."

My eyes fluttered, looking down at the floor. Maybe he didn't see it, but that was all I was capable of. Doubt, fear. There wasn't an ounce of courage in my bones. Monsters had chased it all away.

He lifted my chin and spoke with such conviction. "Promise me that you won't ever doubt yourself."

"I promise," I said and gave him a forced smile, something to reassure him.

With a squeeze of my shoulder and a grin that didn't reach his eyes, he redirected the heavy conversation. "Go help your mother fix dinner. Maybe try and convince her to make cookies tonight."

"You know how stingy she is with her sugar, but I'll see what I can do," I assured, one foot out the door.

"That's my girl," he said with a wink before swiveling back toward the workbench.

———

Steam curled as I set bean salad and sautéed broccoli on the dining table. Mother bustled around the kitchen, skirt twirling at her feet as she gathered plates and silverware. I snatched a stack of cups from the cabinet and walked to my seat, the pain in my foot dulled to a minor nuisance.

The chair creaked under my weight and its uneven legs sent me gently rocking backward. Bill, wearing a grease-free shirt and jeans, eased into his seat and sighed with relief as he leaned back, both he and the chair groaning in harmony. I passed around the cups, then extended my hands toward my stepfather and mother sitting at either end of the table. Liam mimicked me and we all clasped hands and closed our eyes.

"Thank you, Blessed Mother, for this day. Thank you for the food on this table and those gathered around it," Mom prayed. "Thank you for sending Guardian Yllaria to protect us at the market. Watch over her and keep us all safe tonight and all nights to come."

We all nodded, then quickly dug into the steaming food before us. We passed dishes around the table. The clinking of plates and silverware played their melody.

Between bites, my stepfather swiped the newspaper off the counter. Perusing an article with the headline *ANTIC-IPATE FIVE PERCENT HIKE IN TAXES*, he scoffed. "Celepheria's full of selfish crooks."

I glanced over to my mother and shared a knowing look. My stepfather had a special hatred for Celepheria, for what they did—or rather didn't do—for the mainland. Every now and then he needed to let out that frustration, usually in the form of a rant. Bill shook out the paper noisily. When no one took the bait, he cleared his throat and shook the paper out again, waiting for his cue.

With a smirk dancing on her lips, Mom asked, "What are they up to this time?"

"Well," Bill began. "Government is hikin' our taxes again, the greedy bastards. We can barely afford to feed ourselves, let alone protect ourselves or, for Mother's sake, leave this damned land. We're lucky if we get four shipments of supplies a year from Hangrove. 'Too risky for the drivers,' they say, throwing Confinement Laws in our face while there's a bunch of us *living* out here. They don't care if we get picked off one by one by creats as long as they get to live in peace on their damned island!"

His face was deep red, his wrinkles accentuated by his scowl. He was about to start rambling again when Mom warned, "Mind your blood pressure, Bill. No sense in riling up over something we can't change."

Bill sat straighter in his chair and stared at my mother, his eyes wide with rage. I felt his frustration burn in my chest. Even though I found his predictable rants amusing, he had a point.

The Celepherians ruled all of Alberune, but they had no idea what it was truly like for the mainlanders. And since they didn't know, they didn't care. We didn't make up a huge population, mainly because so many had been killed over hundreds of years or had fled to Celepheria if they'd had the means. Just because we were few didn't mean our voices shouldn't be heard—but like Mom said, we couldn't change it, so why worry about it?

I took his pause as an opportunity to change the subject. "Tomorrow is my final Guardian Assessment."

"Oh good! You must be relieved," Mom replied.

"Cassandry, Eithan, and I are planning a celebratory lunch. Could we make cookies for it?" I glanced at my stepfather and his scowl had cracked around a smirk.

"Of course! I'll make sure we have enough sugar after dinner," Mom approved with a smile.

"Can you leave some home, Mom? Please?" Liam begged.

"I won't have any extras if you eat all the cookie dough again," she quipped.

"I'm not making any promises when it comes to cookie dough," Liam mumbled through a mouthful of broccoli, green bits spraying onto the table.

I bit back a laugh. *What a slob!* I couldn't really blame him though. This was cookie dough we were talking about here—the single best creation known to mankind. Bill snorted a laugh too, another break in his glower.

"Don't talk with your mouth full, Liam. How many times do I have to tell you," Mom scolded, straightening in her seat.

"Sorry," Liam mumbled again, covering his mouth this time.

My mother gave him a pointed look, a smirk tugging at the corner of her mouth as she scooped the remaining vegetables onto his and my plates.

After finishing up dinner and doing the dishes for Liam, I hustled upstairs and changed into a tank top and shorts. My ponytail bobbed as I raced back downstairs. In the far corner of the dining room sat my safe runner.

Bill had constructed it for me. He'd welded a slender pipe, adorned with handlebars, to the front of the running platform, a rubber track that revolved like an endless footpath. With a compulsive need to run and build on my speed, I could satiate my need without going outside unnecessarily. After the recent lockdown and market attack, I was in desperate need of releasing pent-up, nervous energy.

Getting the track revolving was always the hardest

part. Once in motion, it became easier, and I picked up the pace. With every step, stress sloughed off. I focused on my feet pounding rhythmically on the track. The dull throb in my sprained foot kept in time with the beat. My mind cleared and the tension that had built up over the past two days drifted behind me as I ran toward nowhere.

Chapter Five

🙊

Cassandry, Eithan, and I walked into the school gymnasium clad in loose-fitting shirts and shorts. My foot no longer hurt, but I'd still wrapped it in the morning—partly for practice as a future nurse, but mostly for extra protection, knowing what horrors awaited me in this harrowing place.

Ropes and swings hung from the ceiling, coated with either slippery oil or tiny barbs and spurs. The indoor track was engineered with a movable wall that raced behind the unfortunate souls assigned that challenge. It forced them to run faster and faster or else it would slam into them and skid their helpless bodies along until the coach turned it off. In the middle of the gym was an elaborate obstacle course ending with the water pit, a cylindrical hole that burrowed twenty feet beneath the gym floor and was filled with either scalding hot or bitter cold water.

In other words, it was a torture chamber

They changed the course often so our bodies wouldn't get used to any particular torment. I cringed at the memory of climbing the rock wall, then being punched by one of the handholds I had wrongly assumed was permanently embedded into the wall. The blow had made me fumble my grip and I'd torn a knee open as I struggled for purchase. The only benefit was that I had gotten dismissed early for my injury.

Painted on the front wall was the Guardian crest. The flames engulfing the bottom started as a deep cobalt-blue and faded to silver. A few students knelt in front of the seal. They whispered prayers of courage, strength, and luck. I rolled my eyes at them and silently wished for my own quick failure.

We moved to a far corner of the gym where we hid in the shadows of the rock wall, hoping the trainers wouldn't spot us. The trainers weren't Guardians but were still experts in strength and combat training. Even with my runner's endurance, I was never prepared for the misery they imparted. The rest of our class was spread out across the gym, most stretching while a few hid like we had.

"I'm not sure I can handle another day on the kill course," Cassandry admitted.

Along with dread for what was to come, Cassandry was somber after our earlier conversation at lunch. Over Mom's cookies, she had apologized for not telling me sooner that she wouldn't be returning to Bellwarn. I had agreed that it really was the best decision for her. It was dangerous to travel on the mainland. After all, Confinement Laws were written for a reason. Then I had apologized for not being happy for her. Cassandry had found a way to escape this monster-ridden world. She could dance through the streets of Celepheria, singing at the top of her lungs, if she wanted. I hadn't mentioned how bitter that thought would be the next time I was cowering under my bed, hoping the locks and shutters kept out the horrors creeping in the night. We'd agreed to make the most of our remaining time together, starting with a second helping of cookies.

Eithan was assessing the kill course as well. With all of his strength in his mind, his lanky body only gave him the advantage of being lightweight. He leaned against the wall in silence, picking at his nails.

When I noticed Victon walking in our direction, I joined Eithan to deflect his attention.

It didn't work.

Victon's beady eyes narrowed on each of us. "Why do you even bother showing up?"

"They make us, genius," I snapped.

He began stretching, twisting his bulky frame while pulling an arm across his chest. "You just waste all of the *actual* candidates' time while we wait for you to stumble through."

"Technically, we are all candidates," Eithan retorted under his breath. "Guardians are born with their powers dormant inside them. This assessment is a way to trigger their release."

Victon bellowed a laugh. "Does twerpy little Eithan Hillem honestly think *he* is a Guardian?"

Eithan folded in on himself, his voice even smaller than before. "No, but Guardian powers are indiscriminate. It doesn't matter how physically capable you are."

"So you *do* think you're a Guardian!" Victon claimed. "Sorry to disappoint, but Guardians are courageous and honorable. Something you'll never be."

"Back off, Victon." I stepped forward. "No one in their

right mind would want to be a Guardian, anyway. It's a death sentence."

"Of course you would think that, coward." His dark eyes squinted down at me.

Cassandry slid between us and pushed Victon back with a hand square to his chest. "Get over yourself and move on."

Before Victon could push it further, the trainers strutted into the gym. Two were brawny men and one was a thickly built woman, all with matching buzzcuts. They immediately began assigning groups to each station. Victon stalked off toward the free weights so he could be assigned to a group with his friends. The trainers didn't miss my friends and me hiding in the corner and placed us on the kill course.

We groaned our protest. Just our luck we'd get assigned the worst challenge for the last assessment.

Making our way to the back of the line, we anxiously watched as the athletes in the class struggled through the course. The kill course was specifically designed to push even the fittest among us to their breaking point: the point where their powers would unleash if they possessed any at all. Last time, I barely made it through the first obstacle, but the trainers forced me to move on even though I was wheezing and wobbly on my feet.

It was my turn too soon. Even though Victon was a jerk, he had a point—this was a huge waste of time. I knew I didn't have powers. All the pain this course had in store would be for nothing. I slowly stepped onto a small podium and hesitated, trying to avoid the inevitable.

The female instructor, Coach Hacket, snarled, "Get a move on, girl."

I glared at her, then took in the first obstacle.

A wooden post was about six feet away and stood almost as tall as the ceiling. Small pegs stuck out along its trunk and led to the top platform. I steadied my feet and lunged, hands outstretched. I grabbed one peg, but my other hand slipped. My body swung and slammed against the pole. I cried out and nearly lost my grip, but I quickly swung my other arm up and grabbed a peg. My feet found their own set and I began scaling the post. Each step was painstakingly harder than the last, from both the physical strain and the pegs becoming increasingly shorter the farther I climbed. By the time I hoisted myself onto the platform, my arms, legs, and lungs were burning. I wobbled onto my feet and took a few breaths, bracing for the next task.

What lay in front of me was pure agony suspended from the ceiling. It had to be breaking some kind of human rights law.

A row of seven metal disk swings swayed in front of me. I'd have to land on one disk, swing to the next, and scale my way across the ceiling to the platform on the other side. A net lay below in case someone fell. I briefly considered free-falling onto it, but knew I'd be forced to start over again if I did. I took a deep breath and leaped from the platform instead.

When I landed on the first disk, my feet slipped and I clung to the central pole while my shoes struggled for traction on the oil-slicked metal. Once I gained purchase, I quickly jumped to the next before I lost momentum. With no traction to launch properly, my jump was more like a sprawled tumble. I grasped the pole on the next swing too low and my hip rammed into the side of the disk. I cried out in pain.

Completey exhausted, I couldn't hoist myself onto the swing platform. Gratefully, I accepted this as a loss and let go of the pole, tucking my knees in as I plummeted to the net below.

Coach Hacket was already yelling at me to get up before I landed. With soundproof walls, the coaches could berate us without fear. Wobbling and stumbling along the net, I made it to the base of the platform I was supposed to land on. There were pegs built into the sides of it, similar to the first post.

Mustering my strength, I climbed up one knob at a time. Sweat coated my forehead and dripped into my eyes. I squinted against the burn. Once I reached the top, I lay on my stomach for a few breaths, but Coach Hacket bellowed for me to get moving.

"Climb up here and make me," I challenged between labored breaths.

"What did you say?" she screamed, a hand already on a peg and feet finding their own.

Oh, Mother, she was actually going to do it. There wasn't enough room on this platform for the both of us. She'd probably toss me over the edge and into the next obstacle without any warning or remorse.

"Okay, okay, I'm going!" I yelled back. "Don't get your gym shorts in a bunch."

I crawled onto my hands and knees, forced myself to stand, and faced the next challenge.

The next three obstacles were more brutal than the last. The platforms were higher, the jumps were farther, and the surfaces were all slick with oil. I was swooping and climbing, but mostly, I was falling. Each time I fell, Coach yelled at me to keep moving. I felt bruises swelling on my face, knees, and elbows. My breath was haggard, my body drenched with sweat and oil. I licked the salt off my lips and brushed away the damp hair pasted to my cheeks. I crawled to the edge of the final obstacle—the water pit. My arms wobbled like gelatin.

"I can't," I panted as I laid my cheek against the cool floor. A bitterly refreshing breeze caressed my burning skin—ice-cold water, then.

"What?" Coach Hacket yelled as she knelt down. "What did you say to me?"

"I . . . can't," I loosed between each breath.

She lay down, belly on the floor. "Don't you dare say those words in front of me. How would you like it if a Guardian said that while you're being ripped apart by some filthy creat?"

Her eyes bore into me, ripping me apart just like that beast would. I closed my eyes and focused on controlling my breathing.

"You get in that water now!"

I opened my eyes and looked at the water. My heart sank as I took in the cold, black abyss. A shiver ran down my spine, fear overpowering the physical pain.

"Don't make me push you in, girl," the trainer threatened.

I knew she would, too. No use fighting anymore—no avoiding the inevitable. I nudged toward the water, fighting against the part of me wanting to flee from the dark chasm. The edge of the water rippled as I breathed over it, revealing nothing of what lay beneath.

"What size is it?" I asked.

"It's the marble."

"What? That's the smallest one!"

"No use complaining." She looked deep into the void, as if she could see the marble lying at the bottom. Then she turned to me, looking deep into my eyes, searching for a hint of the power potentially lying within.

"Prepare for disappointment," I groaned as I twisted my legs around and swung them into the pool.

The bitter cold water was refreshing on my hot, sweaty skin. I dipped into the pool and waded a few seconds before taking a large breath to carry with me to the depths. Closing my eyes, I used the side of the pit as a springboard and launched down the long chasm. The icy water quickly turned from soothing to biting. Cold spiked every pore like needles. I held back the urge to turn around.

As I pushed myself farther through the water, I began to lose my bearings. I felt around for the wall of the tunnel.

I couldn't find it.

In a panic, I opened my eyes to pitch-black. I was lost in the empty, fathomless darkness.

My throat began to tighten.

I waved around frantically for the tunnel's edge. When my fingertips finally brushed the stone, my nerves calmed. Guided along the wall, I swam deeper and faster, knowing I had precious seconds of air left.

I reached the bottom of the pit and instantly began sweeping the floor with my hands, my senses on alert for the smallest bump of a marble. Icy water swept over my hands as I searched. My throat was burning, feeling like it was about to cave in. I gulped, hoping there was a bit of air left trapped in my closed mouth.

I couldn't find the marble. Panic draped over me like a cloak. Icy daggers stabbed every inch of skin. My throat ached for air.

Air.

My head began to ache and spin. I needed to get out of here, but which way was up?

I swirled around, trying to get my bearings with no trace of light to guide me. The floor seemed to have fallen farther down as I searched for any form of contact. My throat burned. My head throbbed.

In the fathomless abyss, something snaked through the water. I froze, eyes locked on the hazy form, willing it to disappear.

It didn't.

An eel-like creature with slick, bruise-purple skin circled me. Its bulbous black eyes hung outside its narrow head, scanning my vulnerable body. Teeth like knitting needles hung out of its jaw at awkward angles.

Coach Hacket put a Portemor monster in the water!? That was too far, even for her. I submitted to all the other obstacles, albeit begrudgingly, but I drew a line at fighting for my life against a creat.

My heart beat faster. I tried to swim up toward the surface, but the beast batted me down with its slimy tail.

All I could do was sob, my tears dissolving into nothing. I prayed for a quick end, a painless death, but my father's crackling scream ripping through the clearing echoed in my memory, and I realized there was no such thing.

Slowly, it closed in on me. It circled closer and closer

until one of its long, needle-tipped teeth brushed my shoulder.

I screamed, opening my mouth, and water rushed in. I gagged and gasped for air. I felt my consciousness wane in and out. The eel faded in and out of nothingness.

Air. I needed . . . *air*.

My body pulsed and time stood still. A raging burst of energy erupted from my chest, rushed down my arms, and out of my hands. Then, the water entombing me was suddenly blasted from the tunnel.

I fell to the floor of the pit and coughed up water from my lungs. Greedily, I gasped for air. The creat that had been about to devour me just moments ago was nowhere in sight. Heads began poking out from the top of the tunnel, so far from where I lay.

Their figures grew fuzzy as my mind was devoured by oblivion.

Chapter Six

S tinging pulses racked my brain and roused me from the darkness. An unyielding pillow under my head perpetuated the pain. The room was too bright. Squinting, I searched for anything distinguishable. My eyes began to focus, and I recognized the nurse's cot beneath me and the scratchy sheet atop it.

Slowly, I propped myself up on my elbows. My arms shook with fatigue as I strained to support myself. I gave up and fell back onto the bed.

Flashbacks of circling monsters and drowning in darkness swarmed my mind. Anxiety rose in my chest. Alongside it, an unexpected thrum reverberated like a second pulse.

Whoa. What was that?

It started in my chest and radiated down my arms, lapping against my closed palms like bathwater sloshing against the side of a tub. My breath hitched in my throat from the sensation—intense and strange, but not painful.

The door creaked open and Nurse Roslyn and Coach

Hacket entered the room. They flanked my bed and examined me.

"What happened?" I breathed, my throat raw.

"Turns out you're the lucky winner there, Baelin," the brute woman said.

"What's that supposed to mean?"

"You have the power. Blessed by the Mother above. Congratulations." Nurse Roslyn's voice was like honey. She grabbed a damp cloth and placed it on my forehead.

Did she just say . . . *power*? Like Guardian power? I must be hallucinating. It had to be a joke. I broke into a weak, cracked laugh. "Good one."

"You don't remember?" Coach Hacket asked. "What's the last thing you remember from your assessment?"

I closed my eyes and searched for my last memories— darkness, frigid cold, and a monster slowly narrowing in. My eyes startled open, my breathing heavier.

"Anora, it's okay. You're safe here," Nurse Roslyn's cinnamon eyes flickered with concern, her thin lips curved into a slight frown.

I ignored her and turned on my trainer. "You put a creat in the pit! You sent me in there to die!" I struggled to hold myself up again, but I had rage to fuel me this time.

"What are you talking about?" Coach Hacket questioned. "There was no creat. We'd never put students in that much danger."

"I saw it! It was going to kill me!"

Nurse Roslyn shushed me and pet my hair like she was cooing a child. "Sweetheart, there was no creat. The lack of oxygen must have triggered a hallucination."

I wanted to argue more. The eel was so vivid. I felt its tooth scrape my arm, its slick tail whack me. But I also knew myself much more clearly than that creature, and I knew they were right.

"Still, you shouldn't have *forced* me in there. I nearly drowned!" I scowled at the coach.

She inclined her head and raised an eyebrow. "Don't give me attitude, Baelin. You better be thanking me. You would've never discovered your power if it weren't for me."

She lifted her chin, pompous like she was accepting an award.

I narrowed my eyes. "Too bad you won't be able to brag to your meathead friends. I don't have any powers."

"Anora!" Nurse Roslyn gasped.

Coach Hacket pinched the bridge of her nose and loosed a breath. "You were in the pit and sent all the water flying out of it. You soaked the entire gym."

"You're lying! That's impossible." It needed to be impossible. There was no other option. I couldn't be a Guardian. That couldn't be my fate.

The nurse gently turned my face toward hers. "It's true. Be honored that the Mother chose you to defend Her creations. We can take you to the gym and show you, if you feel up to it."

My body was exhausted and limp underneath the frail blanket. All I wanted was to curl up underneath the covers and pretend that their accusations were just that—accusations that had no chance of being a reality.

"There's nothing to see. This is a bad joke."

"Anora," Coach said sternly, "it's not a joke."

Nurse Roslyn grabbed my hands with both of hers and forced me to my feet. Every inch of my body was sore with bruises and tight with strain. That abnormal thrum built up in my chest, propelling me as I stood. The nurse assessed me, pursed her lips, and instructed the trainer to fetch a wheelchair from the supply closet.

Coach Hacket wheeled in a rickety wheelchair. The cracked leather backing uneasily supported my weight.

"This is ridiculous," I commented as they wheeled me into the main hallway. "There's no way—"

The words caught in my throat as dozens of eyes landed on me. Students had gathered outside the nurse's office in small groups, whispering. Once I began rolling down the hall, everyone stopped their chattering. My breathing began to pick up and I felt a reassuring squeeze on my shoulder from Nurse Roslyn.

It was a lie, I kept telling myself. My peers were probably here out of concern for me, for the girl who nearly drowned in the kill course. They weren't here to see the girl with Guardian abilities. They couldn't be.

Cassandry and Eithan broke through the crowd to walk alongside my chair. Cassandry grasped my hand and looked down at me with bloodshot eyes. She searched my face and opened her mouth to say something. Her eyes filled with tears and she bit her tongue, fixing her gaze forward as if trying—and failing—to contain her emotions.

Eithan walked behind her, eyes fixed on the floor. He caught my stare and looked down at me. His eyes bore into mine. My heart skipped a beat at the intensity of that look.

We turned the corner leading to the gym. Water pooled in the doorway and drained in several thin streams down the hall. My mouth hung agape as we slowly rolled through it.

Inside, the gym looked as though a river had rushed through. Water dripped from the ceiling like a gentle rain.

The mats, ropes, and weights were slick with water. The pit, once filled to the brim with bleak, unforgiving water, was empty.

It was a coincidence. A misunderstanding. I conceded that Coach Hacket was right about the water, but there must have been another explanation. A logical explanation. One that didn't involve me having Guardian powers —anything but that.

I pointed at the pit and the nurse wheeled me over, doing her best to avoid the largest pools on the floor. I peered down into the abyss.

Not a drop of water was left.

I saw myself sprawled at the bottom, chest heaving. I shook my head and tried to roll away against Nurse Roslyn's grip. She must've noticed my struggle because she ushered me back toward the door.

"Do you believe it now?" Coach Hacket crossed her thick arms.

Despite what I had seen, I spoke with conviction. "Okay, so the pit exploded, but I didn't do it."

She stepped in front of my wheelchair and slammed her hands on its arms. Her face was inches from mine, every wrinkle accentuated by her frustration. "Everyone in here saw you do it. There's no denying it! You're a Guardian now, and you better get used to it."

I turned to my friends, searching their faces for any hint that it was a lie. But Cassandry was crying and Eithan was despondent. Shadows from his glasses hid his eyes as they focused on a puddle at his feet.

"I'm so sorry, Nory," Cassandry sobbed.

"I can't be." Agitation hardened my voice. Conviction. Theirs was a claim I refused to accept.

Coach Hacket sighed in frustration. "I'm not gonna argue with you all day. You did this. End of story. I'm going to radio the Compound and request for a squad to come and take you."

She turned on her heel and left the gym, shoes splashing through the standing water.

Tears dotted my eyes. My jaw was slack. My body trembled. I turned to my friends, and Cassandry came running to me. She slid onto her knees and rested her head in my lap as she cried. I wrapped my arms around her.

I leaned down to her ear and whispered, "This isn't real."

Cassandry lifted her head, squinting through tears. "Nory, I wish it wasn't. I really do."

Eithan stepped by my side and laid a hand on my shoulder. I looked up at him—his eyes were wide and glistening around the edges.

"Eithan . . ." I trailed off, not sure what to say, unsure what to think.

He knelt beside me and leaned in close. My hand gripped his and he didn't recoil. He held my hand firmly, squeezing as if this were the first, and last, time he ever would.

"We're going to figure this out, Anora, together. It's going to be okay," Eithan said softly.

"We won't let anything happen to you. We won't let them take you. They can't force you," Cassandry agreed, trying to convince herself more so than me.

"And once they see I'm not what they're looking for, I'm sure they won't bother."

They both gave me pointed looks.

"Okay, so even if I *did* do this"—I gestured around the

gym—"I'm not cut out to be a Guardian. They'll catch on quick that I'll just be a waste of their time."

"I don't know, you seemed pretty powerful to me . . ." Cassandry trailed off.

"*If* I really did this, it was because I was literally on the verge of death. It's not like I can do it again." My muscles were exhausted, my bones ached—there wasn't an ounce of strength left to call upon my *supposed* abilities. "I bet it was a one-time thing."

My friends exchanged concerned looks but didn't argue. Instead, Cassandry stood and wheeled me out of the gym, Nurse Roslyn having stepped back to give us privacy. Eithan followed close behind.

"I'm sure your parents will have some good advice too," Cassandry chirped, attempting an uplifting tone.

I nodded and sank into the wheelchair, keeping my eyes trained on my shaking hands as I wheeled past settled pools of water flooding the gym floor.

Chapter Seven

Productivity was a lost cause with all of the stares and whispers trailing me down every hall. I complained of fatigue and hid in the infirmary with Nurse Roslyn for the rest of the school day, gorging on bread and berries.

Surprisingly, my limbs didn't ache for very long like they usually did after the assault of the kill course, and I could walk on my own by the time the buses came. My body was probably too preoccupied adjusting to the new, constant rippling of energy in my chest to notice.

I changed into regular clothes—faded blue jeans with a green floral blouse—and went to find Liam. I scoured the crowd of students gathered in the school foyer for bus pick-up, not failing to notice their gazes tracking me. When I finally spotted Liam, I picked up the pace.

His wide eyes were already set on me. Even the little ones had heard about the girl who could move water. I knelt down, pulling him into a tight embrace.

Liam fisted his small hands in the back of my shirt. "Is it true?"

I pulled away a fraction to look into his eyes, so full of fear.

I gave a slight nod. "Let's talk about it at home, okay? I kind of just want to forget about it."

Liam took my hand and squeezed it.

"I drew another picture for Mommy today." He wrestled the drawing from his backpack. "And this time no jerk tore it up."

A smirk broke the frown settled on my face. "So did Thenton end up having a shiner?"

"Yep, and he complimented my drawing, too." Liam flashed a mischievous grin.

"Wow, look at you making friends," I said sarcastically.

Liam laughed. "My friends think I'm a hero now."

Mocking our mother's stern tone, I said, "As your older sister, I must insist you don't resort to violence to deal with your problems." Liam laughed harder and I joined in. "But seriously, kid, it's not the answer."

Liam rolled his eyes. "Yeah, yeah I know. Jeez, you *are* turning into Mom."

The bus parked in front of the school and we all quickly, and quietly, filed in. I left Liam to sit with his friends and joined Cassandry in our usual seat, just as I had every day for the past twelve years. Yet that day, there was tension between us, the air heavy. For the first time in a long time, I didn't know what to say. I didn't want to talk about the gym, about my newfound powers, the inevitable Guardian recruitment, or my eventual gruesome death. But nothing else came to mind, so we sat in aching silence.

Out the window, the tops of the Portemor Mountains

peeking over the forest were visible even from a distance. Some days, you could see gargantuan beasts flying around those peaks with the naked eye. How big would they appear standing right at the base? Would they spot me and swoop down to snatch me up? I shook the image off and turned away from those bleak, imposing mountains.

As the bus jerked to a halt, Cassandry locked me in a strangling embrace. The wind was knocked out of me, but I wrapped my arms around her and squeezed until the bus driver waved for me to hurry up.

Standing at the base of the front porch steps, I hesitated. Usually, I'd bound up the stairs with my little brother, eager to sit down with my mother at her sewing machine and tell her about my day. Instead, I stood staring at the front door, that odd pressure radiating from my chest.

Liam stood a couple steps up, waiting patiently.

"Can I just wait out here all night?" My outside voice was barely audible.

He gave me a sympathetic look. "It won't be that bad. It's just Mom and Bill."

I nodded and took my first step, heart pounding.

I unlocked the front door and leaned inside the frame. The house looked no different. Sun soaked the rug and surrounding hardwood in the living room. The faint sound of my mother's sewing machine and her humming filtered downstairs. My home seemed so ordinary even though my life had completely changed.

Liam scurried past and hopped on the couch. The door clicked shut behind me and I joined him.

As I rustled around in my backpack, a distraction for my buzzing mind, my mother's hands came to rest on my shoulders.

I flinched, and she chuckled as she ran her fingers through my hair.

"Didn't think I'd startle you, Nora bug. How was your day?"

I didn't answer. My mind was too focused on the truth I didn't want to admit to come up with a lie.

She skirted around the couch and perched on the armrest. "Anora, you're shaking. Is everything alright?"

She sunk down next to me, wrapping an arm around my shoulder. That constant vibration in my chest began to strengthen as prickles of energy ran down my arms and into my palms.

What *was* that?

"Did you get a bad grade? I told you there's no need to fret over one little—"

"It's not a bad grade. It's a lot more . . . serious than that." I turned to face her; her brow was set deep.

She squeezed my shoulder. "How serious? Should I get Bill?"

I nodded. She rushed outside to the work shed and brought back my stepfather, coated in fresh grease and wiping his hands on a worn cloth.

"What's up there, squirt?" he greeted and sat on the edge of the chair.

His words had me tearing up. When Bill joined our family, I despised him. No one could replace my father. Slowly, I realized that he wasn't trying to replace him. He simply wanted to love and care for us in his own way. He had become a constant calm and supportive presence for all of us.

I thought of my real father then, how scared he must

be for me, looking down from the Mother's arms. I wished he could be here to hold me and tell me it was going to be alright.

"Kiddo?" my stepfather pressed.

Mom sat beside me again, holding me tight. Liam sat silently on the other end of the couch, the glint of a tear in his eye.

Taking a shaky breath, I admitted, "I've been chosen."

Mom's eyes widened and her mouth fell open. "What do you mean? At your Guardian Assessment? That wasn't today, was it? They have to be mistaken. There's no way. I would've known." She shook her head vigorously, clutching her shirt as if trying to hold herself together.

My stepfather's blank gaze was fixed on the floor, the color stripped from his grease-streaked face.

"I don't want to believe it either, but it's hard to explain away."

I described what happened in the water pit over my mother's sobbing. I told them about the inexplicable resonating energy I constantly felt in my chest.

"Guess that explains what happened to your room," Bill said.

My eyebrows shot up in realization. He had to be right. There was no other explanation for how my room had mysteriously flooded. Maybe that had somehow primed these powers to finally be released in the pit.

Stop, I told myself. Regardless of what happened, how bad things had looked, it would never happen again.

It couldn't.

"So what happens now?" Mom looked to me, then her husband, and then out the window, as if searching for a solution.

Bill's eyes had glazed over from held-back tears. He looked at me like he was silently begging it all to be a joke.

"The school said they were notifying the Guard. Someone will be down soon to evaluate me, then take me."

He stood up at that. "They'd better think twice if they actually think I'm gonna let them take my daughter. There's no way I'm letting you go." He choked up. "I'm not going to sit down while they ship you off to those Mother-forsaken mountains to fight those . . . those things!"

He paced around the room, wringing the bottom of his shirt so tightly his knuckles turned white. He whirled too fast on his heel and winced, bracing his back with one hand while the other caught the back of the chair.

Mother and I jumped up to help him sit. His legs were stiff as he walked around the chair. With a forced sigh, he settled into the cushions.

"I told you to rest your back," I scolded as I fluffed a pillow and stuffed it behind him.

Mom ran into the kitchen and brought back a cup of tea. She set it beside him on a small side table. "You need to take better care of yourself, dear."

Bill brushed her off. "It's just the shock of the news is all. I'll be fine."

"What if you aren't?" I worried.

He rolled his head toward me, his eyes sparkling with the threat of tears. "Don't you be concerning yourself with me, Anora. We've all got bigger things to worry about now."

I nodded and slumped back onto the couch. Their reactions made this seem so *real*. The terror, the carnage, the death. It was all becoming too real.

"I can't face them. They're so much stronger and faster —they'll kill me. Just like they kill everyone. Just like—"

My father's eyes bulged and his face turned purple as the serpent constricted tighter.

My heart began to race and so did the strange thrum of power. It pulsed down my arms and pressed against my palms. What was going on? It felt like there was something squirming beneath my skin and wanted to burst out. When I examined my hands closer, it did.

Beads of water gathered between my fingers. They swirled in a small ball, almost like a miniature storm cloud. I gasped and fanned it away before it grew any bigger.

Okay, so maybe these powers weren't just a one time thing.

Great.

My family stared at me, dumbfounded. Was that amazement or fear in their eyes?

Mom stepped forward and took my damp hands in hers. She took in my features as if she'd never see them again and needed to memorize every detail.

"I'm gonna go whip up something for dinner." Mom kissed my forehead and started for the kitchen.

Before leaving, she half-turned and asked, "Nora bug, can you help me for a second?"

With a weak smile, I followed her into the kitchen.

Chapter Eight

I used to blend in when I walked down the halls at school. I was mundane, not particularly smart, popular, or beautiful. But the several days following my display at the Guardian Assessment changed my status. Everyone parted around me, keeping their distance, either out of fear or respect. The feeling of dozens of eyes trailing me along every corridor, in every classroom, made me squirm like this new energy coursing through my veins.

Cassandry and Eithan didn't leave my side. In the lunchroom, we headed for our small table in the back corner and avoided as many people as possible. I stretched out my legs beneath the table. Even late in the day, they still ached from my run. Every morning since the assessment, I had taken my stress out on my safe runner, and subsequently, my quads. I massaged my muscles as we chatted, trying to ignore the points and whispers, but they were too distracting, along with the grave news I had received.

"Coach Hacket just told me the Guardians will come to evaluate me today."

"What!? It's the day before graduation!" Cassandry exclaimed and was promptly reprimanded by the shushing of an overseer.

My mind was too preoccupied with my uncertain fate to be concerned about graduation or the volume of voices. How would they evaluate me? Leave me on the Portemor Mountains? Force me to fight a monster to the death? Would they leave me for dead if I failed, unworthy to be a Guardian?

I could see claws gripping my throat, tearing open my skin, and savoring the spurts of blood before ripping me to shreds . . .

Cassandry shook my shoulder. "Anora, snap out of it."

My breathing had become quick, my skin clammy, my vision blurry. That foreign wave of energy resonated through my chest and down my arms, beating against my clenched palms. Over the past few days, I had noticed that every time my anxiety surged, so did my power. The only way to stop spontaneous clouds from forming was to keep my palms clenched. Apparently that was the only way it could escape.

Eithan reached across the table and squeezed my fisted hand. "There may be a way out," he said in a serious tone.

I looked at him with sad eyes. "You should join my parents with that talk. I appreciate the wishful thinking, but we can't think of any way out of this."

"But I *really* think I have a good plan, Anora. Just hear me out." His warm eyes looked hopeful as a bright smile spread across his face.

"Okay, what's your plan?"

Eithan inched closer, lowering his head. "Your powers aren't very developed yet, right? They only seem to be triggered by strong emotions or when you're near death. So, during your evaluation, just keep your emotions in check. If you don't get stressed, then your powers won't come out and they won't bother taking you."

I exchanged a skeptical look with Cassandry. For the past several days, my parents and I had stayed up late trying to find a solution. We had sat at the kitchen table, throwing out ideas, everything from packing up the family and running away to faking my death. Either they were too extravagant to pull off, had too many holes and room for error, or presented too high of a risk of being caught.

We had thought of Eithan's idea and already ruled it out, so I challenged, "You really think I'll be able to keep my emotions in check? If you haven't noticed, I've been a puddle of tears lately."

"But your *life* depends on it. I feel like, knowing you don't have any other choice, you should be able to," Eithan countered, just as the overseers patrolling the cafeteria shushed us again.

"Yeah, knowing my life depends on it really won't add any more stress," I added sarcastically.

Eithan furrowed his brow. "Not everything is a joke, Anora. I'm just trying to help you get out of this. I thought you of all people would be trying harder."

"I have been trying. Every morning I wake up thinking about it. I've failed my last two assignments because I spend day and night trying to come up with something, so I'm *sorry* that I'm trying to joke around and give myself a break from brooding."

Eithan's cheeks darkened. "I'm sorry, Anora. It's

just . . . this whole situation is frustrating." His voice softened even more as he offered, "You should come with me to Celepheria."

Eithan's gaze bore into mine. His hand, still holding mine, squeezed even harder, urging me to run away with him. I blushed, and my heart pounded against my ribs in time with that newfound thrum of power.

Cassandry had pulled out a notepad and began doodling, staying out of our conversation, but I could tell she was still listening.

"You want me to go to Celepheria with you?"

"I want you to be safe. I . . . I don't know what I'd do with myself knowing you were on the border."

"What about Confinement? I don't have a travel pass like you guys do."

"We'll sneak out after lunch, take you to my house and hide out there until we can leave. We have a storage trunk under our wagon. No one will think to—"

"Eithan, stop." I cut him short. "Bill told me that when he was in school, a boy and his family tried to do the same when he discovered his powers. A special alert went out over the radio for his capture. Not even two days into their trip, they were caught by a Guardian. He was sent to training *and* wasn't allowed to talk with his family at all after that due to their *bad influence*. I can't risk that happening."

My friends and family were the only thing I wasn't willing to give up. The only thing I couldn't live without. Never getting to write letters to Cassandry or radio with Liam—yeah, that wasn't an option.

I gave Eithan a half-smile, my best attempt at hopefulness. "I'll try to hold it in as much as I can."

His face was grave, optimism washed away by the story. He nodded and let go of my hand. "Good, I really think it might work."

I watched him push peas around his tray, lost in thought. He slid his glasses up his nose, shrouding his eyes. If only I had more time, I could rip that mask off and we could finally be together . . .

I imagined our limbs and lips intertwined for the first time, just to have me torn from his arms by the Guard. And Eithan wasn't all I stood to lose. There was Cassandry, my family, my home—everything I knew. Everything I loved. Determined not to see that become reality, I used them as fuel to rein in my emotions, to dampen the power in my chest until it was barely a flutter against my ribs.

Running away may not be an option, but this might work.

It had to.

The last class of the day was about to start, but I lingered at my locker. Coach Hacket would come for me any moment to toss me into the clutches of the Guard. Sweat beaded my temple as I tried to rein in my anxiety, and with it, my power.

A sudden clatter issued beside my head. I yelped, stumbled backward, and landed on my backside. I looked up to find Victon, his thin freckled lips twitched in a snarl.

"Didn't realize you had a gripe with my locker, Victon," I said as I stood up.

He glared down at me. Even standing, he towered over me.

He rolled his neck along his wide-set shoulders and grumbled through gritted teeth, "You don't deserve it."

He began flexing his hands, then squeezed them into white-knuckled fists.

My throat closed up at the pure rage pouring off of his body. After all those tough words in the gym—for me, of all people, to end up having abilities must've been like a slap in the face to someone like Victon. The low vibration of my power rolled in my chest, growing slowly and steadily. This time, I didn't try to tame it.

I said in a low voice, "Don't start this."

A small crowd grew in the hall, forming a wide circle around us.

He took a step closer. "I've been training my whole life for this. You don't even want it. You stole my purpose. *My glory.*"

I took a measured step back. "Trust me, I wish it had been you too."

He punched the locker door closed beside my head, leaving a dent. I jumped, confident he wished it was my face he'd hit.

I took another step away, gearing my body to run, and then he lunged. He grabbed my wrist then slammed my body into the wall of lockers.

My head burst with pain from the impact, and I put my hands to my temples as I slid to the floor. My power churned faster, building up in my core and trickling down my arms.

Victon grabbed the collar of my shirt with both hands and hoisted me up, my feet dangling just above the ground. I struggled to escape his grasp, trying to peel his iron grip off.

"How dare you take this from me," he whispered as he pushed me up against the locker.

I squirmed under his hold, swinging my legs to kick at him. He pinned me with his body against the wall so I couldn't fight back.

He chuckled. "Where's all that power now?"

It was pounding against my clenched palms, yearning to get out. When Victon's grip grew tighter and one hand slid to my throat, I uncurled my fists.

A burst of wind pushed Victon back with a large, unanticipated force. He let me go and slammed against the far wall. I looked down at my hand. *Wind?* I thought my power had been with water?

The small crowd had grown and together they gasped at the display of my ability. They all turned to me in awe. A few smaller kids ran away; others were frozen in place.

Victon, crumpled on the floor, looked up at me. Fear flashed in his eyes but was quickly covered by a jealous rage.

"I hope they tear you to pieces," he spat as he got to his feet and stormed away.

I couldn't think of anything quick to say, knowing his wish would become reality. I stared out the hallway window to the ominous woods and mountains beyond.

I imagined myself cowering behind a tree, stifling my sobs while creats—and the past—hunted me in the dark. No supernatural power could overcome that paralyzing terror. I was destined to be another fallen Guardian, mangled and torn to pieces, forgotten by the world.

When I finally snapped out of my thoughts, I noticed

my hair was damp and shoes were water logged. Had a sprinkler gone off? I looked up, and found a small rain cloud circling my head.

"Really? Come on," I grumbled.

A few stragglers still lingered a distance down the hall, watching my rain in awe. I clamped my hands into fists and the cloud dissipated into nothing, leaving a small puddle at my feet.

I shook out my hair, hooked my backpack around my arm, and trudged toward class. The squeaking of wet shoes filled the silent hall as I passed my adoring fans.

Water pattered on the floor as I wrung out my soaked shirt outside the classroom door. Just before I stepped over the threshold, there was a tap on my shoulder. I turned to find Coach Hacket hovering over me with a severe look, her features casting long shadows down her rough skin.

"You need to come with me," she ordered, grasping my arm firmly.

She tried to lead me down the hall, but I held my ground.

"No, not yet. I can't," I pleaded. "I need more time."

"You don't get a choice, girl."

My heartbeat pounded in my ears. My power rose in my chest to answer the call and I doused it before it surged into my palms. Why hadn't my gift been the power to stop time? I wasn't ready for this. I would *never* be ready for this.

I fought her grip, but my efforts were futile. She dragged me down the hall toward the gymnasium, my sneakers skidding in protest.

From inside the classroom, Cassandry and Eithan

rushed out to meet me. My friends hurried alongside as our coach pulled me, growling under her breath for me to stop dragging my feet.

"You can do it, Anora," Eithan encouraged. "If anyone can do this, it's you."

"We'll be right here waiting for you," Cassandry promised.

I didn't get a chance to say anything, only to look helplessly at my friends over my shoulder as the doors swung shut behind me.

Chapter Nine

D im lights cast the gymnasium in shadows; the empty water pit was a dismal void. Along the wall, three Guardians stood beneath their seal.

Guardian Yllaria was on the left, casually leaning against the wall. Her silky dark hair was pulled back in a tight bun, no attempt to hide the scabbed gashes on her face from the farmers' market brawl. Next to her towered Guardian Bron, his umber skin glistening in the weak light. His arms crossed his chest, accentuating his bulging biceps through his tight-fitting Guardian jumpsuit. His dark eyes smoldered like embers around his irises. Next was Guardian Leif. He was younger, short copper curls bouncing against pale freckled skin. A mischievous grin crept along his face.

Coach Hacket shoved me in front of them. She bowed her head slightly before abandoning me, shutting the gym doors behind her with a booming *thump*.

Guardian Yllaria bounced off of the wall and strutted toward me. "You look familiar."

My throat dried up. "Uh, hi. I—um . . . you probably remember me from the market attack."

"Oh yeah." Her eyebrows raised in sympathy. "You were the upset one I comforted—well, *attempted* to comfort."

My face rushed with heat, my eyes wide and averting her gaze. "Yeah, I wasn't in the best, um, mental state. It's pretty traumatic watching someone die."

Guardian Bron stepped forward, a soft look on his face. "Of course it is." He threw a pointed look at her. "Yllaria's not judging you."

Guardian Yllaria brushed it off. "So, you're one of us then? What's your complection?"

My *what*? Did she mean my ability? I felt the beat of my power grow alongside my racing heart. I held it in my chest but was unable to snuff it out. A sharp lance of pain spread across my chest at the strain.

I masked my pain and nerves with an exasperated sigh. "I am not a Guardian. Coach made a huge deal out of nothing."

They all gave me an incredulous look.

"We know the story," Guardian Bron said. "That'd be a pretty difficult thing for her to make up."

Anxiety overpowered me quickly. I had never been good at lying—not that I had a problem with fibbing, but it was coming up with one fast enough that seemed to be my downfall.

I stumbled over my words. "Yeah—uh, she just made it up. She wanted to have someone to present to the Guard this year."

Guardian Yllaria gave a skeptical look, turning her

crooked nose upward. "You really think she'd be that foolish, huh?"

"I . . ." I struggled to keep my string of lies together. "I can prove they were wrong about me. Test me and I promise I won't do anything extraordinary."

Guardian Leif slipped out of the shadows. "Are you sure about that? Because your damp clothes would beg to differ."

I flushed, remembering the personal storm I'd conjured just moments ago. Water squished in the soles of my soaked sneakers. My mind buzzed, trying to come up with an explanation, something convincing enough to get these Guardians off my tail and back to the Portemor Mountains where they belonged.

"It was a water fountain mishap."

Guardian Yllaria guffawed. "Yeah, okay, like we believe that."

Adrenaline pulsed and the restraint on my power threatened to snap.

I squared my stance, and with as much determination as I could muster, I challenged. "I swear to you, you'll find nothing remarkable about me."

Guardian Bron gave me a pitying look. "Trying to ignore it, pretending your power doesn't exist, will only make things worse."

"Either test me or leave."

Guardian Bron sighed and waved ahead for the wiry redhead beside him to begin. Guardian Leif's mischievous grin returned for a split second, and then he was gone. I spun around in a circle, looking for the Guardian who was known to be as swift and sly as a fox.

As I searched, Guardian Bron explained, "We are going

to test you against our own powers until yours present themselves."

Peering through the shadows, I tried to spot Guardian Leif. The pillars, ropes, and weights sprawled across the gym created too many places for a slim Guardian to hide. To my right, a rope that hung from the ceiling began to swing slowly as if blown by a phantom breeze. I froze in place, fixated on the swinging rope. My senses heightened and I struggled to dampen the thrum of energy pulsing through my body.

The wind was knocked out of my lungs as I was struck in the back by bony hands. I stumbled, then swung around to see nothing but a faint gray and orange blur rush past. A swift kick to the back of my knees had me tumbling forward, but my hands caught my fall before my face did. Fear flashed and my energy swelled up in defense. I squeezed my eyes shut and balled my hands into fists to focus on keeping my power contained, no matter how much the pressure built.

Distracted, I left myself open to a kick in the side and I toppled over, curling into a ball on the floor.

Guardian Leif materialized in front of my crumpled form. "Come on, you're not even going to try to fight back?"

"I am. Trust me," I admitted through clenched teeth, biting back the pain, my power.

The hard gym floor was cool against my flushed cheeks, but that small comfort was snatched away as Guardian Bron hauled me to my feet.

"Anora, you can't hide it forever," he said. "You can't keep this up."

Bent in on myself, clutching my side, I defended my

lies. "There's nothing to unleash, Guardian Bron. You can beat me up all you want. You still won't find anything."

He sighed, letting go of my arm.

Instantly, Guardian Leif was on me. He hooked an arm around my waist and slid his foot behind my heel, forcing me to trip and fall. I slammed flat onto my back, pain singing out from my spine. I winced from the pain of the blow and effort to restrain my abilities. That abnormal force revved against what contained it—my will and clenched fists. I rolled onto my knees and stood slowly, planting my feet firmly.

It would take more than that to break me.

Blow after blow, I never bothered to defend myself, my concentration solely spent on containing the power held in my fists. My nails dug into my flesh. Hunched over, I wiped away blood trickling from my nose. Frustration grew in the fleeting glimpses of Guardian Leif's face as he tried to tear me down. I threw a smug smile back at him, daring him to try again.

Guardian Bron called the fight to stop, his brow furrowed. Guardian Yllaria stood beside him, her face seething with annoyance.

"Really?" Guardian Yllaria exasperated. "Why try this hard to hide from us? Do you know how many people would kill to be in your position?"

"I'm sure it's everyone's dream to be beaten up by a Guardian."

She scoffed, "Bron, just do it and get it over with."

Guardian Yllaria pitied me once, a weak child trembling in a blood-soaked clearing. Now, she judged me for being that same girl. Why did having powers make a difference? I was still the same person. These powers didn't define me, yet everyone had decided I must've changed. Like I magically transformed into the whole Guardian package overnight, a brave warrior ready to take on any creat.

Newsflash, that was *not* how it worked.

Guardian Bron crossed his arms and faced me, eyes smoldering. His hard-set brow made me tense.

Guardian Leif slid in line with his comrades. "As much as I'd love to keep playing, we need to get going."

Guardian Bron warily stepped forward, regret burning in his eyes. "You can make this quick, Anora."

"I told you. I'm not what you're looking for."

He sighed and inched forward. I held my ground, unsure of what was going to happen. He seemed to be calculating every step as he approached, but why? What did he have planned? When he reached for my wrist, his intentions finally dawned on me. Before I could flinch back, he gripped my wrist, and my scream cut through the gym.

His searing touch burned my skin. The heat, the pain, overwhelmed my senses. I felt my skin boil and peel away under his grasp. Tears swelled in my eyes, and I screamed out in agony. Power coursed through my veins and beat against my still-clenched palms, desperate to escape. I was too consumed with the pain, my only thoughts on how to stop it, so I opened my hand.

When the fist he had grasped opened, a vigorous gust of wind was unleashed. Guardian Bron was thrown off his feet and tossed against the Guardian insignia, his limbs splayed along the phoenix's wings.

We both collapsed to the ground in heaps, me sobbing

and cradling my burnt, blistering wrist and him wincing and massaging his back.

Guardian Yllaria bent down to meet my gaze. "You should've just been honest with us."

I scowled at her. "Screw you."

"This is the start of a wonderful friendship," she sneered.

The gym door creaked open, and Coach Hacket and Nurse Roslyn bustled into the room. The nurse knelt beside me, quick to put ointment and bandages on my mangled wrist.

She was prepared.

Guardian Bron was on his feet and approached Coach Hacket. "She presented with wind. I thought you mentioned water?"

She stammered her reply, face beating bright red. "I-I thought it was, sir. She lifted all of the water from the pit, so I assumed that's what she manipulated. I'm sorry I misinterpreted her element."

"Hmm," he pondered. "No, I don't think you did. There wouldn't have been any air to manipulate at the bottom of the pit. She must have two elemental affinities."

"Really? How wonderful!" Coach Hacket beamed. "Such a rare and powerful Guardian coming from Bellwarn is an honor and a blessing."

I scoffed. It didn't seem like much of an honor or a blessing to me—more like a death sentence.

"Having two affinities isn't that rare, actually, but a blessing all the same," Guardian Bron said. "Thank you for accommodating our assessment. We'll be leaving now."

"I'm not going," I asserted, the intense burning

clouding my senses. "There is no way you can make me come with you after *that!*"

Guardian Yllaria huffed. "Just give up already! You're not getting out of this and now you're just wasting our time. We've got one Guardian covering our base while we're out here, and we need to relieve her."

"I already have plans," I said. "*Life* plans. I'm going to be a nurse. You can't upheave everything like this!"

"This is your life plan now, girl," Coach Hacket spat. "Get used to it."

"What your coach is trying to say," Guardian Bron said, stepping forward, "is that when someone exhibits abilities, their sole duty is to serve the Guard and the citizens of Alberune. That's how it's always been."

"No one ever gets a choice?" I questioned.

Guardian Bron only shook his head.

Nurse Roslyn nudged in. "Anora, you should be proud that the Mother has chosen you to protect Her creations. There are a lot of people who would love to be you right now."

I barked a sharp laugh. "You're right. I should be thankful that I have third-degree burns on my wrist, and that my life, as I know it, is over."

Coach Hacket gave me a stern look. "You better get some sense. We're desperate for more Guardians with the uptick in sightings and attacks, so you should feel honored—"

"Honored? I feel cursed! I don't care if others would love to be me. That doesn't change the fact that *I* don't want this! That I *can't* do this!"

Haggard sobs echoed through the gym as I broke down —from the throbbing burn in my arm, the condemning energy beating in my chest, the upending of my life, and the inevitable end of everything I knew and trusted.

The nurse wrapped a consoling arm around my shoulder, and I flinched away. "Don't *touch* me. None of you."

My power roiled and this time, I let it flow easily down my arms. It pooled in my palms, itching to be released. I flexed my hands at my sides, calmed my crying, and rose onto my feet.

Guardian Bron held up a warning hand. "No one is going to hurt you. Everything is not as bad as it seems. You will be safe with us. We are like you and can teach you how to control your powers, to *harness* your powers. I know all you've known is fear, but now you won't ever have to fear anything again."

"You have no idea what fear is." Venom laced my every word.

Guardian Yllaria and Leif exchanged exasperated looks and whispered to each other. She nodded to him and he blurred into the shadows. My whole body tensed, my senses searching the shadows for the Guardian hidden among them. I held up my palms at my sides and was about to call on my power when a sharp jab to the crook of my neck made me falter. I stumbled to the side and Guardian Leif tied my hands behind my back, not being careful of my injured wrist. I cried out as he tightened the restraints. He jostled me upright, keeping a firm grasp on my arm.

Guardian Bron's eyes burned bright. "What are you doing?"

"You didn't expect her to come easy, did you?" Guardian Leif retorted.

Guardian Bron opened his mouth as if to say something, then closed it again.

"Let me go." I writhed in his grip.

Guardian Leif's lips perked. "Now why would I do that? You seem so pleasant to be around."

"I need to see my family." I scowled. "Now."

Guardian Yllaria piped up, "Too bad, you've wasted too much time. We have to get back to base."

Guardian Bron held up a hand. "We can make time for a farewell. Deshiva will be fine."

He nodded to me and offered a slight smile. I held firm, not giving him the satisfaction of a smile returned. He cast down his gaze. "Let's go."

Guardian Leif nudged me and I stumbled along next to him.

Before, I had dreaded coming to this gym, but in this final moment, I soaked it in. The ropes Cassandry and I struggled to climb together. The mats where I held onto Eithan's shoes as we did endless rounds of sit-ups. The far corner where we always huddled before class, devising ways to escape the assessment. I held fast to these memories, fleeting by with every step I took toward the exit.

Never again would I gossip with my friends about the annoying Guardian worshippers and infuriating coaches. Never again would I toe closer to Eithan, heart racing, hoping our arms would brush against one another.

My head slumped forward and my chest caved in as I traipsed through hallways painted with memories.

Chapter Ten

W e marched into the foyer, Guardian Leif pulling me along like a prisoner. My arms were bound behind my back, my head hung low, and my eyes stared blankly at my worn and squishy shoes.

"Anora, are you okay?" Cassandry called out, voice cracking at the sight of me.

My friends cautiously approached, keeping a wide berth from the Guardians.

"I'm sorry, you guys. I tried."

Eithan inched closer, focused on me and not the Guardian gripping my arm. His brown eyes shined in the overhead light, and my treacherous heart fluttered at the sight. Even though we couldn't be anything more, I yearned to embrace him, to be swept into his arms and kissed softly as he confessed the feelings he'd harbored for so long. My careless heart swelled with longing, then deflated when reality flooded back in.

"I'm sorry, Anora." Eithan's voice shook. "I should've thought of something else. A better way—"

"Eithan, this is not your fault."

Guardian Bron shifted on his feet. "We need to get going."

Eithan reached for me, then let his arm fall when he realized I couldn't meet him with my bound hands.

"I-I won't forget," he whispered.

Tears clouded my vision. "Me neither."

Cassandry burst between us and wrapped her arms around me in a tight embrace.

"You are the bravest, strongest girl I know," Cassandry slurred through her tears. "If anyone can do this, you can."

Guardian Yllaria rolled her eyes. "Come on now. Wrap it up."

Cassandry pulled away to narrow her deep blue eyes at her. Not even a Guardian could intimidate her.

"You're going to do amazing things in Celepheria." I choked up.

"Sorry to break up this sob story, but we're leaving now," Guardian Leif ordered as he dragged me away.

We trudged out the door and down the steps, my friends close behind. They halted on the last step, but I continued toward the forest-covered road where the Guardian jeep was parked. It was nestled in the brush, camouflaged with green and brown paint and lined with windows and mirrors to allow all lines of sight.

As they loaded me in the backseat, I looked back at my friends. I committed Cassandry's sapphire-blue eyes and soft brown locks to memory. I burned Eithan's thick-rimmed glasses and soft features into my mind. The last time I'd ever see my friends was heartbreaking, but it was something I couldn't forget.

Hidden in the trees was my home. The sun peered through the thick branches, painting the rooftop in splotches of light. We parked alongside the road and ascended the porch covered in shadow by overhanging trees. Guardian Bron convinced the others to unbind my wrists on the walk.

I eased the door open and my mother was instantly there, throwing it open. Her mauve dress was covered by a tan apron spotted with stains. She wrung a kitchen towel in her hands, her knuckles white. Distress had set her face into a frown as she regarded the Guardians at my back.

"No, no, no," she whispered. "It can't be today."

"Your daughter, Anora Baelin, has presented with the abilities of an Element Complector." Guardian Bron said. "We are here to recruit and escort her to Guardian Training."

She scrutinized him. "Are you asking for permission?"

"Not exactly, ma'am. We have the Mother's blessing."

"Do you, now?" she posed.

A smile tugged at my lips. Even in the face of despair, Mom was as bold and strong as ever. If I'd inherited anything from her, I hoped it was her fortitude. Before Guardian Bron could reply, my mother swept me into her arms and pulled me into our home.

"What happened?" She inspected my wrapped wrist, the fresh bruises purpling on my arms, and the dried blood under my nose.

"Consequences from their evaluation." I eyed Guardians Bron and Leif sharply.

"Only because she was being difficult," Guardian Leif retorted.

"Don't you *dare* blame her for what *you* inflicted," Mom shot back.

Guardian Leif stepped forward, but Guardian Bron held him back. "We apologize, but it was necessary to confirm her abilities."

"So you have the Mother's blessing to maim my daughter as well?"

I looked up at my mother with pride. She was coming at them with everything she had. When they took me, at least they would leave feeling terrible and guilty—the least of what they deserved.

Guardian Bron was stuttering, searching for a response, when Bill limped down the stairs. He supported himself heavily on the banister as he struggled not to strain his back. Recognizing our uninvited guests, he hobbled over and protectively wrapped his arms around us both.

"We had no heads-up you'd be coming," he said.

"Unfortunately, we can't schedule in advance due to the nature of our duties."

"Her graduation is tomorrow. Surely this can wait 'til after?" Bill asked.

"I'm sorry, but her training begins tomorrow."

"This all seems a bit sudden. It's going to be too much for her." Mom turned to Guardian Yllaria. "You know what she's been through, what she's witnessed . . . and that wasn't even the worst of it."

Guardian Yllaria nodded and replied softly, almost

compassionately. "I'm sure she has witnessed some traumatic things, but that doesn't excuse her from duty."

"But they're the reason why I'm incapable of doing my *so-called* duty," I said. "Those memories—they're incapacitating, all-consuming . . ." I shuddered. "I can't fight. I can only run and hide and hope they don't get the best of me."

"We will help you cope and overcome any fears you have during training," Guardian Bron said optimistically. "You'll be fine, if not better, after you complete it."

"This isn't something I can overcome," I explained. "It's who I am."

"Trust me," he encouraged, "we can get you through anything at the Compound."

"You don't understand." I shook my head. "You're not listening."

Before I could argue my point further, Liam poked his head through the door. He gauged the Guardians towering around him with fearful eyes. Frozen in the door frame, our mother had to guide him to us.

I knelt down and he whispered in my ear, "Do you have to leave now, Sis?"

How I wished I could say no, that I would always be here for him. What if he got into more fights at school? Who would be there to look out for him? He needed his big sister now more than ever.

I looked into my mother's eyes to find defeat. The three Guardians stood opposing and unyielding in their uniforms by the door.

"I think so," I choked out.

Bill leaned down to hug me and cringed, probably from his aching back.

"I'm gonna miss you. I'm not sure when I'll get to see you all again."

Guardian Bron stepped forward. "You are permitted to visit with family twice a year, once you've completed training."

"See there, that's not so bad," my stepfather lied, a ghost of a smile on his stubbled face.

"We have to get going," Guardian Yllaria insisted in a soft voice.

"Be strong. Be safe," my mother urged as she embraced me. "I love you."

"I love you all too." I reluctantly stepped away from them.

Guardian Bron gave them a cordial nod. "On behalf of the Guard of Alberune, I thank you for letting your daughter fight the creats plaguing our country. With the Mother's blessed gifts, she will protect you and our nation from the beasts of the Portemor Mountains."

"Let's be clear, Guardian Bron," my mother spoke with venom. "You *never* got my permission to take my daughter, and you never will."

His response was simply a frown as he took my elbow.

The only sound as I was guided out the door was Liam's sniffling. I kept my gaze locked on my family standing in the doorway as I was dragged to the road. When we reached the vehicle, they tossed me in the back and locked the door. With an inaudible rev of the engine, we started down the road. The thick, overhanging trees quickly shrouded my family, and I was forced to face the road ahead that would lead me to my new beginning. My end.

Chapter Eleven

The sun began to fall behind the trees, staining the dirt road burnt orange. The passing trees blurred into a dark green haze. Guardian Yllaria argued to have me restrained again, not wanting me to delay our trip any more after I tried to force open my door and escape. Guardian Bron gave me a pointed look, then insisted I wouldn't cause a problem. I scoffed. It wasn't because of him that I'd stopped wrestling with the door. I'd realized fairly quick that fighting with a locked door and a shatter-proof window was a losing battle.

Guardian Leif didn't ride with us. He whisked around the surrounding woods like a wisp, racing up trees to look out for any dangers on the road ahead. Guardian Bron drove, throwing me a half-smile occasionally in the rearview. He would open his mouth slightly, like he wanted to say something, but never spoke.

Directly in our path loomed the Portemor Mountains, growing larger with every mile. My foot tapped anxiously on the jeep floor, and I tried to tame my rising fear by focusing on my running shoes.

Most of the shoes delivered to Bellwarn were plain and simple slip-ons or boots. Bill had gone out of his way, and into his pocket, to get me special running shoes for my birthday. They were once white, now stained brown from walking the dirt road to the market countless times. The laces were a dull turquoise with matching stripes running down the sides. The soles were cracked from endless miles on my safe runner.

My stepfather, wearing a goofy grin and holding a gift box, came to mind. My heart ached at the memory of the joy on his face as I opened it. Even though it brought tears, I held that image vividly in my mind as we drove toward those glowering peaks.

We parked the jeep in a thicket a few minutes' walk from the outpost the Guardians operated from.

I followed them up a narrow trail crowded by overgrown bushes. Guardian Leif decided to join us for this final stretch of our journey.

It was dusk and, with the heavy canopy above, I could barely tell where I was stepping. I bumped into Guardian Bron's shoulder, not realizing I had gotten so close.

He steadied me with a hand on my back. "Easy there."

I jolted away from his touch, stumbling sideways into a tree. *How dare he touch me?* He literally gave me third-degree burns, and I'd rather not add more to the count. At the anticipation of a blistering burn on my back, my power churned at the ready.

Guardian Bron held up his hands cautiously. "What's wrong?"

Bristling against the trunk, I felt a jagged strip of bark

poke into my scarred shoulder. I held my palm up to him and cradled my burned wrist against my chest. Guardian Yllaria and Leif hurried to his side, assuming wide stances and readying for action. Power rushed to my hand, ready to take them all on if need be.

"Don't touch me," I warned with an outside voice.

"Why are you such a drama queen?" Guardian Yllaria sighed.

"Sorry that I don't want to get burned regularly from this one." I nodded toward Guardian Bron.

"He can *control* himself," Guardian Leif explained. "Something you know little about."

"I showed control against *you*, didn't I?" I tilted my head in challenge.

A sly grin crept onto his face. "There's a big difference between control and suppression."

Guardian Bron stepped in front of him in warning. "Okay, let's all calm down here."

Calm down? I scowled. If anything, his saying that just made me more irritated.

He looked over at me, arms held firm at his sides. "It *is* something I can control. My skin is only hot at my command. Let's keep moving."

On Guardian Bron's orders, Guardian Leif disappeared on the wind and into the towering pines. He raced ahead to relieve Guardian Deshiva, who was also quick like Leif and would be able to reach her own base by nightfall. Guardian Yllaria let down her long silky black hair, swatting tresses across her shoulder to avoid covering the healing gashes that would soon become scars. She continued up the dirt path.

I cautiously moved back toward the center of the

narrow, winding trail. Guardian Bron kept pace with me, but at a distance.

"So, are you a fan of chowder?" he asked. "The chef at the Compound, Memette, makes the best chowder in Alberune."

"I doubt it's better than my mother's."

"A close runner-up, then." He smiled. "Yllaria and Leif always look for excuses to sneak over to the Compound to have her cooking. I can't blame them. My meals are no comparison."

I simply nodded, unable to force a laugh. "It's weird to hear you refer to them so informally."

"That's one of those things you'll get used to with time. Now that you've been offically identified as one of us, you don't have to address us as *Guardian* anymore."

"I'm not *one* of you."

"I know how hard this is. Believe me, we've all been there. But it will get easier, I promise."

"Not for me."

The sooner he accepted *that* the better. Bron probably thought I'd go along with my recruitment now that he had me at his base—a prisoner—but he had no clue who he was dealing with. Survival had always been my first priority, and battling monsters on the Portemor Mountainside didn't really scream safe and sound. I was nothing if not stubbornly persistent when it came to self-preservation.

Darkness fell heavily as we made our way down the thinning dirt path. Even though Leif was darting around as our lookout, I scanned the brush along the trail myself. Prickles crawled up my spine at the thought of what creature could be squatting in the bushes beside this very path. My feet itched to bolt back home with every step I took closer to the Portemor Mountains. My power thrummed deep within me.

Rounding a bend in the trail, a broad wooden tower stood alongside the pines. A ladder was attached to the front of the structure and led to a wraparound landing as high as the treetops. From the platform, I could see for miles. Bellwarn was simply a gathering of holes in the trees, the homes and buildings well hidden from this vantage. Off to the east was the abandoned shell of Old Bellwarn. What was once a bustling main street filled with shops, boutiques, and apartments was now a disheveled ruin. It served as evidence, a reminder, of those first attacks hundreds of years ago. At my back, the Portemor Mountains loomed. They stood imposingly black against the purple evening sky.

In the center of the platform stood the Guard station. Inside were three small rooms. In the main room, a tiny kitchenette was crammed in one corner, while a large table, strewn with papers and radios, took up most of the space. The other two rooms were a bathroom and sleeping quarters with two sets of bunks on both walls and a thin dresser in the middle.

Yllaria, making an exaggerated point of ignoring me as she moved about, turned on a light above the kitchen sink.

"Aren't you going to shut the blinds before turning on the lights?"

"If there's a creat out there, we want it coming to us," she explained.

I gulped, my anxiety ramming that supernatural energy into my hands. An unnatural breeze swept past my palms and I squeezed them shut.

Yllaria helped herself to a glass of water and a roll

before plopping down at the table. Leif slipped into the seat next to her and they both tuned into the radio, reporting that they'd secured the new recruit.

"Would you like some water or something to eat?" Bron offered.

By now, I would've had a home-cooked meal warm in my belly. I wondered what Mom had made for dinner. Thoughts of her pork and potato roast made my stomach growl. Without needing a response, Bron brought me a glass of water along with a plate of bread and jerky.

He pulled out a chair for me at the table, and I sat down next to him. I nibbled on my meager dinner in silence while the Guardians busied themselves. Bron looked over some papers, transcriptions I couldn't make sense of. Yllaria and Leif checked in with the surrounding outposts, asking if there were any sightings or attacks. I tuned it out, not wanting to hear about any possible monsters lurking in the surrounding woods, and examined my mutilated wrist.

The burn was mostly covered by the wrapping Nurse Roslyn applied. Only a few red, glistening splotches of skin were poking out as I tilted the wound in and out of the light. Oddly, it didn't seem to hurt anymore. There was only a dull sting pricking my wrist. The bruises blossoming on my arms, and probably across my entire body from Lief's assault, didn't pulse with pain either. Nothing seemed to hurt anymore. The sharp pang of loss had ebbed it all away, leaving behind a gaping hole in my chest where my heart should be.

When I finished my meal, Bron suggested, "You should get some rest. Tomorrow will be a long day."

Wordlessly, I followed him to the bunkroom.

"You can have this one." He pointed to the top bunk on the far wall.

In a daze, I climbed up into the bunk without hesitation. Without a fight.

Tomorrow, I promised myself. Tomorrow at the Compound I would set things right and get back home where I belonged.

Bron looked up at me through the short prison-like bars, his dark eyes smoldering. "Anora, I want you to know that we all understand what you're going through. I know you don't really know me, or any of us yet, but if you need someone to talk to—I'm here."

I glowered at him until he slipped out of the room.

Numbness flooded me and I accepted it gratefully. This way, I could pretend being ripped away from my friends, family, and home—the only semblance of safety I'd ever had—was just a foggy, distant nightmare. I could imagine that the harrowing journey ahead was that of a heroine in a book I was reading. A young woman much more courageous, righteous, and honorable than me. Someone I could have unwavering confidence in, knowing, without a doubt, that she could overcome any obstacle. A person I could never be.

Chapter Twelve

I was tightly wound in a blanket after writhing from nightmares of boar-faced creatures chasing me down a mountain. The blanket was scratchy, not the soft cotton touch I was accustomed to. The mattress beneath me was lumpy and squeaked in all the wrong spots. When I opened my eyes, I didn't see a yellow wall or a room cluttered with clothes. I was faced with the bare wooden planks of a Guardian bunkroom.

My parents wouldn't be bursting through the door, giddy with congratulations for my graduation day. There would be no celebratory lunch with Eithan and Cassandry; no send-off as they moved onto bigger and better things. I wouldn't be able to start my training at the Willard's clinic. The future I'd dreamed of no longer lay beyond that door —instead, it was my worst nightmare.

Slowly, I unfurled from the blanket and sat on the perch of the top bunk. My shirt was stiff but dry after my mini rainstorm the previous day. My muted blonde hair hung in tangles around my face. I barely noticed the dull sting pulsing from my burn, and the bruises coating my limbs still didn't ache as badly as they should have.

I remained sitting there for an amount of time that I didn't bother keeping track of. My back slouched, my head hung low, and my vision lost focus. Even the grumbling in my stomach wasn't enough motivation to get up.

The door opened a crack and Bron poked his head in. "Rise and shine."

I glared at him.

"I got something special for breakfast," he enticed. "It's waiting on the table."

I didn't move.

"You have to get up sometime. Might as well be now so you can enjoy it."

When I didn't respond again, Bron opened his mouth to pitch another reason why I should get up. To get him to shut up, I hopped out of bed and shuffled toward the door.

The main room was flooded with sunshine, and I squinted at the sudden severity of it. Yllaria and Leif were nowhere to be seen in the cramped space. On the table was a plate of freshly sliced pear.

I sat and took it without acknowledgment, popping a slice in my mouth.

"Yllaria and Leif are out on surveillance," Bron said, as if I cared. "Throughout the day we scout our perimeter of the mountains. We go in pairs in case something comes up, and one person stays to man the radios."

Bron sat at the table. When I didn't engage, he took it upon himself to carry the conversation.

"Most of us are stationed at posts like this all along the border. Others are sent to Celepheria. Nothing ever bothers them all the way down there, but with such a high volume of people in the city, we want to make sure they're protected, just in case."

Stations in Celepheria? Stations where Cassandry and Eithan would be in a couple months. Where it was *safe*.

"How do you get assigned to these positions? Can you request a location?"

Bron tossed me a smirk. "Nice try, but you can't go to Celepheria right out the gate. They only send the oldest Guardians down there."

"That's not fair."

"Guardians don't age gracefully." Bron took on a serious tone. "Once we reach middle age, our powers dwindle drastically and our health begins to decline. The oldest among us aren't able to handle the border, but they can still be helpful in the city."

"Awesome," I said with sullen sarcasm. "What a wonderful reward for serving the Mother and all Her creations."

Bron leaned back in his chair, assessing me with concerned eyes. "You'll still be able to live a fulfilling life as a Guardian."

"Uh-huh." I dismissed his words as I chomped down on a crisp slice of pear. "Lucky for me, I won't make it to middle age and experience Guardian degeneration firsthand."

"You don't know that. A lot of us survive border duty."

I eyed him incredulously. "There's no way *I* will. If a creat doesn't kill me, my squad will for having a mental breakdown during an attack."

"We will help you get over—"

"You have no idea what I've been through!" I snapped,

my father's face coming to mind. "There's no *getting over* it."

"All of us have a past, Anora. Some of us can relate." When I didn't respond, he sighed. "If you ever want to talk about it, I'm here."

"I need to shower." I shot up out of my chair, sending it screeching across the wood floor behind me.

With a sad smile, Bron handed me a thin towel and led me to the bathroom, making quick work to show me how to use the small corner shower.

"The water doesn't get very hot," Bron warned before shutting me into the closet they called a bathroom.

I quickly wiped off the dried sweat and dust in the lukewarm water. The scar tissue wrapping around my back tightened as I twisted in the compact shower.

Its scaly tail whipped across my back, trying to ensnare me too. I cried out as my skin split open, as my blood splattered next to his on the grass.

But he begged me to run, and I couldn't let him down, so I sprinted away through the trees even as the snap of his bones resonated around me, chasing me home.

The sharp, brief spike of pain from dropping the bar of soap on my toes brought me back. Out of one horror and into another.

My hands shook as I reached for my clothes. They were grimy and stiff, and I scrunched my nose at the thought of having to put them back on.

I called through a crack in the bathroom door, tightening the wisp of a towel around me. "Do you have any spare clothes?"

"Yeah, I'm sure you can borrow one of Yllaria's uniforms."

"Oh no, never mind." I slammed the door shut.

I'd rather smell like a sweaty old gym mat than wear a Guardian uniform. With a sour look, I wiggled back into my dirty clothes.

Yllaria and Leif returned to base shortly after I got out of the shower. I kept to myself and teased the knots out of my hair with a brush I found in their bathroom cabinet. Bron busied himself with gathering new bandages and ointment for my wrist. He handed them to me and I began rewrapping my injury.

Yllaria turned her nose up at me. "You smell terrible."

"Sorry to disappoint," I replied with less bite than I'd intended.

"We'll be leaving now that you're back." Bron said. "Will you be able to man the base alone?"

Leif gave an exaggerated eye roll. "I think you've imparted enough wisdom for us to manage to not get killed in an afternoon."

"I'll be staying overnight, so I won't be back until tomorrow afternoon."

"Oh, in that case—no. I don't think we'll make it," Leif amended sarcastically.

"I'm serious, Leif. You two have never been posted without a senior Guardian before."

Yllaria cut in. "Bron, we'll be fine. We've been active for a few years now."

"Okay, then." He gave a curt nod. "Don't let me down."

Yllaria and Leif saluted him mockingly and he chuckled lightly, saluting in return.

"Don't forget to tell my sister 'good luck' for me," Leif

said. "And that I'll be rooting for her from all the way out here."

"Of course," Bron assured.

Leif turned to me. "You better be nice to my little sister, or you'll have to answer to me."

"If she's anything like you, I can't make any promises."

"Maybe after your training, we'll get to work together," he added with a wink. "I like my squadmates feisty."

With a revolted look, I replied, "For both of our sakes, I hope not."

Without a formal goodbye, we headed down the ladder and along the trail to the jeep. Bron opened the passenger door and extended a hand to help me in. I ignored his offer and hopped into the seat using the overhead handle. He perched in the driver's seat and started the engine. I felt my seat vibrate and barely heard the subtle whine of the engine.

We turned on to a dirt road parallel to the Portemor Mountains. I tipped my head back to take in the expanse of the ominous peaks. They stood about a quarter mile away, the space between pocked with short, thin trees. From this close, the mountains seemed to be never-ending. They were bare of any greenery, draped in pale gray and charcoal earth. Boulders lodged into the side stood out jaggedly all along the steep mountain faces. My power raced down my arms at the sight.

"How do they cross?" I tilted my head toward the deadly mountains.

"It depends on the creat. Smaller ones have burrowed tunnels underneath. Bigger ones, that are agile enough, climb them."

"It looks impossible to climb that."

"It is. Not all of them make it down alive. I've watched hundreds tumble to their deaths. Only the ones with smart footing and fast reflexes make it."

"I'm sure that makes it easier to fight them, too."

"Oh, definitely." Bron chuckled. "Thankfully, you'll take a combat strategy course during training."

I cringed at the mention of training, but I needed to know what I was getting into, so I forced myself to ask, "What can I expect once we get to the training camp—the Compound?"

Bron flashed me a big smile. "You'll be evaluated first thing, along with all the other recruits. Our Commander, Commander Devlend, will assess you. Based on your performance, a training regimen will be set up. You'll take some standard classes too: physical fitness, combat strategy, and theory."

"Will I be evaluated the same way you did it?"

He shifted uncomfortably in his seat, brows furrowed. "Not exactly."

"What's that supposed to mean?" Mild hysteria laced my words. My wrist throbbed at the idea of enduring more.

"I can't say more."

"Why?" I goaded. "Are you sworn to secrecy?"

Bron's voice turned dark and serious. "This is not a game, Anora. He needs to know not only your performance, but how you react. I can't say more than that."

I let the conversation die as I tried to guess what horrible test I'd be forced into. I shrank away from the window facing the mountains and stared at the forest blurring past.

The dirt path wound through the thin woods at the

base of the mountain range. We passed outpost towers similar to Bron's along the way. Occasionally, I spied a Guardian perched on the catwalk surveying the surrounding area.

A tall wire fence ran parallel to the road and interconnected each outpost. Even from this distance, I could make out the thick wires intertwined like vines, climbing up to meet the catwalk floor. Along the top, barbed wire corkscrewed, its metallic teeth thick enough for me to see clearly.

"There's electricity running through the wire. There are doors at each outpost cut off from the current for us to walk through, but some Guardians are able to cross over the top, depending on their abilities."

I could picture Leif breezing over the barbed wire and landing silently with his swift grace.

"Maybe with your abilities, you won't need the door either." Bron inclined his head.

I imagined myself flying over the fence on a gust of wind or pillar of water. At the thought, I felt my power rush to my fingertips, itching to see what it could do. I held it back. Overcoming the urge to release came easier with every passing day, as long as I wasn't suffocating or being burned, at least.

"Doubt it."

"You might be surprised to discover what you're capable of." He flashed a knowing smirk.

"How could you have any idea what I'm capable of?"

"You're not the first of your kind, you know. Element Complectors are actually very common."

"Element Complector?"

"That's what type you are. The Guardians have developed technical terms to describe each type of ability. There's a variety amongst the groups, but they all share a common link. I'm an Energy Complector. My ability manifests in manipulation of my body heat. There are others that can manipulate the energy of the environment and create fire."

"So what do you know about others like me?"

"Element Complectors can control one or two natural elements: earth, wind, or water. There's one, Destrian, who can manipulate natural metal ores, like silver."

I imagined myself accidentally stabbing someone with a silver staff. I shook the terrifying image out of my mind and said, "I'm glad I don't do that."

"You'll learn more from your trainer," Bron said as we weaved down the road, bobbing up and down as we sped over rocks and debris. "We'll be there in about two hours."

My heart and power pounded in my chest, anxiety mounting. I needed my mother's consoling embrace, my stepfather's reassuring nod, my little brother's encouraging smile. An ache cracked through my chest as I felt the distance between us stretch along the road.

"I can't wait to write home," I said.

Bron shifted in his seat. "You can't."

My head nearly snapped off my neck as I turned to look at him. "Why not!?"

"The transition is already hard as it is. Maintaining contact only makes it worse."

I huffed to cover up my whimper. Tears welled in my eyes at the realization. Not only would I not see them, but I wouldn't even be able to talk to my family when I needed them most.

Chapter Thirteen

Bron slowed as we approached the Compound. The surrounding woods receded, forming a wide grassy clearing. A concrete building sat low in the center of the space, surrounded by a tall wire fence similar to the one barricading the border of the Portemor Mountains. Around the Compound was a large field that appeared to slope down in the back with a worn dirt track running alongside the fence. A stubby flag pole sat on the front lawn, flying the Guardian insignia.

Bron rolled up to the gate and waved to a metal box nested atop it. What was it? I'd never seen anything like it. On the front face of the box were layers of black glass that resembled an eyeball with a red light blinking in the corner. After he waved, the gate swung open, seemingly of its own accord, and the jeep eased its way through. Had it come from Celepheria? I tilted my head curiously, wondering how far technology had advanced outside of Bellwarn.

The gate swung back shut, locking us in.

This wasn't going to be as easy as walking out the front door. Once they realized I wasn't cut out for this, though, that I'd be more of a liability than anything, they'd probably send me home . . . right?

He pulled the vehicle in line with the others parked against the cement wall. Overhead, I noted an iridescent shimmer, adding a pinkish hue to the deep-blue sky, and recognized it as a soundproof bubble like the one the construction workers had used at the market. It was the largest bubble I had ever seen.

I got out of the jeep on shaky knees. The warm sun hitting my face did little to calm my nerves or the raging power I struggled to contain.

Bron's non-heated touch grazed my upper arm. "It's going to be fine. There are others in the same boat as you, and I will be here until the morning. You're not alone."

I looked up to find his ember eyes boring into mine, their orange halos flickering.

I sidled out of his touch. "Let's get this over with."

Bron sighed, held open the door, and extended an inviting hand. I inched into the Compound, waiting just inside the threshold for Bron to take the lead.

As the door shut out the sun, my mouth went dry upon seeing the enormous space before me. From outside, the building looked squat, but inside, a stone staircase swept down into a cavernous room. Not a room—an arena. There was a cobalt-blue ring circling the cement floor with several smaller rectangles marked within it. Along one wall was a bench enclosed by plexiglass walls. Painted on the opposite wall was the Guardian insignia. The azure phoenix was framed by a matching blue circle, its beak and wings upturned toward the ceiling. It rose out of flames in shades of bright red, burnt orange, and electrifying white. That looming phoenix seemed to haunt me wherever I went.

As we descended, I looked up at a dome skylight in the ceiling. Sunshine spotlighted the arena beneath. The glass shimmered iridescent pink—either more soundproofing or a reflection of the bubble outside.

There were others already gathered around the ring. A slight girl rocked nervously on her feet, her short blonde hair curtaining the right side of her porcelain face. Next to her stood a tall boy of average build. His stance was confident, golden-brown hands casually in his pockets and wavy chestnut hair brushed back in a quiff. His teal eyes gave away his fear as they darted across the room. On the far side of the group was a pair of towering twins. Planted side by side, their thick biceps strained as they crossed their tan arms across their muscled chests. Their thick brows jutted out slightly, shadowing their eyes in constant scowls. The only difference was the style of their dark auburn hair: one a tight crew cut, the other left shaggy at ear length. They reminded me of Victon with their brutish stance. The only thing worse than a Guardian was an arrogant wannabe—and here were two of them.

Behind them stood their respective Guardian escorts. One I recognized as Guardian Otilia, the solidly built woman that had the strength of twenty. She could toss around monsters like rag dolls, splattering them against the mountainside. The other two Guardians, unknown to me, looked equally as intimidating with their defined muscles framed in tight-fitting Guardian jumpsuits.

Bron approached the two unfamiliar Guardians, and I trailed behind, eyes darting across the room to search for any clues about this suspicious evaluation. While they greeted each other, catching up on how their squads were faring, the other recruits stole glances at me.

The twins couldn't keep their eyes off me, and not in a good way. Their matching scowls traced up and down my form. The boy with blue-green eyes casually swept his gaze over me as he continued his nervous scanning of the arena. The small girl twitched a smile.

Bron grabbed my arm and swung me in front of the two Guardians I didn't know to introduce me. "Cyprian, Destrian—this is Anora Baelin. She's an Element Complector."

I perked up at the mention of Destrian. The one who could manipulate metal.

"Oh, she's like me, eh?" Destrian said as he stepped forward, extending a hand decorated in thick metal bands. Multiple rings adorned every finger, and tight bangles wrapped around his wrists.

Sleek black hair swept across his forehead. His copper-brown skin brought out the flecks of green in his cinna-mon-brown eyes. Several piercings glinted in the sunlight. His ears were lined with gold studs and hoops, and his nose and lower lip were pierced with silver studs.

"Hey," I squeaked out, my gaze lingering on the studs jutting out either side of his lower lip, the subtle weapons he proudly displayed.

He must've noticed me gawking. "My specialty is manipulating metal ore into any form and directing them to move anywhere I want. Hence the killer accessories —literally."

Bron laughed. My eyes widened with fear.

"As long as you don't get on my bad side, they'll stay

here," he assured, tapping his pierced ear. "What's your element?"

"Uh . . ."

"Wind and water," Bron chimed in. "I've only seen her work wind, though. When we first tested her, she blasted me against the gym wall."

"Damn, that's impressive. You must've really deserved it," Destrian teased.

Bron didn't chuckle. "I did."

Destrian flicked his eyes to the bandage at my wrist, then changed the subject. "I think it's almost time. You should probably get in line, Anora."

My feet were rooted to the ground, as if that simple act would stop whatever was about to happen. Bron pulled me by the elbow to the line, my sneakers skidding the whole way, then spun me around to face the arena circle. Once he secured my position, he and the other Guardian escorts retreated a few paces behind us, their chatter echoing off the cavernous walls.

On the wall opposite the staircase, two doors creaked open. The Guardians behind us abruptly ended their conversations and came to attention. A tall, thin man dressed in a fitted charcoal suit entered. His polished black shoes tapped against the stone floor.

Was he Commander Devlend?

Two new Guardians, one with long black hair and the other dark red curls, trailed behind him and stepped in line with the Guardians at our backs. He stood in the center of the arena ring alone. His thinning salt-and-pepper hair and alabaster skin gleamed in the sunshine.

He clasped his hands behind his back and leveled his eyes on us. He scrutinized our faces in silence. My heartbeat thumped against my eardrums. My breathing hitched as my mind began to spiral, thinking of what horrors I was about to endure. Energy surged down my arms and I balled my hands, fingernails biting into my palms.

He took several calculated steps forward and spoke with a smooth, even tone, letting the cavernous room magnify his voice. "Welcome, future Guardians. What an honor it is for you to be here, joining our ranks. I am your Commander—Commander Devlend."

He gestured to the phoenix behind him. "Like the Phoenix, together we will rise above what tries to ruin us, stronger and more determined than ever. Your year of training—and service thereafter—will bring us one step closer to that goal."

His icy blue eyes bore into ours. "I've heard very promising things about all of you and am eager to see what you can do."

The Commander slipped a slender push-button remote control out of his pocket and glided out of the arena circle. He pressed a button and the wide, cascading staircase we had come down retracted into the cement wall, creating a smooth surface. The arena was now a perfect circle. The exit doors taunted me, high on the wall with no staircase now to reach them.

With another click of the remote, the floor in the center of the ring peeled back. The slats in the stone floor grated against each other, retracting to form a gaping black hole into the basement level.

"For your evaluation, you will each battle a creat using your powers only. I, as well as my senior Guardians, will assess your skills and determine how to accurately tailor your training," the Commander announced.

My throat dried shut. Battle a creat—a real live creat!? What was wrong with this guy! Instincts urged me to run, to leave this death trap and never return, but there was nowhere to go. The exit doors looked down with their sunlit window-pane eyes and laughed at me from two stories above.

"I am aware, Mr. Vasterio, that your abilities are not applicable to this style of testing. I will personally see to your evaluation later this evening."

I whipped my head around to the other recruits, and the tall, aquamarine-eyed boy nodded. He gave a sigh of relief. I cursed him under my breath. Why couldn't I be so lucky?

"Out of the rest of you, who would like to volunteer to go first?" the Commander inquired.

The twins stepped forward and declared in unison, "We will, Commander Devlend."

"Very well." A smirk wrinkled his porcelain skin. "Everyone else, sit behind the barrier."

I was first to scurry over to the safety of the plexiglass-enclosed benches. Would the barrier hold against a Portemor monster? Bron slipped in beside me. It was a small comfort to have someone powerful next to me.

The twins split apart, flanking each side of the black void in the center of the ring. The Commander pressed another button once we were all secured behind the barrier. A steel cage, solid except for a few breathing holes on the sides, rose from the ground. Whatever was inside made it shake on the platform.

My knees jittered, restless in my seat. My heart pounded against my chest as I held back fearful tears.

A fury of scales and fangs burst from the brush.

My nails dug deeper into my palms to keep my raging power from spilling out.

Bron whispered in my ear, "The creats brought here for training aren't very dangerous. The barrier is more to protect us from the trainees' uncontrolled powers than anything."

I scoffed, "Easy for you to say. They are *all* dangerous to people like me."

His hand moved to squeeze my frantically bouncing knee, and I flinched away. With a frown, he retracted his hand back to his lap.

With another click of a button, the top of the cage began to open. The twins widened their stances and flexed their fingers. There were no signs of terror on their brutish faces, only smugness. A green, scaly back arched in the cage, pushing against the slow-moving doors. When the door opened fully, a reptilian beast roared out.

I flinched back in fear, banging my head into the cement wall. I winced and rubbed at my scalp. *Please Mother*, I prayed, *let this barrier hold.*

It jumped out of the cage, landing on all fours. Thick, black claws scratched against the cement floor as it jetted around the arena. Its tail, coated in black spikes, swung around wildly. Out of its needlepoint head, a forked tongue lashed out between thin, black teeth. Large, bulbous, yellow eyes rolled in their sockets.

The twins skirted the perimeter to avoid the monster as it darted around. They seemed so sure, so levelheaded. How could anyone be that calm when facing a creat? I'd be lucky if I didn't pass out from one of my attacks, and I was behind the barrier!

One of its yellow eyes locked onto the twin with

shaggier hair. It lowered its belly to the ground, narrowed in on its target, then bolted toward him. He stood his ground with confidence as his brother dashed to stand behind the beast. Once they were aligned, the creature between them, the twins held out their hands toward one another. Beams of energy burst from their outstretched palms and connected to form one solid pillar. It sparked like lightning, flares lashing out from it like whips. The beam caught the beast on its side, burning its legs. It toppled over, issuing a deep, guttural roar. The twins' faces turned deep red, tendons in their necks bulging from the strain, and their pillar of energy sputtered out.

The giant lizard thrashed on its side, its legs a mess of charred scales and claws. The brothers' massive chests heaved, but they forced themselves to circle the beast, aligning themselves with its belly. They raised their hands again, sending out a thinner beam of energy. They missed its torso, aiming too high, and the beast squirmed out from beneath the beam. Its needle-nosed maw snapped at the brother with shorter hair. He bounced back, narrowly missing a bite on the shin.

His eyebrows broke free of their permanent scowl and rose in surprise—in fear.

He sprinted away while the creat limped on its damaged legs. The twins lined up again to deliver another blow but couldn't muster more than a few sparks.

The Commander nodded to the two Guardians that had arrived with him. Together, they left the safety of the box and made quick work of recapturing the beast.

Sweat dripped down the twins' faces as they approached the protected benches. The Commander stepped out to praise them on their unique and impressive ability.

I was rooted in place, my eyes glued to the hole the captured creature had slunk back into. An unnatural wind swirled around my hands, and I clasped them shut in my lap to smother it.

Bron leaned in. "Anora, you need to calm down. Going in nervous is just going to get you hurt."

"Oh yeah, I'm definitely going to calm down after that," I snapped back, gesturing toward the arena.

"You're going to have to go eventually. You have to pull yourself together."

Not if I had anything to do about it.

The brothers, done talking with the Commander, settled onto the bench. They high-fived with satisfied grins on their faces.

The Commander eyed the slight blonde wedged between Otilia and Destrian. "How about you next, Miss Astreya."

I sent up a silent *thank you* to the Mother and prayed that this creat would get out of control and my evaluation would be canceled.

She took measured steps into the arena. Her body seemed so much smaller standing alone. The floor rumbled open again, now with a smaller, solid steel box emerging from its depths. Unlike the last one, this box didn't rattle in the slightest.

The little recruit bounced on her feet, wringing her hands. The box cracked open and a silver-gray mist wisped out. Swirls of thick smoke pooled on the floor. The smoke rose into a column and the girl cautiously inched her way back against the wall. I had never seen that type of creature before. A shiver ran up my spine imagining it roll into the farmers' market as silent as the night, going completely undetected until it made its first kill.

The swirling, silvery fog ghosted toward her. She held up her hands, her thin fingers sprawled out and shaking. The mass of smoke shuddered and came to an abrupt stop, but then quickly pushed forward against whatever force held it. She scowled in frustration.

It cornered her, the gray mist spreading itself wide to cage her in. Panic flashed across her face as it pressed in farther. Through the haze, her shivering was barely noticeable, as was her foggy white breath.

The two recon Guardians motioned to leave the barricade, but the Commander pointed for them to remain seated.

Somehow, the recruit was able to relax her shivering hands, and her eyes fluttered shut. With a wave of her hands, the smoky figure shrunk back from her.

She swirled her hands in a circle and the fog responded by moving not toward her but toward the box. Its movements were not as fluid as when it moved of its own accord, but it was floating away all the same. Slowly, the silvery smoke nestled back into the box and stayed there until the Commander closed the door.

The girl vigorously rubbed her upper arms, her teeth chattering as she shook a chill. The Commander met her at the door, praising her as he had the twins. She settled on the bench.

He turned his icy gaze to me. "Last, but certainly not least—if you'd please?"

He gestured to the open door, but I was frozen in my seat.

The Commander raised a brow at me. "Did you misunderstand, Miss Baelin?"

Bron pressed the small of my back forcefully, pushing me to my feet. I stumbled, my legs stiff and knees locked.

"No, I won't."

"Excuse me?" the Commander asked.

"I won't battle a creat. I, uh . . ."—my voice cracked with fear—"I *can't*. I have this condition—"

The Commander cut me off. "You must take the evaluation like everyone else."

"*He* doesn't." I pointed to the blue-eyed boy. He shrunk on the bench under my gaze.

"Yes, but he's a special case."

"Well, *I'm* a special case too."

"Let's get a move on." The Commander's voice was edged with annoyance as he completely disregarded my plea. "We don't have all day."

Bron pushed me forward, but I fought his grip.

"Forgive me if I'm not eager to jump in the ring with one of those *things*."

He raised an eyebrow. "I understand that this must be quite a shock, but you need to get used to them if you are to succeed. What better time to start than now?"

He gestured again for me to exit the safety of the barricade, and Bron nudged me along, my sneakers squeaking in protest.

"Just focus on your abilities. Once you show him what you can do, it'll be over," Bron advised just before shoving me outside the plexiglass door.

I quickly spun on my heel to find the door already shut in my face. I trudged to the very edge of the arena ring.

My eyes filled with tears, and I squeezed them shut. I tied my hair back with shaky fingers.

When I heard the scrape of the floor opening, I sobbed audibly. Power was at the ready in my fingertips, but I kept my shaking hands clutched.

A large box rose from the ground and rattled violently, a muffled wail sounding from the few small holes drilled in the side. The top began to lift, and I cried harder.

Every nightmare, every trauma I'd ever experienced, flashed before my eyes—all of the teeth, snarls, talons, and howls desperate to tear open my flesh. Somehow, I'd avoided that horrific end. There had been a place to flee, a house to hide within, a man so selfless and full of love to protect me with his own life. Now, there was no place to run, no place to hide, and no one to save me.

A slender creature flew out of the top before it completely opened. Green skin stretched over its bony, humanoid body. The monster had scraggly gray hair, a crooked nose, and bright red eyes.

Slit red eyes trained on me from across the creek.

Not now. I shook the memory from my mind. I couldn't have a flashback here. It would get me killed this time.

As the creat hovered above the arena, reveling in its freedom, I slunk against the barricade in a desperate attempt at camouflage. At the *thump* of my back against the plexiglass, the creature whipped its head down. In an instant, it was flying at me, cackling as it zeroed in. I screamed and barely dodged it, ducking low out of the reach of its slender claws. It whirled around and came at me again. I held up my hands, palms opened. If I didn't use my powers, then this hag was going to kill me. I surged all of my energy through my fingers.

A broad blast of wind shot out and hit the creature, smacking it against the far wall. With no control over my wind, it simply beat against the hag in a continuous wave.

Too quickly, my energy depleted and the gale was snuffed out. No longer pinned, the hag plummeted toward the ground. Right before it collided with the cement, it swooped upward and angled its trajectory for me, shrieking a war cry through the arena.

I crawled away, crouching as low as I could, but the monster still slashed and gouged my upraised forearm. My scream cut through the room as I cradled my bleeding arm. The creature fed off of it, fuel for its cackle. It circled back around, eager for more bloodshed.

I held up my hands again, forcing out whatever power was left in me. Anything to get this over with, to have this nightmare end.

This time, water was called, and a small cloud gathered in the overhead window. The white plumes churned and spread across the ceiling. Rain trickled softly across the arena, then grew into a pummel of coin-sized droplets. I shielded my face from the onslaught and squinted to see if the rain was doing anything. The hag floated stoically, arms outstretched as if embracing the storm. The battering rain seemed to absorb into the creature's skin, strengthening rather than disorienting it.

The cloud continued to swell until I felt the last of my power drain through my fingertips. The storm had sucked every last drop. Without my well of power to siphon from, the storm cloud began to dissolve.

The creature started cackling again. I looked on in

terror as it held up its bony hands toward my cloud and stopped its dissipation.

Oh, Mother save me.

The gray cloud plumed swiftly, filling the entire skylight dome. A low rumble boomed through the room and fissures of lightning danced across the storm cloud. The hag narrowed its red eyes on me, then swept its hands down. Lightning followed its command and cracked a few paces away from me.

Yelping, I scrambled away from the singed floor, and the monster raised its arms again to send another bolt of lightning to deliver my end.

The bite meant for my flesh pierced my father as he dove in front of me.

I knew what I had to do then. What I'd done ever since that day.

I ran.

The front door stood mockingly a floor above with no way to reach it, so I dashed toward the door the Commander had come from. Shouts bellowed behind me, but I ignored them. I burst through the doors just as another bolt of lightning shocked the floor behind me.

Beyond the door was a long hallway sparsely lit by overhead dome lights. I sprinted down the passage, passing several doors along the way. The hall ended, splitting into two, and I veered toward the left without missing a beat. This hallway was shorter with only two doors. The first was a closet stuffed with mops and buckets. The second led to a stairwell. There was another door opposite the stairs and I threw it open. Sunlight flooded the entryway and I smiled at the sight of green grass, then frowned at the formidable wire fence caging me in. But I wasn't going to let that stop me.

I made my way to the front where the jeeps were parked, running uphill as I rounded the Compound. I scoured every vehicle, tearing through every compartment and cushion, searching for a key. All I found was an old pack of jerky and a pile of lint.

Guess I wouldn't be ramming a jeep through the front gates, then. Sitting in the driver's seat, tears welled in my eyes as I realized there was no escape. I banged my fists against the steering wheel, screaming my frustration and ignoring the pain shooting up my bleeding arm.

I heard the back door I had escaped through slam shut.

"Anora!" someone shouted. Was that Bron? "Anora!"

In a panic, my instincts took over again and I hopped out of the jeep and bolted for the wire fence. *I had to get out.*

I went to lace my fingers through the coils, but there was resistance. Where my fingers touched, the iridescent bubble shimmered, not only trapping in sound but me as well. I scrambled to gain purchase anywhere on the fence so I could climb, but the soundproof barrier cloaked every slot.

No, no, no, this couldn't be happening. This couldn't be the end. I pounded my fists against the unforgiving fence, wailing as I threw my whole body into it. The world needed to feel my pain, hear my sorrow, witness my fury.

When strong hands clenched my shoulders, I lashed out. I swung my fists and kicked my legs.

"*No!*" I screamed over and over as I fought.

They wrapped their arms around me at the elbow,

fending off my punches, but I still thrashed my legs, even as they lifted me off my feet. I threw my head back and collided with something soft.

It was Bron, who cried out in pain, but he didn't let go.

"Get Brivania," he ordered in a deep voice.

Slowly, he carried me toward the Compound, struggling to subdue me with each step. I flailed in his grip, fighting with all I had.

"Calm down, Anora," he said. "It's going to be alright."

"Liar!"

A plump woman, accompanied by two Guardians, scurried around the corner of the Compound and headed for us. When they approached, I caught the glint of something in the stout woman's hand.

"Hold her still," she said.

"I'm trying my best," Bron grumbled.

I bucked harder against his hold. Bron faltered and for a moment my arm was free, but then the other Guardians grappled me, pinning me to Bron's chest.

"*Let go!*" I shouted, but no one listened.

"Quick, Brivania, now!" one of them urged.

Then, there was a sharp prick in my arm, and I cried out. Suddenly, a wave of fatigue enveloped me, washing away the fight left in my limbs. It pressed against my mind, consuming the resistance wading there.

"Please," I pleaded, my voice hoarse. "Don't."

But oblivion devoured me anyway.

Chapter Fourteen

"**D**on't come near me," I spat at Bron, who had just entered the bunkroom—or rather my prison cell.

It was a small space with a low ceiling, illuminated by one small window. The room was bare except for a vanity dresser centered on the wall opposite the thin bed I was sitting in. I had changed into a nightgown found in one of the dresser drawers. A fresh bandage was wrapped around my sore wrist and a blood-stained one was around my bicep.

Bron raised his hands up in surrender, a crimson-soaked cotton ball stuffed in one nostril.

"I just came to check on you," he said. "I was expecting you to be scared . . . but *that*?"

"I tried to tell you before, but you wouldn't listen," I said with a fierce glare. "What did you expect to happen? Do you think it's normal for me to fight a creat? What's normal for me is to run for my life. That's what I've always done and always will do."

"You need to get over that instinct." He took a step closer. I tugged my blanket up to my chest like it was a shield.

"It's not that easy, Bron. I don't belong here. I can't be a Guardian. Just send me home."

"That's not an option," he spoke softly. "Do what is asked of you—expected of you—and you'll be fine. Trust me."

"I don't see what the big deal is." I furrowed my brow in frustration. "I'm just one person."

One person that was getting out of this prison—one way or the other.

Footsteps sounded in the hallway. At the sound, Bron stepped away from the bed and leaned against the wall at attention.

Commander Devlend entered the room. The plump woman from earlier, Brivania, was close behind. He seemed taller as he towered over the bed. His graying hair was swept back over the crown of his head. What kind of Commander would willingly put his trainees in danger? Especially on the first day, when we had no clue what we were doing. He basically tried to kill us!

Stark blue eyes roved over me as he said, "What a spectacle, Miss Baelin. I was quite impressed. We haven't had an outburst like that in a very long time."

"Glad I was able to provide your entertainment for the evening." I narrowed my eyes.

"You are a bit scrappy," he said with a dark laugh. "Your assessment was spot on, Guardian Trenton."

I spun around to throw my dagger stare at Bron. He'd talked with the Commander about me? What had he said? Bron turned his eyes downward, saying nothing.

"I've brought our nurse along to check on your wounds." The Commander gestured for Brivania to come forward.

She scurried to my side and sat on the edge of the bed. A few strands of her brown hair, highlighted with touches of gray, fell out of its small bun at the base of her neck. She blew them out of her round, honey-brown face.

"I thought you'd bleed through these quick," Brivania said in her thick accent, unique to the Eterni Peninsula in eastern Alberune.

I had only heard the accent one other time. A traveling merchant had come to Bellwarn selling handmade jewelry crafted from shells and pearls. I had asked the man why he would break Confinement and risk his life traveling alone across the country.

"I want to see everything this beautiful country has to offer, my dear, and I'll be damned before I let any laws or beasties stop me," he had replied with a wink.

He never stopped in Bellwarn again.

The nurse reached over to unwrap my bandage. At first, I flinched away, thinking she would drug me again, but her touch was gentle and her voice was soft.

"I'm just changing the dressing, I promise."

Warily, I let her do her work.

She gingerly unwrapped the gauze. I winced as she cleaned up my wound and coated it with a salve. After the blood was washed away, the gash appeared to be no longer than a couple of inches.

"It's not deep, so you should heal quickly, my dear," she said while applying a new bandage.

Brivania smiled and held the back of her hand to my forehead. Her skin was warm and soft to the touch. I leaned into it, remembering how my mother used to do the same when I was sick.

"She's clammy but not burnin'." She turned toward the Commander. "I think she'll be fine for training tomorrow."

My eyes widened. "Won't it open up again if I start that soon?"

The Commander answered. "We'll start with academics and simple physical training exercises. Nothing too strenuous that would open your minor cut."

"Glad to hear you take it so easy on us." I scowled. He really *was* trying to kill me.

He cut me a hard glare. "Do you not consider your evaluation easy? I think your classmates would disagree."

"*They* didn't have one that could turn their powers against them."

"You each were given a creat that played on your weaknesses. The Fexrunds' weakness is that they have to rely on one another for their power. Against a swift monster, trapping it between them to use their ability is challenging. Miss Astreya is a Mind Complector, meaning she manipulates the creat's own mind to impart her will. One that does not have a traditional body form would make it challenging for her to pinpoint where its consciousness lies. For you, Miss Baelin, the biggest challenge is battling beasts with similar powers to your own. Creats with elemental affinities are particularly common. The fact that you did not overcome this is no one's fault but your own."

I scoffed. "Yeah, it's completely my fault. Someone who has barely used her abilities and has never been in a fight of any kind, let alone against a *monster*."

Bron stepped forward and cleared his throat. "I think what Anora is trying to say is that she hasn't done as much preparation as the other trainees have and may require more basic training."

"What?" I gave him a baffled look. "No, that's not what I'm saying at all—"

Bron cut me off. "Rhismai was the perfect choice for her trainer, Commander, sir."

The Commander nodded. "Yes, Guardian Mojya will have the patience to carry her through her elementary training. I believe my selections for the other trainees will be great matches as well."

"Forgive me, Commander, but I didn't see a trainer here for the Fexrund brothers," Bron said.

Commander Devlend's mouth twitched into a smirk. "Oh, I forgot to mention earlier. I have chosen you to train them."

Bron's eyes widened. "Sir, I don't know how to train a pair of Energy Complectors like them. My ability is internalized."

"There have never been dual Energy Complectors like them before. I suspect their internal energies are calling to one another and externalizing somehow. You are the best internal Energy Complector in the Guard; that's why I need you to train their unique case."

"What about my squad, Commander? I'm not sure they are ready to be by themselves," Bron said.

"Guardians Coracrin and Astreya are more than capable of manning their post without you. You have mentored them well and I have no doubt they will excel in your absence."

Bron slightly bowed his head. "Thank you for your praise, Commander."

I rolled my eyes at Bron's deference. What a suck-up.

Commander Devlend was silent for a moment, assessing Bron. "Dinner will be ready soon. Escort Miss Baelin to the dining hall."

He left the room before hearing Bron's agreement. The nurse handed Bron a fresh wad of cotton, then trailed behind the Commander.

Bron's eyes grew dark, the smoldering edges brighter from the contrast. In those eyes I recognized the look of someone wrenched from the ones they cared for.

"I'm sorry."

Bron nodded, trying to shake off the worry on his face. "The Commander is right. They're capable and will be fine on their own." Then, he added curtly, "There are uniforms in the dresser. I'll wait in the hall."

After he slammed the door shut, I shuffled over to the dresser. Every drawer was stuffed with Guardian uniforms, except for the last, which had nightclothes.

If I wasn't starving, I'd pass on dinner just to avoid putting on this ridiculous costume.

I wriggled and yanked on a tight-fitting jumpsuit. The thick charcoal-gray piece stretched tightly from ankle to neck, squeezing my wound uncomfortably. A thin cobalt-blue accent snaked down my side and wrung my neck. The phoenix insignia set atop my breast and rose up toward me. Completing the ensemble was a pair of jet-black combat boots that squeaked incessantly on the tile floor.

Stepping out into the hall, Bron stomped ahead without any acknowledgment. Fury roiled off his umber skin like steam.

I kept my distance.

Without Bron keeping up his usual conversation, it was hard not to focus on his firm backside as I trailed behind him. Thankfully, he didn't catch my gaze. I might hate the guy for burning me and locking me up here, but I still had eyes. There was no denying that he was attractive.

Self-consciously, I felt down my hips and thought about how wide I must look squeezed into this ridiculous uniform. My cheeks burned when I noticed the glaring curves of my bosom and stomach, and I pulled at the unforgiving material as we entered the stairwell.

We walked down one flight of stairs, passed the door I'd tried escaping through, and entered the main-level hallway. Instead of turning toward the arena, we continued straight. Bron stopped at a set of open double doors and motioned for me to enter.

It was smaller than the cafeteria at school, much smaller. There were four round tables set on a burgundy-tiled floor. A small buffet window opened into a kitchen. Bustling past the window was an older woman with dark, deep-set wrinkles. She was wrapped in a stained blue apron and her white curls were piled atop her russet-brown head.

All of the trainees and their Guardian escorts were seated at one table. At another table sat the two Guardians that had restrained me earlier. Low chatter filled the room as they waited for dinner to be served.

Bron led me to the trainee table and slid out a chair. The table grew awkwardly quiet at my approach and I blushed at the sudden attention. I eased into a seat next to the little blonde that had fought the mist. Her golden eyes wavered and she shifted in her seat.

"Hey, I'm Gwendaliese."

I gave her a nervous smile. "Anora."

"Ah, Gwendaliese," Bron chirped. "Your brother is in my squad. He wishes you good luck with your training."

Her eyes sparkled. "You work with my brother! How is he?"

"He's doing just fine." He smiled. "I do my best to keep him in line."

I guffawed. "There's no keeping Leif in line." Just as the words came out, I turned to Gwendaliese with a stumbling apology. "Oh, sorry. I mean—"

"Don't worry about it, I know exactly what you mean. He's always been a bit . . . mischievous."

"That's a good word for it," I replied, and we shared a small laugh.

Then, the rest of the table sounded off.

"I'm Ander," the twin with the crew-cut hair announced, "and this is my brother, Keldric."

"Blaze, pleased to meet you," the teal-eyed boy said with a smirk.

"Otilia Rutgard," the burly Guardian said. Her dark skin was rough and her brown hair was wrapped tightly in a short braid.

"Cyprian. We met earlier," he said with a ghost of a smile. His warm beige skin, speckled with freckles, complimented his gray-green eyes.

"And I'm Destrian, but you already knew that," Destrian added with a wink. His jewelry gleamed in the fluorescent light.

A heavy silence weighed across the table, the image of my evaluation bearing down on us. Heat crept up my neck and cheeks. I dipped my head low to shield it as much as I could, fussing over my uniform.

Blaze cleared his throat. "So, what's there to do for fun around here?"

Everyone turned to face him, though no one seemed amused by his attempt to break the silence.

"Many of us considered combat training fun when we were trainees," Bron answered. "That's where you really get to test your limits and get creative with your ability."

Blaze nodded, wide-eyed. "Yeah, that sounds like *loads* of fun."

The old woman leaned out of the buffet window, her back slightly hunched. "Come and get it, kids."

We all stood in unison and formed a line. Seasoned red potatoes, broccoli, and cauliflower steamed in large trays alongside barbecued chicken and pork. My plate heaped with generous portions of each. The cook had brought out a jug of water and a wicker basket filled with warmed rolls.

The clanging of silverware and glasses filled the small dining hall. The awkward pressure of conversation was prolonged by the mound of food in front of each of us. The cook hobbled around the room, refilling our empty pitchers.

"Thank you," I said.

"It's no trouble, sweetheart." She smiled widely, deep wrinkles edging her mouth.

I glanced at the two Guardians sitting at the other table. They sat close to each other, shoulders brushing as they giggled privately. Both women were of average build, their subtle curves accentuated by their uniforms. Onyx hair framed one girl's face, while the other had dark cherry curls.

Bron must've noticed my attention and tapped my shoulder. "Let me officially introduce you."

The girls' giggles faded as we approached and the onyx-haired one said, "How're you doin', Bron? I haven't seen you in forever."

She stood and gave him a quick embrace as he replied, "I've been great. Yllaria and Leif have caught on fast. How's your squad?"

"They're amazing, of course. *I'm* the one leading them, after all." She flashed a smile and winked at her companion.

Bron replied with a light chuckle, "I wouldn't expect anything less." He pressed his hand between my shoulder blades, forcing me forward. "Rhismai, this is Anora."

"Nice to meet ya'! I'm excited to get to train another dual Element Complector like me." She held a hand to her mouth to shield her whisper. "Wind and water are the best elements to wield, but don't tell Destrian that."

"I heard that," Destrian called over his shoulder.

"We start next week, officially, but I would like to sit down and chat before then, if that's okay?"

"I'll have to check my schedule," I said.

She laughed. "Okay, I'll hunt you down later this week. When you're free, of course." Rhismai moved to her companion's side. "This is Sephara, she's a Mind Complector from my squad."

We waved, then Bron said, "I heard earlier you were here to be a trainer, too. So who's stationed at your base while you're both here?"

"The Guardians from our surrounding bases volunteered to rotate out monthly to help Garrek this year," Sephara chirped.

"That's a great idea. I wonder if I can convince the Commander to do the same thing for my base."

Rhismai gave Bron a stern look. "They will be fine, Bron. Don't worry about them."

He sighed, but didn't press his concern.

Rhismai looked him over with a pout, then changed the subject. "Blaze, how'd your *personal* evaluation go?"

He ran a hand through his hair. "It was fine, I guess. Definitely not as dangerous as everyone else's, but equally as intimidating."

"So, what is your power anyway?" Destrian inquired, leaning forward to reach the water jug.

"Um, it's kind of hard to explain." His eyes skirted around the room. "I can see people anywhere in the world in the present time. The Commander thinks I'm closest to a Mind Complector but isn't quite sure yet."

Everyone shared a mixed look of wonder and confusion.

"Can we see?" Sephara asked.

Blaze nodded and stood up from his chair. He closed his eyes, then held his palms face up in front of him. Behind his lids, his eyes twitched back and forth. On a whisper of a breath, he repeated a name I couldn't quite make out.

Above his palms, an aura of colors materialized. Swirls of silver and white danced within a sphere of their own making. Shadows appeared in the center, and as the whirlwind settled, they grew in detail. Blaze's eyes shot open and the image became crystal clear under his gaze. A middle-aged woman sat in a rocking chair, knitting by the flicker of a hearth fire. Just as quickly as the woman materialized, she disappeared on a wisp.

My mouth hung agape. Never had I seen something so peculiar, yet so beautiful. Guardian powers were meant to be ugly, chaotic, and deadly. At least, that's what I had thought. I much preferred abilities like his. One that was quiet and innocent. One that brought peace instead of destruction. Why couldn't mine be like that?

"Right now I can only see people that I've met in person. Also, I have to know their names . . . and I can't maintain the image for long."

"That is amazing," Sephara said breathily, eyes wide and mouth slightly agape. "I've never seen a Mind Complector with that ability before."

"Neither has the Commander. He's going to be taking on my training and maybe supplement it with Mind Complectors along the way as we learn more."

"I'm not sure I've ever heard of someone being trained by the Commander primarily," Destrian said, turning to Otilia, the oldest of the Guardians gathered.

She shook her head. "Not since I've been here, no. It is quite an honor."

"Yes, I suppose it is," Blaze agreed, but I saw the truth in his eyes when they locked onto mine—wide with fear. Maybe he didn't see this as being an honor or a privilege, either.

Diverting my gaze, I turned to Bron and yawned. "I think I'm going to head in for the night."

"That's a good idea for all of you recruits. Tomorrow will be a busy day," Bron said to those at the table.

Chairs scratched against the tiled floor as everyone said good night.

Bron led me out into the hall and escorted me back to the bare, cold room where I was bandaged.

"That wasn't so bad," Bron said once we were alone.

"I guess," I shrugged. "Not my kind of conversation."

"It's the first night. It's normal to be shy and unsure of what to say."

"No," I clarified, "I'm not shy. It's that I don't talk about *abilities* or *training*. I'm not interested in any of it. Quite the opposite, actually."

Bron sighed. "You need to get over that, Anora, and quick, if you want to survive this."

"*You* need to get over it if you want to survive me."

A small smile brushed his lips and he leaned against the door frame. "Let me help you adjust. I know how much of a shock all of this is. I'll admit, I've never met a recruit as resistant as you"—his dark eyes searched mine—"but I like the challenge."

"There is no helping me *adjust*. Being a Guardian will never be normal to me."

"With time, it will."

I rolled my eyes but didn't argue further.

When I stepped across the threshold, he reached in to flick on the overhead light. "Can I come in for a minute?"

I nodded, and he closed the door behind him. The room was cold, unyielding. The metal-framed bed felt clinical, the blue walls dusty.

"I want to apologize for yesterday." He frowned. "For the burn." When I didn't acknowledge him, he continued. "It was terrible and cruel. You didn't deserve it, even if you were being difficult. I wish I could take it back."

"I wasn't being difficult." I lifted my chin. "I was tenacious."

"I suppose some could see it that way," he trailed off, his eyes lit like embers. "Can we start over?"

"Are you serious?" I scoffed in surprise. Did he really think I'd forgive him, just like that?

"I'm sorry for how things panned out. I know I can't change what's been done, but I would like to make it up to you—help you get through your training at least."

I narrowed my eyes, scrutinizing him. I was relieved to see his nose was no longer bleeding from when I'd headed-butted him, even if he had deserved it. But Bron had ordered Leif to beat me up, and when that wasn't enough to knock me down, he'd seared my wrists. How could I ever forget that?

Bron did seem to be truly sorry. He'd been thoughtful and concerned for me ever since we'd left Bellwarn. It could all be an act, but if anyone knew how this place ran —and how to get out—it would be him, and that was the kind of ally I needed right now.

"Promise to never burn me again," I said.

He smiled widely. "Yes, I promise."

With that, Bron went to the door and bid me good night. I closed the door behind him, locking myself in my cell. Cold seeped off the walls and into my skin. I welcomed the chill, more in tune with my heart than the forced smiles and small talk. Being alone lifted a weight off my chest rather than adding another layer of fear and uncertainty. The effort of being around them—the Guardians—was taxing. Their enthusiasm for fighting creats and exploring their abilities baffled me and left me feeling more isolated than I ever could by myself. At least with my own company, I didn't have the pressure of conversation—of being someone I wasn't.

Chapter Fifteen

Dust drifted through the sun beaming into the classroom. The light-splashed walls were bare except for the Guardian symbol in the back and a green chalkboard in the front. Six chair-desks were cramped together, facing a small desk in the front corner that was swarmed with papers and books.

Sitting in the back near the windows, I imagined Eithan sitting in front of me and turning around to discuss our homework. My heart ached at the thought of him. I was so used to seeing him every morning, sitting in seats like these. He would be complaining about how uncomfortable they were, how the desk was too small for both his books and his notes. I smiled even as tears threatened to swell.

Gwendaliese sat beside me, her small hands clasped in her lap to hide twiddling thumbs.

"Good morning." She beamed, her golden eyes soaking up the sun's rays.

"Morning. Oh," I said with a lilt. "How embarrassing, we wore the same thing on the first day of class."

She gave me a weak laugh. "I know. I'm not sure I'll get used to having to wear this uniform every day. I miss my long dresses." She tugged at the sleeves and added, "You can call me Gwen."

The door creaked open and the three boys filed in. Blaze slid into the seat next to Gwen while the twins were left to sit in the front row. Gwen bid them all a cheery good morning. Blaze dazzled her with a full smile while the twins gruffed a reply.

"Good morning to you too," Blaze greeted in my direction, leaning back in his seat to meet my eyes.

"Morning," I chirped, fussing with my braided hair.

The Commander swept in shortly after, his cap-toe shoes tapping as he approached the front of the room.

He surveyed each of us before addressing the room. "Welcome to your first day of training. I must say, I was impressed by your evaluations yesterday."

My face burned and I sunk in my chair, scowling at the Commander.

"We'll spend most of today in lecture," he said. "Later this afternoon, we'll do some physical training. By the end of the week, we'll start ability training."

He grabbed a stack of textbooks, giving one to each of us. It was titled, *A Lesson in History: Alberune and the Portemor Mountains.*

"What is our goal as Guardians?" Commander Devlend asked the class.

"To protect civilians from creats," Ander answered in his husky voice.

The Commander nodded. "Yes, but what is the bigger

picture? Do we want to be locked in a never-ending battle with them forever?"

"No, but it's impossible to kill all of them at once," Gwendaliese said.

"Maybe, but what if there was a way to return our world back to the way it used to be? I'm sure your studies have covered how our society used to be over two hundred years ago."

The class nodded together.

"That would be ideal, but that was so long ago," Blaze objected. "There's no way we could go back to that lifestyle."

"So we should simply concede and continue to live shrouded in fear with barely any quality of life?"

"It's too big of a risk to try and change the way things are. It may not be the best life, but it's a safer one," I piped up.

Commander Devlend raised an eyebrow. "On the contrary, Miss Baelin. Turn to page twelve."

The lights dimmed and a plastic box suspended from the ceiling began buzzing softly. Then, there was a flash of white light and somehow the graph in our books appeared on the chalkboard. I hid my shock and wonder at the high-tech display. Gwen and Blaze seemed in awe of it too, their mouths slightly agape. From my vantage point, the Fexrunds didn't look fazed.

The two graphs showed the number of creat sightings and attacks over time. Both indicated a slow and steady incline. The Commander pointed with a ruler to the first year on the graph and dragged it along the board to reach the present year. The drawn-out screech stung my ears.

"There has been an increase in both sightings and

attacks since the first incident back in 1556. In the past few years, the numbers have grown exponentially with no explanation. Guardians have helped reduce the frequency of attacks in relation to sightings, but even so, we cannot stop all of them.

"So yes, we can continue with what we're doing now. Maintain minimal lifestyles and rely on the Guard for protection. But based on these trends, things will not stay the same. In fact, they will only get worse."

He flashed a satisfied smile as if he'd just won a battle. I scowled back. He could throw around facts and figures all day, but the bottom line was that there was nothing more we could do without risking more lives. No matter what we did, what we changed, there would always be death.

I narrowed my eyes. "Then what are we supposed to do?"

"That is the exact question we've been working to answer. I hope your young, bright minds will help us figure it out. Once armed with the knowledge your training will provide, of course." My eye roll did not get past the Commander's quick eye. "I thought you of all people would be more motivated to find a solution, considering . . ." He smirked at me.

I took the bait. "Yes, well I'm a little too attached to my head to go gallivanting around trying to kill every last creat."

"Be creative, Miss Baelin! Who ever said this had to be accomplished with brute force alone?"

"What other way is there?" Keldric inquired.

"We've come up with theories ranging from ways to

build stronger borders all the way to relocation. Unfortunately, none have gotten past the initial planning stages."

"Relocation? I thought Celepheria was overpopulated as it is?" Gwen asked.

"There may be lands beyond our shores, Miss Astreya. We only need to look for them."

"We've tried in the past," Gwen countered. "But the Interminable Storm over the Western Seas makes it impossible."

"Yes, you're correct that we have tried and failed to explore our seas, but you are wrong in saying it's impossible. It is simply a problem to be solved. And, as with solving any great problem, we must start from the beginning. Turn to chapter one."

The entire morning was spent viewing pictures and reading passages about life before the monsters. Bright images of affordable cars driving through bustling town squares lined with storefronts rolled across the board. We read aloud descriptions of how houses were clustered into blocks where the only thing separating their property was fencing. A time when children were free to laugh and run around their yards. A time when a girl could go fishing with her father without fear of a serpent hunting them.

At one time, envy would've enraged me at the sight of their carefree smiles, but now the sting had worn into a jealousy-driven disinterest. I was relieved when he dismissed us for lunch, and I prayed we wouldn't return to the subject again.

I murmured to Gwen in the hallway, "I don't see how rubbing in our faces how great life used to be is supposed to help *expand* our minds."

"Me neither." She shrugged. "Maybe it's supposed to motivate us to want to change."

"If there is an easy way to fix things, then I'm all for it, but I honestly don't see any way to rid our lives of creats without putting people in danger."

Ander glanced over his shoulder. "But it's worth the risk; that's what the Commander was getting at."

"Maybe to some," I countered.

"To sacrifice myself for such a great cause would be an honor," Keldric said, puffing out his broad chest.

Behind his back, I made a gagging gesture. Gwen kept silent, but Blaze snickered to himself. We exchanged glances and smiles.

Ander glared over his shoulder. "So, how are you after your *episode* yesterday, Anora?"

My face heated and I scowled back. "I'm just fine, thanks."

"We were really worried about you," Gwen said. "How's your arm?"

"I'm okay. It was a little cut. The bleeding stopped." I added, "I'm not particularly inclined to fighting of any kind, let alone fighting creats."

"And you shouldn't be expected to," Blaze rallied.

"Yeah, why couldn't I have your gift?" I pointed to him. "You get out of all the fighting."

His aquamarine eyes sparkled. "I guess I really lucked out."

"*And* you get to see anyone you want, anytime you want, while the rest of us can't even write one measly letter. For having to be trapped here, you definitely have it the best."

"Yeah, I suppose I do," Blaze replied softly, looking down at his boots.

"Some people look forward to the fighting," Ander said under his breath.

I rolled my eyes. "Good for them."

Blaze's smirk returned. "The Commander is really going to love you, isn't he?"

"Oh, yes, without a doubt," I said as we made our way to the dining hall.

––––

Sweat beaded my forehead in the blazing afternoon sun as I ran the thin dirt track encircling the Compound. The field surrounding the building was flat, save for the gradual slope along its side. Lush grass blanketed most of the field except for a cement slab jutting off the back of the Compound. Tire tracks matted the grass just before it, most likely leading to an underground garage of some kind.

As I made my final lap down the slope, the other trainees were still yards behind me. In the last stretch, I sprinted farther ahead and left a plume of dust in my wake. With my boots pounding against the earth and fresh air pumping through my lungs, I finally felt a bit like myself again. My mind cleared. All that existed was my body and a path that led to nowhere.

I slowed to a stop near the three trainers and leaned against the fence to catch my breath. The bubble shimmered at the contact, surrounding me in a pink pearlescent halo. When I looked up, Bron was beaming at me in approval.

"I told you," I said between breaths. "Running is what I do best."

"That will be a great advantage." He patted me on the shoulder.

"Have you ever done long-distance running?" Rhismai asked. "In the field, we sometimes have to run for miles to catch a creat."

"I run for a hobby mostly. I use a safe runner at home and the farthest distance it measured was eight miles in just under an hour."

Rhismai bobbed her head in approval. "Do you strength train as well?"

"Eh, not so much." I finally caught my breath. "But it seems those two have got me covered."

I gestured to the Fexrund twins now stretching on the track, flexing their biceps and thighs.

"You better be referring to *these* two," Blaze teased, flexing his toned but comparatively thin arms.

"Clearly." I laughed.

Bron cleared his throat. "Let's move on."

Under the hot sun, we did push-ups, sit-ups, and squats for the rest of our physical training session. I didn't overexert myself, but the sun beaming overhead left me drenched in sweat anyway.

Rhismai stayed at my side, coaching and studying me, as did the other trainers with their respective trainees. Blaze was under Sephara's eye, who was wholly more concerned with Gwendaliese and loosely instructed him on what to do. Dividing his gaze between the twins, Bron stole glances of encouragement in my direction.

"Great first day, recruits. Now go hit the showers."

Bron gestured toward the Compound, cast in the long shadows of dusk.

We lumbered through the back door, up the stairs, and down the long stretch of hallway. At the end of the hall, past all the bunkrooms, were two bathrooms.

On our trek, Bron nudged me. "That was quite the hustle. I'm impressed."

"Oh, please. I looked like an overheated cow writhing out there."

Bron laughed deeply, his coal eyes crinkling at the edges. "At least you can admit it to yourself." He continued with a more serious tone, "I honestly thought you were going to refuse to participate. Maybe you won't be such a challenge after all."

"I haven't gone soft, I just love to run." I faced him. "Trust me, if that fence wasn't there, or if there weren't three Guardians breathing down my back, I'd be long gone."

"I don't think it's possible for you to go soft, Anora," Bron said.

Once in the shower, I let the water wash away my fatigue of body and mind. The scalding water beat against the scar trailing down my back. The steam curled around me and carried away the weight of my mask: the quips, the sarcasm, the laughs, the smiles. They drifted away, leaving behind a hollowness in my chest.

Hunched over a stainless-steel stockpot, the old cook wafted her chowder. Blaze was the only person sitting in the small dining hall, and I joined him. His chestnut hair looked near black after his shower, and without its usual volume, it clung to the sides of his face in wavy locks. Having given my hair a good comb through after my shower, I left it down and draped over one shoulder, my blue shirt underneath growing a damp spot.

"I think those are meant to be pajamas," Blaze critiqued.

"It's comfier than that awful thing." I gestured to his uniform.

"You better get used to it. You'll be living in one next year."

"Not if I have anything to say about it," I muttered under my breath.

"What was that?" Blaze leaned in to hear me better. He raised an eyebrow, curiosity sparking in his eyes.

"Oh, nothing. I just don't care much for the uniforms is all." I smiled and fiddled with my fresh bandages.

I had to be more careful about what I said, and how I said it. The last thing I needed was someone tattling before I even had an escape plan together.

I poured a glass of iced tea and took a sip.

"They are miserable, aren't they?" Blaze said, tugging at his collar. "Maybe we could go on strike."

"We didn't even get a choice in coming here. I doubt they'd let us have a say in the wardrobe," I said, then sipped my tea.

"If we all showed up to training naked, I bet they would." Blaze smirked.

I spat out my tea. "Uh, excuse me?"

"Oh, nothing. Just don't care for the uniforms is all." Blaze winked at me.

A blush warmed my cheeks and we laughed together.

The other recruits and trainers filed into the dining hall intermittently. Otilia, Destrian, and Cyprian had left after breakfast to return to their posts. Gwendaliese, Rhismai, and Sephara joined Blaze and me. Bron sat at the other table with the twins, bonding over discussion of their energy abilities.

The cook struggled to muscle the stockpot into the window, and then set a salad and rolls next to it. She placed plates, bowls, and silverware on the edge of the counter and called, "Come and get it!"

We all rose from our seats and formed a line. When I made my way to the food, I helped myself to salad and bread while the chef served steaming potato and corn chowder.

"Half or full bowl, darling? From the looks of you, you could use a full one," the woman said as she filled it to the brim.

I looked down at my full hips but said, "Yes, please. Thank you, Ms . . ."

"Call me Memette." She gave a wide grin.

"Thank you, Memette," I said as I took the bowl.

Scalding chowder threatened to slosh out as I made my way to the table. The only casualty was a minor dribble which I scooped up with my finger and licked clean. The meal was hearty and full of flavor, just as Bron promised. I savored every chowder-soaked bite of my roll, tuning out the table as they chattered on about training.

I wondered if my stepfather was nagging my mother to make more sweets; if Liam had gotten into anymore fights at school; if Cassandry had found a way to pack all her clothes and was on her way to a new, safer life . . .

"What about you, Anora?" Rhismai asked just as I stuffed my mouth with bread.

Wide-eyed, I swallowed the half-chewed bread. "What about me?"

"How do you feel? About what we're talkin' about." Rhismai gave me a knowing look.

"Oh yeah—that . . ." I took a sip of water. "I feel so good about that—about all of it."

"So you're looking forward to ability training! It's only four days away now. You must be so excited," Rhismai pressed with a mischievous smirk.

Well, that was what I got for not paying attention.

"I'm so super excited about it. Can't wait." I made no effort to hide the sarcasm in my voice.

Rhismai gave me a stern look. "Can we have that discussion we talked about after dinner?"

Heat rose up my neck. "Oh, sure."

An awkward silence settled, leaving only the scrape of silverware against bowls and plates to fill the room. When a knock sounded at the door, we all turned, eager for something to break the silence.

"Sorry to interrupt such riveting conversation," quipped the willowy redhead leaning against the door frame.

"Leif!" Gwendaliese chirped as she hopped out of her chair and crashed into her brother with a strangling embrace. "What are you doing here?"

"Very good question," Bron grunted as he stood, his eyes burning as they pierced Leif.

"Simmer down. Destrian stopped by to see Yllaria and they locked themselves in the bunkroom. I asked if I could join, but Yllaria threw her boot at the door. I took it as they didn't want company."

"So no one has been on patrol at all this afternoon then?" Bron snapped.

"I ran patrol before I left only an hour ago. Did you forget my complection so soon, squad leader?"

Bron narrowed his ember eyes. "I don't need the smart remarks, Leif. You disobeyed orders."

"I would defy any order where my little sister is concerned." He squeezed her against his chest, squishing her dimpled smile.

"Has the Commander come to talk to you yet?"

"Of course he did, and after listening to my plea, he has graciously allowed me to stay for the hour to visit with my sister."

"Yay!" Gwen beamed. "Have you eaten? We can bring some food up to my room and we can catch up on everything."

Leif gave a rare, genuine smile to his sister. "Sounds great."

Brother and sister left, already enthralled in conversation about Gwen's flock of chickens. He asked how her favorite hen, Penelope, was and she dove into a surprisingly thorough answer as they strolled down the hall. Envious tears dotted my eyes. I had to blink them away before the image of Liam being the one to round that corner could settle in.

Soon after they scurried off, everyone began trickling out of the dining room. Before Sephara left, she whispered in Rhismai's ear. My trainer gave Sephara a not-so-subtle squeeze on the bottom before she strutted out the door.

Rhismai faced me. "I may have been sent here as your

trainer, but I also want to be your friend. I want to help you transition into this lifestyle as easily as possible. I've noticed your attitude toward being here is a bit . . . negative. Is it because of your evaluation? If it is, it's completely natural to be afraid when you face one for the first time. But don't let that bad experience affect the rest of your training. It'll only make the process harder."

"It is the evaluation, but it's so much more . . ." I wasn't sure Rhismai would empathize with my situation and be able to help me, but I had to give it a shot. "I'm not simply *afraid*; it's more—intense than that. It takes over my whole body, my mind, and I can't function. I'll be in the way here and on the border. I'll get myself and others hurt—or worse. This is a waste of time for you, me, and everyone here trying to train me to be something I'm not meant to be."

Rhismai leaned forward, lowering her voice into a consoling tone. "Anora, you are meant to be here. You were *born* for this. I know how hard this all must be to digest, but once you get into training and start learning how to control your powers, you'll feel it. You'll feel like you belong and that this is where you're meant to be."

My teeth ground together and I refrained from rolling my eyes. "That will never happen for me."

What was so hard to understand? How much clearer did I have to be? They'd even witnessed one of my attacks after the evaluation and still weren't taking me seriously. There was no bigger sign I could show the Guard that I didn't belong among them.

"It will. It always does, and I'll be here to help you realize it. Training will start slow. We'll focus on controlling and manipulating the elements. Nothing about combat strategy or fighting style or anything."

"I won't make any promises." There was challenge in my voice.

"All I want is for you to try," she said.

"Sure," I muttered.

Rhismai beamed. "I'll take that! I'm excited to see what you can do."

I painted on a smile. "I'm going to head in for the night, if we're all done here."

"Yeah, go ahead. See you tomorrow."

I headed for the bunkroom. It wasn't going to be easy convincing them to let me go. The Guard was determined to cure me of my *simple fears*, but soon they'd realize just how determined I was to get out of this prison.

As I lay in bed with the lights off, my mind was not about to rest.

I began to hatch my escape plan.

Chapter Sixteen

✿❧✿

Drawling lectures about the old world devastated my mornings while calisthenics ruined my afternoons. The nights were spent formulating my escape, pacing the bunkroom as I tried to piece together its perfect execution.

Bron kept his promise. Every available moment, he asked how I was feeling, if I had any questions, or if I just needed to talk—which we did often. It wasn't like I *wanted* to talk, but Bron was persistent when it came to keeping up conversation.

He had started ambushing my evening runs. At first it was annoying having him tag along, but countless stories about his family orchard and his little sister melted my heart.

As the days passed, the laughs came easier and easier with him. A part of me was frustrated because it went against every I-Hate-The-Guard bone in my body. But another part didn't mind so much...

"Did I tell you how I first discovered my powers?" Bron had asked one evening, strolling through the Compound field under the stars and a blue moon. It was strange being outside in the nighttime air and not having to worry about creatures lurking in the shadows. The soundproof bubble overhead was the only redeeming quality of this prison.

"I don't think so." I kicked at some loose stones along the dirt path.

"I had just turned seventeen." He looked up at the stars with glistening eyes. "And my little sister's gift for me was a wildberry pie, my favorite."

"Did a bite of pie unleash your powers?" I had teased.

Bron hadn't laughed.

"She never got a chance to bake it." He cleared his throat and rubbed his eye. "While she was picking berries, a creat came and . . . well . . ."

"You don't need to say." A tear came to my eye. I had felt like I knew his sister after the stories he shared of them running around their orchard. "I'm sorry."

On my next step, I inched closer so our arms brushed. So he knew I was there for him, and that I understood all too well what had happened to his little sister, and his whole world, that day.

"I was so *angry*," Bron said. "My grief unleashed my powers."

"You literally burned through your feelings," I said, then elbowed him in the side.

"Yeah, I suppose I did." He smiled at that. "When I realized what I was, I decided to use my powers to avenge her. To defend Alberune so no other little girls have to be afraid to pick berries."

I only nodded. I saw where this was going but didn't interrupt.

"Anyway." Bron ran a hand along his scalp. "I just wanted you to know that you're not alone here. A lot of us have lost family and friends to creat attacks. A lot of us have witnessed or survived attacks ourselves, too. The best way to work through the past is here, as a Guardian, fighting to create a safer world so no one else has to deal with what we have."

"That's very admirable of you, Bron," I said, and I meant it.

Every Guardian *was* brave for the sacrifices they made to protect Alberune. There was no denying that, but it didn't change the fact that I didn't want to be one. The fear from my past was too consuming, the flashbacks too overwhelming. There was no way I could be a Guardian, but I still appreciated Bron opening up to me. Connecting through our pasts had unthawed my heart a bit. I could tell he wanted to help me, not because it was his job to groom a future Guardian, but because he actually liked me —for me.

He had been right about one thing—I wasn't alone anymore.

———

At the end of the first week, Bron walked me to ability training in the arena. Actually, it was more of a stilted limp. I might be a runner, but my body had not been prepared for a week of physical training with Rhismai.

I lined up along the edge of the blue ring with the other recruits while our trainers stood behind us. Fidgeting, I fought the compulsion to scratch my nearly healed wounds. They no longer needed bandages, but the urge to itch the pink, fresh skin was unbearable.

Commander Devlend stood in the center of the ring with his hands clasped behind his back. The phoenix mural rose behind him. His cap-toe shoes shined under the skylight.

"Good morning and congratulations on finishing your first week of training." Sunlight danced in his icy blue eyes. "I feel you are all well-prepared to begin ability training, but for today, I want you to observe your trainers in combat. Watch how they manipulate their abilities, both offensively and defensively. Also, take this time to learn what other complectors are capable of. When you are in a squad of your own, you will have to work together and harmonize your abilities to take down your opponent."

Our trainers stepped forward into the circle. Bron's muscles flexed underneath his jumpsuit as he stretched. Rhismai rolled her neck and shoulders while Sephara took a meditative stance, eyes closed and head facing the light.

The Commander slid out of the ring and ushered us toward the safety of the covered benches. I sat next to Blaze, who slouched against the wall. He leaned his head back with a sigh.

"Don't you look invigorated this morning," I commented under my breath.

"Oh, and that shamble in here was just your *swagger*, I suppose?" Blaze asked, an eyebrow raised.

I fought back a smirk. "You're one to talk with that *limp* of yours. How's your poor ankle doing?"

"Hey, it may not have looked like much to a track-star like you, but I twisted it pretty bad yesterday!" Blaze defended with a chuckle. "At least today is an observation day and we don't have to do anything."

"I wish every day was an observation day."

Commander Devlend cleared his throat, peering down the bench at Blaze and me. We both stifled our laughs and turned to face the three trainers.

They formed a triangle on the edge of the ring. All of their focus was aimed at the center of the arena where a creature would appear. Panic woke the power in my chest. It raced down my arms and nearly escaped before I clenched my fists.

The Commander swiped a slender remote from his suit-jacket pocket and the floor slowly scraped apart. A large rattling cage emerged from the black depths. The three Guardians readied themselves, loosening their knees and knuckles. Bron's posture radiated confidence. His smoldering eyes caught mine from the other side of the solid steel box just as the top opened.

A piercing screech cut through the arena and a massive bird-like creature burst from the cage, wings outspread and chrome talons clutching the lip of its enclosure. Pewter-gray plumage coated the creature, the slender feathers glinting a metallic sheen in the sunlight. A long and narrow serrated beak with a gleaming hook on its end snapped as the beast cried out. Beady black eyes darted around the arena. Its weighty wings beat a few times, feathers pinging a chime with the motion, and the beast shot toward the ceiling. It circled the perimeter of the skylight as it surveyed the Guardians below.

Bron was iron hot and ready to fight. His skin didn't glow like molten ore, but there were visible waves of heat rolling off his skin. Rhismai held her hands out in front of her, palms facing each other. She waved her hands in a circle, swirling the air between them into a raging ball of wind. Sephara stepped forward and looked up at the vulture. She lifted her hands and moved them in time with the bird's flight. The beast flapped its wings with increasing force and its feathers shook violently, the metallic ping piercing my ears.

Sephara called out over the clanging plumage. "It's going to throw its feathers!"

She pulsed her fingers toward the bird and the strain to beat its wings was immediate. The bird drooped closer to the arena floor as it fought her hold. It must have gotten past her guard, because it violently beat its wings once and two feathers fell like arrowheads toward the ground. They arced as they fell, aimed for Sephara. Rhismai blasted her windsphere at them and knocked them off course. They clattered against the wall and fell to the ground.

Bron raced to grab the feathers. The plumes glowed red hot beneath his touch. Throwing them overhand, Bron aimed for the bird. With the assistance of Rhismai's wind, the scalding feathers pierced the bird, one burrowing into its thigh and the other scraping its cheek. The beast cried out, chrome blood dripping down its face and leg. The blood spotted the arena floor, creating a splatter of liquid mirror.

Swooping down, the bird snapped its jaws at Bron's head. He ducked swiftly and hooked an arm around its leg. A high-pitched screech made the arena shudder as Bron's burning touch scorched the bird's injured leg. The beast swiveled its head back toward Bron, eyes wide with panic and pain. Its saw-like beak pecked at Bron's head, its metallic point hitting his skull with a *thunk*. He let go, stumbling backward. Blood ran down his scalp and he cradled his head but quickly recovered.

Bron instructed his comrades. "Rhismai, you take the air out of its wings. Sephara, you stiffen its limbs."

The girls nodded and did as he said. Rhismai swiped her arms down in an arc and wind followed her. The bird splayed in the air as it tumbled. Before it could regain its bearings, Sephara stiffened its wings. Falling like an iron, the bird crashed to the floor, its feathers clattering against the cement.

The bird whistled a weak coo as it flailed helplessly. A wing, and maybe a leg, were broken, and the beast tried desperately to get up. It squirmed, trying to limp away from the Guardians at its back; its eyes darted around the room. Bron ambled toward the bird, stretching out his arms in front of him and cracking his fingers. With a shrill coo, the bird thrashed, thrusting its broken wings forward in a futile attempt to escape its fate. When Bron reached the writhing bird, he bent down and wrapped his arm around its neck. The feathers there glowed bright red, molten globs sizzling as they hit the floor.

"Don't kill it, Bron. We need to save our beasts for training," the Commander shouted.

"Why not let him put it out of its misery?" Gwen squeaked.

The Commander whipped around. He looked down on her. "Excuse me?"

"It has broken bones and is half melted. How could a damaged creat like that still be useful, sir?"

He towered over her. "I don't care if it's on the verge of death. We can still use it once it heals."

"With all due respect, Commander, I don't see how it

will be able to heal on its own, especially if it's left in that cage." Her voice quavered.

"Do you suggest we keep it out? Maybe send the nurse to set its bones?"

"No! Absolutely not, sir! It's just that I don't think it will heal cooped up in that cage. It might as well be put down now to spare it—"

"Spare it from what? Pain? If it dies afterward, then so be it. But I won't have it killed now out of mercy. You best *kill* that sympathy before it kills you, Miss Astreya," the Commander warned.

"Yes, sir." Gwendaliese slumped on the bench, a rosy blush creeping up her neck and painting her cheeks.

Bron had stopped at the Commander's first order. The bird lay unconscious at his feet, breathing weakly, a silver tongue hanging out of its beak in a pool of melted feathers and chrome blood. Rhismai and Sephara hurried over to Bron and began fussing over his injury. Batting them away, he assured it was fine.

Together, they hoisted the bird and tossed it in the cage. It hit the cage floor with a *clunk*. Gwen winced.

As the cage receded, the Commander led us out onto the arena floor. "What did we learn?"

"That you can transfer energy to an object, like what Bron did with the feathers." Ander spoke up eagerly.

"Yes, sometimes your power alone will not be enough. You must learn how to utilize your surroundings. It's an advantage for any type of complector. Anora, can you give an example of how an Element Complector could use their ability to hone a weapon?"

I shot my eyes to him. "Uh . . . I don't know."

"Were there any examples that Guardian Mojya provided in this exercise?"

From behind his back, Rhismai nodded her head in encouragement.

When asked a question on the spot in class at Bellwarn Central, I would rack my brain searching for the answer. But here, that drive never came.

Blaze stepped in. "Rhismai helped guide the feathers Bron threw back."

Commander Devlend eyed him, and then me. "Thank you, Mr. Vasterio, for helping your classmate."

I muttered a thank you to Blaze, and he smiled.

"I liked seeing all of them using their abilities together to take it down," Keldric blurted out.

"That is a critical skill you will all harness by the end of your training. Playing off of your squadmates' abilities is a key advantage. We're done for the day, but I want you to come up with some creative ways you can use your ability in combat." He faced Blaze. "How about you come up with ways your ability can help aid the Guard's cause, since combat isn't your strong suit."

Blaze nodded and the Commander left. Once the door slammed shut behind him, I moseyed over to Bron.

I eyed his scalp. "Are you okay?"

He flashed a smile. "Yeah, I'm fine. It didn't hurt that bad."

"Really? Because what I saw was the equivalent of getting whacked on the head with a hammer."

"I've suffered a lot worse. I'll be fine."

"If you say so." Then I asked, "Does this mean we have the rest of the day off?"

I faced the warm sun beaming through the skylight,

comforted by the thought of this same sun warming my family home. I wondered what they were up to on such a beautiful summer day.

"You have the rest of the day to work on your assignment," Rhismai pointed out.

"Just how I wanted to spend my night," I muttered.

Rhismai gave me a concerned look. "Try and look at it more as an opportunity to explore your abilities' potential, rather than work."

"That will certainly help me get enthused about it."

"Just give it a try, okay?"

"Oh, right. Sure," I offered half-heartedly as I walked out of the arena.

Her disapproving sigh echoed down the hall, but the usual guilt that accompanied someone's disappointment in me never came.

"Knock, knock," I said outside of Bron's bunkroom door.

The door opened and there he stood, beaming with a thick bandage atop his head.

"What are you doing here?" he asked.

"You're always there for me after a rough lesson, so I thought I'd return the favor." I held out a plate of leftover blueberry muffins.

"Come on in." He held out a hand for me to enter.

His room resembled mine. Nothing decorated the walls or the tile floors. A wrought iron bed and simple dresser sat on either wall. The only addition he had was a set of chairs and a small table in the far corner. I set the plate on the table and sunk my teeth into a muffin as I sat down.

"How're you feelin'?" I said around my mouthful.

"I'm better now that you're here." Bron smiled as he sat down.

"My charm has that effect on people." I winked.

"Oh, I was referring to the muffins," he said as he picked up the biggest one on the plate.

"Ha-ha." I stuck out my tongue. "Very funny."

"Well, it definitely isn't your charm," Bron teased. "You have as much charm as a creat."

"Be nice, or I'll keep the muffins for myself," I threatened.

"Ah, there's that charm." He laughed.

I tossed a blueberry at him and bit down my own laugh. An envelope sat on the edge of the small table. It was addressed to Bron from outpost twelve. I stuffed the last bite of muffin in my mouth and snatched up the letter.

"What's this?"

"Nothing." Bron yanked it out of my hands before I could take the letter out. His big smile was wiped clean as he turned back into the stoic Guardian I'd first met.

I frowned. "Doesn't seem like nothing."

"It's a report from my outpost," Bron said. "It's confidential."

"*Oh!*" My eyes widened. "Big top-secret Guardian business. That's right up your alley."

"It's nothing to joke about, Anora. It's serious." He ran the envelope between his fingers.

Bron was always quick to be the intense, all-business Guardian, but this seemed different. His mouth was set into a frown, his eyes downcast and dark. It was something serious, and it seemed seriously *bad*.

"What happened?" I asked.

"It's Yllaria." Bron sighed. "She was injured while scouting the mountains, broke a few fingers."

"You must be so worried for them." I remembered how upset he was to leave them when he had to stay and be a trainer.

"Yeah, she says she's alright and can still do patrols, but I sent correspondence to the surrounding outposts. They'll send back-up to help out while she heals."

"You've always got their back." I leaned over and put a hand on his shoulder. "You're a good squad leader."

I didn't care about that sort of thing, but I knew Bron did. Being a squad leader was his whole world, and I bet it broke him every day knowing he couldn't be with Yllaria and Leif. Even though he was a Guardian, the reason I was trapped here, and represented the very institution I was trying to break out of, he was still a great person and deserved to know that.

"Thanks." He put his hand atop mine and looked at me, eyes smoldering bright orange around the edges.

My stomach hitched when his eyes locked onto mine, and heat flared in my cheeks. I slid my hand out from underneath his.

"I should get going." I rushed to the door. "Got that big assignment to work on."

"Oh, right." Bron stood. "Thanks again, for the muffins."

"Anytime!" I said, then sprinted down the hall before those fiery eyes could lock me in a trance.

Chapter Seventeen

Fluorescent light beat down on a notebook at the end of the bed. I was lying on my stomach in a baggy gray shirt and sweatpants, legs crossed at the ankle. Instead of writing down creative ways to use my ability, I was drafting a persuasive speech—my ticket out of here.

When there was a faint knock at the door, my heart leaped and power swelled in my chest. I quickly ripped out my speech from the spiral notebook, stuffed it under the mattress, and tiptoed to the door.

Another faint knock sounded and a whisper followed. "It's Gwen, can I come in?"

I hesitated.

What did she want? Regardless of what it was, I didn't need her coming in here and spotting my escape plan. I looked back at the mattress. No stray edges of the torn pages poked out for her to see.

Gwen seemed nice enough. She was a lot perkier than I'd ever be locked up in this prison. She reminded me of

Cassandry and a smile tugged at my lips. What harm could a quick visit do?

I opened the door and she scurried in. She was wearing a matching outfit to mine, the baggy clothes swallowing her thin figure. Her hair was tied into two short pigtails. A pad of paper and pen were tucked under her arm.

"Sorry to bug you so late, but I was having trouble with the assignment and was wondering if you wanted to work on it together?" Her amber eyes looked hopeful.

"Yeah, I could use some help with mine too," I gestured to my newly blank notebook.

Gwendaliese beamed, her smile about to split her dimpled cheeks as she bounced onto the bed. "This is a tough first assignment. It's so hard to focus, too."

"I can't stand these rooms. I haven't gotten a solid night's sleep since I got here."

"Me neither! The beds are horrible. I really miss Henshire."

I remembered seeing Henshire on the map in my geography class. It was a small coastal town near the eastern border of the Portemor Mountains. It was much smaller and sparser than Bellwarn since they lacked the protection of the woods on the grassy plains that ran along the coast.

"Yeah I'm homesick too. I'm from Bellwarn." I lowered my voice to a solemn whisper. "They forced us to come here so quickly. I barely had time to say goodbye."

Her eyes shifted around the room. "Yeah, I heard this was sudden for you. The rest of us had more time to cope. Blaze and I discovered our powers a month before the Guardians brought us here. I think the twins knew a few months before."

I looked at her, wondering how much gossip had

spread when I wasn't in the room. "So that's why you guys are so good with your powers already."

"I did some practicing of my own once I unleashed it. It's pretty cool, huh—being a *Guardian*? When I was little, I always dreamed of having extraordinary powers like them, and it actually happened!"

"I've never really been into the whole Guardian thing . . ."

"Yeah, I've picked up on that . . . I'm sorry."

"I wish the people running this place were sorry, or had at least one drop of empathy or compassion for those that don't dream of becoming a Guardian."

"Yeah . . ." Gwen trailed off. "We should probably try to get at least one idea before tomorrow."

"Oh, right," I sighed. "Sorry I derailed like that. I'm . . . still processing."

Hopefully she wasn't suspicious of me after that rant. Anger had a tendency to run away with my mouth. I should probably work on that.

We bowed over our notebooks. After a short bout of awkward silence from having no ideas on what to write, Gwendaliese turned the conversation to one full of giggles and gossip. We traded stories about our siblings' antics, pestering teachers, and hometown crushes.

Cassandry flashed in my mind throughout the night. Her sapphire eyes would light up at our gossip, eager to jump in with her own. I smiled as I remembered her fervent "whispers"—too loud to be classified as true whispers—from across the desk as she divulged who she'd caught kissing in the hallway. I wondered what colorful opinions she would have of the people here.

What was she doing now? Settling in her dorm, making fast friends with her new roommate. The thought sent a pang of jealousy, but also guilt. Because even though Gwen was fun, I wished it was Cassandry laughing on the other end of the bed.

Chapter Eighteen

"Rough night, ladies?" Blaze asked as Gwendaliese and I stumbled into class half-asleep.

"Is it that obvious?" Gwen feared. "We were up late trying to come up with something for the assignment."

Blaze waved his paper. "I only came up with a few things. I don't think he'll be expecting a lot."

The Fexrund twins turned around to face us and Ander snarked, "It really wasn't that hard."

"We came up with ten ideas each," Keldric bragged.

"Good for you," I sneered, making them both turn away with smug sneers on their faces.

"Just a heads-up," Blaze warned me, "Bron's gonna be asking why you skipped breakfast. He seemed really worried."

I rolled my eyes. "Of course he is; such a mother hen. Every day he asks if I understood the lesson, pulled a muscle, ate enough at dinner."

"I don't think that's the title he's going for," Gwen commented, a playful hitch to her words.

My brows creased with confusion. "What's that supposed to mean?"

"He clearly has a thing for you," she pointed out.

Blaze flushed and swiveled in his chair.

"He just feels like he has to look out for me. He's the same way with his squadmates." As I spoke though, my mind went back to yesterday when we'd nearly held hands.

"Well, I can't comment on that, but what I do know is that smolder in his eyes when he looks at you seems different from when he looks at anyone else. It's more . . . intense." She raised a suggestive eyebrow.

"You're seriously sleep deprived," I teased, even as I remembered Bron's smoldering eyes locked on mine. The thrill it sent up my spine.

"Hey, it may be corny, but it's true!" Gwen insisted.

"Yeah, okay—"

I was cut off by the classroom door creaking open. Commander Devlend ambled to the front of the room, silver buttons on his navy-blue suit glinting in the morning sunshine. With a *snap*, he shut the blinds and, instantly, the chalkboard was littered with light pictures, or so I'd come to call the high-tech display of graphs and tables.

"Do any of you know why you have powers?"

Keldric straightened in his chair. "We were chosen by the Mother to protect Her people."

"Yes, that is true, but I mean in more physiological terms."

The Commander leisurely paced the front of the room. When he was met with a fidgeting silence, he explained further.

"Research conducted at Celepheria University has been looking for what makes Guardians, Guardians. They have uncovered a mutation common amongst us—a mutation coding for a unique hormone."

He continued his discussion, pointing to various graphs and figures as he went. All our mouths hung slightly agape as we digested diagrams of gene codes and protein structures. Not only was the material complex but completely brand new. My eyes glazed over when the lesson was finally over. The Commander whipped open the blinds and I squeezed my eyes shut.

"That lesson is typically difficult for everyone to grasp at first, but we will review this material again. Now, head to the dining hall for lunch, and I will see you all in the arena for your first ability training."

We all remained seated while he gathered a stack of papers on his desk.

He scanned our faces. "Ah, I almost forgot—the assignment."

He sidestepped around the desk and loomed over Keldric's seat. He eyed his paper. "That is quite the list you have there, Mr. Fexrund. I'm intrigued to see what you've come up with."

He held out a hand expectantly for us to pass our papers along to Keldric. My paper only had one idea listed, and Gwen had come up with it for me. But the flush that normally would flood my cheeks after handing in a mediocre assignment never came.

When Commander Devlend received my paper, he met my eyes with a challenging, icy glare. I turned to stare out the window.

"You are dismissed," he murmured.

I was first out the door.

I rushed to the dining hall ahead of the other recruits. Before I could start stuffing my face with the chicken salad Memette had whipped up for lunch, Bron, who now had a small bandage on his scalp, was breathing down my neck.

"Settle down," I urged him. "It was just a late night. Gwen came over and we worked on the assignment together."

Bron leaned back in his chair, shoulders still stiff, but I could see a bit of relief in his eyes. "At least you weren't sick like I thought you were. You can't make a habit of staying up all night. You need your rest."

I looked around to make sure the other students weren't there yet. "I need friends too."

"Yes, you do, but—" He hesitated for a moment then leaned in closer. "I was worried about you. You should let me know when you're going to skip out on things."

He couldn't hold my gaze anymore, turning to look at the lunch spread on the counter. I assumed his treatment of me was like that of a protective friend, but Gwen's words and the intensity between us yesterday whirled through my mind.

I straightened in the chair. "You're not my keeper. I'm free to do whatever I want. I don't have to report my every move."

His dark brows furrowed and the fire-bright rim of orange around his eyes seemed to dim. "Fine, I'll lay off."

"I just mean that I need some room to breathe. It's not that I don't want you around to help me out."

"Huh." Bron gave a nod. "Just around to help you out, got it."

"You know that's not what I mean." I pinned his

forearm to the table, urging him to stay and hear me out, but before I could say more, the other trainees entered the cafeteria. From the doorway, Gwen eyed us curiously and I snapped my hand away from his arm.

"I'll catch you at training." Bron cleared his throat and swept out of the dining hall.

Chapter Nineteen

Traipsing down the hallway behind my peers, dread weighed heavily on my shoulders. The terror of not knowing what would be done during ability training rattled my mind, dredging up painful memories of my past Guardian evaluations.

At the hall crossroads, I halted while everyone else turned left toward the arena. The door leading outside beckoned me, but the image of me futilely clawing at the fence kept me trudging along. There was one kernel of hope though; the start of ability training meant I finally had a chance to enact the first phase of my escape.

When I entered the arena, the phoenix loomed overhead. Sunshine streamed through the skylight and enhanced the bright flames at its feet.

Our trainers didn't align themselves with the blue ring encompassing the arena floor, but rather the smaller squares outlined within it. Commander Devlend and Bron stood in the center block while Sephara and Rhismai stood in those adjacent. I stared at Bron, willing his eyes to meet mine, to give me that silent vote of confidence I had grown accustomed to, but he stood with his arms crossed and looked squarely ahead. He must still be mad about earlier. Maybe Gwen had been more spot-on than I wanted to give her credit for.

I fell in line next to Gwen at the edge of the first block as the Commander began to speak.

"Welcome to your first ability training, recruits. As with your physical training, I leave you in the capable hands of your trainers. Unlike your physical training though, I will be observing you and advising you each personally along the way. This is the most essential aspect of your training." He cut his eyes to me. "I expect you all to put in your best effort."

The Commander left the floor and perched on one of the protected benches. He gestured to Blaze, a silent order to join him. Before Blaze sat, the Commander was already talking to him, his words muted by the plexiglass barrier. I fought the urge to cower behind the shield myself. Out here, the threat of training against monsters and the unpredictable powers of the other recruits weighed on every nerve.

Before heading to Rhismai, I jogged over to Bron. "Can we talk for a second?"

"I have recruits to train." Bron nodded toward the Fexrunds, waiting at the edge of their training square.

"It'll only take a minute." I grabbed his tree trunk of an arm and dragged him to the edge of the room before he could reply.

"I wanted to apologize for how I approached that whole mess of a conversation earlier," I said.

Bron didn't say anything.

"Do you really think I'd let you drag out my runs with your stories if I thought of you as just a bodyguard?" I asked. "Come on."

A smile broke through his stone-hard face. I'd take that as a win.

"Alright, point made, albeit rudely." Bron put a hand on my shoulder, then nudged me toward Rhismai. "Now, get over there and show Rhismai what you're made of."

"Oh, joy," I mumbled as I walked over to Rhismai.

Once we rejoined our respective training squares, the ground began to shake. I yelped in surprise and scoured the floor for any seams where a creature might be released.

Noticing, Rhismai assured, "No creats today. Just you and me."

At the blue seams outlining each training square, plexiglass walls rose around all of us, caging us in.

"It's a barrier to protect us from the other trainees in case they lose control. Nothing to worry about."

She gave me a reassuring smile, but it didn't help.

She pointed to the middle of our training space. "Stand here. I'm going to guide you through a small release. The first thing we need to do is overcome your fear of your ability. You need to trust it in order to control it. Stand with your feet hip-distance apart and close your eyes."

As I closed my eyes, I felt the brush of her hair on my shoulder. The warm hush of her breath brushed my ear, her lips almost grazing it.

She whispered in a sultry voice, almost hypnotic. "Focus on the sound of my voice. Drown out everything else. Only focus on you and me."

Since the training session was just beginning, it was easy to block out the murmurs of the other students and their trainers. My head bobbed, my chin resting on my collar as I slowly fell under her trance.

"Now in your mind's eye, visualize your body: your hair flowing over your shoulder, arms relaxed at your sides, feet rooted firmly on the ground. Home in on your chest as it rises and falls with your breath. See the strong beat of your heart as it pounds against your rib cage.

"Now look *within*. Visualize the power you feel alongside your beating heart. Picture it swirling somersaults within you, dancing alongside every part of you. It *is* you. When you're sad, it ebbs a comforting caress. When you're angry, it surges to your defense.

"Your power shares your wants and desires. It wants to act out all you wish to accomplish. It's an extension of your mind, your will. You are one. Become one and let it flow freely. Visualize releasing those swirls of power throughout your body, filling you from head to toe. In freeing it, through joining with it, you can control it with an effortless thought."

Suddenly I felt it, as if my power was acting in time with her words. My power gently flowed through my arms. It streamed alongside my blood, its strength pooling in my palms. I lurched forward, clenched my fists, and sucked it back into my core. The sudden loss of its strength left me clutching at my chest and gasping to catch my breath. Stumbling back from Rhismai, I attempted to balance myself. I widened my gait and straightened my back. For my plan to work, I needed to appear confident and unbreakable.

Rhismai sighed and pinched the bridge of her nose. "Why did you pull it back in? It was right there."

"I don't want to *become one*," I retorted, trying to hold back my bite. I needed to be confident, not aggressive.

"You do," Rhismai argued. "I know you're afraid of it and what it can do. What it can make you do. But when you were in that state, your body readily let it fill you. That tells me that you want this."

"That's only because of the trance you put me under," I countered, trying to calm my voice.

"Anora, it was not a trance. It was guided imagery, almost like meditation. Whatever happened to you during it was the result of your body becoming relaxed and doing what it naturally wants to do."

"I can guarantee you that my mind doesn't want this. No matter what you put me through, I will never want this."

Her eyes darted to someone behind my shoulder, probably either Sephara or the Commander.

After their silent conversation, she ordered, "Walk with me."

The plexiglass cage trapping us fell as she corralled me, her bony fingers poking into my bicep. All eyes were trained on me as we moved toward the door, and I directed my gaze to the floor, against my better judgment. My eyes snapped up as I passed Bron. His body was stiff as if fighting the urge to run to me. As I turned away from Bron, I caught the teal eyes of Blaze. Unlike everyone else, I didn't sense any pity or judgment from him, only understanding. I flashed him a slight smile.

Once out in the hall, Rhismai guided me down the short hallway I'd tried to escape through. She sat cross-legged on the floor and gestured for me to join her. My uniform was rigid and tight as I squatted across from her, pulling at the fabric in an attempt to get comfortable.

She folded her black hair behind her ears, bringing her ochre face out of the shadows. Her cunning dark eyes softened into concern. "I feel like I don't really know you yet, Anora. I understand coming to a new place and learning all of these new things is overwhelming and everyone handles it differently. I feel like if I got to actually know who you are, it may help me better understand where your anger and resentment comes from." Her voice was soft and compassionate.

I fidgeted in the suffocating jumpsuit as I considered my approach. My ruse worked; stubbornness made Rhismai appeal to her understanding and patient side that the Commander and Bron had spoken of after my evaluation. In the past few days, I'd crafted how to frame my pitiful story in the right light. If she truly did care and really listened, she could get me what I wanted: a ticket out of this place.

"When I was eleven, my father took me fishing," I began. "I thought we had been quiet enough, we were being so careful, but a creat heard us anyway. Across the creek, a huge serpent jumped out of the bushes and aimed for me." My voice caught in my throat at the image of those slit red eyes. "I couldn't move. I don't know how, but it was like its eyes had locked me in place.

"When my father saw I wasn't moving, he . . ." Tears lined my eyes. My throat was heavy with the need to sob, so I coughed instead. "He dove in front of me and the serpent took him instead."

"I'm so sorry, Anora."

I nodded, then continued. "His last words were telling

me to run. So that's what I did, and still do. Whenever there's an attack, or a threat of one, I have these . . . attacks. Flashbacks of that day overwhelm me and I feel like I'm back there and I panic and I run. Running is all I can focus on. It's what I have to focus on or else the flashbacks, or the creats, will catch me."

"It must be so exhausting dealing with these attacks when there are so many triggers in our world," Rhismai said.

"Yes, exactly." I smiled. My plan seemed to be working. "And on top of that, my parents are older and can't keep up with their work. I had a job lined up as a nurse, the highest-paying job in Bellwarn. And now with me and my paycheck not there to support them . . ." I choked up again. "I don't know what will happen. So you see, I don't belong here. I can't do this. So please, let me go back home. Let me live the life I was always meant to."

"I'm so sorry for all you and your family have been through, truly. Now I understand why you've been acting like you have." She looked around thoughtfully before continuing. "Other Guardians have come through here with similar backgrounds, and after enough emotional and mental support, they were able to embrace their destinies and become great Guardians. I think I know how to approach your training now, so don't lose your faith."

Wait, *what*? The genuine smile of promise and encouragement on Rhismai's face left me dumbstruck. I thought my plan was working. She seemed so understanding during my story, so why was she talking about more training?

"Did you even listen to a word I said?"

Her head bobbed back. "Yes . . . I heard everything—"

"And the last part?" I pressed. "The part where I said I don't belong and should be sent back home?"

"Ah, that." She leaned back against the wall. "Anora, I'm sorry, but there's no going back. I thought Bron made that clear?"

"He's mentioned it, but he's so steadfast. I thought someone more understanding would be able to help me."

Rhismai leaned on her hip and peered around the corner.

She shuffled closer and warned in a hushed tone, "You can be the least committed person and still be forced to serve. The Commander doesn't care about our wants, only the needs of the Guard. He makes you serve, one way or another."

Skeptical, I took in her darting eyes. Bron had alluded to a similar fate . . . What did they know that they weren't saying? Whatever it was, I knew I could find a way around it. I had to. Where fear flooded Rhismai's eyes, determination was reflected in mine.

On to the next plan, then.

Chapter Twenty

The next several weeks of ability training left Rhismai frustrated and cursing to herself. When she tried meditation again, I refused to play along. When she flashed a glittering rainbow across the ceiling and coaxed a gentle misting rain, I didn't gawk or beg her to teach me how to create something so beautiful. Attempts to draw out my power from physical blows failed. I was too strong-willed to crack under her whips of wind and rain.

Rhismai didn't try to whisper when she complained about me to Sephara after training, raging that no other recruit had fought her for this long.

One afternoon, I had found them embracing in the upper stairwell landing. Silently, I'd clung to the stone wall. They were so enthralled with one another that they didn't notice me, like a fly on the wall.

"He's disappointed. I know it." Rhismai curled into the crook of her neck, burying her face in her dark cherry curls.

"He sees how difficult she is. He won't blame you." Sephara petted her onyx hair.

"I can't take much more of this, of *her*," Rhismai's voice broke.

"It's going to be okay. Everything will work out as it should," Sephara cooed in her ear.

"I could never survive any of this without you." Rhismai sighed. "You are my gravity."

Sephara looked into her eyes. "And you are my world."

Rhismai cracked a sigh, the kind someone so hopeless, so desperate, would when their savior finally arrived. Sephara lifted Rhismai's chin, and without moving her sparkling gray eyes from hers, she kissed her. Rhismai spiraled into that kiss, clinging to her as if she were her anchor to this earth, and if she let go she'd get caught up in a gusting wind, lost to never be found again.

I had snuck out of the stairwell, a smug smirk tugging at my lips. Rhismai was cracking under my resilience and Commander Devlend was enraged at my insubordination. My plan was working out perfectly.

If I couldn't persuade them to let me go, I'd drive them nuts until they kicked me out instead.

Now, as I left the arena, Commander Devlend's icy gaze met mine from behind the plexiglass, and it threatened to shatter the barrier between us. I took it as a compliment.

The other students were exhausted as we shuffled our way to the dining hall after a long day of training. Gwendaliese was progressing along nicely, gaining more precision over far distances. The Fexrund twins naturally excelled at every task. Their beam of raw energy between them grew in intensity every day. Blaze was mentally exhausted after sitting at the Commander's side and observing our lessons all afternoon. Now, he anxiously awaited his private evening lessons.

We all sat together, our chairs screeching against the cold floor. Ander, Keldric, and Gwen began trading stories of their accomplishments and struggles during training. Blaze was the only one who didn't want to talk about powers and lessons, so I clung to him at every meal.

"I'm starting to get sick of this slop," Blaze muttered as he splashed a spoonful of chowder into his still full bowl.

Looking down at my nearly drained one, I asked, "What are you talking about? It's delicious."

"Not really . . . soup is disgusting." Blaze pushed his bowl away and snatched a roll from a basket on the table.

"Don't say that too loud." I gave a pointed look in Memette's direction. "She might come at you with her ladle again."

We laughed together at the memory of Memette scuffling out of the kitchen, wagging her soupy ladle at Blaze when he requested that she make something other than chowder for dinner.

"I'd never actually had soup before I came here. We don't really make it in Taramora."

Taramora was a coastal town in southwest Alberune where the white sandy beaches and clear ocean water served to distract its residents from the threat of monsters in the north.

I laughed. "What do you eat then? The sand?"

"Why, of course! It's a delicacy." His blue-green eyes glittered like crystals as he smirked.

"Really?"

"No!" He laughed. "Soup just isn't something we make.

We eat seafood, fruits, and vegetables, just never in a liquid form."

"Well, believe me, not much beats a hot bowl of soup on a bitter winter's night. I'd assume this place will have similar weather to Bellwarn."

Worry grew on his face, his smooth jaw tightening. "Is it true you guys get attacked the most?"

"Yep, it's paradise."

"I bet," he teased. "No wonder you're so enthused about being a Guardian and going toe-to-toe with them."

I winked at him. "You've figured me out."

His eyes bore into mine. "Seriously though. I think you're brave for standing up to them." He looked around, ensuring the other students were enthralled in their own conversation. "You should fight for what you want, for what you think is right."

My eyes widened at his bold words. I knew he didn't judge me like the others, but I didn't expect him to blatantly support me. It was no secret that Commander Devlend had it out for me, and Blaze choosing my side probably wouldn't put him in the Commander's good graces.

"Thanks." I smiled widely. "I never thought anyone here would get it."

"They get it. They just don't have the guts to admit it."

"I didn't realize you were so *brave*."

He playfully nudged my arm. "How could you expect someone as dashing as me to *not* be?"

Memette shuffled over with a plate heaping with steaming grilled chicken and fried potatoes. She slapped it in front of Blaze. "I can't stand watching you starve yourself."

"Wow, thank you, Memette." Blaze looked up to the old woman. "It smells delicious."

"Now don't go getting used to this special treatment." She wagged her finger at him. "I won't be making a separate meal for you every day."

Blaze shook his head vehemently. "I would never expect that. Thank you again."

She waved him off and headed to the kitchen. Blaze shoveled the potatoes in his mouth, grease lining his full lips and spotting his stuffed cheeks.

"Jeez, don't choke on it," I said, soaking up the remnants of my soup with a roll.

I overheard Ander and Keldric bid goodnight to Gwendaliese on the other side of the table. Their chairs screeched against the tile floor as they stood to leave.

Once the twins had left, she hopped into the seat next to Blaze. "That was nice of Memette to make you something."

Blaze agreed by swallowing a mouthful of chicken.

"How have you two been?" She glanced over to me guiltily. "I'm sorry we haven't had time to really catch up. I've been so wrapped up in training."

She didn't have to apologize. I wasn't a novice to the ways of cliques. Gwen wanted to do well here, she wanted to be a Guardian, and that was something I could never relate to. She'd found her people in the Fexrunds, and I'd found mine—the boy sitting beside me, stuffing his face with greasy potatoes.

"I overheard Sephara tell Rhismai that she's quite impressed with your progress and thinks you'll do fantastic throughout the rest of training," I said.

"Really!" Gwen's pale face lit up. "I'm so glad to hear. I

feel like I'm not progressing fast enough, especially compared to those two."

"Don't compare yourself to them," I said. "They're way too into this whole thing, in my opinion."

"You'd have to be like one of those crazed Guardian worshippers to reach their level of dedication. Not worth it," Blaze added, his words spraying the table with small chunks of potato.

I wiped up his mess. "Watch where you're talking."

He chuckled and covered his mouth. "Sorry."

"How are your private lessons going, Blaze?" Gwen leaned forward. "I can't imagine a one-on-one with the Commander is easy."

"It's horrible. I feel so much more pressure, you know? He's just staring at me expecting all these great things, but my power is weird. Neither of us really understand it so we don't know how to develop it."

"I'm sure you'll have a breakthrough soon. Commander Devlend has so much experience." Gwen offered an encouraging smile.

"What is it he mumbles to you during our training sessions?" I inquired.

"He says that since I can't help out by fighting, I can learn about all the different complections. He wants me to become like him, I think. Being able to understand and see the potential of every Guardian and being able to pair up squads and stuff like that."

"I wonder if he's grooming you to be his successor."

"Mother, I hope not," Blaze said through another mouthful.

"Blaze," Gwen spoke softly, as if afraid the walls would overhear. "Have you learned what the Commander's complection is? The twins and I have been dying to know, and the trainers won't tell us."

"Not a clue. Never really thought of him having one," he admitted as he licked his dish clean. Honestly, I hadn't thought of him having abilities either. The Commander of the Guard had to have powers, right?

Memette must have been surveilling us because as soon as Blaze finished, she scurried out of the kitchen. "About time. Now head on out so I can get this place cleaned up."

Obliging, we filed out of the dining hall and meandered to the bunkrooms. Before entering the room, I bid them a quiet good evening, but my efforts to be silent were futile. I yelped as I stepped into my room, startled by the sight of Bron lounging on my bed.

"Why are you lurking in my room this late at night?"

"I wanted to talk to you in private." Bron got to his feet. "I didn't realize you'd be at dinner for so long."

"Got caught up talking. Sorry to keep you waiting."

He waved it off. "You really need to quit this rebel act. You're only creating more trouble for yourself."

"If I'm so much trouble, then let me go. As you know, I'm more of a hassle than I'm worth."

"You don't understand, Anora." Bron shook his head, his eyes smoldering with frustration. "The Commander doesn't care how much you protest."

"There has to be a breaking point, even for him."

Bron swept forward in one broad step, his thick body only inches from mine. Heat rolled off his skin. I took in his face, scowled with worry. I moved to step back, but he grabbed my shoulders.

"Anora, please listen to me. You don't know the Commander. You don't know what he's capable of. He will never let you go back home, and the more you fight it, the worse it'll get."

"I think you're overreacting. He hasn't done anything."

"That's only because it's the first few weeks. Trust me, he's noticed your actions and isn't happy. He's giving you time to redeem yourself, and time for Rhismai to get through to you, before he steps in."

"I can't just give up now."

"You need to," he urged. "Give up your pride and selfish wants. It will save you in the end."

I fought against his grip. Where was all this coming from? What happened to the Bron who joked over blueberry muffins? The one who wanted to hold my hand. That Bron would never say something so hurtful.

"My selfish wants? Is that really what you think of me? I'm fighting for what I *need*, for the life I have every right to live the way *I* choose."

"What would happen if every Guardian felt so entitled? There would be no one to defend the border," he countered.

"But that's simply not the case. Ander, Keldric, Gwen: they all *want* to be here. And I'd bet the majority of Guardians, including you, *want* to be here."

"Yes, because we are proud and honored to serve. You should feel the same."

"But I don't, Bron, and I never will. If given the choice, most of you would choose to serve. Shouldn't I be allowed to choose my own path?"

"It's not that easy." Bron sighed.

"And what about my family? They need me." The memory of Bill struggling just to walk down the stairs stirred tears. "You saw my stepfather. They were relying on that nurse's paycheck to make ends meet."

"I understand your worries about your family. It doesn't help that you won't be getting paid until after you finish your training," Bron conceded. "But you have to trust me. I'm just looking out for you, Anora. You don't understand."

"Then make me understand. Tell me what I'm missing here." I anchored my hands on my hips.

"I—I can't," Bron's shoulders slumped. "I've probably already said too much. The Commander made us swear to never talk about it."

I narrowed my eyes at him. What was he hiding?

"Break it. It's not like he'll ever know."

"I can't defy him. I can't break his trust."

"If you won't tell me, then I don't see a reason to stop fighting," I threatened.

"I—" He leaned toward me and caressed my arm with his warm hand. Goosebumps spread across my skin at his touch. "I care about you, Anora. You have to believe me. Stop acting out, follow the rules, and you'll survive this place."

"But you don't understand." I meant to step out of his grasp, but my body didn't want to obey. "If I submit to this place, and to *him*, then I won't survive."

"You have a fire in you." His head tilted slightly towards mine. "I don't want to see it snuffed out."

Now with him so close, I whispered against his lips, "If I stay here, it will."

Bron closed the distance between us, his ember eyes intent on my lips. A tingling feeling danced up my spine. Maybe there had been more between us this whole time, hiding in those little moments where we laughed, where we opened up to each other. I felt it now, a warmth fluttering in my stomach, urging me to bridge the gap between our lips. But all I could think of was what he called me. What he truly thought of me.

Selfish. Entitled.

As he slipped a hand low across my back, I broke away before it went too far.

"I think it's time for you to go." My words were as faint as a breath.

He sighed, hesitant. The burn of his gaze was on me and the parts of my body he'd touched were on fire. After a few moments that felt much longer, Bron slipped out of the room. With his sudden absence, the room grew colder, as if he had sucked out the heat with him.

Chapter Twenty-One

Under the sunshine bursting through the arena's dome window, the Guardian recruits stretched in their training squares. Blaze was anchored to his usual bench seat, bouncing his leg while waiting for the Commander to join him. I sat along the cement wall beside the double doors leading out of the room, twiddling with the laces of my boots.

When Bron strutted in, anger heated my veins from his words the night before, but my heart still fluttered at the thought of our almost-kiss. He walked past with a fretful glance.

Regardless of what had happened between us, of everything said and left unsaid, I needed to press forward with my plan, so I pushed aside his advice and our intimate moment.

Rhismai stood in front of me, cocking her hip to one side and crossing her arms. Her near-black eyes narrowed. "I refuse to go through this childish routine every day. Get up and get to that square. Now."

Commander Devlend breezed into the room, sized up Rhismai, then looked down at me. His face remained neutral, but his electric eyes didn't mask his frustration. Even as he looked upon me, he spoke to Rhismai as if I wasn't there.

"Take care of this Guardian Mojya, or I will."

"Yes, Commander, sir." She glared.

When I didn't budge, she grabbed my arm and yanked me to my feet.

"What is going to get through to you?" She dragged me onto the floor. "The Commander is starting to get mad at *me*. That doesn't happen, and I will *not* let it happen. You got that?"

"Are you threatening me?" I gasped. "Rhismai, I'm shocked."

She dug her nails into my arm. "Don't be smart with me. I'm getting sick of this attitude and won't stand for it much longer."

Bron motioned for Rhismai to come over.

She threw me toward the square. "Get over there and don't move."

I stood my ground and Rhismai tossed her arms up in exasperation. Bron was speaking too low to hear. As Rhismai stormed back, she took a deep breath.

"Okay." Rhismai reined in her irritation. "I don't mean to be so angry. It's just—I'm usually good with the stubborn students. I can get through to them after the first week. But you—you're just so much more . . . determined."

"If *you* can't get through to me, then who will?"

"Oh, I'm not done trying, yet," she sneered.

In an instant, I was trapped in a vortex. Rhismai, arms thrown out in front of her, crafted a hurricane around me.

Bullets of water spat out and battered my skin. Whooshing wind beat against my eardrums and tore at my hair, making it fly in my face and stab my skin. I squeezed my eyes shut and swatted wildly at water and hair. That supernatural force exploded within my chest and surged down my arms. I clenched my fists to hold back the tide Rhismai desperately wanted to be unleashed.

What was her plan? To kill me? I knew frustrating Rhismai was a gamble, but I never thought I'd be risking me life!

The vortex pressed in and water lashed. As the water swirled closer, I realized it wasn't going to stop and gulped down as much air as I could. The whirlpool turned into a solid spinning pillar of water. Instantly, I was taken back to the gymnasium water pit and the dark, icy cold water that forced its way into my lungs.

This water was more vengeful though. I could feel it trying to rip open my mouth. I looked out at Rhismai. Her form wavered in the water clouding my eyes. Her hands appeared to be squeezing and, simultaneously, I could feel the water strangle around my neck. My vision spotted. My lungs and throat burned. Power pulsed in my fingertips as my grip on it began to slip. I used all my strength to rein it in until darkness consumed me.

A throbbing pain spread over my scalp. The space around me was a mosaic of blues, grays, and tans. A starchy blanket slid beneath my fingers. The mattress was stiff and lumpy. I sunk into a thin pillow, barely supporting my head, and squinted my eyes to clear up the image.

Two dark splotches entered the room, one tall and the other round. I cowered under my blanket. Was it the Commander? Was he finally going to do to me what Bron had hinted at? Or maybe it was Rhismai. After she'd nearly strangled me to death, I anticipated the worst.

"No need to be frightened, my dear. It's Brivania and Bron," Brivania said in her distinct Eterni accent.

The round blur bounced over to the side of the bed and I felt the mattress depress underneath her.

"I . . . I . . ." My voice was a painful scratch gouging out my throat. "Can't see."

"Shush, you need to rest your throat. Your vision will clear up soon. No worries. Here."

She grabbed my hand and held it still, outstretched. She cradled a warm teacup in my hand, the heat seeping into my palms. I indulged in a deep waft of the honey lavender tea.

"This will help. Drink up," Nurse Brivania instructed.

The Brivania blob hesitated and hovered at the bedside for a moment, fluffing my scrap of a pillow before bidding her farewell. The door rasped shut behind her. The Bron blob edged toward the bed and knelt down. As he neared, I could make out his features more clearly, like the rounded shape of his nose and sharp cut of his jaw.

"You can close your eyes if you're struggling to see. You don't want to strain them," Bron advised, and I obliged.

All I sensed was the scratch of my sheets and the warmth radiating from my teacup.

"I know it hurts to talk too, so please. Just listen." Bron took in a deep breath before continuing. "I'm sorry for what happened today. I didn't mean—I wasn't intending . . ." His voice quavered. "She never should have done that to you."

"What did—" I squeaked out painfully.

He laid a hand on my arm. "You will be allowed only tonight to rest. You must be ready to train tomorrow and you must fall in line."

I opened my eyes and squinted, trying to read his expression. His blur stood slowly and moved toward the door.

"Make sure to finish your tea," Bron said before he left, shutting the door and turning the light off on his way out.

With only the dim light of the setting sun illuminating the fuzzy room, I closed my eyes and focused on the strands of lavender steam filling my nose, warming my face. The usual frustration at Bron's badgering never came. Instead, betrayal seeded in my gut.

I recalled that before Rhismai had attacked me, Bron spoke with her. What had he said?

I wasn't intending, he had said. Not intending for what? For Rhismai to strangle me? Whether it was what he intended or not, it seemed like he was a part of it.

Bron, my confidant, my support in this torture chamber they called a training camp, had betrayed me.

Chapter Twenty-Two

❧

My vision cleared the next morning and I readied for the day. After a quick shower, I braided back my hair and wiggled into a Guardian uniform. An ache throbbed in my throat and I gulped down as much tea as I could before heading to lecture.

Dizziness waved over me as I ambled towards the classroom. I used the concrete wall to steady myself.

Once in the empty classroom, I shuffled across the room and slumped into the desk beside the windows. I leaned my head against the cool glass pane.

Gwen and Blaze strolled in first, the former rushing to my side. She knelt down and took my hand.

"Are you okay? You should be resting after what happened."

"I've been better, but it's nothing I can't handle," I reassured her, my voice still scratchy.

Blaze stood a few paces back, arms crossed and eyes

haunted. He gawked like I was a trauma patient. He ran a hand through his hair. "I'm glad to see you're alright."

"Are you alright, Blaze?" I asked. "You look like *you* were the one almost choked to death."

He furrowed his brow. "Don't joke about what happened to you like that. I was—we were all worried about you."

"I'm sorry you guys had to see that, but now you see what kind of people they truly are."

Gwen sat straight-backed in her chair without acknowledging my words. Blaze fixed his eyes on mine.

Easing into his chair, Blaze pulled out a notebook from the cubby in his desk and scribbled on the page. He tore the paper and folded it thrice before handing it to me behind Gwen's chair. I snatched it, catching Gwen's wandering eye as I did.

Footsteps echoed in the hallway. I tucked the note into my boot just in time for the twins and the Commander, oddly wearing a Guardian uniform, to march into the classroom. The Fexrunds swaggered to their seats, faces plastered with their usual smug grins. The moment Commander Devlend stepped into the room, his eyes locked on mine like a hunter assessing his prey. Anxiety sent my heart racing, but I challenged his gaze with my own.

"I hope all of you are well-rested after your training," he addressed the class. "You're all exceeding my expectations. So much so, that I think you're ready to scout the Portemor Mountains." He turned to me. "Today."

Adrenaline soared through my body alongside that supernatural energy. My legs and back grew stiff, willing themselves to become a part of the chair. This couldn't be happening. We were going to the actual mountains? *Please be dreaming*, I prayed, because this could only exist in a nightmare.

"I will be accompanying you, as well as your trainers. We'll observe your individual technique as well as your ability to coordinate as a team. Only in the direst circumstances will we intervene."

The Commander beckoned us to rise. The twins shot up and were gearing toward the door. Gwendaliese and Blaze were more hesitant, a trace of fear on both of their faces.

I was rooted in my seat.

As the other students filed out of the room, Commander Devlend approached me.

"Something wrong, Miss Baelin?" he toyed.

I narrowed my eyes. "Nope, everything is just peachy."

"Well, then, by all means, come join us." He gestured towards the door.

"I'm not going to submit myself to this," I spat with my cracking voice.

"Always so hostile, Miss Baelin," he tsked. "I'm afraid you have no choice in the matter. You have been graced by the Mother with your ability and it is your duty to harness it."

"You can't make me go. Just like you can't make me train."

"On the contrary, my dear."

Rhismai and Bron, a thick metal chain wrapped across his chest, appeared in the doorway. Regret smoldered in Bron's eyes while revelry sparked in Rhismai's. The Commander snapped his fingers and the two Guardians approached. I cowered in my seat, my knuckles turning white as I gripped the seat of the chair. Before, I wouldn't have been afraid of Bron, but after our fight, after he'd conspired with Rhismai, I didn't know what to believe anymore.

With startling force, Rhismai grabbed my arm and jerked me up on my feet. I dug my heels into the floor and she tugged my arm nearly out of its socket trying to make me move. I grunted as I poured all my energy into grounding myself.

"Why must you always be so difficult?" Rhismai sighed.

"Sorry I'm not more obliging to someone who strangled me."

She rolled her eyes. "Stop with the dramatics."

"Stop with the attempted murder."

"Would you mind?" Rhismai looked askance at Bron.

Bron hesitated, shifting on his feet. I tried to get him to look at me, but he avoided my gaze entirely.

Rhismai impatiently tugged at his arm. "Snap out of it."

With a tense glare from the Commander, he did. Bron swept me up in his bulging arms, tossing me over his shoulder.

"Hey!" I shouted.

A rush of dizziness sprang at the sudden movement and I fought back a spout of nausea. His arms, warm but not scalding, were locked around the back of my knees. I thrashed against his strong hold. I banged my fists against the small of his back and kicked at his legs.

He heaved me forward, catching my shoulders and hooking his arm around my legs as I swung down. He cradled me against his chest, restricting my limbs. I still squirmed, desperate to break free, as we left the classroom and the Compound all together. The thick links of his chain cut into my arm and side as I wriggled.

"I won't let go," Bron whispered in my ear. "So stop fighting. You'll just humiliate yourself further."

I sneered at him. "I don't care if you think I look like a fool. I'll never stop fighting."

The last time our faces were this close, there was such a different feeling in the air. Dissension, but also the heat of attraction, a spark of lust. In this moment, though, there was only betrayal. As if he could sense the shift too, his eyes darkened.

The other students were lined up at the gate. I flushed when Blaze eyed me trapped in Bron's massive arms. I told myself I didn't care about being humiliated; that it was necessary in order to be the most stubborn trainee the Guard had ever seen. Yet my cheeks still burned as I neared my classmates.

With my broken voice, I murmured, "Put me down."

"I can't do that," Bron said regretfully. "You'll try to run away once we step outside that gate."

"I won't, I promise." I didn't know if I was being truthful. Sensing his hesitation, I guilted him. "I saw you talk to Rhismai before she choked me. Everything you've ever said about being friends, about looking after me, was a lie. After everything, the least you owe me is to set me on my own two feet."

Bron held in his breath, studying me. Then, he turned to the Commander for orders. "Sir, can I set her down now?"

He nodded. "I'm sure between all of us, we can keep Miss Baelin reined if she tries anything."

With that, Bron eased me to the ground. I wobbled on

my feet, trying to find my balance. Bron steadied me with firm hands. I batted him away.

Commander Devlend pressed a series of buttons on a keypad attached to the wire fence gate. I strained to glimpse the code he entered but was too far to see anything clearly. The gate slid open and we slipped out silently just before it locked. Once past the gate, Bron kept a tight grip on my arm, one I knew I could never shake.

My heart thumped like a rabbit's foot as we entered the woods that lead to the Portemor Mountains. The foliage was thick and dark, allowing only small splotches of sunlight to dot the forest floor. Through the thicket, the Portemor Mountains loomed above, their peaks so tall they disappeared into a gray mist of clouds.

I didn't want to give the Commander what he wanted, but I didn't want to die at the hands of those beasts, either. After bottling up my energy for so long, I had no clue how to harness it in a useful way. It would either fizzle or explode with no direction. I could never trust my power, but my feet I could always count on. That reassurance brought little solace, though, as we trudged through the trees.

When we emerged from the forest, the mountain range rose before us. Varying shades of gray and black rock littered the steep mountainside. Jagged shards jutted out of the earth, creating a deadly obstacle for any creature dumb enough to traverse it. Apparently, we were those dumb creatures.

We trailed the Guardian fence until we came upon a camouflaged wire door cut off from the electricity. The

Commander ushered us through and toward the Portemor Mountains.

My body protested, but Bron's grip forced me forward. Every nerve in my body urged me to run. Energy filled my core and roiled down my arms. My nails dug into their permanent imprints on my palms to hold back the tide.

This couldn't be happening. This couldn't be real. These mountains held the promise of death in their slated stones, and I was heading straight toward them. My family came to mind. When would they hear of my downfall? Would it be in the papers? A radio broadcast? I doubted the Guard had time to send in-person condolences. I imagined Mom knitting in one chair, Bill whittling in another, and Liam playing with his toys between them while my name buzzed through the radio speakers . . .

I wasn't sure when I'd started crying, but Bron shook my arm and muttered, "Keep it together."

My boots skidded along the rocky earth. Every step towards the base of the mountains was labored, and mainly driven by Bron.

The Commander ordered us to halt with the flick of a wrist. He addressed us in a level voice, but it seemed booming to me considering we were outside. "I received reports of a creat sighting about a half-mile east. You will proceed in a traditional squad formation with your trainers beside you. Fexrunds will take the lead skirting the base, Miss Astreya will flank their right, Miss Baelin their left."

My knees threatened to buckle. Of course, he set me to scale furthest up the mountainside.

"Mr. Vasterio and I will take the rear. Now, pair up and head out."

Bron took lead in arranging us. We formed a wide set

diamond, the twins at the right-most point while Gwen and I trailed behind with a wide berth. The sneer on Rhismai's face changed to stone-hard concentration as she led me carefully up the mountainside. We ascended methodically, swerving around the rocks. My legs strained as I stretched across a wide band of rocks glittering like broken shards of black glass. Rhismai held up her hand, signaling we were in position, and we started heading east.

My feet itched to run. Instead of surveying like everyone else, I scanned down the mountainside to find a clear path through the squad and to the cover of the forest.

"When scouting, it's important to scan the landscape all around you," Rhismai advised. "Creats tend to come straight down the mountain. The quicker they get to level ground, the quicker a meal. So keep your eyes focused up the mountain, not down, for the most part."

For the first time in weeks, I actually took her advice, not wanting to be caught off guard by a monster. I scanned further up the mountain, glancing occasionally down the slope and at the trail ahead to dodge rocks. While we searched, Rhismai riddled off quick tips on how to use my ability in combat.

"Narrow in on your target and it'll help concentrate your attack. The few wild wind and rainstorms you've done only make the battlefield more chaotic. That can be helpful when working with experienced Guardians, but not with your classmates. If you had participated even a little bit, you wouldn't be so afraid. You'd feel confident and ready to protect yourself."

"I have my own ways of protecting myself."

She scoffed. "If you plan on running, Mother save you."

A flash of brown swept past my periphery and I cocked my head up the slope. About a mile up the mountain, a slender brown creature scurried low to the ground over the thorn-like rocks—right towards us.

The serpent shot out across the brook, fangs unhinged.

Its red eyes were trained on me, my blood.

Adrenaline and power surged and I turned to run down the mountain. I stumbled and stomped my way down, frantically jumping over and swinging around every obstacle. I had to get out of here. Time to test myself and see if I could outrun a creat. Maybe I could make it to the fence door in time, then hide in the woods. That was my only chance of surviving.

Rhismai called out. "To the north!"

She swung out her hands and formed a dark mass of rain clouds above the creature for the squadmates further down the mountain to easily spot.

I was halfway down the slope when a gust of wind thudded against my chest, stopping me in my tracks and pushing me toward Rhismai and the beast.

"*Ahh!*" My arms flailed as I tried to right myself and break through the wall of wind.

The powerful gust swept underneath my legs and pressed against my back. Before I could comprehend it, I was flying. I sailed right back to Rhismai's side.

"You won't get out of this that easily," Rhismai said as she set me down.

I stumbled and plopped on my bottom from the sudden landing. Rhismai gripped my arm and forced me to my feet. Straight ahead, the once small smudge on the side of the mountain was taking shape, a much bigger shape.

The twins and Bron, chain unstrapped and wrapped around his arm, climbed briskly up the mountain to meet us. Sephara and Gwen were not far behind. The Commander stood at the base of the peak, watching intently. At his side, Blaze bounced from one foot to another and kept looking over his shoulder, toward the fence. He probably wanted to bolt as much as I did.

As expected, the twins took the front line and Gwen was a few paces behind them, a mix of excitement and fear. Rhismai shoved me toward them and I dug in my heels with everything I had. Letting out an exasperated sigh, she called over Bron to assist. This time, no level of embarrassment would stop me from fighting them.

As the monster grew closer, Bron struggled to grab me. I ducked and sidestepped out of his grasp—my swift moves against his heavy bulk. I slipped under his chain-wrapped arm and made to sprint down the mountain when a familiar wall of wind slammed against me. My breath was knocked out and I caught myself on a rock before falling flat on my back.

"It's coming, Anora," Bron said. "You don't want to leave your squadmates behind. They need you."

Looking back at the other students, they didn't seem too concerned that I wasn't there as they warmed up their powers.

"I'll just get in their way. If anything, I'll make it worse and someone'll get hurt."

"Such is the burden of the untrained Guardian. Bad things are bound to happen, but as long as you stay and fight, you'll have no guilt," Rhismai said.

Before I could reply, the monster reached us and cried out in a fury. Two spine-like legs arced from its body and anchored into the ground while three other sets rolled frantically. Their needle-like ends jabbed in waves, ready to skewer its next meal. The top set of appendages ended with serrated pincers. Briery claws snapped, emitting a loud *crack* when they came together.

The monster came down hard on its legs, making the ground shudder and loose rocks roll down the slope. Its bulbous head wobbled. Two lobes beaded iridescent black came together to form the top of its head, or rather, its eyes. Just below its eyes was a comparatively small mouth ringed with concentric circles of teeth. Thick antennas twitched at the sides.

Mother, save us, I prayed.

The Fexrunds were first to act, not the least bit shaken. They broke into a sprint in a V formation, easily dodging the deadly spikes of rocks and rounding on either side of the creature. Aligning their hands, a beam of bright, raw energy flashed beneath the monster. A shrill cry erupted as one of the beast's legs was severed. Before any other legs could be lobbed off, the slender creat curved its body, legs dancing, and moved toward Keldric. A snap of a claw at Keldric's back had him cutting off their connection and breaking into a hard sprint.

Sephara nudged Gwen forward. She wrung her hands together, knuckles white, as she stumbled towards the chaos.

At the same time, both Rhismai and Bron were at my back, trying to force me forward too. My stubborn feet dug into the gravelly dirt, making them struggle even more. I'd much rather die fighting these two than that monster.

Gwen, in a sudden fit of courage, threw her palms up

towards the creature. Nothing happened. The beast scurried after Keldric, body snaking and whipping around the slope.

Sephara came to Gwen's back and whispered in her ear. With her words, confidence settled on Gwen's soft features and she threw her hands out once again. The beast lurched, body careening towards the sky as it cried out. It shook its massive head and continued on, but at a slower, labored pace. Keldric took the slight advantage and dashed towards his brother.

Meanwhile, the two Guardians still fought to get me in the action as I clung to a small boulder. I looked up from my perch to see Keldric reach Ander. They stood facing each other, palms raised a few inches apart. Their energy burst outward between their hands, forming a swirling disc of raw power. The beast, slowed by Gwendaliese's hold on its mind, was closing in on the twins. Together, they swept their hands towards it, flinging their energy like a saw blade. The monster curled inward just in time to protect its belly. The energy disc skidded harmlessly along its armored back.

The twins retreated as the beast closed in. Keldric veered to the left, but the creature snapped a pincer at his leg before he could gain distance. The back of his right leg tore open, dark blood spraying across the rocky ground as he collapsed. Ravaged flesh, muscle, and fabric hung in jagged ribbons from his calf. He clung to it, desperately trying to hold the tissue and blood in.

Rhismai and Bron, his chain now glowing red hot around his bicep, sprung into action and abandoned me. Without communicating, Rhismai tossed Bron at the creature on a strong, fast wind. Before it could snap at Keldric again, Bron was on its back. He unfurled his molten chain and whipped it around one eye. The monster reeled and fell away from Keldric, giving Ander and Rhismai an opening to drag him out. I took my opening as well and raced down the slope, leaving the battle behind.

As I reached the bottom, Commander Devlend blocked my path. As suddenly as I noticed him, a crippling pain flooded my body. Not so much pain, but weakness, a bone-deep ache that made me collapse onto the rocky slope.

It felt as if my heart gave out. The breath was crushed out of my lungs. All of my energy seeped from my muscles. I didn't even have the strength to clutch at my chest as I struggled for a breath. What was happening to me? Was this death?

"Even though you cage it up and neglect it, you still feel the pain of its loss. Interesting." The Commander pondered me like a specimen, holding his palm out towards me.

I realized it then. My power was gone. Even though I never used it, it constantly pulsed in my chest alongside my heart. It must have fueled my body somehow without me even noticing. Rage contorted my face but that was all. I couldn't crawl or speak; I was unable to even raise a damning fist.

"You want it back? Do you think you deserve it? You regard your ability with such contempt. It is a gift from the Mother herself and deserves adoration and reverence."

"Stop! Please! You're hurting her." Blaze sprinted over.

He cradled my head in his lap, stroking my sweat-soaked brow with the back of his hand.

"So you do need your power, Miss Baelin. Dare I say,

want it." The Commander flashed a sneer. "Then, by all means, have it."

As quickly as my power was taken, it was given back. My chest flooded with that supernatural force alongside a heaving breath. Strength returned, and at the drastic influx of power, my torso lifted and arced toward the sky. It was too much, a surge more powerful than any before, and it swallowed me up as it raged. All sense of awareness left me —there was only a blinding white light. I felt full and alive, yet strained and expended.

A rush of wind and rain drowned out the screams. A loud crack boomed, making earth and air tremble. After an eternity of conflict, the high of being insurmountably strong yet perpetually drained, I dropped like a ragdoll to the ground. I lay in a heap. My bones felt shattered and my muscles ripped to shreds. My head lolled to the side and I gazed at the battlefield.

All of the Guardians lay on the ground as if they had been thrown back. Rhismai and Gwen's hair stood on end. The creature lay lifeless on a jagged boulder, its body bent over it at a disturbingly severe angle. Its shell was torn open, edges of the gash singed and smoking as its innards toppled onto the rocks below. The reek of it spread fast in the summer air and I gagged. Its bulbous head of eyes lay against the gravel, half-burned and bleeding from where Bron had grappled it.

Not needing much rebound, Bron heaved himself up, clutching his right forearm and limping heavily on his leg. He made his way to Keldric who lay cringing while he held his leg together. Ander, slashes leaking blood down his cheek and torso, stumbled toward his brother. Together, they gingerly lifted Keldric and started down the treacherous slope.

Once the shock had worn off, Rhismai frantically crawled over the rocks to Sephara, who was sprawled across a rough-cut boulder. A burgundy pool of blood spread beneath her skull, matting her curls.

Rhismai's bottom lip trembled. "Sephara. Sephara, wake up."

Sephara remained still, eyes closed and expressionless on the ground.

"*Sephara!*" Rhismai's cries grew louder and more hysterical. Her hands gently inspected her body for any other injuries and vitals.

She turned to the Commander. "Her breathing and pulse are weak, but there."

"Take her to the Compound for Brivania to stabilize her, then transport her to Kinfront infirmary," he ordered.

At his word, Rhismai sprang into action. She spun the wind around Sephara into a protective cocoon. When Rhismai lifted her hands, the shell encasing her love rose into the air. Once Rhismai felt Sephara was secured, they both whisked away into the sky, heading toward the Compound. I watched my trainer fly away, so swift and effortless, like she was born to be one with the breeze.

My gaze came down from the clouds and met the icy smolder of Commander Devlend. Next to him was a dusty and bruised Blaze stunned by the rush of the battlefield. Gwen had come to his side. Cuts and scrapes stained her porcelain skin scarlet.

"See what happens when you don't train," the Commander preached. "You may think your cause is just, but believe me, Miss Baelin, it's only petty and selfish. To spare yourself from battle, you risked your team's lives. You risk not only them but also innocent citizens who have no gift to protect themselves. What makes your life so much more valuable than theirs?"

I couldn't recall when the tears had started. All I could do was stare at the Commander's back as he walked down the mountainside.

Chapter Twenty-Three

The three of us made our way back to the Compound in weighted silence. Gwen's brow was etched in a permanent furrow. Was she simply upset, or was she angry with me? The Commander had implied what happened was my fault, as if I chose to blow up the creat and all of us with it.

I thought of Keldric and Sephara, bleeding and helpless.

No, no matter how much I hated the Commander and wanted out of his training program, I would never go that far

As we approached the gate, it automatically opened for us. Together, we made our way down the hill leading to the back of the Compound, then up the stairwell to the bunkrooms.

Gwen slipped down the hall without a parting word. With my hand on the doorknob, needing to lean heavily against the frame for support, Blaze caught my eye.

His bright teal eyes glittered as he placed a consoling hand on my shoulder. "I'm sorry he did that to you."

My eyes trembled, but I was out of fresh tears. No words came to my lips, so I nodded and placed my hand atop his, giving it a gentle squeeze before entering the bunkroom.

The overhead light was already on and burned my eyes. Squinting, I noticed a familiar silhouette slouched on the side of the bed. I closed the door and leaned against it to stay upright.

"Why do you insist on sneaking in here?" I coughed in my raspy voice.

He cradled his jaw in his hands, elbows propped on his thighs. A brace was strapped around his ankle and a bandage was wrapped around his bicep, a thin slice of blood leaking through.

He scowled at my words. "That's really your first thought? Not 'how's Keldric or Sephara?' Or any of us for that matter."

That stung more than any injury. Did he really think that low of me?

"Of course I'm worried about them." My voice quavered. "How are they—and you?"

He pinched the bridge of his nose and sighed. He took a long, calming breath before speaking. "I'm alright. Keldric is stitched up. He lost a lot of blood, but thankfully he's receiving a transfusion from his brother. He may need some physical therapy; his calf muscle was torn to shreds. And Sephara . . . she hasn't woken up. She's stable though. Rhismai and Brivania are driving her to Kinfront."

"That's terrible." I hung my head. "I hope she pulls through."

Unnaturally warm hands rested on my shoulders and I looked up.

"I know she will." His eyes seared. "What you did today was an accident. Take it as a lesson; a sign that you need to train and gain control so you can help rather than hurt."

I furrowed my brow and stepped out of his grasp. "I didn't lose control. The Commander forced it out of me."

"Only because you refused to cooperate."

"So that justifies what he did?"

"I'm not saying he's innocent, but neither are you."

His accusatory words weighed between us. I took another step away. "Leave. Now."

He advanced, and I moved to retreat, but he grabbed my hand. He pulled me toward him and the unexpected force made me stumble into his chest. He caught me, bracing me with his strong arms.

"Don't push me away."

"Why do you care when I'm so clearly against everything you believe in?"

The question seemed to hold more weight for him than I realized.

His eyes smoldered, the hard edges of his face softening. His lips parted into a small smile. "I—I'm not entirely sure. I'm drawn to you, Anora. Your passion, your fight. Even if it's different from mine."

He leaned down, his eyes angling toward my lips as he gently lifted my chin. Temptation was written in the crease of his mouth. But this time, instead of feeling that tingling rush up my spine, I was overcome with the violating touch of betrayal. I pushed him away.

"How could you possibly think that's okay after all you've done?"

His brow furrowed in confusion.

"You really think I'd forgive you that easily for dragging me out there?" I asked. "You know how I feel about all of this and you still carried me out kicking and screaming to those mountains. You know . . ." I paused at the thought of that cursed terrain, the demons it had sent to torment me and those I love. "You know how terrified I am of that place. And you still made me go."

Bron made to speak but I cut him off. My anger swelled and my haggard voice strained. "*And* you just blamed me for what happened! It was all him! *He* forced that out of me and caused everyone to get hurt, not me."

"Do you think I enjoyed forcing you out there? Do you think I liked putting you in danger? They were his orders. I had to do it."

"Don't pull that excuse. You have a choice, and you always choose to follow him."

"It's not that easy."

"But it *is* that easy to defend what you think is right. I don't understand how you can follow him so blindly."

Bron stepped back. "I'm not a reckless, selfish rebel like you. I actually take pride in my position and have respect for my leader."

"Really, Bron?" I scowled at him. "You just said how much you admired my *passion*, and now you're throwing it back by calling me a brat?"

Bron's eyebrows drooped. "I didn't mean it like that. It's just—I'm not some spineless, mindless drone because I respect the Commander. I know you hate him, but don't judge me because I don't."

I was quick with another accusation. "Well, what about your whispers with Rhismai before she attacked me yesterday, hmm?"

"*That* is not what you think. We had a meeting with the Commander on how to get you to cooperate. I explained what released your powers at the assessment and how I got your powers to present when we picked you up. I suggested we come up with a less severe version of it, but they began planning ways Rhismai could do something equally as . . . impactful. I didn't agree, but the Commander insisted. What I asked her was to go easy on you, I swear."

"You meet with them and talk about me behind my back?"

Bron was supposed to be my friend, an ally. What kind of friend did that?

"Of course that's all you got out of that. You know, even with everything that's happened, I can set aside our differences and still like the person I see. But apparently, you can't do the same."

He limped to the door. He turned back only once, hand resting on the doorknob. When I didn't say a word, he slipped out, letting the door slam shut.

Frozen in place, regret and anger churned immiscible in my heart. Why did I feel so guilty? He was the betrayer. He was the one that schemed behind my back and dragged me to those mountains. I should've known better than to trust a Guardian. Like he said, it was his duty to make me fall in line. I should've realized that was his first priority— not me. No matter how I justified it though, his sad, downturned eyes scorched my mind and broke my heart. No matter how many betrayals and hurt feelings piled up, it seemed those embers between us, those little moments, couldn't be doused.

I'd have to forget about them, I resolved, *put Bron and those memories out of mind and move on, somehow, even though I literally see him all day everyday.*

"Cause that should be easy," I sighed.

Slipping off my boots, a crumpled piece of paper fell to the floor.

I picked up the note, the paper stiff and discolored with dried sweat. I carefully unfolded it and read the scrawl: *I'm in.*

Realization and excitement flooded all at once. It was the note Blaze had slipped me that morning. The phrase was vague, but still, a smile stretched across my dirt-coated, tear-stained face.

He wanted to join me. He wanted out of this prison too, and we would do it together.

Chapter Twenty-Four

T he Commander stomped into class the next morning and announced that training was canceled since Rhismai and Sephara were still in Kinfront. My sore muscles were thankful, but my heart ached thinking about how much pain Sephara was in, how distraught Rhismai must be, and I sent prayers to the Mother for her recovery.

After a droning lecture on different species of creats, Commander Devlend instructed us to spend the afternoon reflecting on our scouting mission and write a paper on what we could've done to improve the outcome. With a pointedly cold look at me, he swept out of the room. Once the tap of his shoes receded down the hall, Blaze and I headed outside to lay in the grass with notebooks and pens in hand.

It was late summer and the heat persisted. Sprawled in the thick grass, head nuzzled atop my crossed arms, I reveled in the soothing warmth of the sun as it beat down on my back. Even though it was noon, my eyelids grew heavy.

"Who knew the outdoors could be so relaxing," I purred into the crook of my arm, my voice recovered from Rhismai's attack.

"You've never laid out in the sun before?" Blaze asked, stunned.

"Living so close, you can't risk being outside more than necessary."

"I couldn't imagine not going to the beach. Feeling the damp sand squish between my toes, the salty spray of the sea . . ." He shut his eyes and smiled. "But we don't get as many attacks as you do. Usually once a year, if that."

"Can you show me?" I inquired cautiously. "If you don't want to use your power, I totally get it. It's just, I've never seen the ocean aside from pictures."

A blush crept on his golden complexion. "It doesn't really work with places. I can only see people."

"Oh—" I began, but he cut me off.

"But I know someone who typically is on the coast this time of day."

Blaze closed his eyes and held his palms out as he had that first day we arrived. His voice, barely a whisper, mumbled a name I couldn't make out and his eyes began twitching beneath their lids. A burst of light danced above his palms, a glittering swirl of tan and pale blues and greens. When Blaze's eyes snapped open, his sight projected crystal clear.

A young boy, wearing only a pair of drenched shorts, scoured a beach on his hands and knees. Fine sand dusted the flat earth in a mosaic of white, tan, and blush tones. Foam lapped against the boy's arms and legs as he searched. Behind him, the sea stretched out for an eternity. The sun danced along the lazy waves, making it sparkle like a sea of aquamarine and peridot gems.

The young boy, his curly black hair matted wet to his dark forehead, dove towards a small burrow in the sand. He emerged with a crab wriggling in his fist. He jumped up with a silent cheer and ran up the beach, his bare feet etching prints in the sand.

The image moved with him. Just past that flat stretch of beach were several small huts with thatched roofs and blue-green painted walls that blended seamlessly with the sea. The boy waved his catch in an old man's face. Dark wrinkles cracked the sides of his face as he smiled at the child, mussing the boy's salty curls.

The scene began to fuzz at the edges and slowly faded away into nothing.

I gawked, still staring at the space where the sea flowed moments ago. No picture in a textbook could ever capture such beauty.

"It's stunning."

"It is," Blaze's eyes softened and grew distant as he, too, stared at where his home had been. "My sister and I used to fish together. We'd walk in about waist-high and cast our nets into the waves." He chuckled softly. "She used to toss it over me. She'd catch me every time and nearly fall over laughing. I knew to expect it too, but somehow she always got me."

Two snapped poles floated among the fish.

I shook the image out of my mind before it could seed. "You must want to get home to her."

"She's not there." Blaze's teal eyes grew dark.

Confusion drew my brows together.

Blaze leaned in to whisper, "My sister was a trainee here two years ago."

"Oh really?" I asked, "Do you know where she's stationed? Maybe she can come visit like—"

"She's not posted anywhere," he said. "She's missing."

"Wait, *what?*" I blurted.

Did I just hear that right? I lunged onto my knees, scooting myself closer to him.

"I think she disappeared sometime during training. We haven't heard from her since the day she left. We didn't suspect anything until a year passed, since there's that ridiculous, 'no outside communication' rule. But after her training, she never came to visit. She didn't even send a letter saying where she was posted."

"So you think she was—what? Ran away, or . . . ?"

A dark shadow fell over him. "We initially thought the worst—that she died during her training. I prayed to the Mother to let me see my sister one more time—and She answered my prayer."

My eyebrows rose at the realization. "Your ability."

He nodded. "I conjured a brief glimpse of her strapped to a metal board in a whitewashed room—screaming. Once I realized I'd unleashed my own ability, every day I conjured her image and tried to figure out where she was."

"Did you find out?"

"I only ever see her in an empty white room. Sometimes it's only her, sometimes there are others . . ." He shuddered, his eyelids wavering.

"You don't need to say anymore." I laid my hand on his forearm and gave a comforting squeeze. "If all you see is a white room anyway, that doesn't provide a huge lead."

"Exactly." He took a deep breath. "My family and I

agreed I would willingly expose my ability at my assessment so I could come here and find out what happened."

"Have you found anything?"

He shook his head. "The trainers and the Commander both claim there was never a recruit named Livi Vasterio from Taramora. It's like she never existed."

Pure rage seethed from Blaze. He brushed a hand through his wavy chestnut hair. "She is the sweetest person I've ever known and they dismiss her existence like it's nothing."

"We can find her, Blaze. Together," I removed his note from my shoe and gave it back. "If you're in, I am. We can escape this place together and go find her."

"You really think we can do it?" Blaze gave a guarded smile. "What about getting back to your family?"

"Of course we can. Between both of our abilities, we can find her and free her. And as for my family . . ." I pictured all three of their smiling faces, unable to fathom the pain I'd feel if something so terrible happened to them. "I would hope, if something so awful happened to them, I'd have a friend that would help me rescue them, too."

Blaze slowly slipped his hand into mine, his skin soft and smooth. An unanticipated spark rocketed up my back, my senses alight from the touch. I squeezed his palm and a blush flourished in my cheeks. I couldn't take my eyes off our clasped hands. They molded together seamlessly and rested perfectly in my lap.

"Thank you," Blaze whispered, his breath a breeze against my cheek.

I raised my eyes to his. The sun seeped through the bubble and lit his skin gold. His eyes glittered like the sea.

A fire fluttered deep inside me and I noticed how close his lips were to my own.

The smack of a door in its frame broke the silence. I flinched and broke away from Blaze, turning to find Bron storming toward us. He tried hard to suppress his limp.

"Glad to see you're both hard at work on your assignment," he barbed. "Commander wants to see you." He gestured for me to stand.

"I got enough shaming from him yesterday, thanks."

"It's not about that—not directly, at least."

I cocked my head in confusion.

"Just come," he commanded impatiently, throwing a glare at Blaze.

"Alright, alright, hold on. I'm still a bit weak." I wobbled to my feet.

Bron grasped my bicep too tightly and cowed me toward the Compound. I peered over my shoulder and Blaze a pleading look.

He chuckled and dusted off his hands in a teasing gesture. "Commander's all yours. Good luck."

－－－－－

Thin strips of light broke through the thick blinds of the Commander's office. Dust floated in and out of the beams. His office was larger than a bunkroom, with one wall solely dedicated to bookshelves. They were over-stuffed but neatly organized. Opposite the bookshelves was a substantial wooden desk that spanned the width of the room. Folders and papers were stacked in every available space in orderly piles. A pincushion chair was tucked behind it, in line with a narrow doorway. Bron ushered me to a wooden chair angled toward the desk and took a seat beside me.

Silence grew heavy with anticipation. I bounced my knee and scratched at my thumbnails. We hadn't talked since our fight—and our second almost-kiss. He was still clearly upset over it, but I was definitely not going to be the first to apologize this time. I was hurt, too. Yes, I regretted some of the things I said. I knew they were too harsh. But he'd betrayed me too, to a much worse end than I had ever hurt him. What made it all worse was that those small embers, those sweet moments, between us in those first weeks were still burning. They wouldn't let me simply be mad at him and forget what we almost had.

"Nice to see you moved on so quickly," Bron snapped.

"Excuse me?"

"Don't play innocent with me. There's clearly something going on between you and Blaze."

Of course that was what he focused on. Not on what he had said, what he had accused me of. None of the things that actually mattered.

"And so what if there is? It's not like we ever were . . ."

He leaned back in his chair and crossed his arms. "No, I suppose we weren't."

"You're the one who betrayed me," I said.

"I guess I shouldn't expect you to see what I did as my way of protecting you." He stewed.

"I can see how *you* would think you were protecting me." I sighed. "But if you really knew me, understood me, you would know that was not the way to do it."

"I wish I did." His inflection lost all of its bite.

Commander Devlend swung the small door open from behind his desk, effectively ending our conversation. As the door clicked, he met my eye and held it as he swooped into his chair. The stacks of papers in front of him were truly mountainous, for I had to crane my neck to see his face.

He moved the piles blocking my view further down the desk. "Is that better?"

I gave one small nod, lounging into the back of my chair, trying to exude confidence. My posture was still stiff, so I rolled my shoulders.

"I did not bring you here to reprimand you further, Miss Baelin. I'm sure you were racked with grief last night over what you caused."

"At what happened, yes, but *not* what I did. *I* didn't do anything to cause that."

"When will you mature and learn to take some responsibility?" Before I could form a rebuttal, he held up a hand. "But I digress. I brought you here to figure out what you've been hiding from me."

"What are you talking about?"

"Don't play dumb with me." His eyes cut like an icicle. "You haven't been playing this game merely for the sake of going home. There is something you don't want me to find out."

I turned to Bron, looking for answers. His jaw was clenched, his face forward and unyielding.

What was he talking about?

"I don't have anything to hide. I really just want to go back to my old life, where I belong."

The Commander waved my words away like a pestering fly. "Drop the act. I know there is more to you. I felt it."

"You felt what, exactly?"

"When I released your power yesterday, I felt something"—he grasped for the right word—"dwelling beneath your wind and water, something more."

"You're joking, right?" I scoffed. "I mean, this is *me* you're talking about. I don't even use the two elements I have. I can't possibly have another ability."

"I'm not so sure. You've suppressed your ability so much that this one is nearly non-existent. I believe it's weaker than your wind and water, but its presence alone is unheard of. No Element Complector in recorded history has had three affinities, and no Guardian has ever held two different complections." He assessed me, leaning back in his chair. "You clearly don't trust me. You don't want me to see how unique your talents are. You're hoping I cast you out as a mediocre complector who's too much of a nuisance to care about. You think if I know this specialty of yours, I'll exploit it."

I sat forward, meaning to interrupt, but he plowed forward.

"I assure you, Miss Baelin, there is nothing to be afraid of. I nurture all of my Guardians, especially the special ones, as long as they cooperate. If you drop this rebel act of yours, I'll be able to help. Who knows what great things we can accomplish?"

My mouth hung ajar, dumbfounded. Where was all of this coming from? He couldn't actually think I, of all people, had a special ability. It was impossible. "Well, I can assure you that I'm not special in any way. Don't make me into something I'm not."

"You shouldn't deny who you are. I know there's something dormant within you, and whether you like it or not, I will draw it out."

"With Rhismai gone, I don't see how that'll happen."

"Ah." He leaned forward, steepling his hands. "I received radio transmission from Guardian Mojya today. Guardian Jayce is still in a coma with no signs of recovery. Guardian Mojya will stay by her side."

"But Commander, isn't that against Guardian protocol?" Bron questioned. "A trainer can't leave during the training year."

"Yes, but I'm making an exception in this case. Guardian Mojya has made no progress with her trainee and has grown animosity toward her. Especially after yesterday's events, I think she would be volatile upon seeing Miss Baelin."

Bron nodded slowly. "I understand your decision, Commander. But if I may say so, respectfully, I cannot train all of the recruits alone."

"Thankfully, that is not your concern, because I will be taking over Miss Baelin and Miss Astreya's training."

My stomach sank. I stiffened, pressing myself into the back of the chair until it nearly tipped backward. *No!* If there was anything worse than being sworn to battle creats on the Portemor Mountains, it was this.

"Glad to see you're so enthused about the new arrangements, Miss Baelin. I know I am looking forward to our time together."

I scowled at him. "Yes, very much so."

"Good." He stood and slunk to his private entrance. "We will resume our normal schedule tomorrow."

With a click of the lock, he was gone. Bron and I remained rooted in place. Horrid memories of what he'd done to me on the mountainside flooded my mind. Would he steal my energy, sucking the very life from me, every day? Would he force me to expend all of my strength until I collapsed on the cold training room floor?

Memories of my family broke through the tortuous images. Mom baking cookies, her face patted with flour. My stepfather, coated in grease, hugging me and smudging it on my cheek. Liam dragging out his toy chest and begging me to play dolls with him. Blaze was there too, heartbroken and searching for his lost sister.

They were my motivation. My reason for living. My reason to escape this miserable place.

Commander Devlend intended to break me, but I wouldn't let that happen. For them, I wouldn't let him win.

With renewed determination, I kicked back the chair and stood. Without giving Bron a second glance, I stormed out of the office in search of my new accomplice.

Out the stairwell window, I spied Blaze still curled up in the warm summer grass. I rushed out to him, bouncing down the steps. He noticed my urgency and stood. I grabbed his shoulder and pulled him close.

My lips brushed his ear as I whispered, "We need to find a safe place to talk."

Blaze nodded. "Act natural," he muttered and started for the Compound.

I followed, struggling to force an ease into my step.

"What are you doing?" He laughed. "You look like a strutting rooster."

"You must know a very graceful rooster, then." I batted my eyes.

"Oh yes, I've never seen such an alluring bird before, until you, of course." He smirked.

"Hey!" I swatted at his arm and pursed my lips, failing to hold in my laughter.

Once we reached the stairwell, the playful air between us became rigid and reality settled back in. We looked up the stairs and waited in silence for a few moments. I glanced down the staircase to the solid metal door at the base. "What do you suppose is down there?"

"Where do you think they house all the training creats?"

My stomach sank. Thinking about how I had been sleeping above a nest of monsters for over a month made me nauseous. I focused on the task at hand before my mind wandered down those steps.

After confirming no one was around, Blaze went to the main floor entrance. We crept down the short hallway, and before entering the main corridor, we scanned to make sure it was clear.

A few dome lights hung from ceiling, leaving portions of the hall in shadow. Doors lined the walls. I only knew where some of them led. At the end of the right wing were the double doors leading to the training arena. Straight ahead were the classroom, dining hall, and nurse's station.

Blaze beckoned me forward, clinging to the shadows. We passed the classroom and the dining hall. The shushing of running water and the clank of pots filtered into the hall. I peered into the dining room and saw Memette scrubbing furiously at her stockpot, suds running up her forearms. From the nurse's station, Brivania hummed an Eterni folk tune. It fluttered into the hall while she stocked shelves with gauze and ointments.

We snuck past her notice and came to a door at the end of the hall. Blaze eased the door open slowly to placate the squeaky hinges. My eyes were trained down the hall, praying no one would spot us. Blaze slipped through the half-opened door and I followed, shutting the door as quietly as possible. The musty room was lit with the *clink* of an old light bulb bursting to life.

The dust-filled air was thick in my nose and I stifled a sneeze. The compact space was filled with rusting filing cabinets and ceiling-high stacks of papers and folders. A thin maze weaved through the forgotten forest of records. I wiped off the grime coating a label on a filing cabinet and read: *Incident Reports: 1560–1565*.

"These records are nearly 200 years old," I whispered in amazement.

I tugged on the handle and the rusty gears groaned, unyielding.

"I've tried; they're too old and rusted to open." Blaze waved for me to follow him further into the ancient labyrinth.

At the back of the room, a filth-covered window was shrouded by thick blinds, dull streams of light barely making their way into the room. The overhead light couldn't reach over the cabinets and towers of papers, so the far corner of the room was layered in shadows.

Blaze took my hand and we sat on the floor beneath the window. Only the glassy reflection of his eyes and the line of his straight nose and strong jaw were visible in the weak light.

"How did you find this place?"

"One night I was snooping in the dining hall for something to snack on and I couldn't find anything good. So, I searched through every room looking for a pantry and found this."

"What's in the other rooms?"

"Most of them are storage rooms like this one, filled

with papers and stuff. One had a bunch of uniforms in it. Another with workout equipment. A couple of them are set up like classrooms but coated in dust. I chose this one because it's the most remote. Hopefully no one will hear us. I haven't seen any cameras in here."

"Cameras?"

"You haven't noticed? There are security cameras everywhere."

My blush was unreadable in the low light—at least I hoped it was. "I don't know what that is."

"You know that box with the black lens perched on the front gate? It records live images of what's happening and sends it to the Commander for him to monitor. There are smaller versions of them posted in the training arena, the classroom, even the dining hall."

"Are you serious? That's creepy. Why does he need to watch us?"

"I have no idea," he said

"How do you know about all of this high-tech stuff? I've never seen a 'cameras' before coming here, or the light pictures."

He chuckled. "It's *camera*. 'Cameras' is plural. And what are light pictures?"

"What he uses for lessons."

"Oh! You mean the projector. The Commander teaches me about the Compound, its functionality and maintenance, during my private lessons. All of this stuff comes from Celepheria. I guess it's commonplace there."

Wouldn't Bill love to hear that? I recalled my stepfather's rants about how Celepheria took advantage of their position and never bothered to give the mainland more than scraps to survive. Maybe he was more right than we realized.

"Sounds like the Commander's grooming you to be his successor."

"Yeah, I'm starting to think that's his intention."

"Well, to add to his horribleness . . ." I transitioned, telling him about what Commander Devlend had told me about my 'secret powers,' and that he would be conducting my training. Blaze listened patiently as I relayed every detail.

"So do you think he's right? About the hidden ability?"

"No. I think he's fishing for an excuse to torment me and take over my power again. But the bigger issue is our plan to escape. I don't think it'll be easy for either of us to crack him with disobedience like I did to Rhismai, and even that didn't pan out how I wanted."

"So if we can't get kicked out . . ." Blaze trailed off.

"We break out," I said.

Chapter Twenty-Five

Gray clouds shrouded the morning sun. A gentle rain pattered against the bubble encapsulating the Compound. Bursts of pink light flashed wherever the droplets landed.

I perched in my desk chair, eyes forward and a slight smile resting on my lips. My hands were folded neatly above my lengthy assignment.

When Gwendaliese entered the room she looked me over warily. "You seem awfully chipper this morning."

I turned to her with a painted smile, a braid bouncing over my shoulder.

This was perfect! Gwen would be the best person to test out my new angle on before the Commander arrived.

"I decided I should finally accept this lifestyle and devote myself to becoming the best Guardian I can be."

"Why the change of heart?" Gwen scrutinized me as she eased into her chair.

"After what happened, I decided I can't be that foolish person anymore. I need to help, not hurt."

Gwen's expression changed from a suspicious scowl to a beaming smile. "That's great, Anora! I'm so happy you decided to join us. I bet you have so much untapped potential; you'll be the best Element Complector yet!"

Gwendaliese fell for my ruse easily. *Good.* I needed to be believable if my latest plan was going to work.

"Well, I'm hoping to at least be the best Element Complector in our class." I winked and jabbed an elbow in her direction.

Gwen leaned in, her tone turning serious. "I know you haven't really been paying attention, but you're the *only* Element Complector in our class."

"I know, Gwen, it was a joke." I smiled, stifling a laugh.

After a second, her honey eyes lit up. "Oh! I get it."

She giggled and leaned back in her seat as Ander stepped in, his brother hobbling behind him on crutches. His calf that had been left in tattered ribbons after the scout was bound with thick bandages. Gwen hurried to his side, fussing and asking how she could help.

Keldric's square face, which I'd only seen scowl or sneer, blossomed a rose color. "I'm alright, Gwendaliese. Thank you."

"Keldric, I've told you before. You can call me Gwen," she insisted as she steadied him into his seat.

He bowed his head, letting his shaggy hair shield his eyes. "But Gwendaliese is such a beautiful name."

Gwen's pale face blushed and she swatted at his shoulder. "Oh, don't be silly." Then, her flirty demure was immediately replaced by regret. "Oh no! Keldric I'm so sorry. Did I hurt you? I don't know what I was thinking hitting you like that when you're in so much pain."

"I'm fine." He laughed it off. "I promise."

She stumbled back into her chair, avoiding my gaze as I gawked at her and Keldric. Apparently, I'd tuned out more than the lessons this past month.

Blaze strolled in next and gave me a swift, subtle nod. Quickly, I turned at attention to the front of the room just as the Commander walked in.

"I hope everyone is recovering after our scouting mission," the Commander said. "I'm confident you all spent yesterday reflecting on what could have been done to improve the outcome." He turned to me with a pointed look. "Let's see what you came up with."

He held out his hand in front of Ander, who swiveled in his chair to collect all of our assignments. He laid the stack in the Commander's hand, and the Commander swiftly flipped through it, glancing at each paper.

He stopped on mine, a surprised eyebrow raised. "A full page, Miss Baelin? I was beginning to believe you were incapable of writing more than two sentences."

"I had a lot to reflect on, Commander, sir," I addressed, biting back my usual sarcastic tone.

His icy eyes narrowed, scrutinizing me for a few moments before placing the papers on his desk.

The dreary morning was filled with talks of strengthening the fences and scouting further into the mountains than ever before. Since numbers of sightings and attacks had been increasing over time, and dramatically so in the past several years, it was important to find a way to staunch the growth before it peaked. And the Commander expected us to do that for him.

"If we go to them, fight on *their* home front, then maybe we can scare them off," Ander stated firmly.

"But no one has ever gone before," I countered. "What

happens when we go to their side and the bigger creats come out to play?"

"And how do *you*, of all people, know how big they can be?" Ander spat. "It's reasonable to think that only the biggest and strongest make it across."

"Where did you grow up, Ander?" I challenged. "How close were you to the mountains?"

"That doesn't matter," he muttered.

"It totally does. In fact, I don't think either of you has mentioned where you're from."

"Like I said," Ander argued. "It doesn't matter where we're from. What matters is our superior power and skill level."

I guffawed. "Where you come from matters. It frames your entire outlook on creats, the Guard—everything."

"They're from Celepheria," the Commander interjected.

The twins' heads snapped toward the Commander, deep red snaking up their necks. The jaws of us three mainlanders dropped. It appeared that Gwen hadn't even known.

"You're Celepherians, and you have the gall to tell *me* what's best for the mainland? I can see the Portemor Mountains on my ride to school. I've seen monsters, ten times bigger than the ones the Guardians fight, fly over the mountains and land at the top. Large enough that they can wrap their tails around it. You've only seen such monsters in your nightmares."

Ander blushed then quickly smothered it with a scowl. "We've been in the simulator before. It's the same thing."

I didn't know what a simulator was, but I knew it couldn't possibly be the same as a real monster. Nothing *simulated* could match the ferocity of a creat. Keldric seemed to agree with me from the way he protectively rubbed his injured leg.

Before I could say anymore, the Commander asked, "So, what would you propose, Miss Baelin?"

Never before had I contributed to any class discussion, so I dug through my mind for a reasonable suggestion, one that would make me appear a thoughtful student. Victon came to mind. A boy consumed with jealousy for my ability. A boy who wanted to serve his country, but couldn't.

"We could open up the Guard to regular people. People eager and ready to defend their country, but who aren't allowed to simply because they don't have a complection."

Ander scoffed. "That's the worst idea I've ever heard! They would all be slaughtered. The border would be a bloodbath."

"That is the main reason we've never allowed civilians in the Guard. No amount of physical training or combat strategy lessons can prepare them for battle against a creat," the Commander said.

I bit my lip as I thought of a solution, and the Bellwarn school patrolmen came to mind. "What about if they didn't have to be in the thick of battle at all? They could be perched atop the fence, or in the trees, with crossbows and throwing knives."

"I know the local guards provide some ease of mind," the Commander commented. "But honestly, their simple weaponry is ineffectual against most creats."

"Then we should develop bigger, more lethal weapons for them to use," I argued. "I know there are a lot of people out there who *want* to serve. There are kids at my school praying every day that their ability is revealed, just so they have the opportunity to defend the border. But when they don't appear, they have to give up on their life-long dream simply because they weren't born with abilities? That's not fair to them, or the Guard, who are under-manned and overworked as it is."

"A very convincing speech, Miss Baelin. But who will pay for weapons development and their training?" Commander Devlend put forth.

"Won't the government fund it? Premier Sevlos knows how important border security is," Keldric answered.

"Are you so sure, Mr. Fexrund?"

He nodded fervently. "He's generous and always giving back to the people."

"He may be gracious to Celepherians, but he allots only the bare minimum funds to the mainland. We suffer far greater than we should because of it."

Even though it made my stomach turn, the Commander's words reminded me of my stepfather. It sounded exactly like something he would say, maybe with a few less *colorful* words.

"But he supports the Guard," Keldric pressed. "He says so."

"He budgets enough to sustain us, but no more. I have requested funds to reinforce the fence, to fortify our base camps, but he always refuses."

"Maybe if we try asking our senator, he could petition for us," Gwen offered.

"I have. He understands its importance but doesn't hold enough power or influence to move it upwards. It was a miracle our last senator was able to get the development of advanced soundproofing technology funded."

"But this would save lives too. Just like the bubbles," Blaze piped up.

"They may argue that it would, in fact, risk lives, and that putting civilians on the border would be a death sentence."

"It's a death sentence for Guardians, too," I said. "If people are willing to make that sacrifice, then they should be allowed to make that choice for themselves."

"Good point." The Commander nodded. "But the Premier focuses on the risks and uses them as fuel to not fund things. The majority of the senate doesn't care to fight for it because they don't know the danger of living on the mainland, nor do they care, I'm afraid."

"So what can we do?" Gwen asked.

"I was going to ask you all the same question." The Commander looked into each of our faces, lingering on mine. "Your proposal, Miss Baelin, is quite unique and may actually be possible if proposed and defended compellingly. Good work."

Then, he dismissed us and strolled out of the room, assignments in hand. My paper winked from the top of the pile.

I was the first to enter the training arena that day. The room was dim and cold, the heavy clouds blocking the sun's bright warmth. A chill rippled off the cement walls and seeped into my skin, stealing my warmth. The other recruits followed suit in waiting for the Commander. As I tugged at the high neck of my Guardian jumpsuit,

Commander Devlend strolled in with Bron hobbling at his heel.

Instead of his usual suit and cap-toe shoes, the Commander was wearing a Guardian uniform and combat boots. The gray and cobalt-blue attire drained any remnants of color from his alabaster skin but drew out the blue of his eyes. Paired with his thinning gray hair, he appeared the ghost of a fallen Guardian.

Bron leaned heavily on his good leg at the Commander's side. His hard chiseled features took on more of a pout as he stared at the wall. He must still be mad over yesterday, over everything. Would he ever be able to get over it? Would I? We were such different people. Our opinions and motivations couldn't clash more. Maybe all we were meant to be were those few stolen, sweet moments in this cold-hearted place.

I stopped fidgeting with my outfit and stepped forward. I joined the other recruits in line, feet spaced shoulder-width apart and hands clasped behind my back. Keldric attempted to match but was forced to keep a hold on his crutches lest he toppled over.

The Commander's eyes swept over us. "Guardian Mojya will not be returning to the Compound. As for Guardian Jayce, it is with great sorrow I say that she has passed on. May the Mother greet her with open arms and praise her for her sacrifice. Let's take a moment of silence to honor Guardian Sephara Jayce."

Even with my feet firmly planted, I stumbled as the news punched me. Righting myself, I dropped my head to pay respects and to hide my tears.

She's dead because of me.

Somewhere inside, I knew it wasn't my doing, that it

was the Commander that caused what happened on the mountainside, but the weight of her loss bore down all the same.

I felt a hand rub my back—Blaze.

I didn't hear the Commander end the moment of silence over the wailing in my head. Blaze wrapped me in his arms and I curled into him.

"I thought she'd be alright," I mumbled. "I didn't think she would—that this could—"

Gwen came up to me, amber eyes rimmed red, and said, "She truly loved being a trainer. Knowing her, she'd be happy to see that her sacrifice has sparked you to become the best Guardian you can in her name."

My chest caved in at her words. Her words that rammed the last nail of guilt into my heart. This was all a façade, an act. I wasn't really reformed because of what had happened at the mountains. Now, my ruse was an affront to Sephara's memory.

How could I move forward with this plan now?

Gwen pulled me from Blaze's arms and into hers. I scuttled out of her embrace. On one side, I blamed myself; the other blamed the Commander. I didn't know which was right.

The Commander cleared his throat. "Today is a day to mourn, but also to honor. Put all of your grief into strengthening your abilities and, in that way, honor the fallen. Let's begin."

He instructed Blaze to observe as he always did, but this time not by his side. Bron had a limping Keldric join Blaze on the bench while he led Ander to the far training square. They began physical combat training earlier than scheduled since Ander couldn't practice his abilities without his brother. The Commander made his way to the center square and nodded for Gwen and me to come forward. I approached him, my head fogged with grief.

"I will train both of you simultaneously. Eventually, it'll be a wonderful opportunity for you to learn how to fight together, but for now, we'll keep to single, separate tasks." He turned to Gwen. "Miss Astreya, I noticed on our scout you struggled to hold your will over the creat. The best approach to tackling this will be to practice on smaller, weaker creatures and work your way up."

He bustled over to the shadow-veiled wall and wheeled over a small wire cage. A small fawn lay in the bottom, its snout tucked snuggly underneath its leg. The movement and dim skylight was enough to rouse the fawn. She blinked her large eyes open, still heavy with sleep. Once she noticed us, her head snapped up, ears perked and twitching.

"Today, practice on controlling its movements." He slid open the cage door.

Gwen knelt down near the opening and gently coaxed the fawn out. Shakily, it emerged and approached her outstretched hand. Gwen's eyes lit up, tears dissipated, as she petted the babe.

"Oh, aren't you the sweetest little thing," she cooed, leading the fawn to the far side of the room.

"As for you." The Commander scrutinized me, an eyebrow raised. "We will start with the basics. Unless you object?"

Not taking the bait, I faced him and wiped the remaining tears from my cheeks.

"Very well," he said as he raised the plexiglass box around us, caging us in together.

"I want you to visualize your energy swelling up in your chest. See it flow down your arms and gather in your fingertips."

I closed my eyes to help me focus. My senses grew fuzzy as I centered on that familiar thrum of power. It felt hot and bubbly in my chest, almost giddy, as if it knew it would finally be released. I lifted my hands, palms facing forward, and allowed it to pool in my fingers. Without a thought, a whirl of wind and rain clustered around my hands.

I cracked open my eyes to tentatively watch the miniature storms swirl around. With my energy flowing freely, my body felt lighter. An ache I didn't realize I had; a coiled knot in my chest, unfurled. It felt foreign and natural at the same time.

My curiosity turned to anxiety as those harmless clouds of atmosphere began to grow, spreading out and engulfing my forearms. Frantically, I batted the wind and moisture away, but it kept expanding.

"Calm down, your panic will only make it intensify. If you loosen your hold on your power completely, it will act on its own accord. It will be natural—chaotic. You must maintain your hold on it at all times."

With a nod, I sucked my power back in. Pain arced in my chest at the sudden rush of power being sealed.

"You're only used to an 'all or nothing' relationship with your ability. You need to learn how to control it without stifling it. How about you try focusing on only one of your elements. It may help to manage a smaller chunk at first."

"I'm not sure I can do that."

"During your evaluation, you were able to single out air and pin the creat to the wall. Just apply that method here."

"That was done in the rush of the moment though. I just opened my hands and hoped for the best, really."

"We'll start with the *basic* basics then." He tsked. "Since you have two affinities that we know of, your power store is divided between the two. The portion able to manipulate wind will seek out and tether itself to individual particles in the surrounding air. Water in the environment is manipulated the same way.

"Element Complectors describe it as casting an exclusionary net into the environment, and whatever it touches, you're able to control. When your power manipulates these tethers, it acts chaotically and drains you quickly. Let your power guide you to your element, but then *you* need to control the tethers."

"Seems easy enough," I muttered.

"Let's just give it a try, shall we?" he suggested, an eyebrow raised.

I wanted to stick my tongue out at him, but keeping to the plan, I maintained the reformed rebel façade. I closed my eyes again and let my power flow freely once more, but this time my awareness went with it. My sense of touch expanded outside my body and traveled alongside my power as it scoped the environment. Individual atmospheric particles stood out to me like the groove of my mother's tweed fabrics. I could distinguish the dry air molecules from the water floating amongst them. As instructed, I tethered all the air around me and tugged.

A forceful whoosh of air encircled me and I was pinned midair, the wind squeezing like a vise. The weight of the air pressed in on my lungs and I gaped like a fish as I tried desperately to breathe.

Just as quick as it started, it ended. The air dispersed and settled in the room, leaving me to collapse on the unforgiving concrete floor. Ragged breaths filled my lungs as I lay sprawled on my back. Tilting my head, I saw a sideways Gwen trying to soothe a squirming, startled fawn.

I propped myself up and found the Commander standing not a foot away. Craning my neck, I looked into his shadowed eyes.

"This is what happens when you suppress your powers. Pent up for so long, they become rather explosive and difficult to manage. You need to release it—drain it to a manageable level before we can make progress. Get up, we're going outside."

After lowering our barrier walls, he ordered, "Guardian Trenton, keep an eye on Miss Astreya."

Without prompting me, he walked toward the double doors.

A faint blush warmed my cheeks as I bustled out of the training room to follow.

———

"Again," Commander Devlend repeated from underneath the shelter of a small umbrella.

I squinted against the raindrops streaming down my face. My braid weighed heavy like a thick rope down my back.

A storm cloud of my own making rolled beneath the bubble, dark and plump with moisture. The cloud pressed against its confines, eager to be free and join the others flying by on the Mother's wind.

"I'm exhausted." I stomped my soaked boots. "Can we *please* be done?"

"You need to expel your pent-up energy. This is the least destructive way to do it. Again."

"I would hardly call this harmless."

"Of all the options, yes, this is the *least* harmful."

"You put too much trust in me."

"My trust is solely in nature, Miss Baelin. Not you."

With a huff, I faced the Compound flagpole. The Commander had pulled down the flag so I wouldn't damage it and kept it tucked safely under his arm.

I focused my dwindling energy on my storm cloud. Within it, I stirred up moisture, revving its potential energy. Crackles of lightning skittered across the cloud. They started sporadic and faint, but I built them up stronger over time. Once I got the technique down, it took me only a few minutes to charge the cloud fully. As my power waned, though, the longer it took. I drained everything I had into the cloud, wincing from the effort until it burst. A crack boomed. A white flash blurred the bleak landscape as a lightning bolt sliced through the air and down the flagpole. The air was warm and heavy, making the hair on my neck rise. My arms flopped like jelly to my sides. My knees wobbled, struggling to keep me upright.

"We've been out here for hours. I need a break."

"It's barely been an hour. You need to work on endurance."

"Yeah, yeah." I waved him off, aggravated. "I need to work on a million things. I can work on it tomorrow."

"Not tomorrow—today. You have a lot of catching up to do."

I sighed, about to argue more, but he cut me off. "Rest for a couple hours, eat a hearty dinner, and meet me in the training room afterward."

Silence was my sign of agreement. I trudged down the hill through the muddy grass, not caring as I dragged it into the Compound with my soggy boots.

Chapter Twenty-Six

"Why are you still in uniform?" Blaze asked as he sat down at the table.

He had a plate stacked high with glazed pork and steamed vegetables. From my own similarly stacked plate, I shoveled mounds of sweet pork and broccoli into my mouth. As my jaw strained to chew, I swiped two of the biggest rolls from the center basket.

"And why are you eating like an animal? That's usually my job." He stabbed a generous helping of meat with his fork.

"You're lucky I had time to shower; I was drenched from being under my own storm for like, five hours. I'm so drained, but he's making me do more after dinner." I continued in a mocking tone, "He says I have 'a lot of catching up to do.'"

Blaze snickered, mouth full and spewing bits of food onto the table.

"You're right. *You're* the animal," I teased.

He elbowed me as I ripped apart a roll.

"Now don't go messing up my table!" Memette shouted from the window counter where she began picking up the leftover food.

Gwen had joined Ander to visit his brother in his room for supper, where he could more comfortably stretch out his wounded leg. Bron was not in the dining room either but must have already stopped by if Memette was already cleaning up. Or he was taking this whole avoiding-me-thing to the extreme.

"I'll make sure he cleans it up!" I called back, my cheeks packed with bread. A few crumbs tumbled from my lips.

His eyes widened in exaggerated horror. "*You're* the one she should be worried about making a mess."

I hushed him and peered through the kitchen window, making sure Memette didn't hear. "Don't get me in trouble too!"

Blaze feigned offense, holding his fork across his chest. "I can assure you, Miss Baelin, the one causing the most trouble here is you."

I laughed. "I think you do a better Commander than the man himself."

Blaze bowed over his dinner. The smirk dancing on his lips threatened to burst into a wide smile. When he whipped his head back upright, his wavy hair swooped back and I couldn't help but stare.

His eyes caught mine, burning bright, and an easy smile settled on his lips. His dark brown skin glowed golden in the low light of the dining hall.

I leaned towards him, wondering how his lips would feel against mine. In that moment, I forgot about our escape ruse, my almost-kisses, as I imagined his lips crashing into mine like his tempestuous sea.

He closed the distance between us. Stiff with nerves, I closed my eyes and braced for the crash of his lips against mine, but instead there was a loud clanging from the kitchen that startled us and we jerked apart. The string of curses coming from the old cook was muffled by running water and banging from restacking tipped over pots.

A flush darkened his cheeks, matching the one burning my own. I cleared my throat, hoping to choke my blush down.

To diffuse the tension, I looked at my nearly full plate. "Because of you, I've barely touched my food. Now I'm going to be late for training."

"I'm sorry. I didn't realize *the Commander* was so important to you. I'll never let it happen again."

"Good, because I definitely don't need the distraction from my studies."

His laugh rumbled deep in his chest. "I couldn't bear to stand in the way of such an academic."

A giggle slipped as I reached for my glass of tea. "Really though, I do need to be leaving."

"Want to meet in the spot later?" Blaze asked, lowering his voice.

"I do have a new goal to add to our operation," my eyes simmered as I remembered the Commander informing us of Sephara's death, the accusatory stare he aimed at me, the guilt weighing on my heart. "But other than that, I don't have anything to report. It's only the first day."

"We could do things other than boring updates," Blaze suggested, his sultry look threatening to bring back my blush.

He leaned closer, laying his hand atop mine and eyeing my lips. Somewhere deep inside, I wanted to join him, but bubbling on the surface was my awkward, inexperienced, too-worried-of-embarrassing-myself side which swarmed and smothered everything else.

"Oh, um, I'm not sure. Who knows what mental and physical state I'll be in after my lesson. How about tomorrow?"

"Fine." Blaze sighed. "I guess that's okay."

"It has to be." I stuffed my reddening cheeks with glazed pork.

"Your allure is hard to resist when you talk to me like that."

I mocked a laugh between bites.

The rest of our meal was filled with lips smacking on food and words. Conversation with Blaze rolled easily like talking with an old friend. We reminisced. My memories flowed readily and I lost all sense of time and space in them. I told him about Cassandry and Eithan's heated banter, Liam and Bill's cheesy jokes, Mom's stern but caring nature. Blaze listened as he finished his meal, tossing in a snarky comment here and there that earned him a playful shove.

An irritated throat clearing brought me back. I turned to find Bron looming in the doorway, arms crossed over his broad chest.

"Forget something?" he asked me, eyebrow raised.

"Oh, crap." I rushed to pick up my dishes and stacked them on the kitchen window. "I'm not that late, am I?"

"He figured you'd try to skip out, so he sent me to fetch you."

"Is he waiting there for me?"

"No, he's been in his office. He sent me ahead to get you down there and ready so he didn't have to sit around waiting."

"Lucky he has you at his beck and call," I commented under my breath as I reached the doorway.

I ignored his scowl as I bid Blaze goodnight.

Bron set a brisk pace even though his limp was not fully recovered. I stretched my legs beyond their gait to keep up. When I reached his side, I grabbed ahold of his elbow, urging him to stop. Unyielding, he shook me off. Heat rolled off his umber skin unbarred, making my forehead bead with sweat.

I had never seen Bron this mad before. He was literally fuming. What had I said to warrant this level of hatred? He was the one that betrayed me. He was the one that dragged me out to those mountains and conspired behind my back. He had said he did all that to protect me. I didn't know in what world bringing someone to the Portemor Mountains constituted as protecting them. Regardless, we needed to make amends. In order for my ruse to work, we had to.

"Hey, slow down." I tugged on his arm.

He brushed me off. "We don't have time to talk."

"You said he's not even down there yet. We can spare a minute." When he didn't stop, I pressed on, "We clearly have our differences in opinion and I don't expect us to ever see eye to eye on things, but I have changed my outlook on how I'm handling things."

Guilt stung my heart at throwing my guise over Bron. No matter what lay between us, when I looked into his eyes, I still saw the friend I strolled through the field with, the one I shared laughs and blueberry muffins with. But I had to convince everyone of my façade if it was going to work.

"After everything that happened in the mountains, I've decided to give up on trying to get out," I said. "You were right, I was just delaying the inevitable and putting everyone in danger for no reason. I want to do what's right. I want to train and use my ability for good."

Bron stopped and scowled at me, probably searching for the sincerity in my words.

"Really? Just like that? After all your tough words, you're going to give up?"

"Blood on your hands is a powerful motivator," I said.

"You better not be playing at something. It would be a horrible disgrace to use Sephara's sacrifice like this."

"I plan to avenge her, not use her." Which actually wasn't a lie. "Bron, I need your support and friendship. Can we just forget everything from the other night and move on? Be friends again?"

That wasn't a lie either.

He scrutinized me, muscled arms folded taut across his chest.

After what felt like an age, a small smile cracked his stone features. "Of course, Anora. I'm always here for you."

I beamed up at him and went in for a hug, but stopped myself. I remembered a heated embrace, a hand beneath my chin lifting my lips towards another's. The spark between Bron and I . . . was it still there for him?

My hesitation did not go unnoticed. His arms were outstretched, but when I held back, he shifted uncomfortably on his feet. His arms fell to his sides.

Trying to redeem our moment, I said, "I'm so glad we're friends again."

A sad smile crept on his face that didn't reach his eyes. "Me too."

I nodded, a heavy silence blanketing us as we continued down the hall.

Even with fatigue racking me after the afternoon's training, Commander Devlend made me sustain a column of swirling wind all evening. Whip-like gusts vortexed through the room, and their harsh gale left my ears ringing. At some point, several tornadoes tore through the space at once. Thankfully, the bench and plexiglass shields were bolted into the ground, so there was no danger of hurtling missiles around the room.

I collapsed to the floor with a *thud*. It was cool on my sweaty cheek. My pulse beat wildly against the stone, stealing the refreshing chill with every *thump*. My chest heaved and my limbs trembled, battered from the latest assault.

Dusk had nearly settled. Millions of stars winked through the skylight. The moon had yet to make an appearance, but I could tell the Mother was sending another sinister omen from the crimson shine gleaming off the leaves.

Halfway up the cement walls, lamps lined the arena, leaving the space lit but dim. Light sprayed up the wall, illuminating the flames the Guardian Phoenix rose from. The longer I stared at it, the more the bird seemed to circle me—prone prey ready to be snatched. Too quickly, I sat up and vertigo leaped up my body.

"You have a lot of energy to burn off," the Commander said, his words echoing through the cavernous arena. "It's both a burden and a good sign of your potential."

"Do you think I'm done? Can I start training without risking blowing up the place?"

"We'll see tomorrow. You'll still be fatigued, which will help temper it. As long as you keep using it daily, it shouldn't pose an issue of building up again. Now we can work on control, how to lessen and build it of your own will."

"Great, I'm heading to bed—I mean if that's alright, sir." I winced.

"Yes, that's fine." He smirked. "I must say, I admire your attempt at being G.I. It has to be a difficult adjustment considering how . . . uncooperative you have been."

He narrowed his eyes, inspecting me for any flaw in my newfound devotion. In the dim light, I hoped he couldn't see my face burn up under his examination.

"It is, sir. I'm trying to catch on as fast as I can to make up for my past behavior."

"Hmm . . ." The Commander trailed. "That's a tall order. I hope you're up for it."

With a clipped farewell, he retired for the evening. In the low light, the high cement walls were like a prison; the front door suspended a story above bore down mockingly. I scurried out of the room before it could lock me in.

Chapter Twenty-Seven

W

ith the sun unbarred by clouds, the following day's training session was slightly more bearable. Gwen went outside to play with her fawn. Keldric slid onto the wooden bench beside Blaze. Ander and Bron were stretching in the farthest training square.

The Commander burst into the arena and called out, "You have run of the room today, Guardian Trenton. I am taking Miss Baelin outside to release what remains of her energy stores. Come meet us in half an hour; I'll be in brief need of your service." Then he turned to Blaze. "Mr. Vasterio, join us."

Without a second glance, Commander Devlend made his way toward the door. Taking a moment to comprehend his orders, Blaze hopped up from the bench and hurried toward me. Catching the door just before it swung shut, we caught up to the Commander before the stairwell entrance.

"Sir," Blaze said warily, "may I ask why I need to join you outside? Am I training with the other recruits today?"

"No, I want you to observe Miss Baelin since you haven't had much exposure to Element Complectors yet. Note her strengths and weaknesses, just as you've been doing with the others."

"Yes, sir," Blaze responded as we stepped out into the bright afternoon.

Squinting against the onslaught of the sun, I spotted Gwen in the middle of the field. The little deer was walking circles around her. The fawn switched from walking to trotting, its gangly legs stumbling with the sudden transition. With each falter, Gwen reached out to catch the deer from falling, petting its neck before continuing the exercise.

The Commander sighed and stomped over to her. Unsure what to do, Blaze and I trailed behind him.

"Miss Astreya, what are you doing?"

Her pale face lit up bright red. "Hi, sir. I was just practicing controlling the fawn's muscle movements like you said."

"I can see that," he smarted. "And how will making a creat *trot* help in battle?"

"I thought this would be a good way to start—"

Commander Devlend cut her off. "It is a waste of your time to practice mental commands that you will never apply in combat."

"I'm sorry, sir, what do you suggest?"

"Suffocate it."

The whites of her eyes showed her surprise and horror. "Excuse me?"

"Suffocate the animal. Not until the point of death, of course, as it can still be a useful tool."

"Sir, I'm not sure I can do that," Gwendaliese admitted.

"That's why you train, Miss Astreya, so you can master these techniques for battle." He explained as if addressing a child.

"No, sir. I mean I won't do it. Pippa is an innocent creature. I won't put her through that much pain."

A vein raised in the Commander's temple. "What did you call it?"

Blaze and I took a few tentative steps back, exchanging a glance. Poor Gwen, she had no idea what she'd just started.

"Pippa. That's what I named her." Gwen's face lit up as she turned to adore the fawn.

"You named it?" he yelled. "This is a tool—not a pet! You're here to learn how to hunt and kill creats. Not make furry friends! There is no room for this kind of weakness in the Guard!"

Gwen cowered, inching closer toward the fawn, whose head hung low, ears bent back in fear. "No, sir! Of course not. But I won't treat an animal like I would a creat."

"You need to in order to learn. Kill this empathy now before it seeds and gets you, and others, hurt on the battlefield." The Commander clenched his fists.

"I don't have empathy for creats, sir. Only for harmless animals."

"So what would you call the mercy you showed the metallic vulture, hmm?"

She stumbled over her words, eyes darting between me and Blaze. "I—uh—that was different."

"How, in any way, was that different? You wanted to end its pain because you *pitied* it!" The back of his neck grew deep red.

I gave Gwen a pitying look, wishing I could help her somehow. He'd never yelled at me so ferociously. Why was he getting so worked up over this? Gwen was talking herself into a hole, but at least she was trying. She was dedicated to the Guard. The Commander had to know that. When I gave blatant disregard to training, he never so much as raised his voice . . .

"It was dying of severe, unhealable wounds," Gwen said. "It was different, and I promise I'll never show mercy towards a creat on the battlefield. I'll prove it to you, sir, somehow."

"And how do you intend to do that?" Commander Devlend asked. "If you cannot practice strategic mental commands on a lesser animal, how do you expect to be able to do it on a creat?"

"I'll figure it out. I swear!"

"You will get over this, Miss Astreya. You must."

Gwen's face paled as she looked up at him, nodding slowly. He stormed away.

"Sorry, Gwen," I whispered.

Her only reply was a soft sniffling as she turned to nuzzle the fawn.

We followed Commander Devlend to the edge of the fence. When he turned to speak, I anticipated his rage to be directed at me. But his skin had returned to its natural pallor, his face forced into an even calm, poised.

"Miss Baelin." The more he talked, the more relaxed he became. "I have not given up on this mystery power you insist on hiding from me. Now that you are more amenable to training, I intend to unleash it."

"Commander, I insist I'm not hiding anything."

"I insist that you are. For what reason, I'm not sure. Regardless, I will find out what it is."

He instructed me to stand in the middle of the field and ushered Blaze to stand back against the fence alongside him, giving me a wide berth. Glancing over my shoulder, I checked that Gwen and her fawn were a safe distance away.

While dread came over my weak muscles, anticipating the demands to come, the small pool of replenished power in my chest churned with excitement. Grounding my heels into the grass, I readied myself for the command.

"Combine your water and wind into a hurricane," he ordered, cupping his hand around his mouth.

That was an advanced move, one that required immense control to not only grasp but weave both elements together. I didn't move. Partly because I didn't want to do it, but also because I didn't know how to begin.

"Is he insane?" I mumbled to myself.

"Visualize it in your mind," Commander Devlend instructed. "See the elements move together and it will happen. In nature they have an affinity for each other, so they won't protest your commands."

"Easy for you to say," I grumbled under my breath, but I did as he said.

In my mind's eye, I saw finite beads of water dance in a synchronous sway, entwining with the wisps of wind filling the atmosphere. When I reached out with my ability, casting my net, I could sense them doing the same. The previous day, I'd grabbed an individual element with one of my powers and parsed it from the other in order to use it. Since water and air naturally harmonized and weaved together, I didn't have that obstacle. Instead, the challenge was managing both of my abilities together, synchronized. When I cast a broad net of energy, lassoing both elements, it was too much to handle and I lost my influence. Water began swirling together to form a cloud while the air picked up in a gale that blew the cloud away.

I reined them back in and tried again and again until I could control what each element was doing simultaneously. I visualized directing the entire air mass as a whole, not as individual elements, and it worked. I rotated it with a fluid sweep of my hands. Slowly, it began to mount into a whirlwind.

I drew in more water vapor from the surrounding air, concentrating enough so that visible liquid spun alongside the wind. Gritting my teeth against the strain, my arms shook with exhaustion from holding so much together. My nearly-depleted energy stores were draining quickly. My whirlwind spun around lazily, not reaching the force of a true hurricane. My power strained to push through, trying to feed it more and build it up to its full size, but there was too much to hold together. The water I forced into the gale began seeping out as mist, laying a dense fog over the field. My tempest dissipated with it and I struggled to grasp it again.

"Quite mediocre, Miss Baelin," the Commander jabbed as he and Blaze approached.

My eyes glazed over and I snapped back between breaths, "Sorry I couldn't put on a better show, your Highness—I mean—Commander."

"I knew your charm wouldn't last." He smirked. "Get

ready for your next training session. We'll be starting shortly."

I glared at him. Why was he so insistent? Clearly, I had no secret hidden ability. He needed to give this up before I literally died of exhaustion.

"There's nothing left in me to train *with*, sir."

"Then I suppose you'll take your combat training lying down?" he asked.

"Combat training?" My brow furrowed with confusion. "What do you mean?"

Movement caught the corner of my eye and Bron, limping slightly, approach us through the fading mist.

"Right on time, Guardian Trenton. You may proceed with combat training."

"Combat training? I thought we weren't starting that for a couple months?"

The Commander sauntered over to him and whispered in his ear. A frown carved into Bron's face.

With a clap on the back, the Commander urged Bron forward, but he didn't move.

"Sir, isn't there another way?" Bron pleaded.

"This way seemed to work perfectly last time." The Commander motioned for him to proceed. "We'll begin after a minute's rest."

Bron shouldered passed Blaze and grabbed my arm, wasting no time ushering me towards the fence. When we were out of ear shot, he breathed, "Show your hidden powers. Now."

"I don't have any."

"You have to." He searched my eyes for any signs of the secret ability.

"I swear, I don't." I shook my head.

Bron sighed. "Then know that I'm sorry for this."

My heart, just starting to ease after my exertion, picked back up again. Sorry for what? What was he about to do? I was too exhausted to interpret his warning, but I'd learned to expect the worst, and I knew enough in my tired mind to be afraid.

Bron left my side and approached the Commander. "She needs a few more minutes, sir. To catch her breath at least."

"Only a minute."

I leaned against the wire fence. The diamond pattern imprinted on my back and the bubble iridescently shimmered in the corner of my eye. My hands shook either with fatigue or nerves or both. My vision shuddered and fuzzed. At my side, Blaze leaned against the fence. He had fear in his eyes but didn't acknowledge it with words.

"Help," I whispered.

With a frown, he nodded and shoved off the fence.

Passably playing as nonchalant, Blaze moseyed along the fence. His fingers caught on the links as he passed, sending a burst of pink in his wake. Using his hand as a visor, he squinted up at the security camera trained on the field.

"I'm not sure we've discussed the outdoor security system yet, Commander. Is it as old as the indoor one?"

"Yes." He strolled towards Blaze. "It was installed when the Compound was remodeled over twenty years ago by Premier Zeckli. He was the only Premier to really understand the importance of the Guard, and he donated the indoor and outdoor surveillance system. Unfortunately, the new Premier doesn't share his values and has yet to donate an updated system."

Blaze feigned astonishment. "I'm surprised it's still running."

"It's an antique compared to the constantly evolving Celepherian tech." He sighed. "Thankfully, I've been able to keep it running. I'll show you how to repair the outdoor system in your next lesson."

Before Blaze could strike up a conversation again, the Commander spun around to face me. Long shadows cast in the hollows of his eyes as he eyed me like an assassin would their target.

"It's time . . . for combat," he added as an afterthought, which didn't help to settle the unease building in my stomach.

Eyelids heavy, I hefted myself off of the fence onto wobbly legs. I managed to take a few steps before a wave of dizziness caused me to collapse to the ground. Bron rushed over and hoisted me up in his arms.

"She's too exhausted," Bron said. "She can't handle this."

"All the more reason to do it now," Commander Devlend said.

Their voices faded in and out as I tried to focus, but all I could think of was drifting off into a rejuvenating sleep. I closed my eyes and nuzzled into the crook of Bron's elbow. He cradled me tighter to his chest. His skin was so soothingly warm. For the first time in a while, I felt sort of safe. Protected.

"I can't do it," Bron said.

"You must," the Commander insisted.

"I—" Bron began, but Commander Devlend cut him off.

"That's a direct order, Guardian Trenton."

Bron let out a long breath that tousled the hair along my forehead.

"Please, forgive me," he whispered.

Just as I was about to open my eyes and ask why he needed my forgiveness, a searing pain jarred my arm.

The fierce burn seared through the jumpsuit and scorched my skin. Fabric and flesh charred. There was shouting off in the distance, or maybe a scream; I couldn't tell over the crackle and sizzle of skin burning and the shriek of singeing pain.

Deep in my chest, I felt a pop, like a ball bursting its shell after being squeezed too hard. A wave of power, bold and strong, surged in my chest and down my arms. I unfurled my palms, hoping it could stop the pain. The blast of energy knocked Bron off his feet and we went tumbling.

Falling onto my ruined arm, an excruciatingly sharp stab reared alongside the burning sting. Overwhelmed with pain, I slowly rolled onto my uninjured side, the rocky ground begging to pierce my skin. My weary, tear-filled eyes were unable to see or comprehend the chaos. I let go of my consciousness and slipped into a peaceful darkness.

Chapter Twenty-Eight

An icy touch dragged me out of a dense slumber.

Brivania held a cold cloth to my forehead. My pulse was so strong it beat against the hand she pressed to my cheek.

I lay on the springboard that somehow passed as a suitable mattress. A deep orange glow cast across the foot of the bed and onto the door from the setting sun. I stretched, and pain streaked down my left arm. I whimpered.

"Don't go doing that now. You're gonna open it up again." Brivania tsked as she inspected my bandages.

"What happened?"

"You got burned, then got cut open with your rocks, and now you have an infection."

My rocks? What was that supposed to mean?.

Once she was satisfied I didn't damage my arm further, she dunked the cloth into an ice water bucket, wrung it loosely, and patted my cheeks with the swollen fabric.

Biting cold water ran down my neck and pooled in the knot of hair at my nape.

"You've been in and out for two days," she said.

"I vaguely remember, but I mostly remember the pain." I turned my arm to view the bandage.

Gauze wrapped around my upper arm, a yellowish discharge soiling them. My wound throbbed against it, constantly sending sparks of pain up and down my arm. It was bearable enough for me to call to mind what happened.

So-called combat training with a so-called friend.

"Where's Bron?" I failed to temper my rage.

"He'll be along soon. He comes by every day, a few times a day." Brivania flashed me a knowing smirk. "He fancies you."

"You know he's the one who did this to me, right?" I pointed to my ruined arm. "And this isn't the first time, either."

"Oh, he's just following orders." Brivania tossed the cloth back in the icy bucket. "Don't be too hard on him."

"That's not an excuse."

I stewed in silence and began mentally preparing what I would say to my *friend* while Brivania packed her gauze and ointments in her satchel. Before leaving, she lifted me into a seated position, situating the pillow so the iron rods of the backboard wouldn't cut into my back.

This could've been me, in another life. A better life. One where I spent the day distributing medicine and replacing bandages, then went home with a whole chicken roast because we could finally afford it. One spent helping people, not worrying about if my supposed friends would give me third-degree burns or not.

Brivania left a steaming bowl of beef stew and bread on a stool beside the bed, then gave me a quick peck on the top of my head.

An hour after scarfing down my dinner, I was nodding off into sleep when a knock on the door echoed. In an attempt to liven myself, I shook my head and called out for my guest to enter. I was geared up to see Bron, but Blaze's head popped in the room instead.

A soft smile warmed my cheeks. "Oh, hey. I wasn't expecting it to be you."

"Sorry to disappoint," he said as he slipped into the room.

He took the tray of now empty dishes off of the stool and sat in its place.

He reached for my hand, then hesitated and drew back. "You must be in so much pain."

I wiggled my fingers at him. "Not enough to ward off hand-holding."

With a grin, he gently took my hand in his. "Once I heard you were awake, I rushed right over. I had to see for myself that you were alright." His eyes grew dark. "What he did . . . what happened. It was awful."

"Yes, I've been meaning to tell my *friend* just how much I value his trust and honesty."

"I'm not sure when you'll be able to. You may be out of commission for a few more days."

"But Brivania told me he's been stopping by."

"Yeah, when you were unconscious. Now that you're awake, he knows the moment he walks in you're going to tear him apart."

"He's not wrong."

"He deserves it, the coward."

"He was supposed to be my friend."

Blaze squeezed my hand. "At least the Commander won't try any more experiments on you."

"What do you mean *experiments*?"

"It worked. The whole burning-you-thing worked, just like before."

What did he mean, it *worked*? Confusion clearly spread on my face, so Blaze asked, "Brivania didn't say how you cut your arm?"

I leaned my head back. "She mentioned a rock, I think."

"And you didn't question why all of a sudden there were a bunch of rocks in the grassy Compound field?"

"I was a little preoccupied, you know, with the excruciating pain."

"When you were burned, your hidden power—the one the Commander kept talking about—was released."

"Oh, please." I scoffed.

"It's true," Blaze said. "You have a third element: earth. You tore up the dirt and tilled up a bunch of rocks; you sent some flying, too."

"But that's not possible," I said. "No Element Complector has more than two affinities."

"An Element Complector has never been documented as having more than two, but that doesn't mean it's impossible."

"There could be a million different explanations for what happened."

Blaze crossed his arms and sat back with a daring smirk. "Like what? Give me one other logical explanation."

I mulled, trying to scrape up anything that might make

some sense. Anything that would mean the Commander hadn't been right.

"An earthquake!"

Blaze laughed. "It's not like the whole ground shook, Anora. Sure, you're powerful, but not *that* powerful."

I scowled at him. "I won't believe it until I see it myself."

"You won't have to wait too long. I'm sure the Commander will have you back at it as soon as possible. You should've seen how excited he was after you threw pebbles in our faces. He was grinning ear to ear; I've never seen him happier."

"My pain seems to give him pleasure for some strange reason." Wanting to change the subject, I asked, "How's Gwen?"

Blaze was quiet for a few long seconds. A frown settled his features.

"What? What happened?" I asked, nerves lacing my words. It must be something bad, but how bad? There seemed to be no limitations on how horrible the Commander could be.

"We need to meet in the spot. I need to catch you up on things—in private," he mumbled as he inspected the walls.

Joining him, I didn't notice any hidden cameras. "Blaze, this is my private room. Surely there are no cameras in here . . . he's not *that* messed up."

"Not cameras. Bugs. Little microphones that are so small you'd never notice them and can pick up sound in a small room like this."

I looked around the room in disgust. There really were no boundaries the Commander wasn't willing to cross.

"I'm not sure when I'll be able to get there. Maybe tomorrow night."

Scooting onto the edge of the bed, Blaze leaned in close. His bright teal eyes took up my field of vision, my whole world. My heart thumped in my chest. Anticipation fluttering in my stomach numbed the sharp stabs of pain in my arm.

His hot breath brushed my lips. "I'll meet you at dusk, in our spot."

Tenderly, his lips brushed mine. The instant they touched, a spark rocketed up my spine. I thought his lips would be rough and worn, but they were soft and light. A new sensation fluttered low in my stomach. It unfurled inside me, like the fanning of the softest painter's brush. My toes curled into the bed sheet. I leaned forward to deepen our kiss but twisted my injured arm instead. Jerking back, I cried out and looked down at my wound. Fresh pus oozed out, dampening the bandage a yellow-green color.

"Oh no! I'm sorry." He slid back, worried eyes scanning over the bandage.

"It's not your fault, don't worry about it," I assured, fixing a smile on my face.

"That looks more like a wince than a smile." He frowned.

"It *does* hurt, so this is the best you're gonna get."

"You should rest. It's getting late."

With a quick kiss on the forehead, he wished me good-night and slipped out the door as smoothly as he entered.

Sleep escaped me as I daydreamed of shared laughs and secret kisses with a boy whose eyes rivaled the effervescent sea.

Chapter Twenty-Nine

❧❦❧

The next day, I indulged Brivania's doting care. She came by four times, bringing trays heaping with various arrays of fresh fruits, vegetables, and baked chicken seasoned with garlic and onion. She cleaned my wound and applied a combination of ointments before bandaging it back up. With a fresh bucket of ice water, she cooled my fever with a plush cloth, dousing my neck and forehead. I leaned into her touch, bittersweet memories of my mother coming to mind.

Secretly wanting her to stay longer, I asked her to tell me about the Eterni Peninsula as she packed up her satchel and gathered the dirty dishes. Her eyes glittered as she recalled her favorite memories of dancing in the foamy spray of the tide under a red moon, quietly chanting to the Mother for guidance and protection. She told me of the time she spent sailing the waves between the mainland and her family's island in the Archipelago of Pardici as they collected supplies and fished. After dinner, I frowned as she bid me goodnight, an unfortunate reminder that she wouldn't be back until tomorrow.

The sun was setting, my signal to start getting ready. I rushed to the dresser to change into a pair of dark blue sweatpants and a black shirt. I wrapped my hair into a bun and slunk to the door, only socks on my feet.

With an ear to the biting cold metal door, I held my breath and listened for any movement in the hall. Once I was convinced the coast was clear, I eased the door open to avoid any squeaky hinges. I inched down the hall, clinging to the wall, and descended the stairs. Sneaking in the shadows, I made my way down the main corridor that would take me to our hideaway. The solitary beam of light spread out across the floor from the dining hall was my only company. A light giggle and a hearty laugh trickled out with the light, most likely Gwen and Keldric flirting. I smiled at the sound—nothing that bad must have happened if she was still capable of laughter. Though, I supposed I was still able to laugh too.

I crept down the hall and slipped into our hideout before any curious eyes could catch me.

An ever-present haze of dust filled the air and I sneezed on my first breath. The light from the lone light bulb reflected off each particle, spotlighting them in their lazy dance. I weaved through the maze of rusted filing cabinets and records until I reached the back wall. Underneath the grime-encrusted window sat Blaze.

He smiled, eyes sparkling even in the dim light. "Good evening, lovely."

I gave him an incredulous look as I looked down at my baggy clothes and pus-soaked bandage. "Who are you talking to?"

"Why, you, of course!" He took my hand, coaxing me to sit.

"I think you need to get your eyes checked."

"Well, it *is* pretty dark in here."

I swatted at his arm and his soft laugh sent my stomach aflutter.

"I heard Gwen in the dining hall with Keldric," I said.

Blaze shook his head. "I hope he's helping her through everything. It can't be easy."

"So what happened?"

Blaze's tone became somber. "He tried to make her hurt the deer again. This time, he told her to make it lay down on a bed of jagged rocks. She refused, and they argued back and forth. He got angry like before, but this time she didn't back down, she got mad right back at him. He lost it and he . . . he slapped her."

My mouth swung open so quickly that my jaw popped. The image of innocent, sweet Gwen being hit by that cretin made my eyes shudder. How could he do such an awful thing? Even for the Commander and all his torturous training practices, this was farther than I ever thought he'd go.

"That's not all," Blaze warned. "After that, she ran back to the Compound and the deer followed her. The Commander held out his hand and she collapsed, writhing in pain. The deer ran around in wild circles—it was chaos. He let go of her, but she lay motionless on the ground. She could barely walk, so I helped her get to her room."

"That's what he did to me!" I exclaimed as I remembered the suffocating, life-draining feeling that washed over me when the Commander took my power away. "I should go talk to her."

"No! You might blow our cover. We're supposed to be on board with this now, remember?"

"Yeah, but she needs a friend right now."

"She has Keldric. From what I've gathered, you're still in the Commander's good graces. He suspects you truly didn't know you had a third affinity and that what was done was the only way to release it."

"I didn't know it was there, but that definitely wasn't the best way to go about releasing it."

"You have to pretend that you do, Anora, or else this all falls apart. He needs to believe you're truly dedicated. How else will you get to train and build your strength enough for us to bust out of here?"

"About that." I cast my eyes downward and slumped my shoulders. "I know what happened to Sephara is because the Commander took over my body, but I can't help but feel guilty and . . . and saying that I'm a reformed trainee now because of what happened—it just doesn't feel right. I feel like I'm disrespecting her memory." I stole Bron's words that rang too true.

Blaze scooted closer. "You feel that way because you're a good person. The Commander didn't even seem fazed by her death and the role he played in it. I think Sephara would know who's responsible and wouldn't want you to feel guilty or hold yourself back."

"You think so?"

Blaze laid his hand atop mine and squeezed it reassuringly. "Of course I do."

With his assurance, my heart felt a little lighter. "I'll get revenge. For Sephara, for Gwen, for me. He needs to know that what he's doing is cruel and completely unjustifiable. His abuse needs to come to an end."

"I'm totally on board with that, but I think it'll blow our cover."

"I'm not saying I'll do it *now*, but maybe after we escape, I can come back and do it—somehow." Changing the subject, I complimented, "That was sly asking about the cameras the other day."

"Why, thank you." His smile dazzled even in the low light. "It's good to know they're old and prone to breaking down; it won't be suspicious when I cut the power."

"Perfect. Now what about an escape route. Found anything?"

"For my last lesson, I got him to move on to the history of the building. So far, the most useful thing he's said is that it was built about seventy or so years ago solely for Guardian use, with some minor renovations and updates since."

"So no chance of a hidden tunnel or mine shaft?"

"As of now, no. But I'll keep digging through these files, wander around the complex. Maybe I'll stumble into something."

"We always have Plan B, even though it'll be difficult breaking into the basement and stealing a jeep."

Blaze nodded. "But with your powers, we should be able to pull it off."

"And free your sister. Any more updates?"

Blaze shifted uncomfortably and didn't respond. In the silence, I could sense the grief ebbing off him.

"I'm sorry. I shouldn't have brought it up."

"No," Blaze sighed. "It's okay. It's all a part of the plan. It's just . . . with my strengthening sight, I can watch her for longer amounts of time."

"You don't have to talk about it. It must be hard."

I couldn't imagine watching as my little brother, terri-fied and screaming, was locked in a blinding white room full of strangers and strapped to a table. Blaze never told me what the strangers did to his sister, but the dark parts of my mind could guess. He must feel so helpless. Maybe he blamed himself in part since he witnessed it but couldn't help her. We were doing something now, though. We were planning our escape. Our mission was to rescue her and we would succeed. Hope and faith blossomed in my chest, because without it, if I wasn't totally confident in us, then what was the point in even trying?

"It is, and I haven't learned anything new. Same white-washed room. Same people dressed in blue gowns. Same . . . everything else." He lowered his head. "The only thing I'm confident of is that she's not being kept here at the Compound."

I lifted his chin. "Don't worry, we'll find her."

With a sad smile, Blaze leaned into my touch. He yanked on the loose folds of my shirt, urging me to come closer. I slid close to him, nestling on his lap and curling against his chest. Our arms entwined, as if this were our natural state of being. The warm scent of cedar and citrus swarmed my senses as I breathed deeply from the crook of his neck. Thoughts of imprisonment and escape faded as my hands focused on how soft the skin at the small of his back was. I strummed my fingers along the trail of his spine.

Dusk turned to twilight as we curled into each other. The twinkling stars and bright blue moon were dull through the dirty window pane. We didn't speak, but there was no silence between us. His heartbeat pulsed in my ear, harmonizing with my own, drumming the beat of our shared desires and intentions. Any refrain waned, and the once distinct lines of our bodies became nebulous.

Blaze leaned against a filing cabinet, making it screech. It startled me, and he wrapped his arms around me tighter. His eyes gleamed in the moonlight, crystals of aquamarine burning through the night and lighting my way to him.

I tilted my head, lips parted, and kissed him softly, slowly. It was thorough, all-encompassing. He laid me down on the cool tile floor littered with forgotten papers. His tongue explored not only my mouth but my neck and collar bone. I ran my hands along his back, lifting his shirt to expose his smooth skin. He tugged on the collar of my shirt, exposing my scar. It peeked over my shoulder, the scar tissue glistening in the moonlight. He ran his finger over it gently.

"From my father's . . ." I couldn't finish, couldn't risk the flashbacks trampling this moment.

He softly kissed my scar and left a trail of them across my chest. I arched into him, his arms slipping around my back and pulling me closer. Then, Blaze's knee slipped out from under him and knocked down a nearby stack of papers. He fumbled to stop the cascade, but it was too late. Our small nook flooded with loose notes and withering scraps of paper, stirring up the scent of mildew and age. He flopped on the floor and accepted defeat.

A hushed giggle escaped my mouth, then grew into an uncontrollable snorting laugh. Blaze rolled onto his side, lips dancing with the threat of a laugh.

"What?" he asked.

I roared with laughter as the scene replayed in my head. Our roaring passion fizzled out by some old files.

His hand came to rest over my mouth and he shushed in my ear.

"You're gonna bring the whole Compound down here." He warned between stifled laughs of his own.

I tried to regain my composure, fighting back a huge grin by biting my lip. "Okay, okay. I'm good."

Blaze moved his hand from my mouth to my cheek, rubbing his thumb over my heated skin. Crystals of blue and green twinkled in his eyes. A trembling rush flooded my body, raising the hairs on my arms. Suddenly, what just happened didn't seem so funny anymore.

"What am I gonna do with you?" He brushed a few wisps of hair from my forehead.

The mood having been thoroughly swept away, Blaze helped me to stand.

We made poor work of picking up the toppled papers, merely kicking them into a pile in a corner of our nook. One paper amid the pile caught my eye.

There was a picture of a young girl's face. She had short, light brown hair sweeping her forehead. With a narrow jaw and slightly sunken cheeks, she looked like a pixie out of a fairytale. Across her eyes was a big, black bar. Turning into the moonlight, I read the few words on the page not blacked out:

CANDIDATE #006

AGE: 17

HEIGHT: 5'2"

WEIGHT: 135

COMPLECTION: MIND

REASON FOR SELECTION: Invaded Guardian Commander's mind, uncovered sensitive information.

Blaze snatched the paper out of my hand before I was finished.

"What's this?" Mild hysteria laced his words.

"I don't know. It was just lying in the pile."

I looked down and found others peeking through the mess at our feet. They all had similar, blacked-out profiles with different Guardian portraits in the top corners of each page.

Blaze didn't bother looking at those. He was too busy inspecting the first one.

"What do you think these are?" I gathered the few I could spot.

"The Guardians that disappeared." His voice cracked, eyes twinkling with tears in the moon's glow. He turned the page around, pointing to the pixie girl with blacked-out eyes. "That's my sister."

Chapter Thirty

O nly one more day of rest and pampering from Brivania and I was told to return to lessons. My muscles ached, but I dragged myself out of bed for the sake of my ruse. After our discovery the previous night, it was hard for Blaze and me to act natural at breakfast. Our usual flirtatious banter was overpowered by the daunting questions we couldn't ask. What were those Guardians selected for? Why were they chosen? Where did the Commander send them?

Even if there was no proof on those blacked-out pages, that was the only thing we were certain of—that the Commander was behind it.

Gwen was also unnaturally quiet as she pushed eggs around her plate, focused on whatever thoughts raced behind her eyes. Her giddy demeanor had been beaten into something more somber.

When the Commander entered the classroom that morning, I thought she would burst into tears at the sight of him, but she held her head high and kept her quivering hands clasped tight in her lap.

She was much stronger than I gave her credit for.

The Commander acknowledged my presence with a tight-lipped smile and a nod. I stared at him, dumbfounded. Was this him being cordial? It seemed so unnatural for him. As the reformed trainee, I should be happy he was smiling at me, right? I returned the gesture a few moments later.

His loathing was now projected onto Gwen, throwing her a disapproving glance every chance he could during the lecture. So badly I wished to encompass him in a hurricane when he crossed her stare. She held her chin up, but I could see her spirit crumbling behind her eyes and I had to dig my fingernails into my palms to stop myself from reaching over and grabbing her shaking hands. She should be proud of standing up to that monster. She needed to know that he deserved what was coming to him, but I couldn't with Blaze's voice in my head warning me not to risk our plan.

So instead, I turned to face Commander Devlend, hands folded neatly atop the desk.

I played my part well, asking questions and answering problems. My hand ached from scribbling notes and diagrams on the lesson packet. The Commander commended me whenever I participated and it pained my face to draw a grateful expression.

At ability training, he nearly skipped over, eager to explore my newfound affinity. It took all my willpower to hold back an eye-roll.

"Miss Baelin! I bet you've been restless locked up in your room these few days. Brivania told me you didn't seem aware of what exactly happened." His voice peaked with enthusiasm where normally he spoke with an imposing monotone.

"Blaze came to visit and told me what happened, sir. But it's still hard to imagine." My voice was wary, not used to seeing the Commander so elated.

"You possess a unique and unheard-of *third* affinity for earth. The raw power and possibilities that come with commanding three elements are astonishing and unfathomable."

I cleared my throat, choking on a sarcastic comment. "I can't wait to see what I can accomplish and what talents I can bring to my squad."

He clasped his hand on my shoulder, looking on with pride, and I flinched. My lips strained and forced a smile. Mother above, playing the eager recruit was going to be way harder than I thought. Swallowing my disgust at his touch, I gave him a quick nod and went to leave the training arena.

I stepped around the Commander and met Bron's eye as he entered the training hall. He halted in the doorway as if my eyes drew arrows and pinned him there. Fury rushed through me at the sight of the friend whose true loyalty lay with the cretin beside me. My first instinct with him had been right. His priority would always be this damned Guard, never me. He never deserved my second chances, my forgiveness.

The Guardian cowered slightly behind the half-opened door but quickly regained his composure. He stormed across the floor toward the twins and I bit the inside of my cheek to keep from shouting at him.

The Commander wrapped an arm around my shoulder.

"I know what he did was physically painful, but you must know now that it was necessary."

I opened my mouth to retort, but Blaze stepped into my line of vision with a pointed cough.

I had to play along.

"Yes, sir, of course," I muttered.

With a pat on the shoulder, he nudged me toward the door.

"Come along, Mr. Vasterio. Miss Astreya." He spat her name with such disgust.

A slight falter in Gwen's plastered composure revealed how badly his inflection stung. With as much ease as she could muster, she fell into our procession.

The moment the door opened to the Compound field, a solid force slammed into my chest and didn't relent, a crushing pressure threatening to snap my bones. I took a step back, Blaze catching me. My hands dropped to my knees and my breathing deepened as I tried to support the unseen load.

Blaze wrapped a supportive arm around my waist. "What's wrong?"

The Commander scrutinized me like a specimen. "Complectors—well the majority of us, Mr. Vasterio— constantly sense our complection. The atmosphere is light and pliable, so she most likely didn't register it since she's been so resistant to learning how to. Those who have an affinity for earth have quite a different relationship with their element. Earth is weighty, solid, and more stubborn when it comes to its manipulation. She isn't used to its presence and needs to adjust."

I clutched my chest as the onslaught of every stone in the vicinity slammed into me. Blaze and Gwen crutched my arms and carried me outside. Using the only skill I had, visualization, I closed my eyes and pictured pushing the weight out beyond my periphery. It offered slight relief, but I began to feel the first pulses of a headache in my temples.

Squinting against the bright, agonizing sun, I took in the Compound field. The once flat, grassy surface was tilled with gravel and rocks. Gwendaliese's deer roamed the outermost edge of the yard, skirting the fence as it grazed the untouched patches of grass. More woodland creatures were scurrying around the fawn, two speckled tan rabbits.

They set me down in the middle of the field and I curled into a tight ball in an attempt to block out the pressure.

"Take some time to relax, clear your mind," the Commander instructed. "Focus on the smallest pebbles littered in the field and push all the larger, heavier stones to the outskirts of your awareness."

I nodded and he left to work with Gwen.

My eyes shot to hers and I reined in my instinct to protect her and take the brunt of his wrath. Blaze nestled in beside me, rubbing my lower back. I closed my eyes, but just barely so I could watch Gwen and the Commander as they neared the animals. At the Commander's approach, the woodland animals' ears and heads drooped. They hurried over to Gwen, nuzzling her legs as they cowered behind her, keeping wary eyes on the tyrant before them.

From this distance, their words drifted away on the wind. Struggling to hear was short-lived as the Commander and Gwen raised their voices in unison.

"That's even worse than what you asked yesterday!

How do you expect me to comply if you keep making things more difficult?" Gwen's face was beet red with fury.

"I'm starting to think that you will *never* comply, Miss Astreya, and it's leading me to more desperate action."

"I would if you gave me reasonable tasks." Gwen crossed her arms.

"Do you think your tasks will be reasonable out in the field? When a creat has you pinned to the ground, how will being *reasonable* fare you?"

"That's a totally different scenario! These innocent animals are not looking to kill me. Give me real monsters to train with and I'll do whatever you ask."

"But you're not ready for them. Your abilities aren't strong enough and attempting to do so will only stall your progress." He tossed up his hands, exasperated.

"I will not convince these rabbits to maul each other. I just won't." Gwen stood her ground, staring down the Commander with a wrath I thought only I could muster.

"You have to do *something*, Miss Astreya." He almost sounded pleading. "Anything to show me that you will be cruel and unforgiving in the field. This is the only way that I know how."

"Let me at least show you with a real creat, sir. I did it in my evaluation. I think I could continue my training with them and not hinder my progress."

"Yes, you did." He then held up a finger. "But your evaluation was a test. Testing and training are two completely different things. It's not feasible to let a creat loose in the arena for hours on end while you try to manipulate it. What happens when you fail at a challenging move and it goes to attack you? What happens when you need a momentary rest? Will it sit on the sidelines and wait for you to be ready? You will not train with creats. It's these animals or nothing."

"Then I choose nothing." As the words slipped out of her mouth, her eyes widened at the realization of what she said, what it meant.

"My, my . . . I thought when Miss Baelin came to her senses I was done with difficult trainees, but I dare say you are worse! A feat I thought impossible." A resolve came to his features that made me uneasy. "Return to your room, Miss Astreya. We are done here."

The twinkle in her eyes betrayed her as she stomped across the rock-strewn field back to the Compound. Poor Gwen, what would this mean for her? I had refused to train and the Commander tossed me onto the Portemor Mountains and manipulated my powers with his own as if I was a plaything. Would he do the same to her?

On heavy feet, the Commander joined us, regaining his composure swiftly. Only with Gwen did he lose his temper so, and I puzzled over why as I continued my meditation.

Pressure from the little pebbles in the surrounding clearing felt like pinpricks on my chest. There were a countless number of rocks scattered in the field and I could feel every single one's presence like a needle taut on thread. The bigger rocks brought the most discomfort. Their full weight pressed on my ribs and it felt like they would snap at any moment. My focus was broad, trying to tame it all at once, so I tried to narrow my focus on the needlepoint of one small pebble. As I tried to grasp that single pinpoint, the other pebbles began to fade away, but the boulders continued to press in, making me uncomfortable, and I lost my focus. After trying and failing to focus, the crushing mass felt as though it was compressing, suffocating me.

Gasping and clawing for air, I struggled to get onto my feet. Blaze sprung up to help me stand. Commander Devlend came to my other side and together they carried me toward the Compound.

"The first day can be overwhelming," the Commander said.

Once inside the walls of the Compound, the weight pressing on my chest seceded. With a sigh of relief, I waved them both off as I filled my newly freed lungs.

After a few deep breaths, I asked, "Why don't they affect me in here?"

"Ah, excellent question." The Commander smirked. "The leading theory is that the distance, as well as the physical barrier of the thick concrete walls, helps to diminish them. We believe the sense is still there, but so faint that you can't really feel them as you do outside."

"But shouldn't she feel the stone in the walls?" Blaze postulated.

"Scientists theorize it has something to do with the manipulation done to the stone. Studies have shown that natural rock has a greater 'essence' compared to rock manipulated by man. But again, these are all only theories. Research on the biology and behavior of Guardians has only really gone into depth in the past few years. Before then, it was only personal records of Guardian and civilian observation that drove our understanding of how we function."

"Regardless if that's right or not, I'm happy to be inside and ready to rest," I said in time with the throb pulsing from my arm.

Outside, the pressure had masked the sting. Inside, the pain sliced through my arm as it came back to the forefront.

"I should go see Brivania about changing the bandage."

With the Commander's permission, we were excused. Blaze was allowed to escort me to the nurse's station but was told to immediately report back to observe the twins' training.

"I won't be there to tutor you though; I have a few transmissions to make. But I will be available this evening for your private ability training."

With that, the Commander strode briskly up the stairs.

Once I was sure he was gone, I turned to Blaze. "How are those lessons going?"

"The same, he asks me to see certain people and I do. The more I practice, the longer and clearer the image becomes. I've even been able to see people with just their name; I don't need to have physically met them in person anymore. Neither of us really understands *how* I do it, though, and that really bugs him. I think he looks at me like a puzzle to solve."

"Who does he ask you to see?"

"All different people. My family and friends. The other recruits' families—"

"Wait—what? You've seen my family?"

Blaze considered me before speaking, unsure and maybe afraid of my reaction. "Yes, I have. Only by his request."

How could he keep this from me? He knew how much my family meant to me. A surge of anger flooded me at first, at the thought of him being able to see my parents and Liam when I couldn't. Then I realized it wasn't anger; it was jealousy.

"Why haven't you told me you could do that?"

"I didn't know if it would make all of this harder—getting to see them but not able to hug or talk to them. But I can show you if you want."

"Uh, yeah!" I beamed and threw my arms around his shoulders, ignoring the slice of pain in my arm. "Before, I think it would've been torture seeing them, knowing I was trapped here." I lowered my voice to the softest whisper in his ear. "But now that we have our plan, I know for a fact I'll get to see them again."

His turquoise eyes sparkled as he pinned my chin between his fingers. "I'm glad I can do this for you. Bring you some happiness in this terrible place." He drew me closer, our lips a hair apart.

"You already have."

With those words floating between us, he kissed me with a crushing force. Thankfully, it wasn't unpleasant like the pressing force of the earth outside, and I easily centered my focus on his soft lips.

Chapter Thirty-One

Swaying leaves on the trees beyond the high wire fence surrounding the Compound began to change from dark green to deep reds and vibrant oranges, a refreshing contrast to the barren, gray Portemor Mountains in the distance. Fallen leaves filled the brisk wind with color and their crisp scent.

Night began to stretch its legs, kicking back the sun as it brought an autumn chill to the evening. Early darkness aided Blaze's and my secret meetings, providing ample time for trading new information about the Compound and how we could utilize it in our escape. We scoured loose files and wrenched open the rusted filing cabinets, searching for more information on the Guardians selected, like Blaze's sister. We found none. We wondered if the Commander was hand-selecting a team to be sent across the Portemor Mountains, and knowing they'd most likely die, it was best to erase their existence. But why would Livi be trapped in a white-washed room every time Blaze conjured her? There were more questions than answers scattered among the crumbling records. When we grew tired of scheming and accumulating more questions than we could handle, we tangled up together in the thin slit of moonlight that came through the storage room window.

In the privacy of our forgotten hideaway, Blaze conjured images of my family whenever I asked. When Mom prepared dinner, still setting out a plate and cup for me, I muffled my sobs in the crook of his arm. When Liam laughed with our stepfather as they smashed toy cars, I laughed along with them, remembering the ridiculous sound effects they both made as the cars slammed together. When Bill struggled to get up from the kitchen table, needing to lean on a cane to walk, my heart splintered for his pain, the struggle his injury bore on my family's survival, and the fact that I wasn't there to help.

Blaze shared images of his family. The woman he showed that first day rocking by the fireplace was his mother. She and his father would go out into the woods and gather firewood, not only for them, but for their entire village. He explained the system set in place among the clan families, that each family provided a specific resource or skill for the whole village. Money was not necessary in his village, as everyone gladly shared with one another. I smiled as I pictured a community not merely surviving like mine, but thriving by helping each other.

Often I thought of my family, and his, during training. Their faces drove me to learn how to control and manipulate all my affinities with precision. They were the reason we were breaking out of this Mother-forsaken Compound. They were my reason to keep going, to keep pushing myself.

In a few weeks, my revulsion to going outside and

feeling the compressing weight of a thousand boulders on my chest diminished to a dull throb pinning against my periphery, alongside my healing burn.

The infection and cut healed, but the burn was persistent, second degree by Brivania's judgment. The random stinging pain it emitted was less frequent as the days passed. Just like my interactions with Bron.

There were several attempts to approach him after training. At first, rage fueled my steps, but with time, my anger extinguished. It was something about him, about those sweet moments we'd shared. We had grown close in those first few weeks, jogging together, teasing each other, and sharing stories of our past, both fun and haunting. I couldn't explain it. I didn't understand it. I should be furious with him and cast him out of my life once and for all. Every time I saw his glowing ember eyes though, I didn't think of all the betrayals, all the hurt. I thought of those moments, those embers between us that somehow kept burning after everything that happened.

Well, they still burned for me, at least.

Even as my fury fizzled, he continued to avoid me. He would slip away with a pathetic excuse about helping the twins study or running an errand for the Commander. After he claimed cleaning the training arena floor was more important than our conversation, I resolved on letting it go. Letting him go.

The support and guidance Bron once gave me was transferred to Gwen. At first, I was jealous, but I knew Gwen needed Bron as much as I had in the beginning. The sweet and perky girl had become fragile and lost. Her amber eyes were glossy during lessons, the Commander making good use of the silent treatment whenever she spoke up. She was no longer permitted in the training arena and every day was sent to her room like a grounded child. Bron and Keldric were there to encourage her, her only reason for trying.

To me, the Fexrund twins were as miserable as ever. With my avid participation in ability training and being personally trained by the Commander, they saw me as competition. At every turn, they tried to make their energy blasts bigger and more intense than my storms or to outrun me during warm-ups. They consistently failed at both, fueling their fury further.

At meals, Keldric was preoccupied with Gwen, but Ander was always up for torturing me. From across the table, he would glare and mumble comments between spoonfuls of soup about how I was a 'kiss-ass' and a fake. At first, I was nervous that he may be catching on to our plan, but Blaze reassured me that there was no way he could know.

After two months of hard training, I was able to manipulate wind and rain into gusting hurricanes that threatened to lift Commander Devlend off his feet. I developed finer, more elaborate techniques, like directing water to form spears that sailed across the room and using wind to suspend small objects in midair. The Commander would beam at me with pride, paying me compliments every day. What brought him the most joy, though, was my third affinity. I was able to lift and hurl pebbles and stones the size of apples across the Compound field.

He referred to me as his gem. He spoke openly about the articles he had written to Celepheria University about me and my three affinities; how well I could manipulate them. This in particular drove Ander mad, turning in class to blatantly glare at me. I would always smirk back at him, making him clamp his lips into a thin line.

Gwen was affected by my praise as well. Instead of filling with anger, she was despondent, almost envious, but I didn't rub it in her face. I could see the way she longed for Commander Devlend to gift her an ounce of my adoration in her glassy eyes. Why someone would seek the approval of such a cretin I would never understand, but I sympathized all the same. So badly I wanted to pull her into Blaze's and my plan, tell her the truth behind my actions and reveal the Commander for the monster he really was, but then Blaze's voice buzzed in my ear to keep up the ruse. So I did.

Since I knew I would soon use my power on my own terms and for my own means, ability training became the highlight of my day rather than the bane of my existence. A thrill of anticipation sparked when I entered the arena or the Compound field to practice new techniques. The churn of energy roiling in my chest revved every time I stepped onto the field, clawing down my arms, impatient for release.

As I walked into the training arena on the chilliest day of autumn, I swaggered to the middle square where scant heat from the sun was magnified through the glass dome overhead. I gathered two swirling balls of water in my palms and tossed them lazily in the air, catching them without losing a drop.

Blaze smiled broadly from his usual bench seat and called out through the open door, "Quit showing off!"

With a wicked grin, I morphed my water into an obscene gesture, earning me a bellowing laugh from Blaze and furious pouts from the twins and Bron, who were stretching on the far side of the room. Gwen leaned against the concrete wall as still and quiet as possible, her usual tactic to avoid being dismissed by Commander Devlend. It never worked.

Just as the Commander waltzed through the large double doors, my water was already forming into a spearhead.

"Nice to see you practicing your spear throws, Miss Baelin. You may actually need them today."

"What's the challenge today? More moving targets?" I asked. Referring to the plastic dummies strapped to a carousel he produced through the large trap door in the floor where he hid all of the monsters for our evaluation.

"No, Miss Baelin, real targets. A real creat."

My heart stopped and my power surged. The water sloshing in my hand exploded into thousands of droplets and darts flew out in every direction. Blaze had the protection of the shielded bench, but everyone else had to duck and cover their faces against the onslaught. Several yelps rang through the cavernous room as water bullets battered their exposed skin. They would have small welts by the evening.

I was so caught up with training and scheming that I forgot what the Commander was truly capable of. Memories of my evaluation sprang up in still frame.

That odious hag cackling as it chased me.

Its thick, cracked nails raking down my arm, drawing my blood hot and sticky to the surface.

Foolishly, I'd let the monotony of the past two months blind me with a haze of hope and assurance. With his few words, my confidence crashed and my anxiety soared. I swiveled around the room, looking to see if he had let any creats out secretly for a surprise attack. When I spotted none, my runner's legs overpowered my common sense and sent me sprinting for the door.

The Commander caught me by the arm and reined me in, nearly tearing my shoulder out of its socket. "I thought we were past this, Miss Baelin. You've been doing so well."

I gritted my teeth. "Sorry, *sir*, old habits."

"Yes, and hopefully we'll break those once and for all." He furrowed his brow.

I reined in my fury, not wanting to let on to my true intentions, and remained silent.

Bron stepped forward. "Is it quarter-term evaluation already, sir?"

"Indeed it is!" the Commander replied with too much enthusiasm. "I will have the Fexrunds battle a creat in stock, but since Miss Baelin needs to be outside to utilize her earth affinity, we will all join her as she scouts her opponent."

My knees buckled; the Commander's firm grasp on my forearm kept me upright. The creatures locked up here were weak from lack of movement and near-starving conditions. Of course *I* would get sent out to find a wild beast that had reached its full strength scaling the steep mountain range.

I cleared my throat to shake the nerves from my voice. "I wouldn't want to inconvenience everyone. I don't mind using only water and wind on a creat you already have."

"Nonsense. I need to evaluate *all* of your affinities, and it will be good to get you all out in the field again," the Commander insisted.

Without turning to acknowledge her, he waved towards Gwen. "Since you have refused to continue your training, Miss Astreya, I perceive you as a liability in the field. You are prohibited from joining us."

"Am I allowed to take my evaluation?" Gwen stepped out of the shadows.

Spinning sharply on his heel, Commander Devlend weighed Gwen with his stare. "You may be a liability in this very room."

Gwen inched forward, the light streaming from the skylight sparkling off the blonde hair shielding her face. "Commander, sir, please give me a chance to show you what I can do—what I am capable of doing to creatures that deserve it."

With a tight cross of his arms, pulling his suit jacket tight across his shoulder blades, he considered Gwen standing before him. Then a wicked grin spread across his face.

"Okay, Miss Astreya, I'll give you one chance," he said. "One."

"Thank you, sir!" Gwen squealed with delight. For the first time in weeks, a genuine smile crinkled her golden eyes.

I bit my lip in worry, not so sure that was something worth celebrating. Not only for the fact that she would have a battle a creat after two months of no training, but I didn't trust the sneer on the Commander's face, either.

The Commander motioned for us to sit on the protected bench while the Fexrunds started their evaluation.

The twins stretched while we situated ourselves behind the plexiglass barrier. Keldric focused on his calf muscle, still weak from his injury on the scout. He stumbled back as the middle of the arena floor gave way and a cage, big enough to hold a jeep, rose from the holding area beneath. The boys separated, standing on either side of the solid steel cage. Once the pedestal stopped rising, its creaking gears done moaning, an odd skittering sound filled the arena. It was as if a thousand little feet were scampering inside the crate.

Terror shivered up my spine, leaving me as rigid as the bench.

Once the cage door inched open, a swarm of white filled the arena. Hundreds of small masses fluttered against each other, giving the illusion of a giant roiling cloud. Squinting, I could make out the individual bodies. A glossy, pearlescent ivory shell with leathery white wings flapping at the sides. Hundreds of them clustered together as their convoy lifted upwards toward the skylight, no attempt to attack the twins.

The boys took the advantage, raising their palms out towards each other. A thunderous bolt of energy snapped and sparked between them. Their beam had grown not just in girth but in intensity, as wide as a doorway. I shielded my eyes against the blinding blast of light. The tiny creats didn't seem to notice the raging, lethal beam beneath them as they rammed as one into the glass ceiling.

Ander yelled a play to his brother over the crackling of their power. "Whip!"

With a flick of their wrists, a thin spark of energy tore from the main beam. Like a whip, it unfurled towards the mass of fluttering creatures and snapped at the bottom of the hoard with a *crack*.

As one, the little monsters unleashed an ear-piercing squeal and scattered across the room. They zipped around the room, no two going in the same direction. In the disorientation, the twins cut off their beam and fell to their hands and knees.

With a *thonk*, one of the monsters crashed into the shield and I jolted back, banging my head against the cement wall. As I massaged the back of my head, I watched the creature sprawled on the ground regain its bearings.

On the ends of its membranous wings were claws of topaz, a vibrant blue glimmering like crystals in the sunlight. They incessantly scratched against the ground as the creature, wobbling back and forth on its bulbous shell, tried to steady itself. Where the gemstone fingertips touched, they left crystalline imprints in the cement that slowly spider webbed outward. Its scrawny legs, also adorned with the same nails, flailed uselessly. Its head was encapsulated within its shell, able to retract and jut out on a long, thin neck. Beady topaz eyes darted across the room as it struggled to get upright. Two gemstone-like teeth protruded from the sides of its mouth like pincers, snapping together to create icy sparks as it squealed.

A shiver ran up my spine at the sound. Thank the Mother for this barrier.

The Fexrund brothers had managed to crawl to one another, swatting at the onslaught of little monsters above them. One winged beast came down on Ander, gemstone talons prone, and sliced at his forearm. His Guardian suit was not penetrated, but along the trail of the cut, a sheet of ice spiraled and spread along his arm. Earnestly, he and his brother batted the cold away before it could spread past his elbow.

Huddled against the cage in the center of the arena, the boys yelled to each other, trying to strategize amid the chaos swarming them. With the frantic beasts still darting around the room, the twins got onto their feet. With swift fingers, the brothers held their palms out a foot from each other and shot out small beams of energy. Impeccably in sync, the twins brought their hands together and then swiftly flung outwards countless spears of energy. All around the room, the winged creatures plummeted to the ground, like pearls falling off a string. Dozens laid motionless on the ground, but the swarm above raged as if none were lost.

Bron mumbled furiously on the edge of his seat, elbows on knees and fingers steepled. Reading his lips, he was silently instructing his trainees to 'do the Blast.' Ander had explained that it was so powerful that if anyone was in the training room when they did it, they would die instantly. He would add, smugly, that it was a level of power Element Complectors could only dream of wielding.

I would roll my eyes. People like Ander, like Victon, were unavoidable, especially in the Guard. I was sure tons of Guardians thought they were superior for their abilities, or cunning, or speed, but at the end of the day, their blood would spill the same as anyone else's at the slash of a creat's claws.

Turning back to the battle, the twins were nearly lost behind the haze of the swarm. They swung their arms to bat them away only to return with icy scratches. One swooped behind Keldric and nipped at the bare skin of his neck with its crystalline pincers. His cry echoed above the cacophony.

As Keldric fell to the floor, gripping at his blue-blackened neck, Gwendaliese jumped off the bench and nearly broke through the barrier between them as she cried out his name. Ander dragged his brother into his lap, tenting him with his body. After examining his brother's neck, he lifted him into a seated position. With both hands on either side of Keldric's face, carefully avoiding the angular veins of sapphire crackling along his skin, Ander motivated his brother to stand and lift his hands.

Strain visible on his face, Keldric did what his brother asked and soon a blaze of pure energy blasted between them. The beasts fluttering about the room shrieked and skirted the arena's edge.

On Ander's command, the twins spread their arms wide, as if opening shutters to a window.

The arena went white.

With an ear-splitting *crack*, the brothers sent their energy cascading through the room. No corner was left untouched by their electrifying, raw power. I cowered against Blaze's shoulder and prayed to the Mother that the shield would hold.

An instant later, the heavy thud of all the winged creatures' bodies filled the room like hail smashing against a roof. Once the last beast fell, the ringing in my ears was the only sound.

The solid metal crate that had housed them was reduced to shrapnel and littered among the dead monsters. Their bodies had curled in death, making the floor look like it was cluttered with massive pearls that had been scorched a livid black. In the center of the room, Keldric leaned heavily on his brother, wincing as he touched his frostbitten neck.

Gwen rushed for the door and hurdled over the bodies to get to him. She helped Ander guide Keldric through the maze of corpses all while blubbering, pleading for him to be okay.

The rest of us met them on the outskirt of the battle-field, Bron beaming at his protégées.

"Did we pass, sir?" Ander asked the Commander.

"You will be given a full report in a few days. But in a general sense, yes, you passed."

"Thank you, Commander." Keldric's smile was laced with pain.

Up close, his neck was a gruesome shade of deep sapphire veined with black. The puncture holes from the pincers didn't leak blood, but rather streaks of blues and blacks.

Ander gave the Commander a curt nod. "Yes, thank you, sir. I was hoping the Blast would impress you."

"It certainly did."

Ander flashed a smug smirk in my direction. I scowled back. I couldn't care less about what the Commander found impressive, but the world didn't need Ander's cocky attitude growing any bigger. It was already smothering.

"You will have follow-up questions about that maneuver to address in an essay after your brother gets examined."

"With all due respect, sir. I'm feeling fine," Keldric said as he bit back the pain.

"Nonsense," Commander Devlend called his bluff. "Go to the nurse's station at once." "Yes, sir, but I'd like to watch Gwendaliese's evaluation and join the scout for Anora's."

After a short consideration, the Commander replied, "We will wait until tomorrow for Miss Baelin's evaluation so you can join. Ander wouldn't be useful alone if things turn bad in the field. But no, you cannot stay for Miss Astreya's. You need to be tended to immediately before it spreads further."

Defeated, Keldric sulked down the hall with his brother and sweetheart on either side.

Gwendaliese was too ecstatic for her evaluation to eat the pan-fried fish and potatoes Memette had prepared for lunch. I was baffled by her lack of concern for what the Commander might throw at his current most-hated student. The Commander would never cave that easily. Had Gwen forgotten all he had done to me? There was no sense in scaring her though, so I nodded along with encouraging words.

When we entered the arena again, her vivacity vanished as she beheld the cage selected for her. The solid steel crate towered before us, almost as tall as a maple tree skirting the clearing and nearly as wide as the span of its branches.

My knees buckled at the size of the crate—the size of the beast within. It had to be about as big as the monster from the scouting mission. For a moment, I praised the Mother above that it wasn't me facing it, but then I remembered I had to go out in the field for my evaluation. That one could be even bigger and more ferocious.

"You got this, Gwen. Show him what you're made of," I said, squeezing her shoulder.

With a faltering smile, she nodded and adjusted the cuffs of her jumpsuit to busy her shaking hands. With Blaze at my side, I hurried to the protected bench, eager to get as far from the crate as possible. Bron sat on the far side of the bench, leaning against the plexiglass and breathing heavily. Probably from having to clean up the last evaluation.

I paused at the door and Blaze bumped into me.

From behind him, Ander snarled, "What's the holdup, Baelin? Decide you want to fight this creat yourself?"

I scowled at him, then said to Blaze with a whisper, "I don't think I should sit by him."

"It's either him or Ander. Pick your poison."

I turned my scowl on him and he simply chuckled and held open the door. Scooting along the bench, I slumped beside Bron. He straightened, flush to the barrier wall to get as far away from me as possible.

I cuddled up to Blaze, encroaching as far as I could into his space before he muttered, "I'd rather not sit on Ander's lap, thanks."

With a scoff, I stopped pushing him and settled in. Bron's arm was so tense at my side that I went rigid as well, face forward but monitoring him in my periphery. The awkward tension between us was thick with unspoken words. Words I wished to speak but he refused, at all costs, to hear. He clearly wanted nothing to do with me. Why, I had no idea, considering *he* was the one who had burned me—literally. After everything, I thought I would be just as stubborn and angry as him, but I wasn't. Against my better judgment, he had wedged his way into my heart and there he remained.

I debated on respecting his wishes or taking the advantage and forcing him to talk to me. When he furrowed his brow over dark, smoldering eyes and let out a huff, my decision was made.

"What are you so broody for?" I asked. "If anyone should be, it's me."

I faced him, and he attempted not to notice by leaning forward to scrutinize the monstrous cage.

"Really? How long is this silent treatment going to last? *I* should be the one mad at *you.*"

With that he turned, his ember eyes burning. "You think I'm mad at you?"

My thoughts fumbled, all the lines I planned to say to him unraveling. Had I hallucinated it all?

"Um—yeah. Why else would you be avoiding me like a disease?"

He shook his head, the words quivering on his lips kept silent.

"How do you expect me to understand if you don't talk to me?"

"I'm ashamed." He turned away, folding his shoulders inward. "Of what I did."

"How could *you* ever be ashamed of following orders?"

"Every minute of every day I regret that I ever followed his orders. I'm sorry, Anora. I hope you can forgive me. Because having you mad at me . . ." His whisper was barely audible. "It's breaking me."

Blaze stiffened next to me, his hand coming to rest on my knee. Instinct was to lace my fingers atop his, but with Bron so close, his confession weighing on my heart, our almost-kisses coming to mind, I didn't.

"I'm not mad anymore," I said. "I haven't been mad for a while, to be honest. I'm not sure I can trust you, though."

"I should've never betrayed you, but there is a reason why I follow his orders."

"Spare me the loyal and respectful Guardian speech."

"No, not that." Bron lowered his voice so only I could hear. "We need to talk, in private, tonight."

Needed to talk about what? He seemed urgent and sincere, but was that my heart messing with me? This could be a trap. I couldn't let myself forget again that his priority was this program, not me.

"You have no reason to trust me, and I don't deserve a second chance, but please, Anora, you need to hear this." Bron pleaded. "I'll bring blueberry muffins if that persuades you."

I couldn't help but giggle. Mother, what had Bron done to me? I'd always been so stubborn, so hard-shelled. How had he managed to burrow his way into my heart? Maybe it was the promise of blueberry muffins.

"Sure," I agreed, just as the Commander swung open the training room doors. We came to attention, standing up in the tight space between the bench and the barrier wall.

Commander Devlend sauntered to the center of the arena, next to the caged creature he selected for Gwen, with a knowing smirk.

"Good luck," he said, then tapped a knuckle against the steel wall of the crate.

A guttural roar rattled the arena. The crate rocked on its platform. I slunk down onto the bench, knees wobbling, and prayed to the Mother that it wouldn't topple over and squash us. Gwen cowered along the curved wall of the arena, desperately trying to meld with the cement.

Once the Commander was securely locked inside our protective shield, he pressed a button on his little remote and the top of the cage began to open. A hunched back, with every jagged groove of its spine accentuated by a taut leathery hide, rammed against the doors, urging them to open faster. Crescent-shaped claws clenched the exposed lip of the crate. Serrated talons screeched against the steel.

All color drained from Gwen's face. Her golden eyes bulged as she inched along the wall on shaky legs. She was faring much better than I would be. If the barrier wasn't between us, I'd bolt down that hallway again. Even with the barrier, I was still shaking, my breaths coming in short bouts. Blaze squeezed my hand, as if that would make everything alright.

The monster's head craned through the opening doors, comparatively small to the massive shoulders still trapped inside. Its ridged scalp led straight into a broad snout. There were no eyes or sockets, just leathery skin that molded into a muzzle with abnormally large nostrils lined with thick folds. Hooked canines protruding past its lower jaw scraped against the crate ledge as its neck craned upward. As its head fully emerged, nonsensically enormous ears popped out from where the doors had held them down. They fanned out, coming to a point like bat ears. Long hairs stuck out of them so far that they visibly swayed when the beast shook its head.

At the sight, Gwen faltered in her steps, skidding her shoe. The beast's head swung around to face her head-on, ears twitching. As the creature waited for its massive body to be released, it sniffed in her direction. At her scent, it howled with renewed frenzy and rattled the crate so viciously that it finally threw open the doors.

In an instant, it was on the floor and on the move, claws scraping against the cement and snout to the ground as it tracked Gwen along the wall. In terror, she sprinted randomly around the room as silently as possible to throw off the creature. It seemed to have worked, and Gwen clung to the wall of the crate, holding her breath.

Hunched over, the beast's broad shoulders lent to gangly arms that curved outward, framing its body with a wide stance. Its scythe-like claws were retracted into its paws, no longer clicking against the floor. Its humped, spiny back dropped prematurely into small and slender hind legs.

Still as fallen snow, the beast stood along the wall where he'd lost Gwen's trail and waited. Her face turned a horrid shade of purple, her frame racked with tremors of fear. She looked at us with wide eyes as she slowly suffocated. She had to do something. The Commander definitely wouldn't. To offer her as much encouragement as I could, I emerged from the cocoon I'd formed behind Blaze, nodded to her, and gave a thumbs-up.

There was nothing 'thumbs-up' about this situation, but it seemed to work. Gwen closed her eyes and held her palms out toward the creature. After a moment, the beast shook its head and swatted as if a pest was buzzing about. She took the distraction as an opportunity to take a few deep breaths. The beast's ears twitched in her direction. She paused, holding her breath again, but it was too late.

The beast lumbered in her direction, head still shaking as it battled the intruder in its brain. Gwen crept along the crate and slipped around the corner. She must have imposed her will harder, for the beast arched onto its hind legs. Its curved spine unfurled as it roared, furiously scratching at its scalp with unsheathed claws to the point of drawing blood.

The monster stopped wrestling itself, seeming to have won the battle, and dropped back onto all fours, mangled gashes adorning its head. Burgundy blood ran along the ridges of its snout and dripped down its hooked canines.

Pure terror etched Gwen's porcelain features as she turned to us once again, not looking for support, but for salvation. Unable to hold back her fear, her knees wobbled as she took cautious steps farther down the crate wall. Her tremors caused her knee to bang against the crate as she tried to cut around the other edge.

Those bat-like ears perked. With claws still extended, the monster gauged the cement as it pursued the sound. Gwen broke into a sprint, not caring about the squeal of her boots as she raced for the exit.

As she dashed across the open arena, we were bound across time, two terrified girls running for their lives.

Rather than the doors swinging wide for her outstretched arms like they did for me, they slammed unforgivingly against her and she crumpled to the ground.

Forgetting who I was pretending to be, pure rage clipped my words as I shouted, *"You locked her in?!"*

Apparently, our protective barrier was not soundproof, because the beast whipped around to face me. With a howl, it barreled across the large arena, driving hooked nails deep into the floor.

I screamed and curled into a ball on the bench. Power surged to my fingertips and whirled the air around me into a defensive shell. *Oh Mother*, this was it. My end had finally come. Why did I ever trust this flimsy barrier to protect me? This monster was about to rip it off its hinges and devour me whole.

Bron sprang up from his seat and went to dash for the

door but couldn't get around my shield. He was yelling something, but I couldn't make sense of the words. My power was out of control and his shouts were muffled by my raging winds.

From across the creek, the serpent lunged.
The carnal desire for my blood reflected in its eyes.

I clammed my eyes shut, wailing as I awaited my gruesome death. My thoughts were consumed by those claws and teeth, begging to shred my skin and muscle to ribbons. It would rip me apart just as ruthlessly as it did its own scalp.

But just as I thought I would meet my fate, the monster squealed.

I opened my eyes.

The beast was so close I could see yellow mucus dripping down the folds of its nostrils, its breath fogging the plexiglass. It reared its head around. Stumbling back, it skidded on small hind legs and fell over as it dug into its scalp. Hooked talons gouged the leathery hide covering its skull. Shreds hung down its snout in ribbons.

Behind the creature was Gwen. Her legs were a bit wobbly, but determination set her brow rather than fear. Both palms were aimed at the beast writhing on the floor. The beast curled into itself. Its spine pulled the leathery skin so taut it threatened to rip on the protruding bone. After a few minutes of intense struggle, Gwen began to waver. Her eyelids were falling heavily and her outstretched arms swayed towards the floor.

As her hold faltered, the beast's convulsing calmed and it came onto all fours. Its gangly arms bowed heavily at the elbow with the weight of its enormous upper body.

Gwen stumbled backward but held her arms out for balance and to maintain her hold.

My air shield had dropped and Bron was able to make it past. He gripped the door handle but was stopped by Commander Devlend, and they began arguing in hushed tones.

Let him go, I prayed. Let him save her.

Gwen, frightened and exposed and exhausted, had just stopped this beast from barrelling full force into the barrier all by herself. She saved not just my life, but all of ours. And what did the Commander do? Sat prim and proper in his seat, enjoying the horror show. I hoped that just this once he wouldn't be such a monster and would let Bron go.

Having regained most of its control, the beast howled a cry of victory. Gwen collapsed, the full weight of her body slapping against the ground. As if it were a dinner bell, the beast turned on her.

"No!" I gasped, jumping up and putting my hands on the barrier.

I started banging on the wall, trying to draw the beast away from her. It went against every fiber of my being to be loud in the presence of a creat, but I had to be for Gwen. At least I had this barrier and my powers. She had nothing left.

The beast stopped and looked back. It seemed tempted to turn on me, but it sniffed deeply and decided the better meal was already out there.

I turned toward the door where Bron stood with his hand on the doorknob.

When his eyes met mine, Bron abandoned his argument with Commander Devlend and threw open the door.

The Commander remained seated, the fury emanating from his icy eyes betraying the neutral set of his features.

Bron sprinted across the arena and climbed up the monster's jagged spine right before it slashed at Gwen. At his touch, the beast cried out and whirled in a circle to shake him loose. Bron's masterfully honed body bucked in time with the beast so he never tumbled. He scaled its hunched back and saddled its neck, then clamped both of its ears with hands rendered from molten iron.

My eardrums split from its screeching cry. It swung its head around, but Bron moved with every jostle. When its claws came out to tear at him, he dodged each swipe so swiftly that the creature ended up gouging its own hunched back.

The stench of burning flesh wormed through the glass and I plugged my nose as I watched its leathery hide char black and flake off. Before burning through the tissue, Bron bent forward and wrapped his arms around its snout, muzzling it with shear strength. Whimpers hummed out of the beast's clenched maw as that too began to scorch and sizzle.

Overwhelming pain blinding whatever senses the creature had remaining, it swung its gangly arms around to no avail. After a few minutes of fruitless fighting, its legs gave out and the monster fell. Bron didn't let go until the beast's arm swung for the last time, landing with a thud on the floor. Once Bron confirmed it was no longer a threat with a few swift kicks to the head, he rushed to Gwendaliese, scooped her up in his cooled arms, and carried her towards the exit.

Blaze, his immaculately coiffed hair now unruly and pointing in all directions, wrenched me from my curled-up position on the bench and nearly dragged me into the open arena.

"Snap out of it. You're a brave recruit eager to defend Alberune, remember?"

"Like anyone will buy that now."

"Humor me."

I forced a neutral calm into my expression and gait, but my knees stiffened as we walked towards the creat. Everyone gathered around Bron, Gwen's tiny frame curled against his broad chest. Blaze nudged me, urging me to stand tall. I gave him a hopeless look. What was even the point anymore? It was obvious I wasn't the reformed trainee I had pretended to be after that. With a pointed glare of his own, he insisted. I stood straighter but couldn't stop my lower lip from trembling.

"What a pity. I was right." Commander Devlend sneered as he stepped forward to assess the unconscious girl.

My scowl burned a hole in his back. He was going to let her die. It didn't matter that these creats were caged, they were still lethal and bloodthirsty. He'd played with Gwen's life just to prove a point. I clenched my fist and opened my mouth. I wasn't going to let him get away with this. Before I could say anything, Blaze put his hand around my mouth.

"Don't, please," he whispered in my ear.

I shook him off but obliged. All the words I wanted to scream at the Commander bubbled in my mind. I would make sure I told him every single one someday.

"Bring her to her room." The Commander ordered Bron.

"But shouldn't Brivania check her over first?" Bron questioned through bared teeth.

The Commander cocked his head to the side at the challenge. "Did you see an attack that I didn't, Guardian Trenton? Because I don't remember the creat laying a finger on her throughout that *battle,* if you can even call it that."

"Claws," I spat.

He whipped around to face me. "What was that, Miss Baelin?"

"That *creat* doesn't have fingers. It has claws." I took a momentary pause and salvaged what was remaining of my dutiful trainee façade. "I mean to say that it should be taken into consideration that not one of them touched her. Especially when other trainees who passed their evaluations *did* sustain injuries."

Ander turned, nostrils flaring, when the Commander spoke. "I'll take that into consideration." His eyes bore into mine, as if trying to spot the truth in them. "I deem all of my *star pupil's* opinions invaluable."

I held his stare until he turned to leave the room. Just before unlocking the door, he smirked at me over his shoulder. "See you bright and early for your evaluation, Miss Baelin."

Those words threatened to break me. Every monster with blood dripping off their chin flashed through my mind. Which one of them would I face tomorrow? Would that be my blood filling their bellies?

He swept out of the room, the whispers of a snigger in the air.

Ander brought me out of my internal nightmare. "How

dare you insult my brother and me in front of the Commander like that!"

"Oh, it's not that big of a deal."

I went to turn from him, but he slapped my shoulder back, forcing me to face him. "For those of us here to honorably serve and not con our way out, it *is* a big deal."

I scoffed. *Excuse me?* I could barely tolerate Ander on a regular day. He pressed his luck with laying a hand on me.

"Simmer down, Ander," Bron said, glaring at his trainee. "No need to make this physical."

"Yeah, especially when you don't have your brother here to help you." A whirling ball of storm squatted in the palm of my hand and I held it up for Ander to see. Water thrashed in time with the whipping vortex of wind, a gray cloud of mist shrouding the chaos within.

"Don't make this any worse," Bron hissed over his shoulder.

With a breath, I blew out my little storm, sending water droplets flying into Ander's face. He cursed and wiped the water from his eyes.

Bron faced me. "What did I just say? That right there could get you reprimanded."

Ander surged toward me and Bron held him off, Gwen still nestled in his arms. "Stop it and walk away, both of you. I need to take Gwen to the infirmary."

With a final damning glare, we both went our separate ways.

Chapter Thirty-Two

The setting sun made the leaves twirling in the breeze bleed the brightest crimson against the dreary sky. I had come to the window for solace, but all it unveiled was the memory of blood sprayed across a creek bed. The whip-like scar scaling my back ached at the thought and I turned back into the dark bunkroom.

A small knock at the door made me tense and hold my breath. Once I heard Bron whisper through the crack of the door, I loosed a breath and opened it.

"Hey," he spoke in the softest whisper, an outside voice used so monsters lurking nearby couldn't hear.

"Come in." I opened the door wide.

He pulled a basket out from behind his back. The scent of blueberry muffins filled the room.

"She didn't have any left over, so I asked her to make some special—for you."

I blushed and snatched the biggest one in the bunch. The dough was warm and sticky with sugar on my lips. He set the basket down on my dresser, then sat down on the bed and gestured for me to join him.

"I'm not sure how much time I have," Bron said, still using an outside voice. "I have a meeting with the Commander soon, but there's something you need to know."

He looked around the room, as if checking to make sure no one was listening. "You're not the first non-conformer. In the past, the Commander would try to persuade the rebels into joining the Guard's cause. If they couldn't be convinced to patrol the border, they became training and teaching assistants. But a few years ago, the Commander became more closed off, less understanding, and those that didn't conform to the Guard's ways didn't become assistants, they just—disappeared."

My heart dropped and my throat dried. Blaze's sister, Livi, came to mind, that black bar burning across her eyes. All those files, all those trainees, tossed aside in a forgotten storage room. Had they all been non-conformers?

Bron continued, "When we asked where they went, the Commander acted like they never existed. A few Guardians really pressed him on it and they . . . they disappeared too. After that, we stopped asking and just accepted it. Now, we're all afraid to get on his bad side."

"That's what you tried to warn me about."

Bron nodded. "I didn't want to tell you all this. I thought it might fuel your rebellion even further and put you in even more danger of becoming the next one to disappear. But now that you're committed to the Guard, I wanted to let you know that *that's* why I followed his orders to burn you. That's why I've always followed his orders, whether I agreed with them or not. I never wanted to do any of those things, but I—I was scared. For you and myself, if the Commander thought I should be disposed of for not following orders. I'm sorry, Anora, for everything."

His head slumped, but he seemed relieved to lift the confession off his chest.

It all made so much sense now. His choices, his actions. I had thought it was all out of honor and duty. That the Guard was his first priority. As it turned out, he was looking out for me all along. He was protecting me from becoming the next Livi, the next missing and forgotten Guardian. Bron truly did care about me.

I placed a hand on his shoulder. "I forgive you. I really do, Bron. Mother knows why. I should hate you for what you've done." I laid a hand on his. "But I don't. I can't."

Bron squeezed my hand back, a bright smile bursting across his face. My heart raced and a blush heated my cheeks. But all I could think of was Blaze's hand caressing my cheek, then my neck, then lower . . . I took my hand away.

"It's probably because you brought me muffins," I teased. "But seriously, I'm glad to know—to understand why you did those terrible things. I . . ."

I debated whether to continue my lie or to share my own truth. I could tell him Blaze's and my plan, ask him if he could help. If I told him about Livi, would he say that he remembered her? Maybe he'd have clues about her disappearance. But then I thought about all of the burns, the betrayals, his deep-rooted fear of the Commander behind them all. Would he keep my secret and help me, or would he deliver me to the Commander on a platter? Would he always be the dutiful Guardian who didn't want to risk vanishing without a trace? Knowing my secret would put him at risk—and that would put me at risk.

I couldn't take the chance.

"You?" Bron trailed.

"I'm happy you confided in me." I flashed a big smile.

"Thank the Mother." Bron sighed. "I couldn't stand you being mad at me. It broke my . . ." He didn't finish, but he didn't have to.

He leaned in closer and reached for my hand again. His rough calluses felt foreign after having Blaze's smooth fingers trail my skin for so long. Our palms connected and I felt a wave, a pulse against his skin. Was that his power? My power washed down my arms to greet it. The sensation was overwhelming and felt more intimate than it should have been. Heat raced up my neck, filled my cheeks. My breath hitched in my throat as a pair of sparkling turquoise eyes battled with the dark, burning ember ones in front of me.

I slipped my hand out of his. "I think Blaze should be done with his lesson by now."

"Oh . . . Do you always see him after his lesson?"

I nodded slowly. He must have taken the hint, because he stood.

"Then I'll let you go. See you tomorrow for your evaluation."

"Right," I said, having almost forgotten after the impact of Bron's information. Of Bron himself.

I would have to face a creat all by myself the next day. In other words, I was probably going to die.

He gave a solitary nod before stepping out into the dark hallway, the bittersweet look in his eyes devoured by shadow.

I paced along the back wall, paper crunching underfoot, as I watched a blood-red moon rise above the chain-link fence.

When Blaze peeked around the corner, I threw my hands on my hips. "What took you so long?"

"Nothing." He stumbled over his words. "He wanted to go over a few extra things."

I brushed off his excuse. "We have to do it tonight."

"Do what?" He grabbed my arm to halt my nervous prowl.

"Our escape. It has to be tonight." I gripped his shoulders. "I can't go out there to fight one of those things tomorrow. I just can't!"

Guiding me to sit down, Blaze said in a soft tone, "Take a deep breath. Everything is going to be alright."

"Are you insane? Everything is *not* going to be alright." I started to hyperventilate. "I can't be on those mountains again."

My eyes whorled wildly around the room as my mind spiraled, thinking about all the possible terrors I would face. Not just the horrors with fangs, but the Commander too. What would he do to a non-conformer like me?

Soft hands caressed my cheeks, forcing me to look at the handsome boy in front of me. Intense teal eyes forced mine to focus. My racing mind settled on those sharp eyes; broken images of an ocean lapping and him laughing at my side washed out my fears.

As my breathing slowed, I said a little more calmly, "Blaze, I can't go tomorrow. I'll run away; it's the only thing I know. The guise I've been fronting will break, if it didn't already this afternoon. And Bron told me something —something about Guardians that disappear without a trace, like Livi. They're all non-conformers that the Commander doesn't want to deal with anymore. That's going to be me tomorrow after I blow my evaluation. We have to leave tonight!"

His knitted brow and frown were almost lost to the shadows blanketing his face. My eyes settled on his teeth gnawing on his bottom lip as I waited for a reply.

"Uh, hello? Any comments? Did you hear what I said about Livi?"

"Yes . . ." he drawled as he looked out the window to gather his thoughts. "It's an explanation, but it doesn't bring us closer to finding where she is. And about leaving tonight . . . I'm not sure I can get the security feed down and the fence unlocked in time. I haven't had any time to prepare."

"What do you need to do? You said before you found where to shut the power off."

"Well, yeah, but it's behind the locked basement door . . . and I still haven't found out if there's a backup generator. I'll have to remember to ask at my next lesson."

I threw my arms up, exasperated. "I told you, I think I can push that lock open with water after practicing on the bunkroom doors. And weren't you supposed to ask him about the generator last week?"

His brow downturned in defense. "I was busy asking him about the surrounding villages and roads. But sure, how about I just rattle off every one of our questions about this place? I'm sure *that* won't send any red flags."

I opened my mouth to argue but stopped. "You're right, I'm sorry. I'm just afraid of tomorrow."

"But you've been doing so well in training. You should have more confidence in yourself." Blaze squeezed my hand for encouragement then quickly pulled away.

Reaching out, I laced my fingers with his and tugged his hand back into my lap. "It doesn't matter how powerful I am. The flashbacks will always be there."

With a quavering sigh, he pulled his hand away and leaned back against a creaky filing cabinet.

"What's wrong?" I closed the distance he created between us, scooching up to his side.

"It's nothing." He tried to loosen his shoulders with a roll, but his form was still rigid. "I'm just worried about you."

With a sad smile, I looked at his moon-washed face, his sparkling eyes gazing gravely off in the distance. Entombed in our silence, my eyes glazed over as I stared at the bright red moon. Its chill seeped into my skin. This time, I didn't question that the Mother's omen was meant for me.

Chapter Thirty-Three

According to Bron, a creat was spotted descending the Portemor Mountains alongside the western coast, an hour's drive from the Compound. He ordered us to finish our breakfasts and congregate by the front gate while he brought the jeep around.

Concentrating on pushing my eggs around my still full plate, it took Blaze hefting me up from my chair to get me to leave the dining hall. He kept a firm arm hooked around my waist as he struggled to get me out of the Compound. My instinct was to resist, to run back to my room and hide under the bed and hope and pray that the monsters would go away. Too bad the worst of them lurked within these walls. The Commander would kill me before he let me get out of this evaluation. The façade of the reformed Guardian trainee was lost on an autumn breeze. Blaze, who always reminded me to play along, didn't bother this time.

A crisp fall chill bit at my cheeks and I took a deep breath. Overcast muddled the sky but drew out the vibrant reds and oranges of the surrounding leaves. The bright canopy was at war with the bleak gray sky, refusing to be dampened or shadowed. It waved to me in solidarity.

The recruits waited as instructed by the main gate of the Compound. Keldric looked lively in his Guardian jumpsuit, a slender strip of gauze around his neck. Gwendaliese was wound tightly around his torso to escape the chill, fully recovered from her fainting spell the previous day.

Gwen seemed okay on the outside, but she had to be scarred by yesterday on the inside. The Commander, the one man she had been desperate to impress, was ready to let her die, simply to prove a point. There was no forgetting such a horrible truth.

With a malicious smirk, Ander leaned against the fence, an iridescent pink halo formed around his body as he agitated the bubble. My stomach and mind were tied in knots, leaving me no energy to address his attitude.

The crunch of gravel underneath tires was the only signal of the jeep's approach as it rounded the hill. Bron drove with Commander Devlend seated beside him, suited in a Guardian uniform. There was a bench seat available behind them. The hatch of a small flatbed was lowered to seat an additional pair.

"Come now. We don't have all day," the Commander urged, waving us in.

The twins hopped onto the flatbed while Blaze, Gwen, and I squeezed into the back.

As Gwen nestled beside me, squished in the middle, the Commander tsked. "Miss Astreya, I thought you would've gleaned from yesterday that you are not to accompany us."

She stiffened, her golden eyes widening as they locked onto mine. I grabbed her hand, not only to keep her pinned in the seat but also to know that I was there for her. I had always been there for her, even when my ruse wouldn't let me.

"Step out of the vehicle, we're running late." He dismissed her like a Premier addressing a lowly housemaid.

"If she wants to come, I don't see the harm," I said.

"Well, then good thing it's not your decision to make, Miss Baelin." The Commander scowled over his shoulder.

Gwen's voice quivered. "Even though I failed to subdue the beast alone, I think my skill, effort, and audacity proved that I belong here, sir."

"Your skill?" He guffawed. "The only skill you possess, my dear, is putting on a spectacular imitation of that fawn you call a pet."

I gasped. Not only was he insulting, but he was wrong. So horribly wrong.

Gwen defended herself. "Considering I haven't been allowed to train for over two months, I thought I did admirably."

"You told me you didn't need to train with the weaker animals I offered. You swore you could handle the real thing. And just as I suspected, you couldn't. So no, Miss Astreya, I do not think your effort warrants my praise or approval. You are a liability." His face grew redder with each word, the temper rising in his voice with each syllable. "*Now get out!*"

Gwen jerked out of the vehicle, letting go of my hand. Tears welled in her eyes. Her delicate character, having hardened to show as much strength as her little frame could muster, fell apart under those final, damning words. All of her light had been sucked away.

"Oh, Gwen." I frowned.

After all she had done to try and get back into his good graces, this was how he treated her? Nothing would ever be enough to soothe that sting.

Keldric leaned over. "Gwendaliese, don't cry. It'll be okay."

Her only response was her soft cries reverberating against the soundproofed dome.

Commander Devlend was unfazed. "Let's get on with it, Guardian Trenton."

"Let me escort her inside, at least," Bron insisted.

"She knows her way. Drive."

Bron's hand was on the door handle, his thumb resting on the unlock button. Would he actually do it? Would he defy the Commanders orders, again? He was probably already on thin ice for disobeying during Gwen's evaluation.

As expected, he took his hand off the handle, clipped his seat belt, and put the vehicle in drive. I watched Gwen make the solemn trek down the hill as we drove down the gravel road.

Flicking past the window were the vibrant colors of autumn swaying from their canopies to the damp forest floor. Birds of browns, reds, and blues flitted from branch to branch, their tweets harmonizing naturally. Above the tree line, the Portemor Mountains towered, dark and oppressive and eager to swallow me whole. Charcoal rock jutted out like spikes and I could've sworn I saw blood dripping down them. Power surged in my chest. I shook my head of the image and coaxed my power back down before I sent the jeep sailing into the wind.

An idea ignited. I could tip the jeep over with a strong gust and never face that monster, then dash into the woods and escape. But just as quickly as the thought came, I realized I would likely leave us all injured and stranded in the woods where a creat was on the loose. Probably not the best idea.

We passed a wooden sign: *Kinfront - 20 mi.*

With a sigh, I hung my head and noticed my hands were shaking in my lap. I turned to Blaze for comfort. His arms were folded tightly across his chest, eyes trained out the window. He had been acting so different, so distant since yesterday. Was it really just that he was nervous for me? Or was it something more?

I slipped my hands under the crook of my arms and huddled against the cold door as we jostled along the dirt road at too fast a pace.

Chapter Thirty-Four

A small village close to the northern border, Kinfront resembled Bellwarn with houses scattered in the thickets and painted in natural hues of greens and browns. One home had a covered front porch and I imagined Liam running down the stairs to catch the school bus with me chasing after him.

How I wished I was looking out the school bus window instead, that life was simple again. Before, I had never felt safe. I thought every snap of a branch was a creat, every trip to the market was a death march. Little did I know how safe I truly was under that bolted up and shuttered roof with my family by my side. All those precautions I thought were not enough . . . I should've been thankful for what I had, for the safety and peace my life offered. Now that I'd been on the mountainside, been face to face with a creat in battle, I knew how much worse it could be.

Kinfront patrons made their way silently down the road towards the farmers' market. Some eyed us with suspicion, others with fear. As we ambled through their market, I gawked at what ingenuity crafted it.

Expertly constructed huts encompassed the tree trunks on the clearing edge. The walls were painted, carved, and bent to resemble actual bark. No seams were evident from the road, but I could tell that the small knots conveniently at waist height on every tree in the clearing were no random acts of nature. Having grown among similar trees, I could tell their girth was far too big, but to a monster, it would be another empty lot to pass by without a second glance.

How had we never heard of this? If Confinement laws weren't so strict, if communication wasn't so limited, maybe we would've. If I ever made it back to Bellwarn, I would tell my stepfather and his construction crew of the ingenious design.

Once we cleared the village, Bron radioed the nearest squad outpost asking for the latest whereabouts of the target. He took the next right turn on the bumpy dirt road.

"About ten minutes or so and we'll be there," Bron announced, sparing a quick glance back at me.

Energy plumed in my chest, racing down my arms, ready to be unleashed from my fingertips. I directed my focus at keeping my power in check rather than on the beast prowling in these woods. Progress in training these past months made my power grow—deepen as if it were stretching its legs after being crumpled for so long. It consumed me as we neared the coastline budding through the thinning trees. A bead of sweat rolled down my temple as I struggled to contain it pounding against my palms, begging to be set free.

Across a stunted expanse of the beach was the dull sparkle of a dark blue sea, like diamonds skittering along an undulating surf searching for the sparse sun peeking through the clouds. My shoulders sank at the sight, wishing I could've seen the dazzling, near-blinding glimmer of Blaze's ocean. Far off in the distance was the Interminable Storm. I had only ever seen the neverending storm in pictures, in lessons about why exploring ours seas was impossible. Seeing the dark, roiling clouds that never dissipated, never moved across the water, in person sent a shiver up my spine.

Bron stopped just before the front wheels sank into the mushy sand. Everyone hopped out of the jeep, except for me. The Commander swung open the door and gestured for me to step out.

I didn't.

The Commander pinched his nose. "I swear you recruits are trying to kill me."

My mouth twitched into a devilish grin.

He glanced at Bron across the vehicle's hood. "Guardian Trenton, escort Miss Baelin from the jeep since she is too stubborn to do it herself. I don't want to waste any more time."

Through the windshield, Bron's smoldering stare locked with mine and I held it with as feral and true of a fire in my own.

"I will not force her, not again."

My breath caught in my throat. Did I hear that right? Bron was defying the Commander . . . for me? That would put him in so much danger. Why would he risk it?

The Commander was about to bark at his Guardian

when Ander shouldered forward. "I don't have any problems doing that, sir."

Before I could duck out of his reach, Ander hooked under my arm and yanked me out of the jeep. Tripping over my own feet, I fell to the ground, twisting just in time to avoid cracking open my nose on the road. By the back collar of my jumpsuit, Ander lifted me up, the fabric cutting into my throat.

After a few coughs and beating off dust, icy blue eyes burned into me.

"Now what exactly happened to my *star pupil?* I thought she was eager to serve? Ready to atone for what she did to Guardian Jayce?"

Rage hazed my vision and I forgot about who I was pretending to be. How *dare* he put all the blame on me for Sephara? He'd brushed her off so easily, wiping the blood staining his hands onto mine. The Commander seemed to have a habit of brushing off the Guardians he found to be pests, but we were never meant to be pawns for his game.

It was about time Commander Devlend was reminded of that. My true mission washed over me like a balm, a shield. Energy thrummed in response, building up in my core to its greatest extent.

My nature was not to serve the Commander or his Guard, but to make my own choices and live my life the way I saw fit. My purpose was not to patrol an outpost, but to see to it that every Mother-gifted person was given a choice before being chained to one. My destiny was not to fight the monsters from beyond the Portemor Mountains, but the one standing before me.

"Oh, I planned to avenge Sephara." Venom laced my

words. "I just didn't realize I'd get the opportunity so soon."

A crushing wind burst from my hands and wrung the Commander. I lifted him off the ground, his writhing body only able to twitch under the immense pressure. I kept his arms and hands pinned to his sides so he couldn't use his power to snuff out mine. With a roar, I released the entire force of my power on his frail body. Through the wind, I felt a bone snap.

Either from my fierce loathing, the amount of power I unleashed, or a combination of both, I could sense not only the surrounding air but the air nestled inside the Commander's lungs. Just as the individual particles of atmosphere brushed against my power, so did the breath in his throat. With a small tendril of influence, I reached out, gripping that breath like a tether, and pulled. His face contorted and his cheeks sunk into his opened jaw, making his gaunt face even more skeletal.

There was muffled shouting far off in the distance, or was it the crashing waves of the ocean? I could only concentrate on making that evil thing in my clutches suffer. Fury narrowed my vision. My surroundings blurred behind my whirlwind.

Only a little bit longer and I'd let him go. Enough to avenge Sephara, Gwen, Livi, and the countless others that disappeared by his hand. I needed to avenge myself. Not who I was now, but the terrified girl who just wanted to be heard.

He needed to hurt as much as he'd hurt us.

Just as I felt him wane, the fight leaving his thrashing legs, I began to alleviate the pressure. Before I could let go completely, a searing burn raked my back. I dropped the

Commander, losing all of my focus as I fell to the ground. The scent of charred flesh singed my nose.

Overhead, I expected to see Bron's stone-hard face, but it was an electrifying white beam raging above my head—and descending.

I rolled out from beneath it. By the time I was on my feet, Bron had Ander in a headlock. A burning one from the sound of his screams. Ander swung his meaty fists back, breaking their energy beam. While they wrestled, I turned to find Keldric and Blaze both standing utterly still, shock gleaming in their wide eyes.

In the patchy grass on the side of the road, the Commander was on wobbly knees as he gasped for breath, one arm cradling his torso. Keldric rushed over to their fallen leader only to be swatted away. Bron released Ander, leaving behind harsh pink flesh on his neck and cheek.

Bron rushed over to inspect my back and winced. "That looks pretty bad. We need to go back for Brivania—"

"Oh no." Commander Devlend, having given up his stubborn pride, stood up with the twins supporting either arm. Even with his body still recovering, his words came out with as much bite as before. "That burn will be your punishment. Less than you truly deserve, you treacherous little thing."

"Why not just kill me now then?" I yelled, my power already having rebounded and racing through me.

"Unfortunately, Miss Baelin, you are more useful to me alive than dead."

"I told you it was all an act, sir," Ander sneered.

"Yes, and I'm sorry I let her third affinity blind me to it."

"There is no sense in you keeping me. I will *never* bend to your will. I will always keep fighting."

"We'll see about that," was all the Commander said through ragged breaths, a wicked smirk on his face.

As I opened my mouth to argue, a single, slight crack broke through the forest.

Bron and I were the only ones to whip our heads toward the tree line.

"What is it?" Blaze asked.

Bron and I both shushed him, and I waved for him to go behind the jeep. With an agitated grumble, he obliged.

The subtle shuffle of leaves and rustle of a bush wormed through the woods. Peering through the thin tree line, I spotted a ruffled shrub, its leaves quivering. There was no sign of what caused it and I slowly slid behind Bron as he scanned the forest. Off to the right, another crack of a splintering branch echoed and I snapped my head towards it. A dark shadow scurried across the forest floor, ducking behind the brush.

Across the creek, a creature lurked, slithering through the bushes.

My heart reared in my chest. The fresh burn across my back didn't so much as tingle as terror consumed me.

I retreated to the jeep. "Let's get out of here."

"We can't. The local squad has been called off on account of your evaluation. Even if we called them in now, they won't get here in time," Bron explained.

Ander shouldered forward, leaving Keldric to bear the Commander's weight. "We can handle it ourselves, Baelin. Go cower in the jeep and wait for us real Guardians to take care of it."

Did he honestly think that would get under my skin?

No need to ask me twice—I was sprinting for the jeep before he even finished the jab.

"Keldric," Bron ordered, "get my chain out of the back."

With a swift nod, Keldric lumbered towards the jeep, Commander Devlend a dead weight on his side. After aiding the Commander into the jeep, Keldric joined his twin standing beside Bron, passing the latter a thick-linked iron chain. Bron wrapped the chain around his forearm and began heating the iron against his skin.

Blaze jumped into the back seat next to me and locked the door. The Commander seethed from the front seat while I stewed in the back, my power swelling in my chest. Then, all at once, that raging power was doused from within. I clutched at my chest and gasped for air at the sudden loss.

"You will never make a fool of me again," the Commander said between ragged breaths.

Over his shoulder, I could see his hand upraised and shaking as he funneled every ounce of energy he had into suppressing my power. I slouched in my seat and labored to breathe. I looked to Blaze, silently pleading for him to do something, anything, to stop the Commander.

He remained seated, avoiding my gaze entirely.

What was wrong with him? Why wouldn't he help me? I wanted to shake him by the shoulders and ask what happened to the boy who was willing to take on the entire Guard so we could be free.

I turned to look out the window in an effort to distance myself from the monster in front of me and the coward beside me.

Through the glass, Bron's hurried commands were

muffled as he instructed his trainees to flank the woods. They took wide positions flush to the broadest trunks they could find. Standing in the center, Bron hollered to draw in what lurked beyond.

From the corner of my eye dashed a dark blur among the trees. I glimpsed the predatory flick of a reptilian tail before it sank behind the brush. Bron noticed as well and turned to face it, yelling again to lure it out into the open. Above a bush at the clearing edge, a set of slit yellow eyes narrowed on Bron. Raising his right arm, he warned his trainees to ready themselves for his signal.

When I looked back to the bushes, those reptilian eyes were gone and I scanned the brush line. My heart galloped in my chest and it felt odd to not have the thrum of my power revving alongside it.

The only sound was the pulse beating in my ears, until Bron brought down his fist in an arc and shouted, "*Now!*"

Just as the Fexrunds reached out towards one another and their energy beam fused between them, a giant creature darted out of the woods and got caught in the surge of raw power. The beast's round head stretched towards the sky on an elongated neck as it roared in pain. Protruding on either side of its neck was a transparent, fleshy orb with liquid sloshing around inside. Green scales, with patches of wiry, knotted growths that resembled moss, singed black under the blast. After the initial hit across its long torso, the beast fell onto all fours. Spindly limbs tipped with yellow claws dug into the soil, and it scurried back towards the cover of the woods.

The twins apparently hadn't cut off their beam fast enough, for Bron slid underneath to give chase to the beast. Just before the creat ducked into the shrubs, Bron grabbed the tip of its tail. Another guttural cry echoed across the beach as Bron's fire hot fingers dug into scaly, mossy flesh. The chain was still black, showing it wasn't ready as he struggled to wrangle the serpent.

The Fexrunds had called off their beam and helped Bron drag the beast back into the open. It dug its claws into the ground to slow the men down. As they hauled the beast, its maw spread wide. Rows of needle-thin, curved teeth were strung with saliva. My breath caught, thinking it was about to twist and bite their legs, but instead it retracted its head and neck as if it were about to retch. A bubble of water flowed out of its throat from that spherical reservoir embedded in its neck.

The water ball split into three, spiraled in the air, and encased their heads. The twins immediately dropped the monster's tail and stumbled backward onto the ground, swatting at the water drowning them. Bron kept his grip on the beast, holding still and tense. The water bubble steamed as the intense heat from his face slowly evaporated the water—too slowly.

Blaze finally shouted at the Commander. "Let her go! She needs to help them."

"You think *she* will help them? She would rather commit murder than face a creat."

"But they're going to die! At least give her a chance, give *them* a chance."

I was still under his hold and unable to speak, but in my mind, I was torn between crippling fear and blood-soaked guilt. Whenever I'd faced a creat, all I ever did was run away. What would make this time any different?

"Please, Commander. You can't let them die, too."

With a sigh, the Commander threatened, "If you try *anything*, it will be the last thing you do."

Instantly, power flooded my veins. It rushed through my chest and arms, rejuvenating me.

"Blaze." Terror clawed up my back, along my scar. "I can't go out there."

"You have to!"

The Commander only stewed in his seat.

I shook my head. Images of all the creatures that had terrorized my life flashed before my eyes. All of the death, destruction, and chaos they'd caused, that I'd witnessed firsthand. I saw my father's warm, beaming face become purple and blood-splattered. Those memories kept me cowering lower into my seat.

How was I supposed to defeat that monster if I couldn't destroy the ones in my own head?

Blaze grabbed my hands, holding them palms up. Water droplets I didn't realize I'd conjured whizzed around my fingertips, winding up and ready to spring into action.

"You can do this, Anora. Your ability is ready. All you need is the confidence to wield it."

Deep in his shimmering eyes was hope. My fear ramped up, but so did the tang of guilt. Unlike Sephara's death, all of their blood would dry on my hands and my hands alone.

When a blood-soaked memory sprang up, I replaced it with one from training. A hurricane thrown together with ease. Darts of water zinging around the arena. A memory of me—strong and powerful.

Out the window, the twins lay on the ground, the fight leaving their sluggish limbs. Bron stood tall as he struggled to evaporate the water enveloping him, his hands grappling with the serpent trying to escape. The iron wrapped around his arm was not yet red hot. The creature was too wide and long in the torso to bend back and bite him, but he still tried, and with every wrench of that scaly tail, Bron's grip slipped.

My heart sank at the sight. If anything happened to Bron . . . I would never forgive myself. Maybe I was walking to my death, but for once in life, I didn't care. I had to try to save them. I had to be strong—for Bron.

With a quivering hand, I opened the door and slid out. Hovering near the door, I held my palms up toward the chaos and prayed that Bron kept his hold.

My power brushed against the water bubbled around Bron's head, investigating what hold the creature had over the element. Where my hold on an element felt like millions of threads cast out to control each individual molecule, the creature's was like a coating encapsulating the mass as a whole. I poked at the shell with a minuscule funnel of wind, a drill of air to break it apart and free the water underneath. There was resistance, and from this distance, I could barely make out the tiny indent my wind pressed into it.

The monster halted its flailing to search the beach for what pressed against its hold on the water. Just as the beast locked its eyes on me, I popped the capsule. Quickly, I harnessed the water inside and forced it through the puncture. With no more water to wield, the creature's influence vanished and Bron was free. He gasped audibly, his chest expanding to the point of busting his ribcage.

Without any hesitation or moment of triumph, I tossed the ball of water down the beach with a sweep of my arms and moved on to the twins. Once they were both freed, they came onto hands and knees and heaved in the dirt, clutching their stomachs as their bodies tried to inhale fresh air and cough up the water in their lungs simultaneously.

Having lost whatever focus I had while strangling the Commander, I couldn't grasp the water in their throat and didn't want to risk bursting their lungs by forcing air down them. So, I retreated to the jeep and locked the door behind me. Once I was back in my seat, that curtain of suppression fell over me again. Honestly, I didn't care, because I'd done it! I had actually done it.

For the first time, a flashback hadn't overwhelmed my senses. For the first time, a hallucination hadn't taken hold of my mind.

For the first time, I hadn't run away.

Bron had recovered quickly and worked his way up the beast's tail, limiting its range of motion with every inch gained. He walked his hands slowly up the length of its tail, charred scales peeling away in his wake.

The serpent roared and squirmed, failing to bend back far enough to wrap its needle-lined jaw around his calf. Its hind leg batted blindly at his ankle. Razor-sharp talons easily tore through the tough fabric of Bron's uniform and he bit back the pain as blood gushed down his boot from the thin slashes peppering his skin.

Bron made it to the base of its tail. He wrapped his unadorned arm around it to anchor the beast and then unraveled his chain, finally glowing red, from around the other. As quick as a whip, he lashed the chain down the creature's spine, the last link whacking its skull. The creature wailed, its limbs giving out. With a thud, the beast collapsed, a plume of dust billowing around them.

Through the haze, I could see Bron wrap his chain, glowing like an ember, around one of its hind legs and pull tight. Ear-splitting squeals raked the sky. Frail and useless, the serpent's leg kicked to free itself of the burning chain. Bron's biceps bulged, teeth bared, as he pulled tighter on the chain. The mossy flesh sizzled where the chain cauterized, and the scent of charred flesh scalded the air. Eventually, the kicks slowed into twitches as the iron cut in deeper. With one final yank, the leg detached fully from its body and lay still in the patchy grass. The creature had stopped fighting; its head rolled to one side and its yellow eyes closed.

The twins had recovered from their coughing fits and sat in the sand, chests heaving, as they watched their trainer. He motioned for them to come near, and they both jumped up.

With the beast incapacitated, Bron took time to teach his wards, pointing and gesturing at various vulnerable areas on the serpent. A twitch of the beast's arm had Bron hastily finishing his lecture and instructing the twins to end it.

On either side of it, the Fexrunds angled their palms slightly downward between them. Their conjoined energy beam was set at a downward angle, creating a cone of churning, raw power that cut through the beast's neck.

When it was done, Bron jogged to the jeep, radioed the local squad that all was taken care of, and notified the Kinfront Clean-Up crew. Without a word, he turned on the vehicle, and we took off down the road we had come from.

I struggled to keep myself sitting upright as we jostled

down the road, my muscles refusing to cooperate while my powers were being smothered. I felt the charred flesh of my burn rub against the upholstery, but it still didn't hurt.

Bron looked down at the Commander's raised hand, then to me in the rearview. "Let her go."

"She tried to kill me. *Your Commander*. Or have you forgotten where your loyalties lie?"

There was a pregnant pause. Was he standing up for me again? What had gotten into him? He was putting a target on his back, between helping both Gwen and me— the Commander's two least favorite people. Bron was an outstanding squad leader, but that only gave him so much push back. Why would he risk it, after all the sacrifices he'd made to remain in Commander Devlend's good graces?

He met my eyes in the mirror. "No, I haven't," he declared.

My heart beat faster in my chest, caught on a thread of hope that maybe, perhaps, I could believe him.

Chapter Thirty-Five

P ulling into the Compound, Keldric didn't wait for the jeep to come to a complete stop before running inside to greet Gwendaliese. Once parked on the rear side of the building, Ander aided the Commander out of the jeep and guided him toward the Compound. Too fatigued to suppress my power and walk, the Commander released me. I was relieved when power swirled in my chest.

After Blaze and I stepped out, Bron went to park the jeep. He pressed a button on its roof and the cement slab at the back of the Compound slid open to reveal a narrow ramp leading into the pitch-black basement. My heart pounded harder knowing what was housed in that darkness. Shaking the thought away, I ambled to the door.

Before any of us could enter, Keldric came bursting out. Shaggy hair whipped across his thick brow and a look of shock was on his wide-set face.

"I can't find Gwen."

"We just got back, Kel. She could be anywhere," Ander said.

"She's not in her room and she's not in the dining hall. There's no other place she would be."

"Maybe she's visiting with Brivania," I suggested.

"We're going to the infirmary now. I'll see if she's there," Ander huffed as he shouldered the door open.

The Commander leaned heavily on him, grimacing.

"We'll take a peek in the other rooms on the first floor," I offered.

"I'll check upstairs again." Keldric's words clung to the wind as he sprinted back through the door.

I stayed back while Blaze held the door open for Ander and the Commander to limp through, the latter holding back a wince and cradling his side. They headed down the corridor for the nurse's station and I dragged Blaze to the right, toward the training arena.

"That was the worst ride ever." I threw a look over my shoulder. "I'm surprised I didn't pass out from him holding my powers for so long."

"Can you blame him? You tried to kill the man."

"I didn't *actually* try to kill him." I rolled my eyes. He couldn't be serious.

He gave me an incredulous look. "It sure looked like you were. You sucked the air from his lungs, Anora. You really didn't think that would kill him?"

"I—I wasn't going to do it for *that* long. I just needed him to understand how I feel, what he's put me through."

"It didn't look that way." Blaze shook his head. "I'm really surprised he didn't blow up on you more than he did."

"I think his injury stopped him from doing much more

than suppressing me." We reached the arena double doors and I shouldered one open. "He said I'm more useful alive than dead . . . I bet he's planning to make me disappear like the other recruits."

Our steps echoed in the vast space, the towering walls shadowed under the overcast weighing on the domed skylight. Dim light seeped through the windows on the front door suspended high on the wall, stretching down the expanse where a sweeping staircase should be. With no sign of Gwen hiding along the walls, I turned toward Blaze, realization dawning.

"Oh no, do you think he already took Gwen?" I asked, panic racing through my heart.

"Of course not," Blaze scoffed. "He was with us all afternoon."

"True . . ." I trailed off, scrutinizing Blaze. His response came across like he was *defending* the Commander, but that couldn't be right.

Blaze remained silent, distant, as his eyes scanned the room.

"I think I'm next. We have to escape tonight, there's no other option."

"Okay." His tone was dismissive.

"What's your deal? You've been distant and weird all day. You didn't even try to help me when the Commander first took my power. You left me there to struggle."

Blaze halted near the doorway, his body tense. Neglecting to face me, he answered with clipped words. "Nothing is wrong."

"You are *such* a bad liar." I let out an even breath to calm my voice. "Be honest with me."

With a sigh, he shifted just a fraction, the profile of his

face cast in shadow from the hallway lights shining in front of him. "I feel powerless to help you. What could I have *honestly* done to save you from him? I may have abilities, but they are useless compared to yours and everyone else's. I'm just an ordinary guy. I can't stand up to the Commander, or anyone. I can't protect you."

He hung his head and I frowned, hating to see him so defeated. Knowing that he had wanted to help me, but didn't know how, cleared the air and warmed my heart. I approached him on silent feet. I wrapped my arms around his waist and nuzzled my cheek against his back.

"Your support is a form of protection. One that rivals any complection in my eyes."

Hesitant hands slid over mine, interlacing our fingers and tugging me closer.

He spun around in my arms. "I'm sorry. For everything."

"It's not your fault," I said with a soft smile. "No need to apologize."

He cleared his throat and stepped out of our embrace. "You should go see Brivania."

"Oh, right." I nodded. "I almost forgot about my burn. It really doesn't hurt that bad at all, surprisingly."

"Pretty sure that's a sign of some serious damage."

"Hopefully she's moved the Commander to his room already."

"Oh, I bet that was his first demand. He would never deign to lay on an infirmary cot."

We chuckled and walked through the double doors together, letting them swing closed behind us.

Commander Devlend had been moved to his room and Brivania was still attending to him. Blaze left me waiting in the infirmary while he continued the search for Gwen. I wandered the nurse's station, perusing her various salves and medicines scattered across shelves lining the wall. Dozens of white bottles of varying sizes were stuffed onto the shelves haphazardly, and I stood on my tiptoes to read a label.

A glimpse at what my life might have been. Sorting pills. Applying ointments and bandages. How impossible that all seemed now.

Brivania bounded into the room. She bustled over to her desk, arms overflowing with bundles of bandages and vials. She hastily listed off all of the things she had to prepare for her latest patient, not sparing me a glance.

Startled by her burst into the infirmary, I had fallen off my tip-toes and knocked a few bottles from the ledge. I bent down to gather them before they rolled away, and my charred skin pulled taut, a ring of pain sparking across my lower back. I felt hot trickles of blood running down my back as I stood.

"Sorry to impose, Brivania. But it seems I've gotten myself burned—again."

Brivania dumped her supplies onto her desk and scurried over, twisting me around to analyze my burn.

"Oh, dear child, what happened to you?"

"The Fexrunds. How bad is it?"

"It's bad. You need a skin patch. Do you feel dizzy?"

Pulling me away from the shelves and into direct light, Brivania made quick work of cutting away the top portion of my jumpsuit. It felt like a heavy weight off my chest as I peeled it over my head.

"Not really, no."

"Hmm, must be that your powers are masking it." With a light touch, she cleaned the wound, covered it with a salve, and bandaged it.

"You must be used to this by now, my dear," Brivania said while securing the bandage.

"This one doesn't hurt as bad, thankfully."

"This is a severe burn. Nerve damage."

She handed me a bottle of antibiotics. "Make sure to drink your fluids and take these."

I took the bottle just as Bron stalked into the infirmary, shoulders bowed and bloodied footprints trailing behind him.

"You too?" Brivania didn't hide her exasperation as she tossed me an oversized shirt to slip on. "You all are running me ragged."

"It's just some minor cuts. No need to fuss," Bron huffed as he slouched on the end of a cot.

When Brivania bustled away, I whispered to Bron, "After today, I'm pretty sure the Commander is going to make me disappear."

Bron's ember eyes flared bright orange. He wrung his hands and tapped his foot, flicking blood onto the floor.

"I won't let that happen."

"What can you do to stop it?"

"I . . . I'll think of something."

"I have an escape plan in place. I think it will work."

Bron scrutinized me, doubt in his eyes.

"It's better than sitting around here." I tossed my hands up.

"Fair point. I can visit the Commander this evening and keep him occupied while you get out of here."

"Thank you." When I looked into his eyes, I felt those embers still burning. "I know things have been weird between us. But looking past all the conflict, all the differences we've had . . ." I stole his words. "I like the person I see."

"The person I've become." Bron mended, taking my hand in his. "Because of you."

That strange, intimate thrum of our powers coalescing sent a soothing warmth up my arm and into my chest, my heart. In that moment, our souls bonded, finally in tune. After all our misunderstandings and betrayals, we had come to an understanding and appreciation for each other.

I blinked away the tears welling in my eyes. "I should go."

With a sad smile, he wished me good luck and kissed my hand.

My heart fluttered at the brush of his warm lips against my skin. Then, the memory of Blaze and I tangled up came to my mind. I could only manage a weak smile in return.

I turned towards Brivania and wished her a good evening. She must have overheard us, because she crushed me in a hug and kissed my forehead. I imagined my own mother mirrored in her sentiment, bracing me with strength and courage.

With a final look back at Bron, I snuck down the hallway to find Blaze.

The mildew scent of molding paper was stirred up for the last time as we initiated our plan. We ran over all the steps again and decided to meet in the basement stairwell at dusk.

When we were done and I went to leave, about to weave through the maze of files and paper stacks I'd come to memorize one final time, Blaze tugged on my arm. Looking back, his somber eyes glimmered like aquamarine crystals in the dying sunlight. The scratch of his scruff against my forehead as he pulled me close triggered a smile. With his thumb under my chin, he lifted my gaze to meet his. In that moment that felt both like an instant and eternity, his breath melded with mine, my body molded into his.

"I love you, Anora. No matter what happens, remember that."

My heart thundered against my chest, beating in time with his own. "I love you too."

His mouth devoured my confession with a deep, urgent kiss. He clung to me as if this were our last embrace, pressed his lips against mine as if they would never meet again. My back pulled taut and pain seared the edges of my burn, but I ignored it as I leaned into him further, not able to get close enough.

He broke us apart, saying it was time to go, and led me through our maze and into the darkness beyond.

Chapter Thirty-Six

A t the base of the staircase we so frequently climbed, fear crept into my chest as I beheld the locked door. An iron door lined with thick bolts and no window or slot to peek through at what prowled behind it. A chill bloomed across my spine even though I was layered in a charcoal gray thermal and matching sweat-shirt. An image of a solid steel crate being lowered into the black depths below the arena flooded my mind and paralyzed my body.

Blaze fumbled to fit the key in the lock, hands shaking.

Trying to shake that burned image from behind my eyes, I whispered, "I still can't believe you were able to swipe that. At least we have a little luck."

Blaze nodded gravely, focusing on the lock as he slipped the key in and set the tumblers inside clinking.

Before he opened it, he turned to me with reassurance. "Whatever is down here—don't look at it. We need to find the jeep and get out of here."

"And you can shut down the security grid power, right?

We'll be able to get through the gate?"

"Yes. Once I find the breaker, it should shut down easily. There's no back-up generator."

"Okay, then we shouldn't waste any more time." I beckoned him forward with a jut of my chin.

Darkness bleaker than a starless night leaked from the doorway. The stench of rotting meat wafted with it. My white-knuckled hand dug into Blaze's shoulder while the other covered my nose.

The door grated open, allowing the darkness to drag us in. Every cautious step into its clutches was heavy, as if my shoes had become leaden, begging me to reconsider each step I took. With the waning light from the stairwell, I could see Blaze reach into the shadows, hands roving the walls in search of a light switch.

After what felt like hours, a click of a switch had the room lighting up. The space was the length of the entire Compound. Cement walls climbed high to meet a matching ceiling lined with dome lights. I followed the string of lights as each one turned on in succession down the length of the room. Once the last light flickered on, my gaze fell on what lined the walls.

Solid steel cages sat along the edge of the warehouse. They were varying sizes, the smallest the size of a refrigerator, the largest as big as a towering pine—that had to be the one housing the creat that Gwen had battled. Twin metal rails ran down the middle of the room, a new pair diverting in front of each crate to form a network of tracks that culminated at a wide platform. On the left, parked in the shadow of the last cage on the far wall, was the jeep and a rusted van. Opposite the staircase was the crest of the ramp leading out onto the lawn above.

The room was eerily silent, no shrieking from the dozen or so cages.

Terror froze me in the doorway, and subconsciously my power pulled water into my palm. A ball of water formed in the hand covering my face and swirled up my nose. I coughed and spat out the water. The boom of my hacking bounced off the cement walls and stirred the beasts lying in wait in their cells.

Guttural roars rumbled inside my chest and high-pitched shrieks rang in my ears. We both stumbled back by the unexpected onslaught. Meaty paws pounded against their prison walls. Claws squealed as they dug into steel.

Please keep them in their cages, I prayed to the Mother.

Blaze overcame the trance first and tugged on my arm, pulling me toward the vehicle. I followed blindly, ears bombarded with wailing and nose swamped with festering rot. As we neared the jeep, Blaze left my side to find the breaker and shut down the power to the security system.

With the jeep in front of me and no one around to hold me back and force me to stay, salvation was finally tangible. Tears welled in my eyes as I thought of those first days when I battled the hag, the Commander, everyone that said this was my destiny and to accept it blindly. *This* was my destiny, to escape and fight for others like me to have a chance to choose their own fate. A life we chose for ourselves, not one forced upon us.

All of those moments and emotions culminated as I seized the driver's side handle. As the growls and snarls seemed to fade, filing away with the rest of my nightmares, a vice grip locked around my collar and waist, pinning my hands firmly to my sides.

Chapter Thirty-Seven

With a curdling scream, I kicked the beast ensnaring me.

How did a creat get out? It must have knocked over its cage or busted open the doors. Either way, it grappled me, but I refused to die this close to freedom.

I thrashed my body to loosen its grip. It only got tighter. Swinging my head backward, I collided with a small protrusion with an audible *crunch*. The agonizing groan it let out was almost human—too human. My suspicions were confirmed by the stubby human hands cinched around my shoulder and wrist. Who was it? How did they get down here? It was just Blaze and me down here a second ago, or so I thought. Confused, but oddly relieved it wasn't an escaped monster, I called out for Blaze.

The person swiveled and revealed Blaze standing behind us.

"I'm sorry," Blaze said, his voice cracked with the threat of tears.

I shook my head in confusion. What was going on?

From behind the van, someone limped forward. Blue eyes cold as death bore into mine as the Commander emerged from the shadows, gripping a polished cherry wood cane.

My heart sank. No, no, no, this couldn't be happening. Freedom had been right there, within my grasp. Now it skittered away with the *click-click* of Commander Devlend's cane.

"What an unfortunate turn of events, Miss Baelin. I would've rather enjoyed having such a rare gem as my protégé." His voice was pitying.

"What's going on?"

"I thought you would have posed more of a challenge to subdue than Miss Astreya, but this was far easier than I anticipated."

"What did you do to her?!" I roared alongside the beasts pounding against their cages. I reared my head and squirmed, fighting for freedom.

"Why spoil the surprise?" he taunted with a devilish grin.

What kind of monster smiled thinking about all the torturous things in store for his former students? I'd rather die before I found out what it was.

I wriggled my unbound wrist and flashed my palm outward toward the Commander. With a flick of his wrist, all of my power was stolen. My mouth gaped. I slackened against my holder like a feeble fish left on a riverbank for far too long. My vision blurred. The dome lights above became fuzzy ovals of light in the darkness.

"You despise your gift, Miss Baelin, but look at how

much you've come to rely on it. Some would see that as weakness, but when I felt it earlier today, when I feel it now, I know what it truly means—strength. Yours is a power so fierce it rivals any that has passed through the Compound." He broke into a cough, weak and wheezy. "And I curse the Mother every day for bestowing that great power to *you*."

He smothered more of my energy, my life force, than he ever had before. The light was beginning to fade entirely as I grew weaker; only the growling of captive monsters was clear. Before I could slip away, a small pulse beat back into my chest, a tiny kernel returned. My breathing steadied, and my head and vision cleared, but my power remained slumbering in the pit of my chest.

"I am not through with you yet."

"What is it that you want? Why are you doing this?"

"You fooled me. I thought I broke you and could sculpt you into the most fearsome Element Complector in history. But it was all a ruse. You're still the selfish brat you came here as. You're a liability and a danger to all Guardians and civilians alike, and I refuse to condone it. I will not be responsible for letting a rogue complector out into the world to wreak havoc."

"How did you know?"

"The day quarter-terms were announced, I saw it— your façade fell. I didn't want to believe it, but I convinced Mr. Vasterio to not only confirm what I suspected but to deliver you to me so I could dispose of you properly."

My heart cracked, a physical pain in my chest, and I whimpered as I absorbed his words. Blaze *helped* him? Blaze was working for the Commander this whole time?

All of our plans, all of our dreams, all of those moonlit kisses in a forgotten records room . . . all of it was a lie, a ruse of its own to lure me into the Commander's trap.

I turned to Blaze, tracks of tears making his golden cheeks shine silver in the light.

"Say it's not true," I pleaded, broken.

"He told me he would reunite me with my sister if I helped. I didn't want to, I would never want to hurt you, Anora. But I need to save my sister, more than anything— I need to get her back."

Was Blaze really that big of a fool? The Commander would never truly mean such a promise. Blaze had to be blindly optimistic, since his sister was on the line. If it had been Liam, I might have faltered, too. Maybe taken a second to consider joining the Commander. I knew who the Commander truly was, though. A man willing to let Gwen die in the arena to prove his point. A man who smiled thinking about making his rebellious recruits disappear.

He'd never let Livi go.

How could Blaze believe such a snake? And why was he so willing to sacrifice me, the person he claimed to love?

"Say it's not true!" I cried over and over as I thrashed against my captor. "*Say it's not true!*"

My voice broke through sobs of a heart that had seen too much betrayal.

"I needed Mr. Vasterio to lure you down here. I didn't want to fuss with your kicking and screaming all the way down the stairs."

With a nod of his head, the lights of the van flashed on. The vehicle rolled forward until the back doors were beside me. A brutish man hopped out of the driver's seat and opened them. With a second nod from the Commander, he approached Blaze. The man grabbed him by the wrist, twisting it backward as he circled him. With Blaze slow to process what was happening, the man easily grabbed his other wrist and began tying his hands together behind his back.

"Wh-what's going on?" Blaze asked tentatively, as he slowly began to struggle.

"You honestly didn't think I'd keep you around, did you?" the Commander replied pitifully, as if addressing a naive child.

"You said I would be your second, your wandering eye that kept tabs on the Guardians. You said I was an asset!" Blaze's voice became hysterical as he pulled against his restraints.

"You were too curious about your sister, never dropping the matter even after I told you I didn't know anything about a Livi Vasterio. You should've taken the hint, I'm afraid. And seeing how quickly you sold out the woman you love, how could I ever trust you by my side?"

"But my sister!" His turquoise eyes went wide as he beheld the Commander for what he truly was. "You swore you'd reunite me with my sister!"

"I'm an honest man, Mr. Vasterio, and I intend to uphold my end of the bargain." He waved toward the open van door.

"No . . . *No!*" Blaze made to run away, but his handler grabbed him before he could take a step.

Distracted by the exchange, my captor loosened his grip. I took the advantage, slipping my arm out and jabbing him in the ribs. He stumbled back, but before I could take a step, the Commander seized that little kernel of power keeping me upright and I fell in a heap to the ground. The holder knelt over me, bloodied nose dripping as he made quick work of tying my ankles and hands. One knot went around my wrist and another above my knuckles to keep my palms wedged together.

No, please. Anything but this. I'd welcome death over the horrors the darkness dwelling in that van promised.

He hoisted me up by the arm and tossed me into the back of the van. It was near black, the light only emanating through the back door. The floor was slick and smelled of urine. The Commander restored my power fully, seeing I was no longer a threat, and I wiggled onto my bottom. As I righted myself, I kicked a mound hidden in the back of the van, and it whimpered.

"Gwen? Is that you?"

As Blaze was hefted into the van, she leaned forward. In the dim light, the bruise inking her right eye melded with the black of the van as if slowly consuming her.

"Anora?" She then asked with desperate hope, "Are you here to save me?"

My bottom lip quivered, unable to admit our fate.

The silence was answer enough and she receded back into the shadows, crying, her throat hoarse. With a resounding slam of the van doors, all I could hear were the sounds of our cries and the muffled growls of the monsters locked inside similar cages.

The engine revved and I solemnly closed my eyes, willing my spirit not to shatter entirely as the van began to roll. My hope for freedom, for my family, for saving others like myself dissolved in the depths of this van. How foolish I was to believe I could outsmart the Commander. He beat me at his own game, one I hadn't realized I was playing. I never stood a chance.

Above the roars of monsters, a more human shouting match began and we came to a halt. Muffled, but loud enough for me to recognize, I heard Bron's deep voice calling for me, pleading my name. "Anora!"

"Bron? Bron!" I cried out as loud as I could. "In here!"

Beside my head, something slammed against the van wall. Two handprints burned into the side, heating the metal bright orange. I cried out in joy, but just before my savior's hands could break through, they fell away. Bron made a choking sound I knew too well as the sound made when all your powers were taken from you.

"*No!*" I screamed. "Bron!"

The orange glow within those handprints faded to gray as the van trekked up the ramp and out of the Compound.

Bron had come for me. He'd fought the Commander to save me. He wasn't just another Guardian drone; he was selfless and brave. He believed in doing the right thing and had found the strength to actually do it—for me. But now his life was in danger. Would the Commander forgive his treachery? Bron was at risk of disappearing now, just like I was. If only we could've vanished together.

Every bump in the dirt road sent us toppling over and we wrestled our way up into seated positions again and again. Eventually, Gwen stopped struggling and Blaze was soon to follow. They curled up on their sides, their sobs ushering them into unconsciousness.

With every jostle, I continued to right myself. The rope knotted around my wrist and knuckles dug in deeper each time I heaved myself up. I got up regardless, time and again, even when hot blood trickled down my fingertips.

Eventually, the road smoothed and our speed picked up. My mind threatened to crack under the weight of despair, my spirit ready to fade into the shadows looming in the depths of the van. But I held onto a fraction of myself staring at the hanprints that would be forever reaching for me.

Chapter Thirty-Eight
SOMETIME AFTER

❧

Restrained on that freezing metal table, I often wondered: am I dead?

Pure white flooded my vision, my senses, my mind. It washed me clean of every desire for revenge, every hope of freedom. But then they'd come back, their faces made indistinguishable by blue masks, and I'd remember that I had only wished for death. It hadn't graced me quite yet.

One pair of eyes, such a comforting shade of brown, seemed familiar, and I would beg them for mercy. It took me a while to realize they wouldn't grant it.

I became the girl strapped to a table in a white-wash room. I no longer had to rely on my mind to imagine what happened.

At first, when they'd prodded and stabbed me, draining the life out of my veins, I would scream until my voice was a whisper, thrash until my muscles gave out. As time blurred into that blank white nothingness, I learned to stop fighting.

Livi had endured this for two years? How did she manage? How did she make it through? She was so much stronger than I gave her credit for. Every now and then, I turned to face the wall and wondered if Livi was on the other side. Did I have enough strength? Enough will to make it through? I asked Livi these questions through the wall, or maybe it was Gwendailiese, or another forgotten recruit. I never got a reply.

Sometimes, I wondered how life would be if I had stopped fighting long ago, when the only thing holding me back was one zealous man. I would face the chance at a terrifying death every day, but at least I would be able to eat real food that didn't come from a tube. I would freely walk through the trees, mapping the uneven terrain of rocks and roots through my boots—not this smooth white tile as blinding as the ceiling, hands shackled, escorted by three guards.

I could speak.

Would it have been worth it if I had known what awaited the rebel I had become? A life where time stood still, where the only things that marked the passage of time were the injections that made me spit up blood and shock treatments that left me twitching. A world where the only trace of my existence was a forgotten record gathering dust. Another anonymous picture of a girl with black smeared eyes.

But somewhere rooted deep in my mind, where the drugs and electric shocks couldn't quite reach, I held fast to a memory, the reason I was here. The tricks orchestrated by a twisted man.

The betrayal. The heartbreak.

The retribution I sought not only on the Commander,

but the boy who had won my heart, my faith, my trust, and then surrendered them so easily to a vicious monster.

That was the only thing that kept me going. Not the rhythmic beep of the instruments strung to my chest or the tube lodged in my throat. It was that spark of vengeance that fueled me. That drive to show them they can't tear me down. They could rip me open, shock me until I was numb, but they would never sear out my will to fight. To persevere.

The marred girl hiding in the woods, desperately searching for somewhere safe, was gone. I was still scarred, still broken. I always would be. But they had seared out the part of me worried with self-preservation. The girl who was left only craved revenge.

Thank you for reading Creatures
Most Vile

Please consider leaving a review so that other readers can find this title. Not only does it help an indie author and publisher make more books, but you'll also be helping other readers find their next favorite book.

About the Author

Microbiologist by day, author by night, Chelsea enjoys crafting, watching cheesy monster movies, and fangirling over her favorite fantasy novels and Marvel superheroes. Most days she can be found cuddling up with her beagle-mix Otis and a good book. *Creatures Most Vile* is her debut novel.

About the Publisher

ZENITH is a YA/NA imprint of GenZ Publishing, launched in 2019 and growing more every day. We believe in the importance of reading and writing in shaping the future. As such, we focus on publishing debut, emerging, or underrepresented authors whose voices are ready to be heard.

Find out more and submit your story:
www.zenithpublishing.org

Other Zenith Titles You May Enjoy

Casting Shadows by Dziyana Taylor

Exordium by S.N. Jones

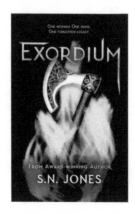

CPSIA information can be obtained
at www.ICGtesting.com
Printed in the USA
BVHW081916121021
618744BV00002B/8

9 781952 919374